THE MAID, THE MILLIONAIRE AND THE BABY

MICHELLE DOUGLAS

HER RIGHT-HAND COWBOY

MARIE FERRARELLA

MILLS & BOON

First Published in Great Britain 2020
by Mills & Boon, an imprint of HarperCollinsPublishers,
1 London Bridge Street, London, SE1 9GF

The Maid, The Millionaire And The Baby © 2019 Michelle Douglas
Her Right-Hand Cowboy © 2019 Marie Rydzynski-Ferrarella

ISBN: 978-0-263-27863-7

0120

MIX
Paper from
responsible sources
FSC C007454

FSC
www.fsc.org

This book is produced from independently certified FSC™
paper to ensure responsible forest management.

For more information visit: www.harpercollins.co.uk/green

Printed and bound in Spain
by CPI, Barcelona

Michelle Douglas has been writing for Mills & Boon since 2007, and believes she has the best job in the world. She lives in a leafy suburb of Newcastle, on Australia's east coast, with her own romantic hero, a house full of dust and books, and an eclectic collection of sixties and seventies vinyl. She loves to hear from readers and can be contacted via her website: michelle-douglas.com

USA TODAY bestselling and RITA® Award-winning author **Marie Ferrarella** has written more than 250 books for Mills & Boon, some under the name Marie Nicole. Her romances are beloved by fans worldwide. Visit her website, marieferrarella.com

Also by Michelle Douglas

Snowbound Surprise for the Billionaire
The Millionaire and the Maid
Reunited by a Baby Secret
A Deal to Mend Their Marriage
An Unlikely Bride for the Billionaire
The Spanish Tycoon's Takeover
Sarah and the Secret Sheikh
A Baby in His In-Tray
The Million Pound Marriage Deal
Miss Prim's Greek Island Fling

Also by Marie Ferrarella

Coming Home for Christmas
Dr Forget-Me-Not
Twice a Hero, Always Her Man
Meant to Be Mine
A Second Chance for the Single Dad
Christmastime Courtship
Engagement for Two
Adding Up to Family
Bridesmaid for Hire
The Cowboy's Lesson in Love

Discover more at millsandboon.co.uk

THE MAID,
THE MILLIONAIRE
AND THE BABY

MICHELLE DOUGLAS

For Millie, who is ever-generous with her smiles.
We're so happy to welcome you to the family.

CHAPTER ONE

Imogen adjusted her earbuds, did a quick little shimmy to make sure they weren't going to fall out and then hit 'play' on the playlist her father had sent her. She stilled, waiting for the first song, and then grinned at the sixties Southern Californian surf music that filled her ears.

Perfect! Threading-cotton-through-the-eye-of-a-needle-first-time perfect. Here she was on an island, a slow thirty-minute boat ride off the coast of Brazil, listening to surf music. She pinched herself. Twice. And then eyed the vac-uum cleaner at her feet, reminding herself that she was here for more than just tropical holiday fun. A detail that was ridiculously difficult to bear in mind when everywhere she looked she was greeted with golden sand, languid palm trees, serene lagoons and gloriously blue stretches of per-fect rolling surf.

Still, in a few hours she could hit the beach, or go ex-ploring through the rainforest, or…

Or maybe find out what was wrong with her aunt.

Her smile slipped, but she resolutely pushed her shoul-ders back. She'd only been here for three days. There was time to get to the bottom of whatever was troubling Aunt Katherine.

Switching on the vacuum cleaner, she channelled her inner domestic goddess—singing and dancing as she pushed the machine around the room. This was the *only* way to clean. Housework was inevitable so you might as well make it as fun as you could.

She'd been *so* quiet for the last three days, but the lord of the manor, Jasper Coleman, didn't like noise, apparently.

Each to his own.

She shrugged, but the corners of her mouth lifted. At eleven o'clock every day, however, he went for an hour-long run. A glance at her watch told her she had another fifty minutes in which to live it up before she'd have to zip her mouth shut again and return to an unnatural state of silence—and in which to dust, vacuum and tidy his living and dining rooms, his office and the front entrance hall. She meant to make the most of them.

She glanced around at the amazing beach-house mansion. While she might refer to Jasper Coleman as lord of the manor, his house didn't bear the slightest resemblance to an English manor house. The wooden beams that stretched across the vaulted ceilings gave the rooms a sense of vastness—making her feel as if she were cast adrift at sea in one of those old-fashioned wooden clippers from the B-grade pirate movies starring Errol Flynn and Burt Lancaster that she used to love so much when she was a kid. A feeling that was solidly countered by the honey-coloured Mexican tiles that graced the floors, and the enormous picture windows that looked out on those extraordinary views.

She angled the vacuum cleaner beneath the coffee table. She should *love* this house. But the artfully arranged furniture and designer rugs looked like something out of a lifestyle magazine for the rich and famous. Everything matched. She repressed a shudder. Not a single thing was out of place.

Now if *she* owned the house… *Ha! As if.* But if she did, it'd look vastly different. Messier for a start. Her smile faded. There were shadows in this house, and not the kind she could scrub off the walls or sweep out of the door. No wonder Aunt Katherine had become so gloomy.

And those two things—Aunt Katherine and gloomy—just didn't go together. The weight she'd been trying to ignore settled on her shoulders. She had to get to the bottom of that mystery, and not just because she'd promised her mother. Aunt Katherine was one of her favourite people and it hurt to see her so unhappy.

Another surfing song started and she kicked herself back into action. She had a house to clean, and she'd achieve nothing by becoming gloomy herself. She turned the music up and sang along as if her life depended on it, wiggling her backside in time with the music and twirling the vacuum cleaner around like an imaginary dance partner. While the rooms might be tidy, they were huge, and she had to get them done before Mr Coleman returned and locked himself away again in his office to do whatever computer wizardry he spent his days doing. In a suit jacket! Could you believe that? He wore a suit jacket to work here on an island that housed precisely four people. Just…wow.

The second song ended and her father's voice came onto the recording. This was one of the joys of her father's playlists—the personal messages he tucked away in among the songs. 'We miss you, Immy.'

She rolled her eyes, but she knew she was grinning like crazy. 'I've only been gone three days.' She switched off the vacuum cleaner, chuckling at one of his silly stories involving the tennis club. He recommended a movie he and her mother had seen, before finishing with, 'Love you, honey.'

'Love you too, Dad,' she whispered back, a trickle of homesickness weaving through her, before a movement from the corner of her eye had her crashing back to the present. She froze, and then slowly turned with a chilling premonition that she knew who'd be standing there. And she was right. There loomed Jasper Coleman, larger than life, disapproval radiating from him in thick waves, and her mouth went dry as she pulled the earbuds from her ears.

Her employer was a huge bear of a man with an air of self-contained insularity that had the word *danger* pounding through her. A split second after the thought hit her, though, she shook herself. He wasn't *that* huge. Just…*moderately* huge. It was just… He was one of those men whose presence filled a room. And he filled this room right up to its vaulted ceiling.

A quick sweep of her trained dressmaker's eyes put him at six feet one inch. And while his shoulders were enticingly broad, he wasn't some barrel-chested, iron-pumping brawn-monger. Mind you, he didn't have a spare ounce of flesh on that lean frame of his, and all of the muscles she could see—and she could see quite a lot of them as he'd traded in his suit jacket for running shorts and a T-shirt— were neatly delineated. *Very* neatly delineated. *That* was what gave him an air of barely checked power.

That and his buzz cut.

So…not exactly a bear. And probably not dangerous. At least not in a 'tear one from limb to limb' kind of way. None of that helped slow the pounding of her pulse.

'Ms Hartley, am I right in thinking you're taking personal calls during work time?'

He had to be joking, right? She could barely get a signal on her mobile phone. She started to snort but snapped it short at his raised eyebrow. It might not be politic to point that out at this precise moment. 'No. *Sir*,' she added belatedly. But she said it with too much force and ended up sounding like a sergeant major in some farcical play.

Oh, well done, Imogen. Why don't you click your heels together and salute too?

'Not a phone call. I was listening to a playlist my father sent me. He's a sound engineer…and he leaves little messages between songs…and I talk back even though I know he can't hear me. So…' She closed her eyes.

Too much information, Immy.

'I expected your aunt to have made it clear to you that I demand peace and quiet when I'm working.'

Her eyes flew open. 'She did!' She couldn't get Aunt Katherine into trouble. 'But, you see, I thought you'd already left for your run.'

She glanced at his office door and had to fight the urge to slap a hand to her forehead. She was supposed to check if that door was open or closed. Open meant he was gone and she could clean this set of rooms without disturbing him. If it was closed that meant he was still working… and she had to be church-mouse quiet. Biting her lip, she met his gaze again. 'I'm sorry. I forgot to check your office door. It won't happen again, Mr Coleman, I promise.'

He didn't reply. Nothing. Not so much as a brass razoo. Which was an odd expression. She'd look it up…if she could get an Internet connection. She eyed him uncertainty. He might not be a big bear of a man, but he fitted her image of a bear with a sore head to a T. Which might not be fair as she didn't know him, but she wasn't predisposed to like him either, the horrid old Scrooge.

He turned away, and she sagged with the relief of being released from those icy eyes. But then he swung back, and she went tense and rigid all over again. 'I'm going for my run *now*, Ms Hartley. In case my attire had slipped your attention.'

His sarcasm stung. Her fingers tightened about the vacuum cleaner, and suddenly it was Elliot's voice, Elliot's mocking sarcasm, that sounded through her head. She thrust out her chin. 'Did you just call me stupid?' She might only be the maid, but she didn't have to put up with rudeness. 'Look, I made a mistake and I apologised. It doesn't mean I'm stupid.'

'Oh, Imogen!' She could practically hear her mother's wail. *'What about Aunt Katherine? You promised!'*

Jasper Coleman had been in the act of moving towards the front door, but he turned back now with intimidating slowness. Rather than back down—which, of course, would be the sensible thing to do—she glared right back at him. She knew she might be a little too sensitive on the topic of her sharpness of mind and her reason—her *intelligence*—but she wasn't being paid enough to put up with derogatory comments directed at it.

At least, that was what she told herself before she started quaking in her sensible ballet flats. Her sense of self-righteousness dissolved as Jasper drew himself up to his full height. Any idiot knew you didn't go poking bears.

'I don't know you well enough to make a judgement call on your intelligence, Ms Hartley.' He gestured to his office door. 'A question mark does, however, hang over your powers of observation.'

She bit her tongue and kept her mouth firmly shut. Thankfully it appeared that he didn't expect an answer, as, without any further ado, he strode from the room. A moment later she heard the click of the front door closing. He didn't do anything as uncouth as slam it.

'Of course your attire hadn't slipped my attention,' she muttered, pushing her earbuds into the pocket of her skirt. She was a dressmaker. She noticed what everyone wore.

Though for some reason she'd *really* noticed what he'd been wearing. Which didn't make a whole lot of sense because his attire had been so very generic. Those nondescript running shorts had come to mid-thigh and were neither ridiculously tiny nor ridiculously tight. His T-shirt, though, had hugged his frame as if it'd been spray-painted on, highlighting the flex and play of firm muscle.

Oh, Imogen, who are you trying to kid?

It wasn't his clothes but the body inside the clothes that had held her attention so avidly.

Scowling, she pushed the image of her perplexing boss from her mind and completed the rest of the cleaning as quickly as possible, vacuuming and dusting immaculate surfaces. But, as her aunt said, they were immaculate because they were cleaned five days a week. Without fail. Because it was what the lord of the manor decreed, apparently.

Jasper's office was as immaculate as the rest of the house. And just as cold. Unlike her workspace at home, he didn't have any photographs sitting on his desk, no sentimental knick-knacks or anything personal. His room was functional and blank. He was supposed to be some kind of computer *wunderkind*, though how on earth he could create in a space that was so *beige* was beyond her.

She gave a final flick of her duster to the enormous desk, glanced around the room with a critical eye, and was about to leave when her gaze shifted to his computer... for the third time in about as many minutes. She bit her lip. She'd bet—given all the fancy tech gadgetry he had in here—he could log onto the Internet without a single problem.

She'd been trying to find out—for three days now—if the waters surrounding the island were safe. Aunt Katherine had no idea. She preferred the calm waters of the lagoon to the surf.

Jasper swam in his twenty-five-metre pool twice a day—from six to seven each morning and again in the evening. The man was obviously a fitness freak—three hours of cardio a day. Imagine? 'Kill me now,' she muttered. Not that she disapproved of fitness. She just couldn't do fitness for fitness's sake. She had to do something fun or it just wouldn't happen. Give her a Zumba or dance class, or the surf. She loved swimming in the ocean.

If it was safe.

Not giving herself any time to hesitate, she slid into her boss's chair, woke his computer from sleep mode and clicked the Internet browser icon. Surely he wouldn't mind? It'd be in his best interests to keep his staff safe, right? Occupational health and safety and all that.

She recalled the look in his eyes less than thirty minutes ago, and her own churlish, 'Did you just call me stupid?' and grimaced. He might make an exception in her case and feed her to the sharks.

'So just hurry up and find out what you need to find out,' she ordered, typing in: Swimming in Brazilian waters.

The search engine results loaded onto the screen. 'Eureka.'

She leaned forward, intent on clicking the link to a website that looked as if it would give her the information she needed.

'Do *not* move a muscle, Ms Hartley,' a deceptively soft voice said from the doorway.

Imogen froze. She moved nothing but her eyes to meet her employer's gaze. 'Is there…?' She swallowed. 'Is there a snake or a scorpion about to pounce on me?' Her voice came out hoarse, but she was too afraid to cough and clear her throat in case she incited some animal to attack.

'Don't be ludicrous. Of course there isn't. Unless you call yourself a scorpion or a snake,' he added, striding towards her with a purposeful step, his lips pressed into a thin line.

Danger. The word whipped through her for the second time. This man was dangerous. She should've followed her first instincts. Leaping to her feet, she shot around the farthest side of the desk, keeping its wide expanse between them. She grabbed a paperweight in one hand, and then seized a pen and held it like a dagger in her other.

He slammed to a halt so quickly he swayed where he stood. 'What are you doing?'

'I don't like the look in your eyes.'

For some reason, her words made him pale. His chest lifted as he dragged in a breath. 'I don't like undercover journalists.'

'I'm not a journalist,' she spluttered, 'undercover or otherwise!'

'I hold the same contempt for industrial spies.'

She pointed the pen at his computer. 'You think I'm snooping in your personal files or...or your work files?'

Lips that shouldn't look quite so full twisted. 'The thought had crossed my mind.'

Wow, was this man paranoid or what? No wonder he lived on a desert island. And no wonder her aunt had warned her to be circumspect around him—*difficult* and *temperamental* had been the words she'd used.

'We seem to be at an impasse, Ms Hartley. I never for one moment meant for you to think that you were in physical danger from me.'

Oddly enough, she believed him.

'But I want to look at that computer screen to see precisely what it was that had you grinning like a Cheshire cat and shrieking "Eureka".'

That was probably a very good idea. 'How about I go this way until I'm standing in front of your desk?'

'And I'll go this way—' he gestured in the opposite direction '—until I'm behind my desk.'

'I want it on record that I take exception to the charge of shrieking, Mr Coleman. I don't shriek.'

'Duly noted, Ms Hartley.'

'Right, well...let's call that Plan A, shall we?' Imogen Hartley's lips lifted, but that didn't assuage the acid burning in Jasper's gut. The fear in her eyes as he'd started towards her had nearly felled him. What kind of brute did she take him for?

'Do you want me to count?' He didn't want to give her any further cause for alarm. 'On the count of three—'

With a frown in her eyes, as if he puzzled her, she shook her head and started moving around the desk. He kept his own steps measured and unhurried as he moved in the opposite direction.

Once they'd switched places, rather than looking meek and mild, or guilty and ashamed, Imogen Hartley made an exaggerated flourish towards the computer like a model in an infomercial.

He muffled a sigh and took his seat. At least she didn't look frightened any more. Steeling himself, he turned to his computer. He stared at it for several long moments, blinked, and then eased back, his shoulders unhitching. 'You're checking the surf conditions?'

She nodded.

He tried to keep a frown from forming. 'Did you really think Ilha do Pequeno Tesoura—' he used the full Portuguese name of the island '—would be in the database of some surfing website?'

'Well, no, not exactly. But we're only a leisurely thirty-minute boat ride from the coast. Which means it'd be quicker by speedboat,' she added with a shrug, as if that explained everything.

A speedboat would reach the island in less than fifteen minutes. And her shrug explained nothing.

'So I thought that checking the surfing conditions on the coast might tell me what I needed to know.'

'Which is?'

She gestured, presumably towards the Atlantic Ocean on display outside his office window. 'If it's safe for me to swim on your beach.'

'Why?'

Two vertical lines appeared on her brow as if he'd just asked the most ridiculous question ever put to her—as if two seconds ago she'd considered him a sensible man and now she didn't.

Two minutes ago, she'd thought him a scary man. He'd never forgive himself for that.

Still, those lines on her brow were oddly cute…and kind of disturbing. Disturbing in the same way that seeing her dancing and singing while she'd been vacuuming had been disturbing. This woman was full of life and energy and spontaneity—full of unguarded reactions. It reminded him of normal people, and the outside world, and life. It was why he'd been so unforgivably short with her. The ache she'd unknowingly created inside him—an ache he'd thought he'd mastered a long time ago—had taken him off guard. It was why he'd come back early from his run—so he could ask Katherine to apologise to the girl on his behalf.

Apologise yourself now.

He opened his mouth. He closed it again. Katherine had rolled her eyes when she'd spoken of her niece—had said she was flighty and impulsive…recovering from the latest in a string of unsuitable relationships…had hinted, without saying as much, that her niece would find him irresistibly attractive. Be that as it may, while she might be irresponsible this girl was untouched by all the ugliness that surrounded him. And he'd like to keep it that way. It'd be better for all concerned if she considered him a temperamental grump rather than a reasonable human being.

He watched, fascinated, as she forced her face into polite lines. 'The reason I was checking the surf conditions is because I want to swim on the beach out there. My aunt couldn't tell me. She doesn't like the surf. If she wants a dip, she swims in the lagoon. You only swim in your pool. So…'

It took an effort of will not to lean towards her. 'So?'

'So I wondered if there was something wrong with it. Is there a great white shark colony camped just off the reef? Are there hidden rips or strange jellyfish? I mean, I've not noticed anything unusual, but…'

She trailed off with a shrug, her meaning clear. She'd evidently grown up with the same 'swim safe' messages that he and most other Australian children grew up with. The main beach here on Tesoura was a sheltered haven with rolling breakers created by the offshore reef, but the thought of her swimming alone disturbed him. 'Are you an experienced surfer?'

'I'm not a board rider, but I swim a lot at the local beaches back home.'

He searched his mind for where it was that Katherine's family called home.

'Wollongong and Kiama way,' she clarified. 'The beaches an hour or two south of Sydney.'

He'd swum those beaches once upon a time. A lifetime ago. A life that felt as if it had belonged to somebody else.

He shook the thought off. 'The beaches here are similar to the ones you'd be used to back home.' Tesoura's beaches were probably safer than most.

'Thank you.' The smile she flashed him pierced beneath his guard, making that damn ache start up in the centre of him again. Her smile faded, though, when he didn't smile back, and he did his damnedest to not feel guilty about it. 'I'm sorry, I should've asked your permission before using your computer.'

Which raised another question. 'I don't want you touching any of the equipment in this room, Ms Hartley.'

She nodded and apologised again, hesitated and then said, 'I guess there's no chance of you calling me Imogen, is there?'

'None whatsoever.' He did his best not to feel guilty

about that either. 'Didn't you bring a laptop or tablet to the island?'

For some reason that made her laugh. 'Ah, but, you see, I haven't been given the keys to the kingdom.'

What on earth was she talking about?

'The Wi-Fi password,' she clarified.

Why on earth not?

'Apparently I don't have the right security clearance.' Her lips twitched irresistibly. 'It must be above my pay grade.'

She quoted that last sentence as if it was a line from a movie, but he wasn't familiar with it. Then again, he couldn't remember the last time he'd watched a movie.

He pushed that thought aside. Why on earth hadn't Katherine given her niece the password?

None of his business. He knew Katherine was keeping secrets from her family, but he had no intention of getting involved. Without a word, he wrote the login details down and pushed them across to her.

She glanced at them and her eyes started to dance. 'Does that mean I just got a promotion?'

He resisted the urge to smile back. 'It now means you can log onto the Internet using your own devices rather than mine, Ms Hartley.'

The smile dropped from her lips. Again. Banter with the boss wasn't going to happen and the sooner she understood that, the better.

Something rebellious and resentful at the strictures he'd placed upon himself prickled through him, but he squashed it. It was for the best.

She shifted from one leg to the other. 'Look, I wanted to apologise again about earlier. I—'

'It's all forgotten, Ms Hartley.'

'But—'

'I'd appreciate it if you'd close the door on your way out.'

He turned back to his computer and opened a fresh spreadsheet. She stood there frozen for a moment, and then shook herself. 'Yes, of course, sir.'

And if her *sir* held an edge of sarcasm, he didn't bother calling her on it. He wasn't interested in winning any Best Boss of the Year awards. Imogen was only here temporarily while Katherine sorted a few things out. She'd be gone again in a flash. And peace would reign once more.

The moment she left he closed the spreadsheet. He'd only opened it to look busy and get Imogen to leave his office. Ms Hartley, he corrected. *Not Imogen.* He checked his Internet browsing history more thoroughly.

She'd started precisely one search. That was it. She'd wanted to know the surf conditions. As she'd said. She wasn't a journalist. She hadn't lied.

Good. He hadn't relished the thought of telling Katherine her niece was a thief, liar or cheat. He eased back in his seat, glad that the open friendliness of Imogen's face wasn't a front for deception. He was glad his instincts hadn't let him down.

You could've made an effort to be a little friendlier.

He squashed the notion dead. No, he couldn't. It started with a couple of shared jokes, and evolved to shared confidences, and before you knew it a friendship had formed—a friendship you'd started to rely on. But when it all went to hell in a handbasket you found out that you couldn't rely on anyone. Not your friends, not your girlfriend and sure as hell not your family. He wasn't walking that road again.

It was easier to not start anything at all. He'd learned to rely on nothing beyond his own resources. It'd worked perfectly for the past two years, and if it wasn't broken...

A sudden image of Imogen's face—the fear in her eyes as she'd edged away from him—speared into his gut, making a cold sweat break out on his nape. Who was he kidding? *He* was broken.

And a man like him needed to stay away from a woman like Imogen Hartley.

Shooting to his feet, he strode to the window, his lip curling at the tropical perfection that greeted him. He should've chosen the site of his exile with more care—picked some forlorn and windswept scrap of rock off the coast of Scotland or…or Norway. All grey forbidding stone, frozen winds and stunted trees.

Two years ago, though, all he'd cared about was getting as far from Australia as he could, as quickly as he could.

He wheeled away from the window. He'd never cared that the island was beautiful before, so why wish himself away from it now? He should never have cut his run short—that was the problem. Running and swimming kept the demons at bay. He should've stuck to his routine. And a hard forty minutes' worth of laps would rectify that.

He flung the door of his office open at the exact same moment the front doorbell sounded. He blinked. He hadn't known that the doorbell even worked. It hadn't rung in the two years he'd been in residence. All deliveries—food and office supplies, the mail—were delivered to the back door and Katherine. The villa was huge and sprawling, and the back entrance was closer to the jetty, which suited everyone. Nobody visited Tesoura. *Nobody.*

He'd bet his life it was Imogen Hartley. She'd probably rung it for a lark. She was exactly the kind of person who'd do that—just for the fun of it, to see if it worked. He waited for her to pop her head into the room and apologise. She'd probably feed him some story about polishing it or some such nonsense. He'd even be gracious about it.

Imogen came rushing through from the direction of the kitchen. 'Was that the—?'

The doorbell rang again.

'—the doorbell?' she finished.

He gestured towards the front entrance, his gut clenching. 'I'd appreciate it if you'd answer it, Ms Hartley.'

Those vivacious eyes danced as she started for the door. 'Butler is definitely a promotion.'

Even if he hadn't put his 'no smiling' rule into place, he couldn't have smiled now if he'd wanted to. Somebody ringing the front doorbell here on his island miles from civilisation could only mean one thing—trouble. 'If it's the press…' he managed before she disappeared into the front hall.

She swung around. 'Short shrift?'

'Please.'

She gave him a thumbs-up in reply before disappearing, and despite himself a smile tugged at his lips. The woman was irrepressible.

He stayed out of sight but moved closer so he could listen.

'I understand this is the residence of Jasper Coleman,' a pleasantly cultured male voice said.

'May I ask who's calling, please?'

He couldn't fault Imogen's tone—courteous, professional…unflappable.

'I have a delivery for him.' There was a series of dull thuds, as if things were being dropped to the ground, and then a softer click and scrape. 'Don't worry, he doesn't have to sign for it.'

Unflappable disappeared when Imogen yelped, 'That's a baby!'

What?

'Hey, wait! You can't just leave a baby here.'

'Those were my instructions, miss.' The voice started to recede. 'Just following orders.'

Jasper shot out from his hiding place in time to see his *butler* accost a man almost twice her size and pull him to a halt. 'What is wrong with you? You can't just go around dumping unknown babies on people's doorsteps.'

'The baby is neither unknown nor am I dumping him. I was hired to escort the baby to Mr Coleman. And I'm rather pleased to have managed it before his next feed is due. As far as I'm concerned, my job here is done.'

Ice trickled down Jasper's spine. Ignoring it—and the baby capsule sitting on his doorstep—he forced himself forward. 'There has to be some mistake.'

'No mistake,' the man said, turning towards Jasper. 'Not if you're Jasper Coleman.'

Imogen released the man's arm and stepped back to let Jasper deal with the situation, but she didn't disappear back inside the house and he didn't know whether to be glad of her silent support or not.

'You *are* Jasper Coleman, right?'

He wanted to lie, but there was a baby involved. 'Yes.'

'Then there's no mistake.'

His gut clenched. There was only one person who would send him a baby, but… It was impossible! She'd said she hated him. She'd said he'd ruined her life.

The man gestured to the baby capsule. 'Mr Coleman, meet your nephew.'

On cue, the baby opened his eyes and gave a loud wail.

Jasper couldn't move. 'What's he doing here?'

'Your sister hired me to escort the baby here from Australia.' He pulled a card from his pocket and handed it across. 'Belforte's Executive Nanny Service, sir.'

'You're a nanny?'

'One of the best. If you check with the office, you'll see that everything is in order. I believe you'll find a letter from your sister in one of the bags. I expect it'll explain everything.' And then he frowned as if suddenly recalling something. 'Mrs Graham did say that if I saw you to say the word *Jupiter*. She said you'd know what that meant.'

His gut twisted. Jupiter had been their password as kids. The baby's cries grew louder and more persistent.

He was aware of Imogen glancing from him to the nanny and back again, but he couldn't meet her eye. He couldn't move.

'You'll have to excuse me. I'm expected in Rio for my next assignment by nightfall. Have a nice day.' And then he turned and strode away, evidently washing his hands of them all. And who could blame him? It wasn't *his* baby.

It didn't stop Jasper from wanting to tackle him to the ground and force him to take the baby back. *Damn!* What game was Emily playing now? He swallowed down his panic and channelled the coldness he'd spent the last two years perfecting. He would find a way to deal with this and—

Imogen pushed past him to sweep the crying baby up into her arms and cuddle him. 'Hey there, little dude, what's all this fuss about? You feeling a bit discombobulated? I don't blame you.'

The baby batted his face into her shoulder a couple of times, rubbed a fist across his eyes, while Imogen cooed nonsense, and then he finally looked up at her. She sent him a big smile before blowing a raspberry into his hand. To Jasper's utter astonishment the baby not only stopped crying but smiled back, as if Imogen was the best thing he'd seen all day.

And Imogen Hartley visibly melted.

Right, she'd said she'd wanted a promotion. He wondered how she'd feel about the position of nanny?

CHAPTER TWO

IMOGEN BOUNCED THE baby on her hip and winced at Jasper's white-faced shock. A baby turning up on his doorstep was obviously the last thing he'd expected. Cool eyes darkened and a bitter resignation twisted his lips, making her heart thump. She fought an urge to go over and put her arm around him, to try and comfort him the way she did the baby.

But why should he need comforting?

She moistened her lips. 'This is your nephew?'

He nodded.

She waited, but he didn't offer anything else. 'What's his name?'

'George.'

It was too hard to look at Jasper, so she smiled at George instead. 'Hello, gorgy Georgie!'

Jasper swore. Not particularly badly, but with a venom that made both her and the baby jump. *Okay.* So he *really* hadn't expected the arrival of this baby. And he was *really* unhappy about it.

But little George stared at his uncle with wide fear-filled eyes and looked as if he was about to start crying again. So she bounced him gently and started singing, 'I'm a little teapot.'

The baby turned to her again and his face broke out into a big smile. He waved his hands and made lots of inarticulate noises. What an adorable bundle of chubby-cheeked cuteness!

'Hey, you going to be a singer, little guy?' She glanced at his uncle. 'How old is he?'

'Nine months.' Jasper stared at her oddly. 'You're very good with him.'

'Back in the real world I'm Auntie Immy to four of the cutest babies on the planet.'

'I thought you were an only child?'

Ah, so Aunt Katherine had told him a little about her, then. What other confidences had she shared? 'An honorary aunt.' She stuck her nose in the air. 'Which everyone knows is the best kind.'

He stared at her for a moment before one side of his mouth hooked up. Her heart stilled mid-beat, before pounding again with ferocious abandon. That half smile transformed him completely—the stern mouth curved with a sensual lilt that chased away some of the shadows in his eyes. It made her think of summer and fun and…ice cream. She fought to catch her breath. From the first moment she'd clapped eyes on Jasper, everything about him had screamed undeniable maleness. But now he was also unmistakably gorgeous.

He sobered, the frown returning to his face, and she dragged her gaze away. Dear God, please don't let him have misconstrued her scrutiny.

She scuffed a toe against the ground and tried to hide a grimace. What was there to misconstrue? She'd been ogling him, which was seriously poor form. But it didn't mean she had designs on him or anything, and—

'Are you feeling all right, Ms Hartley?'

She realised she'd scrunched her face up, and immediately set about un-scrunching it. 'Thought I was going to sneeze.'

He raised an eyebrow.

'It didn't seem like a good idea with an armful of baby,' she improvised. She wanted—no, needed—him to stop looking at her in that way. She gestured to the series of bags that George's minder had dropped to the doorstep. 'I guess we should get these out of the sun.' Without another word, she grabbed the baby capsule at her feet and strode through into Jasper's impeccable living room.

She grinned at the baby. 'Oh, you're going to mess this up perfectly, master George.'

'How is he going to mess it up?' Jasper said, coming in behind her. 'Is he old enough to walk?'

'Unlikely, though he might be crawling. Hey, little dude, are you speeding around yet?' She sent Jasper a grin. 'I'll show you what I mean.' She went to hand him George, but he took a physical step away, a look of horror speeding across his face.

Whoa.

She gulped down the words that pressed against the back of her throat. There was something going on here that she didn't understand, and the last thing little George needed was for her to make it worse. So she instead pointed to the bags. 'In one of those there are bound to be some toys and a baby blanket.'

Without another word, he started rummaging and eventually found what she'd asked for. Handing her the blanket, he held a toy out in each hand—a plastic set of keys on a key ring in primary colours, and a plush bunny rabbit with long ears. With a squeal, George reached for the keys.

Very carefully, Jasper handed them over.

Imogen spread the blanket on the living room's thick designer rug and then upended the rest of the contents of the bag across it.

'What the—?'

Setting a boomerang pillow in the middle of it all, she very gently settled George into its curve before pulling the toys closer. He threw the keys, waved his arms about and started making *broom-broom* noises.

She reached for a toy car. 'Is this what you're after, little guy?'

He grabbed it, immediately shoving one corner of it in his mouth.

Imogen rose and gestured to the baby, the rug, and the assortment of toys. 'Hey, presto, your living room isn't quite so immaculate.'

He eyed her carefully. 'You sound as if you approve of the change.'

'It's very hard to disapprove of babies, Uncle Jasp—Mr Coleman,' she amended in a rush, heat flushing through her cheeks.

What on earth…? Just because there was a baby in the house didn't mean she could dispense with normal boss-employee formality.

He let her near slip pass, just continued to stare at her. Um…?

Oh! She was supposed to be working. He was probably wondering what on earth she was still doing here lingering in his living room as if she owned it. Swallowing, she backed up a step. 'I guess I better get back to work and—'

'No!'

She halted, mentally tutoring herself on the appropriate levels of deference due to an employer. 'Sir?'

'I have a proposition to put to you, Ms Hartley.'

She glanced at baby George, who was happily banging a plastic hammer against his foot, and she started to laugh. 'I just bet you do.'

Damn! Couldn't she maintain a semblance of polite dutifulness for even thirty seconds?

He eyed the baby and then her. 'You did say you wanted a promotion.'

She'd been joking! And while it hadn't been a joke that'd

made him laugh, or even smile, she knew he hadn't taken her seriously. 'Is nanny a promotion?'

'Absolutely. It comes with a higher pay grade, for a start.'

She didn't care about the money. The money wasn't the reason she was here.

'With all the associated security clearances.'

Had he just made a joke? She grinned—partly in shock but mostly in delight. 'Now that *is* an attractive fringe benefit.'

'Is that a yes, then?'

She glanced at the baby. It'd be way more fun to look after George, but it wasn't why she was here.

'You're hesitating. May I ask why?' He gestured to the baby. 'You seem a natural. While I understand there may be some allure to dancing with vacuum cleaners, you did seem to enjoy singing nursery rhymes too.'

She'd definitely rather look after George than dust and vacuum, but she'd promised her mother she'd find out what was troubling Aunt Katherine. Looking after a baby 24/7 could put a serious dent in the amount of time she could give to that.

'Ms Hartley?'

'Mr Coleman, I have a feeling that your idea of what being a nanny involves and my idea of the same are worlds apart.'

He blinked.

She nodded at the letter he held—the letter from his sister that he still hadn't opened. 'You don't know how long George is here for. You don't know what his mother's wishes are and—'

'How will our ideas about a nanny's duties differ?'

She eyed him uncertainly. 'I think you'll expect me to be on duty twenty-four hours a day, seven days a week. And I'm sorry, but I'm not interested in working those kinds of hours. That's not the reason I came to Tesoura. I'm here to spend some time with my aunt. And in my free time I plan to lap up all of the tropical gorgeousness that I can.' Until she returned home, and her real life started. A thrill rippled through her at the thought…along with a growing thread of fear. 'The former is going to prove difficult and the latter impossible with a baby in tow.'

He tapped a finger against his lips. 'Asking you to work those hours would be completely unreasonable.' He said the words with such a deep regret that in other circumstances she might've laughed.

She didn't laugh. She edged towards the door before she weakened and did what he wanted—became a full-time carer to that gorgeous bundle of baby.

'Where are you going?'

His sharp tone pulled her to a halt. 'To go and perform the duties you're currently paying me for.'

'You can't leave me alone with the baby.' Panic rippled across his face. *'Please.'*

That *please* caught at her, tugged on all of her sympathies and completely baffled her. 'Why not?'

'I don't know a single thing about babies.'

George had been staring at them as if aware of the tension that had started to zing through the air, and he promptly burst into tears. She didn't blame him. She swooped down and lifted him in her arms, patting his back as he snuffled against her neck. 'Well, lesson number one is to not yell around them. It upsets them.'

Aunt Katherine came into the room with her brisk step. 'Goodness, I thought I heard a baby. So the cot and pram that were just delivered weren't mistakes, then?'

Jasper gave a curt shake of his head and gestured towards George. 'Emily's baby.'

Her aunt's eyes widened. 'Well, now, that's a turn up for the books.' She moved across and clasped one of George's hands. 'Hello, little man, it's nice to meet you. I knew your mummy, back in the days before you were born.' She glanced back at Jasper. 'Poor little tyke looks tired. How long is he here for?'

He shook his head. 'I don't know.'

Imogen refrained from pointing out that if he read his sister's letter, they might get an answer to that particular question.

Katherine pursed her lips. 'Right.'

Imogen glanced from one to the other, trying to make their relationship out. Katherine had been on the island for the past two years. Before that she'd worked for the Coleman family for seventeen years. Were they friends? She bit her lip. Were they lovers? The question disturbed her, though she couldn't have said why. At forty-nine Katherine was still young, and she was certainly attractive. While Jasper would be what—mid-thirties? It didn't seem outside the realm of possibility.

Her aunt was keeping secrets. Every instinct Imogen had told her that. Was Jasper one of those secrets?

If he were either a friend or a lover, though, he'd have given Katherine the week's leave she'd requested at Christmastime.

Her aunt's laughter hurtled her back. 'Don't look at me like that, Jasper, because the answer is a big fat no. If I'd wanted to look after a baby, I'd have had one of my own.'

That made Imogen smile. Katherine didn't have a maternal bone in her body.

'But—'

'No buts,' Katherine said without ceremony. She glanced at Imogen and then Jasper again, and her eyes started to gleam. 'I'll let you continue your negotiations with Imogen, shall I?'

'What negotiations?' he grumbled. 'She's as hard-headed as you.'

Imogen surveyed her perplexing boss. For someone who'd been shocked into white-faced silence at the arrival of the baby, he seemed to have taken it into his stride now, seemed almost…resigned. Why—if he didn't want the baby here—wasn't he making arrangements to send the child back?

Katherine turned and patted Imogen's arm. In a low voice she said, 'Get him to help with the baby,' before disappearing into the kitchen.

If she did what her aunt asked, would Katherine stop avoiding her and tell her what was wrong?

'What did your aunt just say to you?'

She did her best to smooth out her face. 'Only that lunch is ready.'

His eyes narrowed, but he didn't call her on the lie. She pulled in a breath. 'Mr Coleman, I think between the three of us we can work something out.'

He widened his stance. 'You heard your aunt—she'll have nothing to do with him.'

'She won't change dirty nappies or bathe George. But she'll give him a bottle and be happy to keep an eye on him when he's napping.'

'There's one other thing you need to take into consideration, Ms Hartley, and that's the fact that I'm *not* looking after that baby.'

'Mr Coleman,' she said very gently, 'that's not my problem. It's yours.'

He knew he was being unreasonable—not to mention irrational—but he could barely check the panic coursing through him. It'd smashed through the walls he'd put up to contain it, and while part of him knew the panic was illogical, another part understood all too clearly that he had every reason to fear the consequences of his nephew's visit.

Aaron wanted revenge, and Jasper didn't doubt that his

brother-in-law would use George as a weapon—to hurt him or extort money from him. That was the best-case scenario he could come up with—that Aaron wanted money. And Jasper would give money—a lot of money—to keep this child safe.

But he'd learned to not rely on best-case scenarios. With his luck in another day or two police would show up and arrest him for allegedly kidnapping the baby. And then he'd be charged, and there'd be court proceedings…again. The thought had exhaustion sweeping through him.

Ms Hartley was right, though. This wasn't her problem. It was his. He dropped to the edge of the nearest sofa.

Focus.

Fact number one: the baby was here now, and arrangements needed to be made for his care. Fact number two: he didn't want the press getting wind of this—whatever *this* was. Instinct warned him it'd be wiser to scotch any rumours before they started. He had to keep this as quiet as possible, which meant the fewer people who knew, the better. *Those* were the important facts for the moment. He could worry about the rest later.

'Can…can you just stay there with the baby while I make a phone call?'

She frowned but nodded. Not giving her a chance to change her mind, he grabbed his phone and speed-dialled his assistant in Sydney. He needed information. 'Evan, my sister has just had a nanny service deliver her baby to my house without warning.'

Two seconds of silence greeted him before Evan said, 'What do you need me to do?'

'Can you find out what Emily and Aaron's movements are at the moment? *Discreetly.*'

'I'll be in touch as soon as I find anything out.'

'The sooner the better, please.'

He tossed his phone to the coffee table and scratched a

hand across his head. It was entirely unreasonable to ask Imogen to be on call with the baby all the hours of the day and night. It contravened every workplace agreement he subscribed to. It was unethical. He'd taken great pains to ensure his company's workplace practices were above reproach. It was especially important now to continue in the same vein.

Besides, neither Katherine nor Imogen were the kind of women to be browbeaten by a domineering boss. Not that he was domineering, but he wouldn't be able to cajole either one of them into doing something they didn't want to do. There was a part of him that was glad about that. It indicated that they had integrity. It was important right now to surround himself with people of integrity.

The sofa dipped a little as Imogen sat beside him. 'I want to pat your back much the same way as I am little George's at the moment.'

He met warm brown eyes flecked with green and filled with sympathy. He straightened. 'Please don't.' The thought of her touching him…

He cut the thought off.

George had nestled his head in against her shoulder and noisily sucked a dummy, while she rubbed slow, soothing circles to his back—lulling and hypnotic. It took a force of will to lift his gaze back to her face. Up this close he could see the light spattering of freckles across her nose.

'Of course I'd not do anything so forward. But it's obvious your nephew's arrival has come as something of a shock.'

Understatement of the century.

'I think I should leave you in peace for the next hour or so to read your sister's letter, and to take stock of the situation. I'll keep this little guy with me for the present.'

That was kind, but…

'Wait,' he said as she started to rise.

She subsided back to the sofa. He let out a low breath. He wasn't ready to read Emily's letter yet. He wasn't sure he'd be able to believe a single word it said. 'You honestly believe that between the three of us, we'd be able to look after the baby?'

'Yes.'

'How would you see that working?'

She shrugged, and her chin-length hair—a mass of dark curls—bounced and bobbed. 'A little bit of give and take on all sides, I expect. Though probably mostly from yours.'

He didn't like the sound of that much. Still…needs must. 'In what way?'

'You'd need to cut down on some of your working hours to help out with George.'

He'd expected that.

'Mind you, that could be a good thing. Seems to me you work too hard anyway.'

The moment the words left her mouth, she shot back in her seat. 'I can't believe I just said that. It was way too personal and completely out of line. I'm sorry.'

She was holding his nephew, rubbing his back—and she spoke the truth—so he let it pass. He worked long hours because, like the swimming and the running, it helped to keep the demons at bay. Keeping busy kept him sane. For the duration of the baby's stay he'd simply be busy helping look after him instead of wrestling with complicated computer code. It wouldn't have to be any different from his current routine.

'And while George is here, you might need to…'

He raised an eyebrow.

'Lower your standards of cleanliness.'

He blinked.

'If I'm looking after George for part of the day and night, I'm not going to have the same amount of time to devote to cleaning your house.'

'That's fine with me.' In fact, it was more than fine. 'Ms Hartley, you've vacuumed and dusted these rooms every day since you arrived. Now far be it from me to question your work practices—I've never been to housekeeping school, so I don't know what the norm is—but don't you think vacuuming every day is overkill? I'm tidy in my habits, don't tramp mud into the house on a regular basis, and don't have children or dogs—' He broke off to glance at the baby in her arms. 'I don't *usually* have children or dogs to stay.'

'But Aunt Katherine said you had the highest expectations when it came to—' She broke off, biting her lip.

What on earth had Katherine been telling her niece?

He pushed the thought away. He had more pressing concerns at the moment. 'I'm happy to relax the current cleaning standards.' He pulled in a breath. 'There's just one other little problem in your proposed plan.'

'Which is?'

His stomach churned. 'I don't have the first idea about babies. I don't have a clue how to feed them or what to feed them or how to prepare whatever it is that you do feed them. I've never changed a nappy. The thought doesn't fill me with a great deal of enthusiasm, admittedly, but evidently it's a chore I'm not going to be able to avoid. And precisely how do you bathe a baby without drowning it? Don't they get slippery and hard to hold? That sounds like a disaster waiting to happen, if you ask me.'

She smiled, the green sparks in her eyes dancing, and the impact of it hit him in the middle of his chest, making his heart thump.

'I can teach you all of those things easy-peasy. But there are a couple of other things you'll need to learn too, like cuddling and playing. Both are vital to a baby's development.'

Before he knew what she was about, she'd leaned for-

ward and set the baby on his lap, and he wanted to yell
at her to take him back. But recalled, just in time, that he
wasn't supposed to yell around the baby. He wanted to
shoot to his feet and race away. But he couldn't because
he had *a lap full of baby*.

He wasn't sure how the kid would've reacted if he'd been
fully awake—with a loud verbal protest he suspected—
but, drowsy as he was, he merely nestled in against Jasper's chest. The warm weight made his heart thud, made
him wonder when was the last time he'd actually touched
someone? *Hell!* He—

'Stop frowning,' she chided gently from where she'd
moved to kneel in front of him, adjusting his arm so it went
fully around the baby with his hand resting on the child's
tummy. 'We don't want George glancing up and being
frightened out of his wits by the scary man glaring at him.'

The thought that he could so easily frighten his nephew
sickened him.

'I mean, that's hard enough for a grown-up to deal with.'

Her voice held laughter, but that didn't stop his gaze
from spearing hers. 'I'm sorry I scared you earlier. I really didn't mean to.'

'I know that now. I overreacted, but—'

He looped his fingers around her wrist. 'Never apologise for trusting your instincts and being cautious. It's
better to feel a little foolish than it is to get hurt—every
single time. No exceptions.'

She stared at his hand on her wrist and nodded. She'd
gone very still. Had he frightened her again? He didn't
hold her tightly. She could move away at any time… Her
tongue snaked out to moisten her lips and something hot
and sweet licked along his veins.

He let her go in an instant.

She eased away, colour high on her cheekbones. 'Do

you mind if I check the bags?' She gestured to the muddle of bags that apparently came with a baby.

'By all means. Are you looking for anything in particular?' If she took the baby back he'd look for her.

'George's schedule.' He must've looked clueless because she added, 'Feed times, nap times…those sorts of things.'

He tried to do what she was doing—focussing on the situation with the baby rather than that moment of…

He didn't know what to call it. A moment of awareness that had taken them both off guard. He pulled in a breath and counted to ten.

Emotions were running high, that was all. He was holding his nephew, for heaven's sake. A nephew he'd thought he'd never get to meet, let alone hold. It was making him hyper-aware of everything. What he didn't need to notice at the moment, however, was the silkiness of his housemaid's skin or the shininess of her hair. He gritted his teeth. Or the beguiling shape of her mouth.

He forced his gaze to the baby who, with half-closed eyes, continued to suck on his dummy with a kind of focussed fierceness. His chest clenched. What kind of unfairness or…or whim had turned this little guy's life upside down? The innate fragility and helplessness of the baby, the sense of responsibility that suddenly weighed down on him, had his former panic stirring. How could he do this? How—?

'I didn't go to housekeeping school either,' Imogen said out of the blue. 'Just so you know. In case you hadn't worked that out for yourself yet.'

She sat cross-legged on the rug, going methodically through each of the bags. And she was telling him this because…?

'I wouldn't want you accusing me at some distant point in the future of being here under false pretences.'

He recalled how she'd puffed up earlier when she'd

thought he'd been slighting her intelligence. Did she feel lesser because she'd not been to the right school or wasn't properly qualified or something? Focussing on her issues was certainly better than focussing on the baby he held. 'It doesn't necessarily follow that you're not a hard worker, though, right?'

'Exactly!' Her smile was so bright it could blind a man. He blinked but he couldn't look away. And then she grimaced. 'I don't have the subservient thing down pat yet, though.'

His lips twitched. 'I hadn't noticed.'

'Ooh.' Her grin widened and she pointed a finger at him. 'You just made a joke.'

He ignored that. Making jokes at the moment was no doubt highly inappropriate. For heaven's sake, *he was holding a baby.* 'Ms Hartley, let me put your mind at rest. I trust Katherine's judgement.'

'Even though I'm family?'

She's a bit flighty and irresponsible.

He didn't see any evidence of that. 'Even then,' he said. He spoke without hesitation. He'd trust Kate with his life. He knew she was keeping secrets from her family, but they were harmless enough. He couldn't blame her for protecting her privacy when he'd all but exiled himself to a remote island.

She's a bit flighty and irresponsible. He suspected Kate had lied about that to put an invisible wedge between him and her niece. He didn't blame her for wanting to protect Imogen from a man like him. He didn't consider himself a good prospect either.

Imogen halted from her rifling of bags. 'I want to apologise for my rudeness earlier.'

She'd been rude?

'I shouldn't have jumped on you like that for calling me stupid.'

'I did *not* call you stupid.'

'You know what I mean.'

She'd only been responding to his rudeness. 'I shouldn't have been so short with you.'

One shoulder lifted. 'I'm a bit sensitive on the subject, and I shouldn't have flared up like that.'

He stared at her for a moment. 'Why are you sensitive?'

She ducked her head. 'It doesn't matter.'

He had a feeling it mattered a great deal.

He wasn't sure what she saw in his face when she glanced back up, but whatever it was had her heaving out a sigh. 'I don't think I'm stupid, Mr Coleman. I know I'm not. I'm just a bit sensitive about it at the moment because last week, before I came here, I ran into an old boyfriend—my high-school sweetheart.'

From the look on her face he'd been anything but a sweetheart.

'When he found out I had no plans to go to university—like him—he told me I was…'

'Stupid?'

'I believe the words he used were *uneducated yokel*.' She shrugged. 'Naturally I kicked his sorry butt to the kerb.'

'*Smart* move.'

'But, you know, that was seven years ago, and people grow up, so when I saw him last week I said hello.' Her lips thinned. 'That wasn't quite so smart.'

A hard ball settled in the pit of his stomach. 'He called you stupid again?'

'Implied it.'

What a jerk! 'Why?'

She shook her head. 'It doesn't matter.'

He didn't believe that for a moment.

'I'm *not* stupid and what I'm doing with my life *isn't* stupid or risky. It's just…his voice has wormed its way inside my head, and I haven't been able to shake it. I'm sorry you were the one who had his head snapped off, though.'

'I have broad shoulders.' He shrugged. 'And if you want the truth, I came back early from my run to apologise for being so grumpy.'

She folded her arms and stared at him. 'You know what? You're not the slightest bit difficult or temperamental.'

What on earth had made her think he was?

Katherine. The answer came to him swiftly. Katherine didn't want him messing with her niece, and he had no intention of giving the older woman cause for concern. He might not be difficult and temperamental, and Imogen might not be flighty and irresponsible. But their lives were poles apart. And he had every intention of keeping them that way.

CHAPTER THREE

THE MYRIAD EXPRESSIONS that chased themselves across Jasper's face pierced Imogen with unexpected force. Her heart beat too hard—a pounding that rose into her throat and made it ache.

She didn't bother tempering the sympathy that raged through her. She doubted she'd be successful even if she tried. He'd stared at his nephew with a mixture of such shock and wonder, pain and hope and desolation, that it had almost overwhelmed her. She understood the shock and the hope, but not the pain and desolation. And certainly not the fear.

A bit of panic—yes.

Worry and anxiety—absolutely.

But not that bone-crushing fear that had seemed to be directed both inwards and outwards at the same time. She'd been desperate to rid him of that expression, so she'd overshared. Again.

But that was better than staring at his awful expression and doing nothing about it. The lines fanning out from serious grey eyes were still strained and the grooves bracketing his mouth were still deep, but he no longer looked so worn or overwhelmed.

The grey of those eyes was quite extraordinary. She'd never seen eyes like them—silver in some lights, they held a hint of blue in others, but could deepen to charcoal and concentrate so intensely you felt spotlighted…and seen, *really* seen.

'All right, Ms Hartley, let's try your suggestion and see if, between the three of us, we can manage. I'll increase your and your aunt's salaries for as long as the baby is here and—'

'Oh, that's not necessary.' He was already paying her a generous salary.

'You'll both be taking on extra duties and I have no intention of taking advantage of your good natures. We'll do things by the book. You'll be compensated accordingly.'

He wanted this to be a work arrangement, rather than a favour between friends. Which suited her fine because they *weren't* friends. She recalled the awful expression that had overtaken his face and couldn't help thinking that the one thing Jasper Coleman could do with at the moment, though, was a friend.

She glanced at George, noting the way he worried at his dummy. 'He's due for his bottle.'

'You'd better take him, then.'

She suspected that if he'd had more confidence in handling babies, he'd have simply handed him over, and she'd have had no choice but to take him. As it was, he stared at her expectantly, evidently expecting her to obey him immediately, and she had to fight her instant response to do exactly that. 'I will, but first I want to make a request.'

His brows rose. Yep. He'd expected her to jump to do his bidding immediately.

It's what he's paying you for, Imogen.

'Is it possible for us to drop the Mr Coleman and Ms Hartley and call each other by our first names? I know I'm only a housemaid with a promotion to a third of a nanny's position while you're a genius billionaire, but I can promise you I won't forget the distinction. The thing is, I've never worked in an environment that maintained such formalities, and I just know I'm going to slip up and call you Uncle Jasper to little George here at some point. "Go to Uncle Jasper, Georgie,"' she sing-songed to demonstrate what she meant. 'It'd be really nice if we could eliminate that worry right now.'

She couldn't work out if he was trying not to smile or trying not to frown.

'You don't look particularly worried, Ms Hartley.'

Was that a no? 'I can assure you that I'm shaking on the inside.'

She bit back a sigh when he didn't smile. Mind you, he didn't frown either. She tried again. 'You and my aunt call each other by your first names. I promise not to take any liberties just because we move to a more informal mode of address.'

He stared at her for several long seconds. 'Are you familiar with the movie *The Sound of Music*?' he finally asked.

'Intimately.' It was one of her favourites. 'An oldie but a goodie.'

'I'm vividly reminded of the moment in the film where the captain asks Maria if she was this much trouble at the abbey.'

A bark of laughter shot out of her. 'And she answers, "Oh, much more, sir."' She glanced at the baby in his arms. 'I have to say I'm *very* glad you weren't just landed with seven children.'

As if they couldn't help it, his lips lifted. Her pulse shimmied and all the fine hairs on her arms Mexican-waved.

'Very well, Imogen, first names it is. Perhaps now you'll be good enough to take the baby?'

He angled the side holding the baby towards her, and she moved closer, ordering various parts of herself to stop tripping the light fantastic. 'Hey there, beautiful boy.' George came willingly, but not before Imogen had sucked in a deep breath of Jasper-scented air.

He smelled of the sea and the sweat from his run and

something darker and spicier, like cardamom. The smell of sweat especially should've had her nose wrinkling, but it didn't. She edged away before she could be tempted to drag in another appreciative lungful.

His sister's letter still sat unopened on the arm of the sofa. Why hadn't he torn it open and devoured its contents yet? She adjusted her weight from one leg to the other. 'May I make a suggestion?'

'You may.'

'I think you should read your sister's letter. And before you accuse me of taking those liberties that I promised I wouldn't, I want to assure you that I'm not trying to pry. Your family's concerns are none of my business. But we need to know if George has any medical issues or medications that he's taking or any allergies.' She lifted the schedule of feeding and nap times she'd found in the same bag that held some ready-made bottles of formula. 'None of those things are mentioned here, which probably means that there's nothing to worry about,' she added quickly at the look of absolute horror that passed across his face. 'But with knowledge being power and all that,' she finished on a weak shrug.

Surely no mother would send her baby somewhere so remote—so far from medical facilities—if he had a known medical condition like asthma, though. At least…not a good mother. She glanced at the baby in her arms. Sympathy, compassion, pity and foreboding all churned in her stomach. Why on earth would *any* mother send her child away? Was Jasper's sister a good mother or—?

'Why are you frowning, Imogen?'

She started. 'Oh, I…'

'I'd rather know. Especially if it pertains to the baby.'

He hadn't called *the baby* by his name yet—not once. What was that about? Though she wasn't silly enough to ask that question either…yet.

'Your sister would tell us if there were any issues we should be aware of where George is concerned, right?'

She waited for him to reassure her. He didn't. His shoulders didn't slump, but it felt as if they ought to, that they were only remaining in place due to some superhuman effort on his behalf. 'I don't know. My sister and I have been estranged for the last two years.'

Why?

She didn't ask that either. He didn't look as if he had the heart for it. She focussed her attention on the baby instead. 'How about we make a pact, little George? While you're here you're only going to get all good things. What do you say to that?'

He spat out his dummy and gave a grumpy grunt that reminded her so much of his uncle it made her laugh. 'I'm glad we got that sorted. It's going to be nothing but sun and fun and kisses and cuddles and good times, right?'

He nodded, copying her, and he looked so darn cute she found herself automatically swinging back to Jasper to share the moment. She found him staring at them with an arrested expression on his face, and it had her smile freezing and all of that shimmying and Mexican-waving happening all over again.

She had to get that under control because *that* wasn't going to happen here. Instinct told her that if Jasper thought for a single solitary second that she was attracted to him, he'd boot her off his island faster than she could sew a side seam. She couldn't let *that* happen until she'd found out what was troubling Katherine.

She swung away, grabbing up the bag with the bottles and formula. 'I'll go and warm up George's bottle.' And she didn't glance back once as she marched from the room. She kept her gaze trained on little George, who clapped his hands together and chanted, 'Yum, yum, yum.'

Both she and George were chanting, 'Yum, yum, yum,' as they entered the kitchen.

Katherine glanced up from where she sat at the table with a glass of iced tea. 'I expect you're both hungry.'

'Ravenous,' she agreed, pulling a bottle from the bag and setting it in the microwave.

'Here, give him to me,' Katherine said when the bottle was ready. 'I'll feed him while you eat your sandwich.'

Imogen did as she bid. Maybe little George here could be the icebreaker she needed with her aunt?

They both watched as the baby fed greedily, his eyes closing in bliss. 'Eat up, Immy, because you're burping him. I don't do vomit. Or nappies.'

Imogen grabbed her sandwich from the fridge—chicken salad, her favourite—and started eating too.

'What's been decided?'

'I told Jasper that between the three of us, we'd be able to manage. I thought he was going to explode.' She winked. 'But he eventually saw the wisdom of my suggestion.'

Katherine snorted.

'We're both being paid higher duties for the duration of George's visit. And before you ask, I've no idea how long that's likely to be.'

Katherine raised an eyebrow. 'He's really agreed to help with the baby?'

She bit into her sandwich and nodded. 'He wasn't what you'd call enthusiastic—' *resigned* might be the appropriate term '—but he agreed to let me teach him what he needs to know.'

'Good for you.'

He hadn't been the least bit unreasonable or temperamental. She glanced at her aunt before feigning interest in her sandwich again. 'While I'm more than happy to pull my weight and do the job I'm being paid for, I'm not prepared to be turned into an on-call round-the-clock drudge. I came here to spend time with you, Auntie Kay.'

Katherine's face shuttered at her niece's words, and Imogen set her sandwich down and gripped her hands in her lap to counter the painful tightening of her throat. Had she done something to disappoint her aunt, to alienate her somehow? She swallowed hard and did what she could to keep a cheery expression on her face. 'Why did you tell me to get Jasper to help with George? When I dumped the baby on his lap, I thought he was going to pass out. What's the deal with his family?'

Her aunt gave her one of *those* looks. 'Imogen, I don't gossip about my employer.'

'I'm not asking you to. It's just…he seems a bit hung up about it.'

'People's lives can be complicated.'

Was her aunt's life complicated? Was that the problem? 'You think well of him, though, right? I'd even go so far as to say you care what happens to him.'

'I've known him for nearly twenty years. I worked for his family for a long time. Of course I care what happens to him. But he's shut himself away for far too long. It'll do him good to have a bit of contact with the outside world.'

'Are the two of you more than friends?'

Shocked eyes met hers. 'Are you suggesting what I think you're suggesting?'

'I know it's none of my business, but—'

'It most certainly isn't. But, me and Jasper? The idea is ludicrous.'

That made her frown. 'Why? You're both young and attractive. And you're stuck out here together all on your own and—'

'I don't feel *that* young, Imogen, I can assure you. The idea is preposterous. I've known the boy since he was twelve years old.' Katherine's eyes narrowed. 'And I'd advise you not to get any ideas in that direction either. Jasper Coleman is a troubled man. Like the rest of his family.'

'Is there anything I ought to know? Is he...' she hesitated '...dangerous?'

'Of course not. I wouldn't hire any young woman to work here if I thought that, and certainly not my own niece.'

Of course she wouldn't.

'It's just that young women have always fallen all over themselves to impress him. I'd rather not see you join their ranks.'

'Oh, you don't need to worry about me, Auntie Kay. I have plans and I'm not letting any man derail them.' Plans she and her best friend and now business partner, Lauren, had staked their entire life savings on. Elliot could take his *stupid* comments and choke on them, because Imogen *was* going to succeed.

She glanced at her aunt again, swallowed. 'I've been playing around with some new designs and I'd love to show them to you after dinner—get your opinion, throw around some new ideas.' Katherine was the reason she'd learned to sew as a fresh-faced nine-year-old. She'd always encouraged Imogen's creativity.

'I'm sorry, but I have to keep going over the household accounts. I promised Jasper's accountant I'd have them to him by the end of the week.'

It was the same excuse she'd given last night. Imogen did her best to stay chipper, to give her aunt the benefit of the doubt. Maybe she *wasn't* purposely avoiding her. 'Can I help?'

'I expect you're going to have your hands full tonight.' She handed George over. 'Time for me to get back to work.' With that, she strode in the direction of her office.

Imogen watched her go and pursed her lips. As soon as her mother had found out that Katherine was looking for a temporary maid, she'd badgered Imogen to take the position and make sure all was well. And for the first time

Imogen was glad she'd promised to do what she could. Because her mother was right—something was wrong.

She stared down at the now content baby. 'I'm going to get to the bottom of this, George.' Her aunt was acting out of character, and she was going to find out why.

'Are you sure this is the first time you've changed a nappy?' Imogen demanded, moving in to run a finger around the waist and legs of the nappy Jasper had just put on the baby.

She smelled of oranges and vanilla. He frowned; dumbfounded that he'd even noticed what she smelled like. 'The very first time,' he promised, edging away a fraction.

Chagrin flashed across her face and it almost made him smile. So far today he'd learned how to prepare a bottle of formula, though he'd managed to get out of feeding and burping the baby. She'd accepted his 'I'd prefer to watch the first time' excuses, though he doubted he'd get away with that at lunchtime, especially as she'd given him a free pass for the entirety of yesterday. He'd told her he'd needed to put some work measures in place before he could concentrate more fully on helping her with the baby.

It had been a lie, mostly. He owned the company. He employed other people to manage its day-to-day operations. He didn't need to check in daily. A simple email had taken care of business.

But he'd needed the solitude—had needed to get his head around the events of the previous day. He'd need a whole lot more than a day and a half of solitude to make that happen, though.

He forced himself back to the present moment to find Imogen still staring at his nappy attempt. 'What? There's nothing wrong with it.'

'I know. That's the problem.' She wrinkled her nose. 'You're one of these perfect people who get everything spot-on first time, aren't you?'

Nope, that didn't describe him at all. 'I'm good with my hands.' He'd allow that much. He'd spent far too much time as a kid making paper planes and kites. He'd eventually graduated to assembling model airplanes and ships, and then disassembling computer motherboards and putting them back together—activities that had kept him out of sight and out of the line of his father's fury.

The baby chose that moment to wave his hands in the air with a series of excited gurgles, and Imogen swooped down to kiss those little fists and tickle his tummy, making him chortle. He was a sturdy and happy little chap. *Not* what he'd have expected from Emily's child.

Imogen sent Jasper a sidelong glance, the green in her eyes sparkling with devilment. 'So, you're *good with your hands*, huh?'

He didn't have a collar on his T-shirt, so it had to be an imaginary collar that tightened about his throat. 'I, uh…'

She straightened, laughing outright. 'When I first met you, I dubbed you Mr Cool and Mysterious, but I think I need to revise that to Mr Clueless and Out of His Depth.'

He stiffened, trying to resist the pull of her teasing. 'I *am* still your employer, remember?' But his words didn't carry even a quarter of the weight he'd meant them to.

'Yes, sir!'

She saluted and all he could do was shake his head. Where did all of her irrepressible sense of fun come from?

She stepped away from the change table. If nothing else, the baby had certainly arrived well equipped.

His jaw suddenly clenched. A change table. In his house. On an almost deserted island. It'd look as if he'd planned for the arrival of this child.

Try explaining that to a jury.

'Right, seeing as though you're so good with your hands, you can carry George through to the living room.'

He crashed back and pushed his dark suspicions to the back of his mind.

He hadn't had to pick the baby up yet. Other than the time she'd plonked him on his lap, he hadn't touched him until the nappy change. Jasper had spent the last two nights at the other end of the house from Imogen and the baby, but Imogen had been adamant this morning that they set up a proper nursery in one of the upstairs guest bedrooms. At *his* end of the house. He'd wanted to protest, but on what grounds?

He couldn't keep taking advantage of Imogen's good nature. And the light in her eyes had told him not to bother trying. She might have an irrepressible sense of fun, but if she was anything like Katherine, she'd have a will of steel too. And instinct told him she was definitely cast in the same mould as her aunt.

So, he'd helped to shift all the associated baby paraphernalia, had unpacked tiny romper suits and little short sets into a chest of drawers. There'd been something about those tiny clothes that'd had his chest clenching. He'd done his best to ignore it. He couldn't afford emotion and sentiment. Not in this situation.

Swallowing back an automatic objection, he took a step closer to the baby.

'What are you afraid of?' she asked softly at his elbow.

Too many things, and all of them too personal to share. But he had to say something. 'I don't want to drop him. I don't want to hurt him.' Both of those things were true.

She didn't laugh, and something inside him unhitched. He suspected he deserved mockery, but he was grateful to be spared it all the same.

'George isn't a newborn, so you don't have to support his head when you lift him. His neck muscles have developed enough to support that weight on their own.'

'Okay.'

'Once you pick him up, you can either balance him on your hip, like you've no doubt seen me doing.'

She seized a teddy bear to demonstrate. He did his best not to focus on the shapely curve of her hip.

'Or you can hold him against your shoulder.' The teddy went to her shoulder where she patted his back. 'Or you can hold him in front of you with his back against your chest.'

The teddy bear was pressed to her chest. But it was smaller than a life-sized baby and holding the toy there highlighted her, uh…curves. Rather deliciously.

Don't ogle her chest.

'Of course, you shouldn't hold him too tight.'

She demonstrated by pulling the soft toy hard against her and it was all he could do not to groan. He would *not* notice her physical attributes. It'd be wrong on so many levels. He was her employer, for heaven's sake. He might've been stuck on this island for the last two years, but he read the news, kept up with what was happening in the world—the *#metoo* movement had *not* passed him by. And he was not going to join the ranks of men who used their positions of power to prey on young women sexually. The thought sickened him.

He forced his mind back to the task at hand. 'Isn't he going to squirm and throw himself about and…?' He trailed off with a shrug.

'Have you ever held a puppy or kitten?'

'No.' He and Emily hadn't been allowed pets when they were growing up.

He turned to find her mouth had fallen open. A beat started up somewhere in his chest. Her eyes softened and she lifted her hand as if to touch him, and then seemed to recall herself. Stiffening, she eased back. 'Not everyone is an animal person.'

'I'd have loved a dog as a kid.'

Where on earth had that come from?

But it earned him a smile and he couldn't regret it.

'All I was going to say is that puppies and kittens wriggle a lot when they're excited. George here is a whole lot easier to hold than an overexcited puppy.'

'Okay.'

'So...' She gestured for him to pick up the baby.

He and the baby stared at each other. Carefully, he eased forward and slid his hands beneath the baby's armpits and lifted him. The weight of the baby was somehow reassuring. He dangled him at arm's length, getting used to the weight, noting how large his hands looked around the baby's middle. Little legs kicked as if they had an excess of energy, but they didn't make him feel as if he'd drop the child.

Swallowing, he moved him to rest against his chest and shoulder. The kid grabbed a fistful of Jasper's shirt and bounced, but Jasper kept a hand at the baby's back to steady them both, and then slowly let out a breath. 'Okay, that wasn't so bad.'

He turned to Imogen, expecting to find her smiling, but she wasn't. She was staring at him, hands on hips. 'What?' he asked, suddenly defensive.

'Do you know you haven't spoken to him yet?'

He scowled. Yeah, he knew. It was another one of those threshold moments, and he'd had enough of them for one day. 'Did you have a lot of pets growing up?'

Her face relaxed into a smile. 'I can't imagine not having a dog.'

'You have a dog...*now*?'

She started to laugh. 'Relax, Jasper, I've neither abandoned my dog nor brought her with me and hidden her in your garden shed. She's the family pet, and lives with my parents and has done so for the last ten years. Lulabelle the Labrador cross is adorable and spends most of her days dozing in the sun. I couldn't imagine not having a dog,' she repeated.

He'd ached for a dog as a kid, but he hadn't thought

about that in years. He rolled his shoulders, keeping a firm grip on the baby. 'Why not?' What was so good about having a dog?

'They're great company.'

Yeah, well, he didn't need any of that. He liked his own company.

'They're a lot of fun.'

He didn't need fun either.

'And they don't judge you. They just love you unconditionally.'

He couldn't think of anything to say to that.

She started to laugh again. 'And in addition to all of that they'll keep you on your toes as they chew your shoes, dig up the garden, traipse mud into the house and pee on the carpet. A lot like kids, I guess.'

'Oh, now I'm really going to rush out and get a dog,' he said wryly, trying not to notice the way the ends of her hair danced whenever she laughed.

She sobered and nodded at the baby. 'You're going to need to talk to him.'

Damn. He'd thought he'd distracted her from that. 'Why?' Why did he have to talk to the kid? It'd be in everyone's best interests if he could maintain his distance. He'd make sure the baby's physical needs were met—why couldn't that be enough?

'Because he needs to know he can trust you. Besides, it's friendly and polite.'

He wanted to stop his ears and close his eyes.

'He needs to feel comfortable around you, not frightened or intimidated.'

He pulled in a breath. Okay, her words made sense. He could make small talk with the kid, right? It wouldn't kill him. It wouldn't bring the walls he had firmly in place crashing down. He glanced down to find the baby staring at him. 'Hello, baby.'

George shoved a fist in his mouth and eyeballed him.

'George,' she sighed. 'His name is George.'

A scowl shuffled through him. Who'd chosen the name—Emily or Aaron? 'George is too big a name for a baby—too adult.'

'Which is why I sometimes call him Georgie…or Gorgy Georgie.'

The baby pulled his fist from his mouth to smile at her, but Jasper shook his head. 'I am *not* calling him that.' He must've spoken too loudly, because the baby gave a start. 'Sorry if that offends you,' he muttered, patting the nappy-clad bottom. 'What about kid?' he said, hoping to avert some very loud crying. 'Are you all right with me calling you kid?'

To his utter amazement, the little guy threw his head back and laughed. As if Jasper had just told him the funniest joke he'd ever heard. He tried to stop his chest from puffing up, tried to not feel so pleased when a little hand slapped his chest, right above his heart. 'He's a happy little guy, isn't he? Doesn't seem to cry much.'

Her lips curved into the most bewitching smile that he did his best to ignore. 'You sound surprised.'

'I am.'

'Not all babies fuss and cry a lot.'

But he'd never thought for a single moment that Emily's baby would be one of the contented ones. He pushed the thought aside. 'What now? What are we doing next?'

'We're going to the beach.'

He stiffened. 'You just want to go for a swim. You're going to abandon me on a beach with a baby I barely know, while you get to live it up.'

He took one look at her face and he wished he could haul the words back. He'd planted that idea well and truly in her head, and he could see now that she meant to run with it.

'How very perspicacious of you,' she said, mock sweetly. 'I've been on call with the baby ever since he arrived. I deserve a swim. And I'm not exactly abandoning you. I'll be within shouting distance.'

He tried not to scowl.

'And while I'm swimming you might want to give some thought to how you'd like our schedule to work.'

'What do you mean?'

'I'm not leaving Aunt Katherine with all the house-work. I'll need a few hours each day to dedicate to my housekeeping duties. I suspect you'll want a few hours each day to work too.'

Um. 'I…' He didn't know what to say, what to suggest.

'For the moment, I'm just saying think about it.'

She turned and left the room. 'Where are you going?' he hollered after her.

'To put my swimmers on,' she hollered back.

'What am *I* supposed to do?'

She moved back to stand in the doorway. She glanced at the baby and then around the room. 'You'd better pack him a bag—some toys, his teething ring, a blanket…and a hat.' She glanced at him, her eyes tracking across his head, and he had to fight the urge to run his hand across his buzz cut. 'You might want one of those too. I'll bring the sunscreen and some cold drinks,' she tossed over her shoulder before disappearing.

Jasper huffed out a breath. 'You wouldn't believe it from the way she speaks to me, kid, but I'm *her* boss.'

He set the baby carefully into his cot while he gathered a few things together. He found a tiny cotton sunhat and set it on the baby's head.

The baby frowned and pushed it off. 'So…it's going to be like that, is it?' Jasper's hands went to his hips. 'She's going to insist on it, you know.' Shoving the hat in the pocket of his cargo shorts, he hiked the bag over his shoulder, lifted the baby out of the cot, and went to find a hat for himself.

CHAPTER FOUR

IMOGEN CHANGED INTO her swimming costume and tried to make sense of the expressions that had flashed across Jasper's face whenever he'd glanced at his nephew. Consternation was ever present, which she got. But she didn't understand his… She didn't know what to call it— calculation, maybe? As if he viewed his nephew as a piece of problematic computer code he needed to decrypt. Or a to-do list he needed to tick off.

Beneath that, though, she also sensed the wonder George stirred in him. And the fact it was an ever-present threat to his detachment. It was as if Jasper was afraid to care even the slightest little bit for his baby nephew.

Maybe he was, but why? Because of his sister?

She slathered on sunscreen. It was none of her business. She knew that. But if George's sister was an irresponsible piece of work or in some kind of trouble, then little George was going to need someone to rely on. Someone like Jasper.

She snapped the tube of suncream closed with the heel of her hand. Surely Jasper didn't mean to abandon George at the end of all this—just hand him back to his mother when the time came and be done with him? Not without some follow-through. Not without making sure George was going to be okay. He had to maintain some contact with his nephew, even if it proved difficult. Right?

But even as she thought it, she was far from convinced Jasper saw it the same way. In fact, she was almost certain he saw it in a completely opposite light.

'*He's a troubled man.*'

Her aunt's words played in her mind, and she found herself nodding.

'*He's demanding and difficult.*'

That had her shaking her head, though. He valued his privacy, and she doubted he'd suffer fools gladly, but he wasn't unreasonable, and while he could be remote and aloof he wasn't surly or supercilious. Those things gave her hope because she hadn't imagined the surprise in his eyes, or the pleasure, when George had smiled at him.

If it hadn't been for those glimpsed flashes of warmth, the thawing she sensed him trying to fight, then she'd…

She jammed a hat to her head.

Then you'd what? She mocked her reflection, rubbing in a dollop of cream still left on her nose. She wasn't making a dent in Katherine's aloofness at the moment, so what impact did she think she could have on Jasper?

The one thing she *could* do was to ensure little George's stay here was as lovely as possible. And she meant to do that to the best of her ability.

Grabbing a tote, she tossed in a T-shirt and the sunscreen, before stalking into the kitchen to grab some cold drinks and a bottle of cold boiled water for George. Katherine, sitting at the kitchen table, gave a start and pushed the letter she was reading back into its envelope and slid it beneath the newspaper.

Imogen's chest tightened, but she pretended she hadn't seen the furtive movement. 'We're heading down to the beach. Want to join us?'

'Imogen, I'm working!'

She seized a couple of pieces of fruit. 'You're entitled

to some R & R. And I bet Jasper wouldn't mind. In fact, I expect he'd welcome your company.'

'I'm sorry, Imogen, but even if I wasn't busy, I'm not a fan of the beach and all of that sand.' She eyed the fruit Imogen still held. 'And if you're going to feed any of that banana to the baby, you better pack some wet wipes.' She pointed. 'In that cupboard to the left of the sink.'

With a sigh, she grabbed them and then gathered up her things. She paused in the doorway. 'Auntie Kay, is everything okay?'

'Of course it is,' Katherine said brusquely. 'Why wouldn't it be, you silly child? Now, you'd better get your skates on. Jasper won't like kicking his heels for too long. Enjoy your swim.'

She had no choice but to submit. But as she walked away, her mind raced. She needed to find a way to break through her aunt's atypical reserve. Doing housework and looking after a baby were all well and fine, but she had to remember the real reason she was here on Tesoura.

They spread the blanket in the shade of a stand of palm trees that swayed gently in the breeze like something from every hopeful daydream she'd ever had about tropical islands. 'Smell that glorious sea air, George. Feel how warm it is. Hear the sound of the waves.'

She closed her eyes and inhaled. *Glorious.*

When she opened her eyes, she found Jasper staring at her as if she'd lost her mind. George was clapping and beaming. George was the easiest to deal with, so she kept her gaze on him and clapped too. While she might've addressed the baby, her words had been aimed at the man. She wondered if Jasper ever did relaxed and casual. He might've changed into shorts and a T-shirt, but for all intents and purposes he might as well have still been wearing a suit jacket for all the relaxation he radiated.

Pointing that out, though, would be impertinent, and it'd achieve absolutely nothing. So, she kept on clapping her hands. 'This was the game George and I played last night. For a very long time.'

'Looks riveting.'

'It's just as well babies are so cute, because so much of their care falls into the categories of the mundane and downright boring.'

'Which is the real reason you didn't want to take on the job of full-time nanny?'

There was no censure in his voice, just curiosity, and she found her gaze swinging up. 'Do you think housework is any less boring?'

One shoulder lifted. 'Given the way you do it—dancing and singing off-key at the top of your voice—perhaps.'

His words made her laugh, but his almost-smile had things inside her wobbling. She dragged her gaze away. 'Like I said, I just don't want to lose all my leisure time.' She needed the time and headspace to keep chipping away at her aunt.

'So what now? I get the great good fortune to play the clapping game while you enjoy your said leisure time?'

The question could've sounded sulky and petulant, but it didn't. He just looked—and sounded—at a genuine loss. She made a mental note not to swim for too long. She had no intention of abandoning him, not when he evidently felt so out of his depth. 'There are lots of other games too. For example, we like playing choo-choo trains.' She seized the bright red plastic train and pushed it across the blanket, making train noises.

George pursed his lips and made *choo-choo* sounds too, and then clapped and grinned.

Jasper shook his head. 'I'm *not* doing that.'

Imogen gurgled a laugh at George. 'Uncle Jasper thinks choo-choo trains are beneath his dignity.'

George bent at the waist, leaning towards her to laugh too, laughing because she was laughing. He was the sweetest little guy.

Her employer glared. 'I'm wondering how you got to twenty-five years of age without someone throttling you, Ms Hartley.'

'I'm guessing it's because of my sparkling personality.' She hummed a few bars of 'How Do You Solve a Problem Like Maria?' from *The Sound of Music*. Without giving him time to respond, she pulled the bag he'd packed towards her. 'Right, you have a couple of books here—' the thick cardboard ones that were almost indestructible '—so you can read one of those to him. But you have to point to the picture and say the word. Making the appropriate sound will earn you bonus points.' She pointed to a chicken and made chicken noises.

He opened his mouth, but she pushed the book into his hands before he could speak. 'It also makes the game last longer and that can be a blessing when your hands are sore from the clapping game.'

He didn't sigh, but it looked as if he wanted to.

'First and foremost, you need to keep him safe.'

His shoulders immediately tensed. 'What dangers am I guarding against?'

'Well, he isn't crawling yet, but he can roll and he can do a funny kind of tummy crawl. So he can get himself to the edge of the blanket…and there's all of that sand…and everything he picks up goes in his mouth.'

He nodded. 'No sand eating.'

'Once babies begin to move, they can do so surprisingly quickly.' She pointed to the water behind her.

He pointed a finger at her and then the water. '*Not* going to happen.'

'I know. You'll keep an eagle eye on him.'

He blinked.

'Insects can be a problem too. We don't want him bitten by an ant or stung by a bee or anything along those lines.'

He immediately traced the blanket's perimeter with eyes that made her think of laser beams. She pulled in another of those wobbly breaths. His worry, his vigilance, his desire to do this thing—a thing he apparently didn't want to do—to the very best of his ability, touched something inside her, made it soft and breathless. 'And…um… finally…the sun. We don't want him getting sunburned.'

His hands slammed to his hips. 'Then why don't we just take him back inside where it's safe?'

'Jasper,' she said gently, 'he's *your* nephew. You're free to take him back into the house whenever you want. But how would you feel cooped up inside all day? Besides, there are things you need to protect him from in there too—the sharp edges of coffee tables, making sure he doesn't put something he shouldn't in his mouth.'

He dragged a hand down his face, making her heart twist. 'I'm sorry. It's just…there's a lot to consider.'

And he'd never expected to be in this situation. That much was apparent. She forced her lips upwards. 'If it's any consolation, vitamin D is most excellent for growing bones, and sunscreen will help take care of the sunburn.' She raised an eyebrow. 'As will a hat.'

'It's in my pocket,' he muttered. 'He doesn't like wearing it.'

She didn't say anything, simply poured some sunscreen into her hand. 'I've never put this stuff on a baby before, so it could prove interesting.'

He looked as if he wanted to run away. 'How can I help?'

'I don't know. You might need to hold him. Let's see how we do first.'

She smeared a line of the lotion down George's nose and across each cheek, and started to rub it in. He gave a squeal of outrage and tried to turn his face away, but she was too quick for him. When she did it again, he frowned at her and then he opened his mouth and…well, he yelled at her to stop. It was the only way she could think to describe it, and she found herself laughing. 'He reminded me of you then.'

'I don't frown like that.'

'I beg to differ.'

'And I would certainly never yell at you.' He then seemed to recall that moment in his study when he'd found her sitting in front of his computer, and winced, scrubbing a hand across his hair.

She took pity on him. 'Not without provocation,' she agreed. 'And in George's eyes, sunscreen apparently provides ample provocation.'

His nose curled. 'I can understand that. The stuff is sticky.'

If she didn't still have a handful of sunscreen she'd have slammed her hands to her hips. 'Are you telling me you're not wearing sunscreen?'

'I…' His mouth opened and closed. 'There wasn't time.'

Without thought, she reached across and deposited a liberal amount of lotion to his face. George let loose with a long, 'Ooh!'

'Exactly, Master George, Uncle Jasper needs to set you a good example.' But as she said the words, her stomach was clenching up tighter and tighter. She should never have touched him. What on earth had she been thinking?

She hadn't been thinking. She'd acted on impulse. And in this instance, impulse was bad. *Really bad.*

Or really divine. Depended on which way you wanted to look at it. Beneath her fingers Jasper's skin felt warm and vital, vivid, and the strength of him seeped into her fingers and all the way through to her bones, making her feel buoyant and alive. Which was crazy. The scent of him—warm cotton and cardamom—had an unfamiliar yearning stretching through her.

She couldn't look at him; afraid she'd betray the need racing through her. She stared doggedly at George instead. 'I'm really sorry. I shouldn't have drowned you in suncream, but your nephew is watching this exchange intently. And I'm thinking that if I dab a final bit on your forehead and rub it in, then maybe he'll be a bit more amenable and let me do the same to him.'

'Right.'

That was said through a clenched jaw, and she did her best not to wince. She tried to not feel *him* as she did it, but her fingers were tingling by the time she'd finished.

Little George blinked when she repeated the procedure on him, and frowned, but he didn't squeal or holler.

'Okay.' She gritted her teeth. 'Let's try arms next.'

Without a word, Jasper held out an arm, but she couldn't help noticing the way his eyes had turned remote and distant. Cold. It was all she could do not to shiver.

To her amazement, though, George also held his arm out in imitation of his uncle. Holding her breath, she squirted lotion on both arms—man's and child's. 'Quick,' she murmured to Jasper. 'Give me your other arm.'

Again, George copied, and she laid a line of cream down both arms—one strong and tanned, the other tiny, plump and pale. 'Right, we're ignoring your arms for the moment, Jasper. You take one of George's arms while I do the other. You can rub yours in once we're done.' Which meant she wouldn't have to touch him again.

Without a word, and with quick efficient movements that made her own efforts seem clumsy, Jasper gently rubbed the cream into George's right arm. Wanting to distract George while she did his legs, she said, 'Help Uncle Jasper rub the cream on his arms.'

She gave a quick demonstration, not actually touching Jasper, just pretending to, and George immediately leaned forward and started patting his uncle's arm. Jasper turned to her, his eyes wide. 'He…he understood exactly what you wanted him to do!'

'He's smart…and utterly adorable. And that—' she pointed to his arm '—will keep him occupied for ages.'

While the lotion on Jasper's other arm was about to drip onto the blanket. With an apologetic grimace, she reached across and rubbed it in. The action brought her face in close to his and she wondered if the consternation—the turmoil—in his eyes was reflected in hers. She edged back, her mouth going dry, and the shutters slammed down over his eyes, leaving her confused and flailing.

'I think it's time you went for your swim, Imogen.'

'I think that's a very good idea.' She nodded. 'Before you throttle me.'

Did she imagine it or did his lips just twitch?

She started to untie her sarong and his gaze immediately swung away to focus on the baby. It made her heart thump too hard. She swallowed and forced herself to focus on the reason she'd brought him and the baby out here. 'What are you going to do if he cries?'

Jasper did his level best to keep his eyes on the baby. Imogen's touch—on his face and his arm—had been innocent, almost absent-minded. But it had woken something inside him, and he desperately wanted to lull it back to sleep. Ogling her, near naked in a swimsuit, would *not* help him achieve that particular objective. Besides, he didn't ogle. He'd never ogled. And he wasn't starting now.

'And here's a hint. Calling for me is the wrong answer.'

Her voice was filled with laughter and he wanted to lean into it, play along, but experience warned him not to. While he might have to face the fact that he could like Imogen Hartley—quite a lot actually—there was no place in his life for her. He'd trusted a woman once—had foolishly come to rely on her, had thought they were a team.

But she'd left, frightened off by his father's threats. He didn't blame her for leaving, not for a moment. But it'd taught him two hard lessons. The first—that he couldn't rely on anyone but himself. The second—that it'd be wrong of him to put any woman in a position where she could be hurt by his father.

'Jasper?'

She could whisper his name in a way that made the surface of his skin come alive.

She knelt back down to the blanket in front of him and the baby. 'If you're that uncomfortable with this, I'll stay. I don't have to go for a swim.'

'No, you go for your swim.' He didn't want to deprive her of such an innocent pleasure. She'd been looking forward to it—had definitely earned it—and he'd do whatever he could to facilitate it. He made himself swallow, pulled his face into neat lines. 'I'm just...out of practice at talking to people. Evidently I've been spending too much time in my own head.'

He couldn't believe he'd said that out loud. He wanted to check his words, choke them back, but it was too late. Gritting his teeth, he forced his mind back to her original question. 'If the baby cries, I'll make sure nothing is hurting him, and then I'll check his nappy.' Um... 'I saw a bottle of something in your bag...?'

'It's just cold boiled water.'

Right. 'Well, I'll see if he wants that.'

'And if that doesn't work?'

He tried not to scowl—neither she nor the baby deserved his malcontent. 'I'll distract him by playing choo-choo trains or something equally inane.'

The green flecks in her eyes shone bright and clear. She stared at him steadily now and he didn't know if she was amused by him or concerned.

Don't be an idiot.

If she was concerned about anyone it'd be the baby.

'And if that doesn't work,' he added, doing his best not to frown, 'I'll sing to him.'

Her lips parted. 'What a lovely idea.'

He stared at those parted lips and that monster he'd been trying to lull roared back to life—fierce, hungry and primal. Her eyes widened at whatever she saw in his face, and her tongue eased out to moisten her lips. They stared at each other, lost in some strange in-between world— but in between what he couldn't say—and then the baby squealed, and she jerked back, and he could breathe again.

She leapt to her feet. 'If he cries, pick him up and give him a cuddle. That might be all he needs—a bit of reassurance that he's safe.' And with that, her sarong floated to the ground and she set off towards the water.

He did his best not to notice her bare legs and arms or the curve of her hips. She wore a seriously sedate swimsuit, and a sun shirt. It shouldn't make a man's mouth dry with longing.

It shouldn't.

Keep your head.

He'd been on his own too long, that was all. This was just an...adjustment.

A squeal at his elbow snagged his attention. He glanced down to find the baby pointing a wobbly arm after Imogen and frowning. 'Immy's going for a swim.' He called her Immy to the baby because it was what she called herself. *Come to Immy; Immy's getting your bottle now.*

George looked as if he might cry. 'She'll be back soon. It's not worth getting upset about, kid, believe me. Look—' he held out his arm, shuffling closer '—we haven't rubbed all of this goop in yet.'

The baby gave a toothless grin and started patting Jasper's arm with an enthusiasm that tugged at the older man's heart. He was a clever little kid. Were all babies this smart? He'd bet they weren't.

They spent a leisurely few minutes making sure it was all rubbed in, and then George stared at him expectantly. Right... He cleared his throat. 'Do you want to play the clapping game?' He clapped his hands together a few times. Nothing. 'What about your train?' He seized the train. 'Would you like to play with that?' No way was he making *choo-choo* noises, though.

The train was tossed across the blanket. Uh-huh...

The hat! He pulled it from his pocket and set it on the kid's head. The kid immediately sounded a protest and went to pull it off, but Jasper whipped out his own cap and waved it about.

'Look, I have a hat too.'

And he set it on his own head.

The baby pointed to it and bounced. 'Um! Um! Um!'

He wanted Jasper's hat? He handed it over. The kid pulled his own hat off and gave it to Jasper, and then tried to put Jasper's cap on. He finally managed it, with a bit of help from his uncle, and did his best to look up at Jasper, but the brim covered his eyes. Fat hands lifted the brim, and when he finally made eye contact with Jasper, he laughed hysterically. Jasper couldn't help but laugh too. The kid had a weird sense of humour. And that was the game they played for the next twenty minutes—swapping hats and laughing.

Boring and mundane? Perhaps. But he'd attended board meetings that had dragged worse and achieved less. And at least he was sitting in the sun on a beautiful beach.

The thought gave him pause. Since when did he care where he was or what the weather was like? Though a bit of sun was good for the baby. Imogen had said so. Personally, he didn't care about either the beach or the sunshine. At least that was what he told himself.

He glanced back at the baby. Okay, this whole 'looking after a kid' thing wasn't rocket science. It was something he *could* learn. He could make sure all the kid's physical needs were met, and be friendly with the little guy, *and* keep his distance. He didn't need to engage his emotions towards the baby any more than he did towards his staff back in Sydney. He cared about their well-being, naturally, but it didn't matter to him on a personal level if they decided to leave his employment or anything. Just as it wouldn't matter when Emily demanded the return of her child.

And as far as Jasper was concerned, that was the best-case scenario he could think of.

'Look.' He pointed down the beach. 'Here comes Immy.' She moved with an unconscious grace that had his chest drawing tight, making it hard to get air into his lungs. He swallowed and looked away. 'I hope she enjoyed her swim, kid. She's earned it.' He had to do better where she was concerned. She'd gone above and beyond these last two days.

George glanced up at Jasper, eyes wide, and then his face split into a grin and he clapped his hands. Jasper found himself smiling back and clapping his hands too.

'How was the water?' he asked when she reached them, doing his best to look—and feel—unaffected.

'Freezing!' she said with her usual irrepressible cheerfulness, grabbing her towel and drying her face. 'Makes you tingle all over.'

Tingling was the last thing he needed to think about, but she literally glowed from her swim. Something inside him responded to it. And there was nothing he could do about it. Other than try and ignore it.

'Hey, Georgie, did you have fun?' And then she squeezed a drop of water from her hair and let it fall to the baby's foot.

George squealed. And when she made as if to drip more water on him, he squealed louder, seized a handful of Jasper's shirt and hauled himself upright on wobbly legs. He'd have fallen, would've pitched forward to smack his face against Jasper's knees, if Jasper hadn't caught him. The kid then stood balanced on Jasper's lap, and he bounced and chortled and waved his arms in glee that he'd evaded Imogen and her antics.

Jasper could barely draw breath. The baby had *trusted* him to catch him—to protect him and keep him safe.

George laughed up at his uncle now as if they'd shared a joke. Jasper's mouth dried. That…that was just fanciful, right? Nine-month-old babies couldn't share a joke with you.

The baby's legs gave way, and he plopped down on Jasper's knee, snuggling into him…and then he wrapped an arm across Jasper's tummy and he cuddled him. Every hard thing inside Jasper's heart melted to a puddle, and his arms went around little George of their own volition.

He stared down at his nephew, his heart filling with too much emotion. He said the rudest word he knew. Very softly.

He glanced up to find Imogen watching. She didn't remonstrate with him for his bad language. Instead, she asked, 'What just happened?'

The soft warmth of her voice helped to soothe the ragged edges of the panic pounding through him.

He didn't bother trying to deny it. 'I'm falling for him.'

She wrapped her towel about herself and sat on the edge of the blanket. 'What's wrong with that?'

His chest ached. His throat ached. And his head pounded. 'I have absolutely no jurisdiction over this child, Imogen. When one of his parents demands his return, I have to hand him over. I won't be able to keep George here.'

She sucked her bottom lip into her mouth, her gaze never leaving his. 'But you can visit him, can't you? And he can come for holidays here to Tesoura, right?' She searched his face. 'I'm not getting something. What am I not getting?'

A breath rattled out of him. 'My sister is married to a man who beats her. I tried to help her break free of him, but she didn't want that. Instead, she cut *me* from her life and said she never wanted to see me again.'

Her hand flew to her mouth. When her gaze lowered to the babe in his arms, her eyes filled. He wanted to hug her for her concern, for the way she worried about George. For her kindness.

'No matter how much I might want to, I can't protect George. Not from his own parents.' And yet how on earth could he abandon George to a lifetime of fear and abuse?

Nausea churned through him. History was going to repeat, and he was powerless to stop it. The thought nearly broke him.

'Despite all of that,' Imogen said slowly, 'your sister still sent the baby to you. That has to mean something, don't you think? What did her letter say?'

'Next to nothing!' It hadn't provided him with an ounce of reassurance. George jumped at his tone and started to fidget, Jasper soothed him the way he'd seen Imogen doing—holding him against his shoulder and rubbing his back. '"Dear Jasper,"' he recited through gritted teeth, '"I know you've probably not forgiven me, but there are some things I need to take care of. In the meantime, I need someone to look after George. Please keep him safe until I can come for him. Emily."'

She hadn't signed off with 'love' or 'best wishes' or 'sincerely' or anything else. And she hadn't given him any further explanation. He wasn't sure why he'd expected more. His lips twisted. Hope sprang eternal, he supposed.

Imogen had stiffened. She stared straight at him as if

expecting something more from him—in the same way he'd expected something more from Emily. 'What?'

'It sounds like she's in trouble.'

He hated the way her words made his gut clench. 'What makes you think that?'

Her hands lifted. 'What makes you think there could be any other possible explanation?'

'Experience.'

She blinked and eased back. He was going to have to explain, and he didn't want to. But George needed all the allies he could get, and Jasper had no intention of ostracising a potential ally as kind and generous as Imogen. She made his nephew smile and she made him feel safe. That was worth more than gold.

He did what he could to find his equilibrium. 'My father and brother-in-law are both shaped in the same mould.'

Her bottom lip wobbled. 'They're both…violent?'

'They're both miserable excuses for human beings.'

Her eyes filled again, and it made his chest twist. 'I can't stand either one of them,' she said with quiet vehemence, and for some reason it warmed up parts of him that had started to chill.

'My father wanted all of my mother's attention. He resented Emily and me for taking up so much of her time. Sometimes, when it all got a bit too much for her, she'd farm us out to relatives for a couple of weeks or would send us off to some holiday camp.'

He'd hated it, but at the same time he'd welcomed the reprieve from his father's anger.

Imogen worried at her lip. 'She was probably trying to protect you.'

His head felt too heavy for his shoulders. 'Or saving her own skin.' And he didn't blame her. But when he'd offered her a chance to escape her husband—when he'd offered her refuge and a chance to start a new life—she'd spurned it, had rejected him. Just like Emily.

'That's what you think Emily is doing with George?'

'I know that on the day she sent George here, she and Aaron attended a big charity ball in Sydney—one of the biggest events of the social calendar—filled with all of the powerful and well-to-do. I also know that in the coming week Aaron is going to the States. No doubt Emily will be going with him.'

She pressed a hand to her brow. 'What if you're wrong? What if she's in trouble and trying to break away from her husband? Him going to the States could provide her with the perfect opportunity to do that. Does she have anyone she can turn to? Would your parents take her in?'

'My father would order her to return to Aaron.' The two of them had always been as thick as thieves.

'Friends?'

'Aaron vets all of her friends—in truth he's probably isolated her from them all by now.' In the same way his father had his mother.

'So she has no one to turn to?'

She had him! She had her brother. He broke out in a cold sweat. Despite everything she had to know that, didn't she?

CHAPTER FIVE

'I'VE BEEN THINKING about what you said.'

Jasper came striding down the path towards her and Imogen halted in her pegging out of George's tiny clothes, momentarily transfixed. The back garden was a riot of shrubs, palms and flowerbeds, but none of that could hold a candle to the man moving with such easy grace towards her.

He carried George in his arms, completely at ease as if he'd been born to it. The image of a little baby held against a pair of broad, sigh-worthy shoulders—all of George's small helplessness contrasted with Jasper's power and strength—had the potential to do crazy things to a woman's insides. Protectiveness and nurturance all wrapped up in a single glorious package. Was there anything more attractive—?

She broke off, realising that Jasper was staring at her expectantly. She tried to click her mind into gear. 'You've been thinking about what I said?' she parroted, hoping she didn't look completely at sea.

'About Emily.'

She eased back to survey him more fully. 'About the possibility of her being in trouble?'

He nodded.

She glanced at George, currently fascinated by a bird singing in a nearby shrub, before turning back to Jasper with his serious grey eyes and mouth that was made for smiling but so rarely did. She was becoming too invested here, but how could she not? The way these two had bonded in the last couple of days amazed her. They adored each other. And it made her fear for them both.

She swallowed. 'And…?'

'I have a favour to ask.'

Her heart leapt. Which made no sense. She bent down to retrieve a tiny pair of shorts from the laundry basket. 'Okay.'

He took the shorts from her and handed her George. 'I need your help.'

'Okay.' She focussed on the variety of romper suits, bibs and singlets that waved in the breeze like colourful bunting and tried to get her racing pulse under control.

He pegged out the shorts and then reached into the basket for a bib and pegged it out too. She wanted to tell him that she was paid to do the laundry, but didn't because… well, he was the boss and she guessed he was also paying her to hold the baby.

'Does that mean you'll help?'

'Of course I will.' A woman could be in trouble, and there was a baby involved. How could she refuse?

And just maybe the warmth from a pair of grey eyes as they rested on her didn't hurt either.

That's shallow, Imogen. Seriously shallow.

But Jasper's eyes *weren't* shallow. They hinted at depths she found intriguing…fascinating.

He reached out and clasped her forearm in silent thanks. The heat of his touch penetrated through skin, muscle and sinew, making her want more. She sucked in a breath as the ground beneath her feet shifted. It took her so off guard she didn't have time to hide her reaction. His gaze narrowed and his nostrils flared. She recognised the same need and hunger coursing through his eyes.

Everything inside her clenched. She forgot to breathe.

He stepped back, distancing himself behind a mask of stern calmness, and she gulped in a breath, reminding herself that he was her employer and she was his employee. And even if that weren't the case she wasn't getting involved with someone who'd marooned himself on a desert island.

She had plans. Lauren was relying on her. She was relying on Lauren. As soon as she left here she was throwing herself wholeheartedly into those plans. If she didn't she and Lauren would lose everything they'd worked and saved so hard for—it wasn't just her money they were risking, but Lauren's too. They'd made a solemn promise to give this new business of theirs every chance they could—to give it their very best efforts. She squared her shoulders. She wasn't letting Lauren down, and she *would* prove the naysayers wrong.

Tesoura was idyllic for some holiday R & R, but there was no way she'd ever live in a place like this.

Not that he'd ever ask her to.

Which was exactly as it should be.

She retreated to a nearby stone bench and busied herself bouncing the baby. Tried to quieten the clamour flooding her veins.

'I didn't realise how much laundry a baby could generate.'

Jasper surveyed George's clothes flapping in the breeze, obviously not finding it difficult to move on from thoughts of touching her. Well, she could move on too—with the same super-duper ease. She pasted on a bright smile, which admittedly was a little difficult when she was gritting her teeth, and tickled George's stomach. 'Messy little tyke, aren't you?'

Jasper continued pegging out the clothes. She kept her gaze trained on a nearby hibiscus flower in bright red.

'Is there a trick to it?'

Jasper, with the now empty basket clasped to his side, stared at her. She moistened dry lips. 'A trick to what?'

'Washing George's clothes.'

She tried to stop her eyes from staring. 'You want to do the laundry?'

'*Want* is too strong a word, but you said you'd teach me everything I needed to know. I want to know how to do it *all*. And it doesn't seem fair that you get landed with all the boring, mundane bits.'

That was the problem. Right there. In that one gloriously generous sentence. He said something like that, and it turned her to mush. He acted all lord of the manor one moment, and then…and then the opposite of that. It could knock a girl sideways if she was taken unawares. She did what she could to stiffen a backbone that wanted to melt. 'Jasper, stuff like doing the laundry is what you're paying me for.'

'But if something were to happen to you or Katherine—say you both got a tummy bug—or were simply busy with other things, I'd need to know how to do something as basic as wash George's things.'

She knew he came from a privileged background, but surely he knew the fundamentals. 'You, um…have done a load of washing before, right?'

He looked momentarily horrified, and then he laughed. 'It's true that my family had household staff when I was growing up, but seriously, Imogen. Your aunt was my family's housekeeper for nearly twenty years. What do you think?'

She bit back a grin. 'I expect she made sure you and your sister learned a few life skills.'

'Precisely. I know how to operate my washing machine. I do my own laundry when your aunt takes her annual leave.'

Why hadn't he granted her leave at Christmastime? The more she learned about him, the more of a puzzle that became. She couldn't imagine him denying her aunt any request for leave.

Which maybe meant Katherine had lied to them. It

maybe meant her aunt hadn't wanted to spend Christmas with her family.

She swallowed.

'Imogen?'

She shook herself. 'The only difference is in the laundry powder. We use a milder detergent for George's things. A baby's skin is more sensitive than an adult's.' She led him into the laundry room where she pointed the relevant washing powder out to him.

He nodded. 'Okay, got it.'

The laundry was generous by laundry room standards, but far too small to be confined in with Jasper and her own see-sawing hormones. Especially when he leaned in close to take George from her arms. The scent of warm spice invaded her senses. She took a hasty step back and spun on her heel to lead the way into the kitchen. 'So how can I help? What's this favour you want to ask?'

'I want to set up a fake social media account. I've spent the last two days trying to contact Emily, but with no luck. It could be that she's simply wanting to avoid me.'

The worry in his eyes belied that, though, and it tugged at her heart. 'You think you'll be able to reach her via social media?'

'It's worth a shot. I suspect Aaron monitors all her phone calls and social media accounts. He'd never allow her to friend me or anyone associated with me.'

She still wasn't a hundred per cent sure what this had to do with her.

'But he probably wouldn't look twice if she received a friend request from Jupiter Collins, who attends the same gym.'

The penny dropped. 'You want me to pose on social media as Jupiter Collins.'

'Complete with a profile pic, history and a social calendar filled with all the things young women your age like to do.'

'I already have social media accounts, though. My picture is already out there in cyberspace. Won't that…' she lifted her hands '…cause problems, blow our cover?'

'I have computer programs that will help with that. When I'm finished with your picture, you won't recognise yourself.'

'Okay, let's do this.'

They left the baby with Katherine. Once in his office, the first thing Jasper did was position Imogen against a wall without windows, so there was no possibility of the view giving away their location, and took a photo.

She watched in amazement as he hunkered down at the computer with her image before him on the screen and changed her dark brown hair—all wild curls—to a sleek blonde shoulder-length bob. Her hazel eyes became blue and he lightened her skin tone. She tried not to grimace as he then did odd things, like lengthen her face, widen her smile and enlarge her eyes.

She pressed her fingers to her face, to reassure herself that everything there was unchanged. 'Me, but not me. It's amazing.'

Jasper studied the image on his screen. 'I like the real you better.'

'Yeah, right,' she snorted. 'She's thinner, has beach-blonde hair and big baby blues. And is a gym junkie!'

Jasper laughed, and for a moment it felt as if she were catching a big wonderful wave that rolled you gently all the way to shore. 'While you're sassy, funny and cute. And a surf junkie.'

He thought she was cute? Really?

She tossed her hair. '*Sassy* is just another word for "lack of subservience", right?'

He chuckled again, his fingers typing away furiously.

'I'm not all that interested in subservience, Imogen. Your good heart is of far more value to me.'

Don't melt. Don't melt.

He suddenly froze. 'This—' he gestured to the screen '—isn't some weird male fantasy of mine. I wouldn't want you thinking that this is a… I mean…'

She took pity on him. 'That's good to know, Jasper.'

He eyed her uncertainly and then turned back to his computer. 'I made up a short bio for our Ms Collins last night.'

Jupiter Collins's biography appeared on the screen, and Imogen leaned in closer to read it.

'I have her living in a neighbouring Sydney suburb to Emily, and she goes to the same gym. I made her five years younger so they can't be old school friends.'

She read the bio, and something tugged at her. 'Give her a baby too.'

'Why?'

'So, we can tell her how George is doing.'

He swung to her. 'That's a really nice idea. Boy or girl?'

'Girl.'

'Name?'

'Georgia,' she said immediately. 'Georgia… Jas…' She tried to think of a feminine version of Jasper. 'Jasmine! Georgia Jasmine.'

He huffed out a laugh but sobered almost immediately. 'A baby will provide another point of contact. They both go to the gym *and* have babies of a similar age. Jupiter's friend request shouldn't raise Aaron's suspicions.'

His fingers flew across the keyboard. They looked sure and capable and she'd never realised before how sexy a man's hands could be. The thought of those hands on her body—

Heat exploded through her and she had to look away.

Inappropriate. Seriously inappropriate.

'How…um…?' She cleared her throat. 'If you and your sister are estranged, how do you know what gym she goes to?'

'I rang her best friend yesterday.'

He'd been busy.

'Aaron hates Prue. Has forbidden Emily from having anything to do with her.'

Imogen's nose curled. 'I *really* don't like this man.'

'I hate him.'

He slumped as if all the energy had drained from him at that admission. Imogen found herself reaching out to clasp his hand.

'You're doing what you can. You're keeping George safe and you're giving Emily a way to contact you if she needs to. One step at a time.'

His hand tightened about hers. 'I shouldn't have leapt to conclusions so quickly—shouldn't have been so caught up in my own bitterness that I discounted the possibility that she might be in trouble.'

He glanced at their joined hands and then released her so fast it made her blink. She pulled her hand into her lap, her heart starting to pound. 'What matters is that you're doing something now.'

He went back to his typing, his mouth set in a straight line. 'Emily and Prue *accidentally* bump into each other every once in a while. Prue makes sure of it. She agrees with you, by the way. She said the only reason Emily would send George away was if something was wrong.'

And he'd immediately leapt into action to help a sister who hadn't spoken to him in two years.

'I'm giving Jupiter three months' worth of history.'

'How on earth can you do that if you're only creating the profile today?'

He glanced at her from beneath his brow. 'It's probably better not to ask.'

Right.

'Any suggestions for things Jupiter might've posted?' he asked.

'Absolutely.'

The corners of his mouth twitched. 'You didn't hesitate.'

'I'm a very social person. I have a phone full of photos that I've shared on social media.'

'Social, huh?'

'I take pictures of movies I've seen, books I'm reading—usually for my book club—pictures of my toes after I've had a pedicure. Cocktails make great pictures to share. And the beach. I share oodles of pictures of the beach. And my softball team's scores.'

'You play softball?'

'Yep. It's off-season at the moment, but I'm a halfway decent hitter and—' she waggled her eyebrows '—I'm third base.'

'You don't say?' Those delicious lips curved upwards. 'You lead a full life.' The smile faded and his brow knitted together. 'You must hate it here.'

What on earth…? 'Of course I don't hate it. Tesoura is paradise, and Aunt Katherine is here. It's the perfect spot for a mini-break.'

'But you'd never settle in a place like this for good?'

'No way. I'd holiday here again in a heartbeat. But I couldn't live the kind of life you do, Jasper. I love my softball team and my book club. I'd miss my family and friends too much. I love my life. Why would I give all that up? Even for an island paradise?'

I love my life. Imogen's words rang through Jasper's mind. Had he ever loved his life?

The answer came swift and sure. *No.*

He'd been fiercely glad when, at the age of eighteen, he'd broken away from his father's control. In retaliation, Keith Coleman had refused to pay for his son's university studies, had refused to introduce him to the so-called 'right people' and had refused to put his name forward at his exclusive gentlemen's club. Jasper didn't regret any of it.

He'd used the modest legacy his grandmother had left him to help fund his studies. He'd worked part-time and had flat-shared with three other guys. He'd got by just fine.

He'd loved being free of his father. But he hadn't loved his life. His victory had been bittersweet. Neither his mother nor Emily had ever managed to escape, despite all of his begging, despite the detailed plans he'd given them to prove they could make it work. He'd had to continue watching from the sidelines as his father had directed their lives with a filthy temper and an iron fist.

At the age of twenty-five he'd invented a universal print drive that had made him millions. He'd renewed his petitions to his mother and Emily to come and live with him, or to let him buy them houses of their own away from Keith and Aaron. He'd promised them money and whatever else they needed, had sworn to protect them. But again, they'd both refused.

And then everything had blown up in his face and…

And he'd come here.

Luckily he'd had the means to do that!

But while he'd been free, he hadn't been happy.

His money meant he'd been able to put together a crack team of computer programmers. His company made some of the market's bestselling computer games. That gave him satisfaction. There'd been a couple of women he'd imagined himself in love with over the years. Those affairs had been exciting. But he'd never experienced the kind of bone-deep contentment with his life that Imogen evidently did with hers.

And while a part of him envied it, he also suspected a life like that could never be his. A person needed a better childhood than he'd had to achieve that kind of happiness—the sense of security that such happiness could last and was worth investing in.

It was a timely reminder of the gulf that lay between him and his intriguing part-time nanny. He was in danger of finding her too interesting, too...*desirable*. And he needed to annihilate all thoughts in that direction. Mentally girding his loins, he glanced across to find her scrolling through pictures on her phone.

'I can't use photos you've already uploaded to social media,' he felt bound to point out.

'But there are oodles and oodles that I haven't used. I took some of the gardens in the local park.'

They'd be suitably generic. Jupiter could be interested in gardening. Excellent.

'Here's a lovely glass of Sémillon.'

She liked Sémillon?

'Wait, what was that?' He touched her wrist as a couple of photos whizzed past.

She went back and a picture of a formal dress appeared. 'This?' She turned the screen more fully towards him. 'We're not sharing that. It's one of my new designs. I've been snapping the odd shot to share when I open my school in May.'

He sat back. He didn't know why he was so shocked. 'You're a designer?' On some level he'd always known she wasn't actually a housemaid, but... 'You're opening a design school?'

'I'm a dressmaker,' she corrected. 'And it's more a sewing school than a design school. We'll teach sewing, dressmaking, pattern making and so forth. We'll also offer a bespoke dressmaking service.' She shrugged. 'We're hoping it'll keep us busy.'

'Us?'

'A girlfriend and I are going into partnership.'

'Why are you waiting till May? Why not now?'

'The premises we've leased don't become available until then. And Lauren is on contract in the UK until March, so…'

He didn't know what to say. 'I had no idea.'

'There's absolutely no reason why you should.' That cheeky smile peeped out, making things inside his chest fizz like champagne. 'So maybe now you can see why I have such a problem with subservience. I actually want to be the big kahuna.'

She winked as she said it, though, and he knew she was simply teasing him. But… 'Launching a brand-new business. It's—' He snapped his mouth shut.

None of his business.

Those green sparkles in her eyes dimmed as if she knew exactly what he was going to say. 'Why aren't I back home frantically preparing for the launch of my school?' She started flicking through her photos again, but her knuckles had turned white. 'Lauren and I have been working towards this launch for two years. We've got everything in place, ready to go. I'll be back home in March, maybe sooner, to do all the pre-launch stuff.' She glanced up as if she was going to say more, but then shrugged. 'This will be my last chance for some R & R for some time to come, I expect. I mean to enjoy it while I can.'

But she wasn't getting R & R, was she? She was working as a maid and nanny. He glanced at his watch.

The woman opposite him gurgled back a laugh. 'Is there somewhere you need to be?'

He liked her laugh, and he liked it when he could make her laugh. He pulled in a breath—mentally pulling back. He had no intention of getting too used to that laugh. It was a temporary treat, like ice cream or cake.

When was the last time you had ice cream?

He rolled his shoulders. That didn't matter. It just proved how easy it was to give up unnecessary treats—like ice cream, cake and a woman's smile—and not miss them. And he had no intention of missing Imogen when she was gone either.

In one sudden swift movement, she pushed away from his desk. 'Oh, you probably are busy! Probably have video conference calls planned and all manner of things. I—'

'Not today,' he assured her. 'I just wanted to make sure we weren't running late for your daily swim.'

She eased back down into the chair. 'You don't have to work that into your schedule, Jasper. It's my job to work around yours.'

She was already going above and beyond. And he didn't like the thought of her swimming on her own. He didn't say those things out loud. He simply said, 'George enjoys his time on the beach.'

She looked as if she wanted to say something but turned back to her phone instead.

'What were you going to say?'

The green lights in her eyes caught the sun pouring in at the windows, and it made him suddenly glad that he'd chosen to live on a tropical island rather than some frozen rock in the North Sea.

'Just that we can take it in turns if you like? Swimming, I mean. You have this amazing beach at your disposal. Why not take advantage of it? It's way more fun than laps.'

For the past two years he'd exercised—hard. But he'd chosen the gruelling and effective over the fun. He hadn't felt like having fun. But today her suggestion appealed. 'You wouldn't mind?'

Luscious lips broke into a broad smile. 'Would I mind sitting on the beach, here in paradise, playing with George while you have a dip in the ocean?' She shook her head. 'You're a seriously hard taskmaster, Mr Coleman, but I'm up for that particular challenge.'

He tried not to grin. And failed.

She rested her chin on her hands and pursed her lips. 'I don't have the subservient thing down, but you don't really have the boss thing down either, do you?'

'My philosophy is to hire the best people, tell them what I want, and then leave them to get on with it. I find that works ninety-nine per cent of the time.'

'Nice philosophy.'

She gazed at him with frank admiration and it made perspiration gather at his nape. 'It doesn't mean I can't pull rank when I need to.'

'I already know this about you.'

Damn. Was she never going to let him forget that unfortunate morning when he'd growled at her? He opened his mouth to apologise—*again*—when he recognised the teasing laughter in her eyes and something inside him eased. 'Very funny, Ms Hartley. Now if you'd be kind enough to send me some of those photos…?'

She turned her attention back to her phone. 'I'm sending them with captions.'

'Because you don't think I can manage a twenty-five-year-old woman's voice?'

'Because it'll be quicker, and I want to get down to the beach.'

'That definitely wasn't subservient.'

He was rewarded with a tinkle of delighted laughter as he watched his email program and waited for the first of her photos to come through. They hit his inbox in quick succession. Her captions were short and sparky and the voice was better—younger—than he could've ever managed.

'So?'

She stared at him with an angled chin, evidently waiting for feedback. He was a firm believer in giving praise where it was due. 'These are perfect.'

'I should've been a writer.'

For a fraction of a second, he stilled. Did she know

Katherine's secret? Had her aunt finally confided in her? Whether she had or hadn't, it wasn't his place to give the game away. 'It's not too late,' he said instead. 'Though you might be pressed for time with the opening of your new school.'

'Yeah, nah.'

His lips twitched. 'Was that a yes or a no?'

'It's a maybe.'

She'd gone back to her phone and an influx of new pictures arrived, along with suggestions for status updates. All spot on and useful. He suddenly frowned. 'Would it be asking too much for me to have a look at your profile?'

'Friend me.'

Not a good idea.

Her fingers stilled. She glanced up. 'You don't have a profile on social media, do you?'

'No.'

'Of course he doesn't,' she murmured, before gesturing to his keyboard. He opened another browser window and handed the keyboard over, careful to glance away when she typed in her password. Her feed promptly appeared on his screen and as he scrolled down it, he found it as fun and vibrant as the woman herself.

He let out a breath. 'You and Jupiter don't sound anything alike.' It was the reason he'd wanted to check her account.

Liar. You wanted a voyeuristic glimpse into that life she loves.

'You made it pretty clear you didn't want anyone being able to trace Jupiter to me—or to link us together in any way.'

'I wish some of the people I work with were as quick to read between the lines as you.'

'Ooh, do I sense a promotion to Marketing Manager?'

'Not a chance.' He channelled his best Captain Von Trapp impression to counter the overwhelming desire to reach across and slam his lips to hers. 'Way too much trouble for the abbey.'

She didn't laugh as he'd expected. Her gaze was focussed on the computer. She pointed. 'That's my family. At Christmas. The holiday is a big deal for us.'

She had a big extended family. And every person in the photograph wore a big grin and a silly paper hat—the kind that came from Christmas crackers. There were pictures of huge platters of king prawns sitting either side of a baked ham that held pride of place on a table groaning with baked vegetables and salads. There were pictures of a game of backyard cricket and a water fight. It was about as far from the Christmases of his childhood as one could get.

He thought of George and his heart burned. What would his nephew's future Christmases be like?

'Of course, Aunt Katherine wasn't there, which put a bit of a dampener on things.'

Katherine hadn't been there? Why not? She'd told him—

He gulped the question back and glanced up to find Imogen… Well, she wasn't actually glaring at him, but it was only one level away. There was definitely puzzlement in those eyes, and a lurking resentment.

Katherine hadn't been at the Hartley family Christmas. And Imogen blamed him for it. *He's difficult and demanding.*

'What do you do for Christmas, Jasper?'

'Nothing.'

She straightened. 'What, really? Nothing? No roast turkey or ham or…or a plum pudding or presents?'

'Nothing,' he repeated, a bad taste coating his tongue.

'You don't have your bachelor buddies come to stay or…or…?'

'Nothing.'

The single word sounded stark.

It *was* stark.

He glanced back at the photographs on the screen. All that laughter and fun… He could never re-create that in a million years—he wouldn't know where to start—but in the future he could at least make an effort. He had to. For George's sake.

'What happened to you, Jasper?'

He glanced across at her whispered words. Her eyes had welled with such sadness he reached out to touch her cheek, aching to offer her some form of comfort. He wanted to tell her not to cry for him, but the words wouldn't come.

He pulled his hand back and lifted his chin. 'Nothing of any note.' It'd be better for her to not get involved in his life. Much better. 'C'mon, it must be time for that swim.'

CHAPTER SIX

IMOGEN SLATHERED SUNSCREEN across her cheeks, surreptitiously watching her aunt as the older woman jiggled George on her knee. Despite Katherine's no-nonsense briskness and seemingly cheerful demeanour, it couldn't hide the tired lines stretching from her eyes or the occasional slump of her shoulders when she thought no one was watching.

Ever since Imogen had arrived on the island, she'd told herself to go slow, that there was time for her to win her aunt's confidence, but she was coming to the conclusion that she'd chosen the wrong approach.

Except…

Her chest squeezed tight. Except the expression on Jasper's face when she'd blurted out her question not ten minutes ago—*what happened to you?*—had shown her the folly of the direct approach.

The darkness that had stretched through his eyes… It had made her throat burn and her eyes sting. She'd have done anything in that moment to make him feel better.

That's not what you're here for.

With a sigh, she glanced at her aunt, who was playing some game with George that involved his fingers and toes. 'Auntie Kay, what made you come to Tesoura?'

Katherine raised an eyebrow. 'I didn't want to work for Keith Coleman any more. I liked his wife, and I'd liked both Emily and Jasper, but they'd left home by then…' She ran a gentle hand over George's hair. 'And after the blow-up, I thought Jasper could use a friendly face.'

She plonked herself in a seat. 'What blow-up?'

'Honestly, Imogen, it was in all the papers at the time.' Her aunt turned to face her more fully. 'Your lack of interest in current affairs is appalling.'

She wrinkled her nose. 'I keep abreast of world affairs. And two years ago, I was in Paris.' She'd been doing an internship at one of the big fashion houses there. Australian news didn't rate much more than a line or two in the European papers. She racked her brain for what her mother must've told her at the time, but she'd been so full of the excitement of living and working in Paris—all that she'd been learning and experiencing—that if her mother had told her anything, it certainly hadn't stuck.

'There was a falling out between Jasper and the rest of his family. His brother-in-law accused him of assault and Jasper was charged—it was all set to go to court—but the charges were dropped.'

Her heart hammered against her ribs. 'And?'

'And that's all anyone knows. Other than the fact that none of them have spoken to Jasper since. Or he to them.'

Had Jasper given his brother-in-law a taste of his own medicine? She hoped so. She *really* hoped so.

'But as Keith is one of Australia's leading politicians, the tabloids had a field day with the story—it seemed that every day there were front pages splashed with claims and counter claims. It was ugly, and an unpleasant time for the family.'

No wonder Jasper had leapt to the wrong conclusion the day he'd found her sitting at his computer chortling, *Eureka*.

'Don't you find yourself going—I don't know—a bit stir-crazy here?'

Real amusement lit her aunt's eyes. 'You've only been here a week. You can't be bored already.'

'Of course not! This place is amazing, beautiful. But I couldn't live here for good. It's so…' *Empty.*

'I enjoy the peace and quiet.'

'But don't you miss catching a movie whenever you want, and seeing your friends—' she went straight for the jugular '—and browsing bookstores?'

'Are you trying to steal my staff, Ms Hartley?'

She swung around to find Jasper striding into the kitchen wearing a pair of brightly coloured board shorts, and both her and her aunt's mouths dropped. Her pulse did a funny little cha-cha. 'I, uh…' She swallowed. 'Well, I'd be fibbing if I said the family wouldn't love it if Aunt Katherine came home.'

'I'll offer you double whatever she's offering, Kate.'

'Very funny.' Katherine's gaze raked up and down his length. Imogen tried not to follow suit. 'But let me see if I have this right. You're going swimming? With Imogen?'

'Not at the same time.' He flicked a glance in Imogen's direction but just as quickly looked away again. 'We'll be taking it in turns to sit with George on the beach.'

Katherine's brows rose. 'But you're going swimming… for fun.'

He stretched his neck first one way and then the other. 'Imogen pointed out, quite rightly, that I have a perfectly good beach sitting on my front doorstep that I hardly seem to use. So I thought I'd…use it.'

Katherine took them in with one glance before giving a smile so blindingly bright Imogen had to blink a couple of times to clear her vision. 'I see Imogen has been working her magic on you.'

Heat flushed up Imogen's neck and into her face. What on earth…?

'I'm glad to see you finally taking a bit of a holiday, Jasper.'

'It's not exactly a holiday. We—'

'The two of you look the picture of youthful holiday fun.'

In her head, she begged her aunt to stop.

'Why don't you leave George with me and go enjoy yourselves?'

The look she sent the two of them was so arch Imogen prayed for the ground to open up and swallow her.

'Wouldn't dream of leaving you with the baby, Kate,' Jasper said, not looking at Imogen. 'Besides, George loves his daily romp on the beach.'

Without another word, Imogen grabbed her tote and the baby bag and led the way to the front door and outside. She didn't want to meet Jasper's gaze but ignoring him would only make things more awkward.

If that were possible.

She glanced up, but instead of derision or embarrassment she found laughter in those cool grey depths.

A breath whooshed out of her. 'Wow!' Jamming her hat to her head, she pulled it down low on her forehead. 'Just. Wow. That was so not subtle.'

'You can say that again.'

'She used to be the coolest person I knew, but now...' She shook her head.

Spreading the blanket beneath the palm trees in what had become their usual spot on this glorious stretch of beach, she scattered several of George's toys across it, her mind racing. 'It doesn't make sense.'

Jasper lowered George to the blanket. 'Why not?'

She started, realising she'd spoken her concern out loud. 'It's just... I could've sworn when I first arrived that she was warning me off you.'

He eased down onto the blanket too. 'How?'

No way was she telling him that. She adjusted her hat and sat. 'Just telling me to be careful not to bother you. Things like that.'

'She told you I was difficult and demanding, didn't she?' *Damn.*

'She told me you were flighty and irresponsible.'

Her mouth fell open. His gaze lowered to her lips for a fraction of a moment, his eyes darkening, before snapping away again. Heat flared in her stomach before charging out to her extremities, making her swallow compulsively. If the man could create that kind of heat in a woman, just from a single smouldering glance, could you imagine—?

Don't imagine.

'You're not flighty and irresponsible any more than I'm difficult and demanding.'

'Exactly.' With a superhuman effort she reined in her pulse. 'So why…?'

'Your aunt is a clever woman. I suspect she's been hoping we'd keep our distance from each other, but George's arrival has put paid to that plan.'

'So why do such an about-face now and literally throw us together?'

He quirked an eyebrow, and she rested back on her hands. 'She *wasn't* trying to throw us together,' she started slowly. 'She was hoping to embarrass us and make us feel so awkward that we'd barely be able to look at each other.'

'That'd be my guess.'

'Why on earth would she do that? I know how well she thinks of you, while I used to be her favourite niece.' But maybe she wasn't any more. She rubbed a hand across her chest. Maybe somewhere along the way she'd lost her aunt's love and respect.

'Imogen, she could think well of me and yet at the same time not think we'd make a good match. She knows the kind of family I come from. I don't blame her for not wanting that for you.'

'Auntie Kay doesn't judge people on their families. She—'

'Go for your swim, Imogen. You've earned it. It doesn't matter why Katherine would prefer not to see us hooking up together, because it's simply not going to happen. It's one of those ridiculous hypothetical scenarios that we needn't concern ourselves with.'

A short sharp jab of pain went through her. It took an effort to keep her voice quiet and measured. 'I don't need warning off, Jasper.'

'That's not what I was doing.'

'Yes, it was.'

He opened his mouth, hesitated and then dragged a hand down his face. 'I'm sorry. I didn't mean to offend you. And it's probably closer to the mark to say I was warning myself off.'

That didn't seem very likely and her disbelief must've shown. He picked George up and held him in front of him—almost as if he were using him as a human shield. 'You're an attractive woman, and you make me laugh. Now, I don't mean to make your aunt sound asexual, but I've known her since I was twelve years old. She practically feels like *my* aunt.'

She frowned, not sure where he was going with this.

'So, in essence, I've spent the last two years on this island without any female company that I'd classify as beguiling or tempting.'

He thought her beguiling and tempting?

'I can't deny that I enjoy your company. I also appreciate all you've done to help George. I'm just reminding myself not to enjoy it too much.'

He thought her beguiling and tempting?

She moistened her lips, and just for a moment wondered

what it'd be like if they did allow themselves to enjoy each other's company *too much*.

She tried to shake the thought off. It was crazy—and crazy-making. She wasn't interested in a fling, and instinct told her he wasn't a fling kind of guy either. Neither of them needed that kind of complication in their lives. He needed to focus on his little nephew—and she wanted to help with that, not become a hindrance.

'You know what?' She rose. 'I might go for that swim now.'

He didn't say anything, just nodded, but she was minutely aware of her body as she untied her sarong—her fingers fumbling with the knot. Jasper thought her beguiling and tempting? The thought awakened something inside her—a sexy siren who wanted to tempt and beguile and make a man lose control—and while she did her best to ignore that siren call, she was unable to keep the sway from her hips as she walked towards the water.

She did her best to lose herself to the push and pull of the waves, to the invigorating assault of cold water on overheated flesh, and to the thrill of catching perfectly formed waves until she'd worn that siren out—or, at least, had numbed her with cold and exercise. Only then did she emerge back on dry land—out of breath and ready to drop.

Jasper tossed her a towel. 'How was that?'

The siren snapped to attention and Imogen could've wept. She dried off her arms and legs extra vigorously. 'Brilliant. Just give me a moment and you can tag-team me.' She pulled her sea shirt over her head and reached for the dry T-shirt she had in her tote but froze at the hunger that blazed in Jasper's face. Every desire she'd ever had roared to life in an instant.

With a tensing of his jaw, he dragged his gaze away, and, giving herself a mental slap, she scrambled into her dry shirt, wound her sarong back around her waist—not bothering to tie it, knowing her fingers wouldn't work—and knelt on the other side of the blanket from him, careful to keep her eyes fixed on George.

'Your turn!' Her voice emerged too loud and the brightness she injected into it jarred. She'd meant to physically tag him—slap her hand to his—but she changed her mind. One touch and he'd realise she was burning up.

Blowing out a breath, she smiled at George, picked up his teddy bear and danced it along the blanket. 'Water's great once you get in.'

Jasper shot to his feet as if he couldn't wait to be away from her, and she was really careful to keep her gaze from him as he shucked off his shirt, but couldn't resist glancing behind her as he jogged straight into the water without breaking stride, the shock of the cold barely seeming to register.

'Oh, my, George,' she murmured, pushing his toy train towards him and fanning her face. 'Your uncle is hot, hot, hot.'

But off-limits. Definitely off-limits.

Her employer swam for a good twenty minutes.

He's your boss. Don't forget he's your boss.

'Water's pretty damn fine, right?' she said, doing her best to look unaffected by the perfect line of his chest when he stood by the blanket again. The way the towel rubbed across defined pecs and honed abs made her mouth dry.

'Imogen, it's freezing!'

He dragged that towel over his hair before pulling his shirt back on and hiding all of that gloriously masculine muscularity.

That was a good thing.

He sent her a grin and she was relieved to see the strain had faded from his face. It helped ease the tension that had her wound up tight.

'But I know what you mean. I forgot how invigorating

that could be.' He spread his towel out beside the blanket and collapsed onto it. 'Did you and young George here have fun?' He tweaked his nephew's toes.

'I had a good think while you were swimming.' Was it her imagination or did he tense at her words? 'About Aunt Katherine,' she added quickly. She didn't want him thinking she was referring to anything else. 'I'm worried about her.'

He sat up, giving her his full attention. 'Why?'

'She told us all back home that she couldn't get the time off at Christmas, that she was needed here on Tesoura. I know that you're not going to give me an answer to this, but I'm starting to suspect that you did give her the time off, and she simply chose not to spend it with us.'

He watched her carefully but didn't say anything.

'She's been avoiding me since I arrived. During the day it's all work, work, work, and at night she tells me she has to get the household accounts into order for your accountant.'

She was doing what?

That was an outright lie. Not that Jasper could say as much to Imogen.

'I think the real reason she's trying to keep us apart is so we don't start comparing notes, realise there *is* something wrong and put our heads together to try and figure out what it is.'

That made a disturbing amount of sense. He knew at least one thing that was troubling Katherine. But was there anything else?

Shame hit him. He hadn't been paying attention. He'd been far too focussed on… He swallowed. He'd been too focussed on himself. Misfortune made some people more empathetic. He, though, had become more self-absorbed.

Look at the way he'd immediately jumped to the conclusion that Emily had sent George to him as part of an elaborate plan of revenge. It still might be, but that didn't change the fact that it shouldn't have been his first concern.

'Jasper, I have a feeling you know more about this than you're letting on.' She stared at him for several long seconds. 'Relax, I'm not going to ask you outright. I understand you have a duty as Katherine's employer and friend to keep her confidences.'

He let out a careful breath.

'But I am going to ask you if I should be as worried as I am.'

His gut clenched at the anxiety reflected in her hazel eyes, at the way her teeth worried her bottom lip. He wanted to ease her mind. He'd do just about anything to make her smile again. But he couldn't lie to her. 'I don't think you should be as worried as you are.'

She let out a long breath and closed her eyes. 'Thank you.'

'But I'm not a hundred per cent sure.'

Her eyes sprang open.

'Would it help if I had a word with your aunt?' He could at least urge Kate to confide in her niece.

She nodded without hesitating. 'Thank you.'

Jasper didn't approach Kate until after dinner, after he'd put George down for the night. Only then did he set his feet in the direction of the kitchen and Katherine's domain, but raised voices had him halting short of the doorway.

'For heaven's sake, Imogen, for the last time nothing is wrong! I'm getting tired of you harping on the subject.'

'But I'm worried about you.'

'That doesn't give you the right to pester me or pry into my personal life.'

What the...?

'Pry? I haven't pried.' Imogen's incredulity mirrored

his own. 'Auntie Kay, we're family. I know Mum's worried about you too, and—'

'While *I* know your mother sent you here to try and pressure me to return home. She's always known how to play the guilt card, but I'm not falling for it this time.'

'That's not fair!'

'It's more than fair. And you coming here as her proxy… It disappoints me, Imogen. I thought better of you.'

'What on earth are you talking about? I—'

'Enough! Yes, your mother and I have had a falling-out, but it's not your place to make me feel guilty about that or to play go-between. I have the right to live my life as I see fit. You're here to work—end of story. I'd appreciate it if you did that without interfering in my personal life.'

Jasper's head reared back. He'd never heard Katherine use that tone before, and he moved forward without thinking, aware of how gutted Imogen must be, and then had to take a step back when Imogen pushed past him with her head down. But that didn't prevent him from recognising the devastation on her face or the betraying sheen in her eyes.

A moment later the front door slammed. He wanted to go after her, make sure she was all right.

He shot into the kitchen and glimpsed Katherine's troubled expression before she quickly masked it again. She wiped the kitchen counters down vigorously. 'Did you want something, Jasper?'

He didn't bother pussyfooting around. 'That seemed unnecessarily harsh.'

'I don't appreciate Gloria's tactics.'

Gloria was her sister—Imogen's mother. 'Imogen isn't Gloria.'

'But she's acting as Gloria's envoy.'

He considered the charge. It didn't add up, not after

their conversation earlier on the beach. 'Are you sure about that? Because I'm not.'

Katherine's eyes flew to his. She straightened, setting the dishcloth in the sink. 'What other explanation is there? Why else would Immy be here?'

'For all the reasons she's stated—that she's between jobs, that she wanted to see a little more of the world, that she wanted to spend some time with her favourite aunt.'

'But she keeps asking annoying questions and saying she's worried about me, and—'

'Because she *is* worried. I know that for a fact. Look at it from her perspective. She's come all this way to see you—it's obvious that she adores you—and you're refusing to spend any time with her. And you're using the lamest excuses to avoid her. Now *I* know why you're busy, and *I* know why you're worried, but Imogen doesn't have a clue. And neither does Gloria.'

She pressed a hand to her forehead.

'Is it possible her mother didn't tell her about your argument?'

She blew out a breath. 'Yes.'

'So…?'

'So I'll apologise when she returns and smooth things over.'

'Why don't you tell her the truth? She'll be thrilled for you.'

'Because that will simply give her mother another weapon to use against me. She'll say I don't need an outside job to support myself any more, and that I can just as easily move back home and write there.'

'You can ask Imogen not to tell her.'

'That doesn't seem fair—asking Imogen to keep secrets from her mother.'

'She's a grown-up, Kate. I suspect there are lots of things she doesn't tell her mother.' He hesitated. 'Is there anything other than the book that's bothering you? Because I can—'

'Of course not!'

Her reply came too quickly. Unease circled through him, though he couldn't explain why.

'I can see, however, that you're worried about Immy.'

His shoulders went tight. He didn't like being so easy to read.

'Why don't you go after her and make sure she's okay? Let her know I'm sorry and fill her in on my secret. It's been exhausting to keep it and I'll be glad for her to know the truth.'

'Wouldn't you prefer to do that yourself?'

She shook her head. 'Off you go.' She shooed him out of the kitchen. 'I'll keep an eye on the baby.'

He found Imogen walking along the beach, her hands shoved into the pockets of her shorts and her shoulders hunched. The water lapped at her toes, but she barely seemed aware of it. He moved in next to her, and they walked in silence for a bit. The faintest blush of mauve lingered in the sky to the west as the last of the day's light faded.

'Did you hear all of my exchange with Aunt Katherine?'

She didn't look at him, just kept her eyes trained straight ahead. 'I heard enough to get the general gist.'

A huge golden moon hung low on the horizon, casting a path of dancing light on the water and turning the sand silver except for where the silhouettes of the palm trees made dark shadows. 'I didn't know that she and my mother had fallen out.'

'A fact that occurred to her only after you left.'

She stopped then, her eyes searching his face. The hurt mirrored inside them made his heart burn. 'Really? Or are you just trying to make me feel better?'

He crossed his heart.

Her gaze raked across his face again before something inside her seemed to relax. 'And I'm guessing she perhaps reached that conclusion with a little gentle persuasion from you?'

He didn't answer and she started walking again.

'She is sorry, you know?' he ventured.

She nodded, but still didn't speak. He touched her arm to make her halt. The silk of her skin an invitation hard to resist. 'I saw how upset you were when you left the house, Imogen. I…' He didn't know what it was he wanted to say—that he was worried about her, or that he was sorry she'd argued with her aunt, or that he thought her the most beautiful woman he'd ever laid eyes on?

He tried to dismiss that last thought to some dusty dungeon of his mind. It was just the moonlight talking.

'It's sweet of you to worry about me, Jasper, but I'm fine. To be perfectly honest I'm a bit cranky with both of them for turning me into piggy in the middle.'

She stared out to sea, her hands on her hips. 'Do you know what they fell out about?'

He stared into the dark waves. 'All she said is that she was tired of Gloria pressuring her to return home for good.'

'They've always been chalk and cheese, you know? Mum's the extrovert who's super social while Katherine's the one who has always relished peace and quiet. Mum's also seven years older and still sees Katherine as her little sister who needs brisking up.' She wrinkled her nose. 'It makes her bossy. I don't blame Katherine for getting her nose out of joint and telling Mum to pull her head in.'

'But?'

She shrugged. 'Despite all that, they're really close. I mean, they bicker, but it really rocked everyone when Katherine didn't come home for Christmas. It sent Mum into one of her panics. She was convinced something was wrong.'

And she'd infected her daughter with her own anxiety. 'About Christmas…'

She glanced at him. 'What about it?'

'Your aunt does have something on her mind, and she's given me permission to share it with you.'

She turned to face him fully and it made him hyper-aware of the warm breeze brushing against his calves and the lazy, languid elegance of the nearby palm trees and the rhythmic sound of the sea.

'Which is?'

He snapped back to attention. 'She wants to keep it just between us for the time being. So if you have a problem keeping things from your mother…'

Her eyebrows rose. 'I'll respect my aunt's confidences.'

This really should be coming from Katherine, but he knew how much the older woman hated fuss of any kind. He sympathised with that. He preferred to avoid the spot-light too. 'Well, the truth of the matter is a couple of years ago your aunt had a novel accepted for publication.'

Imogen stared at him in incomprehension for a mo-ment and then everything inside her seemed to electrify. She straightened, her shoulders shot back and she stared at him with huge eyes. 'She's been writing a book?'

'Well, a series, actually. She's had three books accepted so far and is working on her fourth—pulp fiction.' He grinned because he couldn't help it. 'Imogen, you have to read her stuff. It's so much damn fun. A crazy blend of zombie horror and romance, but it works.'

Her jaw dropped. 'You've read them?' And then she thumped his arm. 'I'm *so* jealous.'

'But now you can read them too.' Warmth radiated from where she'd touched him. He tried to ignore it.

She jumped up and down then, clapping her hands. 'Oh,

this is the best news. So exciting.' She stopped bouncing to purse her lips. 'She's been keeping it a secret because she thinks my mother will poke fun at her. Mum's a high school English teacher with a high regard for the classics, but she's not a literary snob. In her spare time she reads...'

'Zombie horror?'

A laugh gurgled out of her and it washed over him, rich and warm. 'Cosy mysteries and family sagas. I bet she'd love Katherine's stuff.' She lifted her chin. 'But you know what? They can sort that out for themselves. I'm not getting involved.'

Good for her.

Her face clouded. 'So that's why she didn't want to come home at Christmas?'

'Not exactly. Her publisher wants her to make significant changes to her latest manuscript before they'll agree to publish it. She's been trying to make those changes and struggling with it big-time.'

Comprehension dawned across her face. 'And that's what she's been doing in the evenings—not working on the household accounts but working on her book.'

He nodded because it was too hard to speak when he was fighting to get air into his lungs. The play of emotions across her face in the moonlight, the bounce of her hair and the vulnerable mobility of her lips all held him spellbound.

'Jasper, thank you. I—'

She broke off as their gazes caught and clung.

CHAPTER SEVEN

JASPER WANTED TO kiss her. She recognised the desire alive in his face. It shimmered like the light on a piece of Thai silk—prisms of luminescence arcing delicately against fragile cloth to form rainbows of luxuriant colour. Her every atom yearned towards him. She didn't just *want* him to kiss her—she *ached* with it.

Hovering between breaths, she waited, but he blinked, and she saw him fight to find the strength to gather his resources and step back.

A protest keened through her, but she understood why he did it. He was her boss. Making a move on her would be dishonourable, even though her employment status in his house fell firmly in the temporary category.

But she could make a move on *him* first, right?

She moistened her bottom lip. His gaze zeroed in on the action, hunger darkening his eyes and making his breathing ragged. The pulse at the base of his throat raced.

Why, yes. Yes, she could.

A thrill raced through her. 'Have you ever seen a more glorious moon?' she whispered, pointing to it though her gaze didn't leave his.

His gaze didn't leave hers either. 'No.'

'I once strolled along the Seine in the moonlight on a warm spring night, and I didn't think there could be a more romantic setting in the world. But I was wrong.'

His nostrils flared. 'You think my island is romantic?'

She nodded. 'Standing here on this beach now with a moon like that—all bright and vibrant—hovering just above the horizon like some kind of jewel, and with a warm breeze playing across my bare skin, that gorgeous perfume I've never smelled before drifting across from the forest and mingling with the scent of the sea...'

His Adam's apple bobbed.

'It feels like magic. And *very* romantic.'

His eyes throbbed into hers.

'I want to kiss you, Jasper.'

'Imogen.' Her name was barely more than a groan wrenched from his throat.

'I won't if you don't want me to.'

He closed his eyes, all the muscles in his jaw bunching.

'You know those moments you wished you'd taken, but you let slip away? And then spend the rest of your life kicking yourself for?'

His gaze returned to hers.

'This feels like one of those moments.'

A slow breath eased out of him, drawing her attention to the strong column of his throat and down to broad shoulders that made her mouth dry.

She forced her gaze back to his, not bothering to hide her need. 'I know it can't be anything more than a kiss. I'm not usually impulsive like this. I'm not into flings. But once I leave your gorgeous island, I'm starting a new phase of my life. This might be my last chance...'

He edged closer. 'To?'

'To seize the perfect moment—to live in it—without worrying about the consequences. To revel in a moment out of time one last time.'

His face gentled. 'A moment out of time?'

'A moment that, even when we're old and grey, will still put a smile on our faces whenever we remember it.'

His knuckles brushed across her cheek, firing her every nerve ending with heat and lust. His smile, when it came, made her thighs tremble. 'Then we'd better make it memorable.'

Her pulse started to gallop. She did what she could to get it under control—at least a little—because she didn't want to rush this moment. She wanted to savour it and imprint it on her mind for all time.

Which sounded crazy and overly dramatic, but she didn't care. She was following her gut all the way on this one.

Lifting her hands to touch his face, she revelled in the feel of his day-old growth as it scraped across her palms. He held still, waiting. 'What?' he eventually whispered, and she realised she'd been staring.

'There's something else that makes this moment incredibly romantic.'

'What's that?'

'You,' she murmured. She couldn't believe that she was touching him; that she was going to get to kiss him. 'You're beautiful, Jasper.' She could've chosen any number of words. *Gorgeous. Hot. Sexy.* They all fitted. But the one she'd uttered felt perfect. 'Beautiful inside and out.'

His lips parted as if in shock. His eyes had grown soft. 'Imogen…'

But she was done with talking. She slid her hands around his neck and pulled his head down to hers, reaching up on tiptoe to touch her lips to his.

The spark that ran through her made her tremble, but his hands at her waist held her steady. It gave her the security, and the boldness, to lean farther into him and move her lips across his more firmly. He was an intoxicating mixture of softness and strength, and kissing him was as invigorating as swimming in wild surf. It electrified her. And it must've electrified him too because it was as if their blood started racing at the same speed and to the same beat; their mouths opened at the same time and their tongues tangled as they tried to devour each other.

Wind roared in her ears, blocking out the sound of the surf. One of his hands pressed against the small of her back, urging her closer. The other flattened between her shoulder blades, hauling her against him. Every inch of her from the hips up could feel all of him. She wrapped her arms around his neck and tried to get even closer. The kiss went beyond anything she'd ever experienced. As if together they'd become the sea, sand and sun. As if crashing against each other, washing against each other, and heating each other up was what they were designed for.

She wrapped one leg around his waist to angle her pelvis more firmly against his. One large hand splayed beneath her thigh to hold it in place, and with a guttural groan he thrust against her. She threw her head back with a cry of pure need, arching into him.

She didn't know who stilled first. The way it felt—as if the moon had cast some spell on them and had cosmically attuned them to each other—they might've stopped at exactly the same moment. They stared into each other's stunned eyes. At least, she expected she must look as shell-shocked as him. She felt as if she were in a snow globe and someone had just shaken it—and the landscape of her life would never settle into the exact same contours again.

He let go of her leg. She lowered it to the ground.

He unwrapped his arm from her waist. She removed her hands from his shoulders.

She touched her fingers to her lips. He swallowed. 'Did I hurt you?'

She shook her head. 'No, but...wow.' Heat continued to spark across her skin like a tropical storm. 'I mean...wow!'

He nodded.

'No.' She shook her head. 'I mean a real *wow*.'

'Imogen—'

'I really wasn't expecting *that*.' She knew she was babbling but couldn't stop. 'I thought it was going to be some really sweet kiss that…' She shook her head at his pulsing, dark-eyed silence. 'But that wasn't *sweet*. I was ready to tear your clothes off and do things to you and with you that I've never—'

He reached out and pressed his fingers to her mouth with a low curse that made her close her eyes. Eventually she managed a nod. 'Sorry. Too much information.'

'For the record, I wasn't expecting things to get so intense so quickly either.' His hands clenched. 'I've been on this island too damn long.'

She gulped in air. 'Oh, no, you don't. You're not taking *all* the credit for that. It had just as much to do with me as it did with you. And I don't care what stupid excuses you want to make, but together we…*rock*.'

Bracing his hands on his knees, he huffed out a laugh. 'That's one way of putting it.' He straightened and met her gaze. 'But we both know it can't go beyond that, right?'

'I know.' She scratched both hands back through her hair and then frowned. She bit her lip and stuck out a hip. 'Why not?'

Her question slipped out without her meaning it to. Maybe the kiss had short-circuited her thought processes. His face grew grim and for a moment she thought he might revert to the wounded bear she'd met when she'd first arrived here, that he'd turn around and stalk off without another word. But then his face gentled again and he almost smiled. 'Because you're not romantically impulsive?'

And neither was he?

'You don't do flings.'

And he wasn't offering anything more.

Got it.

'You're only in Tesoura for a short time. You have big plans for your life. Exciting plans.'

She did. And she'd never be so foolish as to sacrifice those plans for a love affair. 'That's right.' She slapped a hand to her forehead. 'I remember now.' She eyed him carefully. 'And you have no plans to leave Tesoura?'

'None. This is my home now.'

She pulled in a breath. 'You're right. This can't go beyond that kiss. Sorry—' she shot him what she really hoped was a smile '—the oxygen is finally reaching my brain again.'

He laughed, and she wished she couldn't feel its rumble all the way to the centre of her being.

'There are other reasons too, Imogen. Many reasons. I'm going to tell you a story so you can understand what I mean.'

A story?

He pointed at the moon, and she turned to look. 'It still looks amazing,' he said.

But not as amazing as it had a moment ago. As it had moved farther into the sky, it had diminished in both size and colour. It looked neither as big nor as vividly yellow, as if it had lost some of its heat and energy.

Jasper surprised her when he moved behind and wrapped an arm about her shoulders and drew her back against him. She didn't resist, just let his warmth surround her. It was a protective gesture, a gesture of camaraderie, and it was kind. He didn't want her to feel alone, and he didn't want her to feel rejected.

The moon blurred and her throat ached.

'Do you remember asking what had happened to me?'

She nodded, not trusting herself to speak.

'I think if I tell you that story, you'll understand—and agree—that it's better for me to be on my own.'

She frowned out at the dark water, lifting a hand to

squeeze his forearm in a show of silent support. She couldn't see how she was ever going to agree that he should be *on his own*. Not forever. She got the fact that he might not want to be with her, but this self-imposed exile? He deserved better than that.

'I've already told you my father was physically abusive. He had a big leather belt that he wielded with great… authority. When he wasn't using his fists.'

She flinched, and his arm tightened about her.

'My mother copped most of his anger, though she's spent her entire life trying to placate him. I stepped in when I could…when doors weren't locked.'

She closed her eyes, but the image of the young boy he must've been was burned onto the insides of her eyelids. She forced her eyes open again. 'And then *you* copped it.' He didn't say anything. He didn't need to. 'Emily?'

'Mum and I did our best to protect her. She's a couple of years older than me, but she's always been a tiny little thing.'

Her heart burned.

'They say history never repeats, but they're wrong. In Emily's case it did. I never really liked Aaron all that much—thought him kind of smarmy—but I figured Emily was better off with him than at home where Dad was liable to lash out without warning. I'm guessing that's what she thought too.'

If Emily had never had a strong female role model like Imogen, then…then she'd have never really stood a chance.

'I dropped in on Em and Aaron unexpectedly one evening. I could hear raised voices upstairs, so I let myself in and followed the ruckus to its source. Where I saw Aaron backhand my sister. I saw red.'

'What happened?'

'I punched him, but evidently not hard enough because he got up and came at me. Emily was screaming at us to stop.' He paused. 'He charged. I sidestepped. Don't get me wrong, I had every intention of beating the living daylights out of him, but not in front of Emily. She'd been traumatised enough.'

He went so still she started to worry. She wrapped both her hands around his forearm and held on tight, pressed back against him, wanting him to know that he wasn't alone.

A breath shuddered out of him. 'His momentum sent him crashing across the landing and down the stairs.'

She gave a slow nod. It evidently hadn't killed the guy as he was still making Emily's life a misery… 'I'm finding it hard to feel any sympathy for him.'

A low chuckle broke from his throat, disturbing the hair near her ear and making her break out in gooseflesh. 'I can't say I felt too much of that at the time either. He broke his leg badly in two places. He walks with a limp and still needs a stick to get around. He's lucky to not be in a wheelchair apparently.'

She had a feeling he was lucky Jasper hadn't managed to get his hands on him good and proper.

'He accused me of assault. I was charged and a trial date was set.'

All Aunt Katherine had told her earlier came back now. She spun in his arms. 'But it didn't go to court.'

He stepped away and she immediately missed his warmth. His laugh held a bitter edge. 'He knew his charges would never stick. His fall down the stairs was an accident of his own making, not mine.'

So he'd dropped them, but… 'Why didn't Emily break free of him when she had the chance?'

This time his laugh held even more bitterness. 'Believe me, I wish I knew. I tried to get her to leave him.'

Her heart pounded so hard her chest hurt. 'But?'

'She told me she still loved him. She said he'd only forgotten himself that once, had only hit her that one time, and that it had been her fault for goading him into it.'

Imogen covered her face with her hands.

'She told me her relationship with Aaron was none of my business, that she hated me for what I'd done.'

She pulled her hands away to stare at him in disbelief. She felt suddenly and utterly exhausted. He must feel at least a hundred times worse.

'She said she'd never forgive me for hurting Aaron, and that she never wanted to see me again.'

And he'd not heard from her until last week? 'Your parents?'

'They took Aaron's side. My father and Aaron were always as thick as thieves, and my father had been looking for an excuse to sever all ties with me for years. He seized this one when it came along, lost no time in telling the tabloids my temper had always been a problem.'

'What an absolute pig of a man!'

'He forbade my mother from having any contact with me.'

It wasn't her place, she knew that, but she was angry with his mother too—*livid*. She pressed her lips together as hard as she could for a moment before releasing them. 'Do you miss them?'

'I don't miss my father.' He glanced at her with shadowed eyes. 'I have no love left in me for him. He destroyed that a long time ago. But my mother and sister…'

He missed them. She could see it. He'd banished himself to this island in despair because he hadn't been able to save them.

'I call my mother twice a year. I ask her the same questions. Can I come and get you? Is there anything I can do to help you get away from him?'

He was keeping the lines of communication open. Letting her know she had an escape route if she needed it. Imogen wanted to hug him.

'She refuses every single time. She tells me she likes her life.' He was quiet for a moment. 'I made her memorise my phone number in case she ever needs to call.' He shook his head. 'Emily still refuses to speak to me.'

For the last two years he'd been on his own, with no one to talk to about any of this. It had to have been festering away inside him like poison. She wanted to cry for him. 'Jasper, I'm so sorry.'

He nodded. With what looked like a concerted effort, he pushed his shoulders back and smiled. The sadness in his eyes, though, pierced her soul. 'So you can see why I think it best that I remain on my own.'

She didn't bother fighting her frown. 'Actually, I'm afraid I don't.'

His jaw went slack. 'Imogen—' he leaned towards her '—my family is complicated…ugly.'

'So what? It's not who you are. If a woman cared about you, she wouldn't give two hoots about your complicated family. She'd care about you—that's what would matter. I'm sorry, Jasper, but I don't get that reasoning at all.'

Jasper pinched the bridge of his nose, tried to ignore the way his heart leapt at her words. 'I missed out one important thread in my story.'

He called it a story because he desperately wanted to put some distance between it and him. But it didn't seem to be working.

Imogen pressed her hands to her abdomen as if she were fighting nausea. 'There's more?'

'I had a fiancée.' He forced himself to straighten. 'It wasn't public knowledge—we hadn't announced it yet. Bronwyn was, and still is, a cellist with the Sydney Symphony Orchestra. My father threatened her career—told her he'd have her dismissed from the orchestra—if she didn't break things off with me.'

Bronwyn's betrayal was still a raw ugly wound, though he'd never blamed her for her decision to walk away from him—not in the least. His father had threatened her career, her livelihood…her dream. 'He told her he'd see to it that she'd never play again.'

'So…she broke up with you?'

'I don't hold her responsible for that.'

Her eyes filled and his throat thickened. 'I can see that. Though, I'm not sure I'd have been so forgiving in your place.'

Imogen thought she'd act differently, but she didn't know Keith Coleman. She didn't understand how dangerous he could be. And Jasper had no intention of her ever finding out.

'*That's* why I need to be on my own, Imogen. *That's* why I can't have any ties. My father will go after the woman I love and do whatever he can to destroy her.'

'So you're not even prepared to risk it? Even if this hypothetical woman you love—and who loves you—not only has her own resources to rely on, but yours as well?' She leaned towards him. 'You're a wealthy man. That gives you a measure of power and protection.'

'It's not worth the risk. We're not just talking about someone's livelihood here, but their dreams—things they've been working towards their entire lives.' He could never ask a woman to give that up for him. 'My father has political power. His connections include key industry and business figures. He wields his influence with about as much care—and as much gusto—as George does his toy train. I will never put a woman in a position where she could be hurt by him.'

'Then your father has won. You're letting him win.'

Her words had a resonance that sounded through him.

Maybe she was right, but at least he could prevent his father from hurting another woman.

'No woman needs that hassle in her life. It's not a war she should be forced to fight. It wouldn't be fair. I refuse to be the catalyst for that kind of damage. It wouldn't be fair,' he repeated, before drawing himself up. 'Have you heard the mantra "do no harm"?'

She stared out at the water for three beats and then turned back with a nod.

He slapped a hand to his chest and met her gaze. She pulled in a breath as if she understood everything he was trying to say. For some reason that only made his heart burn harder.

'Life isn't fair, Jasper. No matter what you do, life isn't fair. It's not fair that you have such a father. It's not fair that a jerk of an ex-boyfriend of mine calls me stupid. It's not fair that my mother—'

He jerked to attention. 'Your mother?'

She shrugged. 'It wasn't fair that she and my aunt had to watch my grandmother die from breast cancer.'

Some sixth sense told him it wasn't what she'd originally meant to say. She turned on him, though, before he could challenge her. 'The thing is, whatever you do—you're not going to be able to protect everyone from everything. And you don't know what unforeseen consequences your attempts to keep everyone safe—your attempts to *do no harm*—could have either.'

'What are you talking about?' The decision he'd made was the right one, damn it.

'The day after you'd broken up with her, Bronwyn could've just as easily tripped and fractured a wrist. Hey presto, she can no longer play in the orchestra. That stuff happens all the time. But if you'd still been together and you'd been walking beside her, you might've caught her. And hey presto, no broken wrist.'

He rolled his eyes. 'You're being ridiculous. You're creating imaginary scenarios that may or may not happen and—'

'So are you!'

His head rocked back. He felt as if she'd slapped him.

'You're saying *if* you let a woman close, and *if* your father finds out about it then he *might* threaten her in some way. And *if* that happens, you're saying she's going to walk away from you…and *if* she doesn't then she's going to get hurt because you and her don't have the power to fight your father.'

His teeth ground together.

'That's a lot of *ifs* and *mights*, Jasper.'

He counted to ten. 'You haven't lived the life I've lived. And you don't know my father the way I do. This is no longer up for discussion.'

'But—'

'Look, I know that kiss was spectacular. But spectacular kisses don't necessarily lead to spectacular relationships.'

She drew herself up to her full height, which meant she reached the top of his nose. 'This isn't about me.'

'Are you sure?' He knew it wasn't, but he asked the question to deliberately anger her, to distance and alienate her. It'd be much better that she think him a jerk than for his father to—

His hands clenched. He would *not* let his father hurt her. He would not allow that man to dim this woman's fire or to crush her dreams.

Her soft laugh jerked him back. 'You're being a deliberate jackass now.'

His jaw clenched before he forced it to relax again. 'We really need you to work on that subservience thing.'

'You're being a deliberate jackass, *sir*.'

He had to cover his mouth to hide a smile.

She turned and started back along the beach in the direction of the house. He fell into step beside her, doing his best to not breathe in the notes of vanilla and citrus that seemed to be a part of her. Water foamed up suddenly around her ankles, making her smile. It was such a simple pleasure, and in that instant he felt bad for being, as she'd put it, a jackass.

'That kiss, Imogen…'

Was it his imagination or did she stiffen? 'Hmm…?'

'You're right, you know? It's not the kind of kiss one forgets.'

'Burned on my brain,' she agreed.

He envied her that cheerful candour. 'And when I'm old and grey and I remember it, it's going to make me smile. Every single time.'

'Me too.'

She sent him a smile full of warmth, but a new distance lurked at its edges, a distance he'd created, and his heart protested. A defiant part of him wanted to smash the barriers he'd forced her to put into place. But to what end? So he could hurt her more?

He clenched his hands. Sometimes spectacular kisses did lead to spectacular relationships, but mostly they didn't. He and Imogen didn't have a relationship—not in that sense—and they weren't going to. A man who couldn't find a way to protect his own mother and sister didn't deserve love and romance. His chest burned. He wasn't worthy of a woman like Imogen.

He pulled in a breath and steeled himself. He couldn't kiss Imogen again. He *had* to resist.

CHAPTER EIGHT

IMOGEN HAD HEARD about raging emotions—had read about them in books, and had even experienced them a time or two, but not like this. She felt as if she were being battered by cyclonic winds and stinging rain. A part of her wanted to seek shelter, to lick wounds that had started to throb with a nagging persistence that made her temples ache.

Another part of her wanted to seize Jasper and kiss him again, to drag him into the maelstrom with her. If he kissed her back it would make all those aches go away. She knew that on a primal level.

But if he didn't kiss her back…

She pulled in a breath and swallowed. If he didn't kiss her back it'd make everything hurt twice as much. And she couldn't kiss him again. Not after he'd told her he didn't want her to.

When they reached the edge of his garden, she halted and closed her eyes. 'That birdcall is lovely,' she said on the pretence of listening to something rather than calling attention to the effort she was making to calm the storm raging inside her.

She needed to compose herself before she spoke to her aunt.

She could feel Jasper's eyes on her, assessing her, so she did what she could to smooth out her face. 'Do you know what it is?'

She opened her eyes to find him shaking his head. She resisted the urge to point out that he demonstrated a remarkable lack of interest in his idyllic island retreat—the place he now apparently called home. She'd bet a therapist would have something insightful to say about that.

She pressed her lips together to stop herself from playing therapist.

He opened the front door and ushered her ahead of him. She refused to notice the warm spicy scent of him—or his beguiling heat—as she slipped past.

Don't think about Jasper. Focus on Aunt Katherine.

Katherine and George were in the living room, and, with the windows dark now from the night, the room reminded Imogen even more of a ship. George, looking sleepy on his blanket on the floor, cuddled his toy rabbit with its super-long ears. Katherine, looking worried, leapt up from the sofa the moment they entered.

'Imogen, honey, I'm sorry about earlier,' she started at the same time Imogen spoke.

'You've written a book!'

And then they both laughed and hugged.

'I shouldn't have said what I did,' Katherine said, pulling Imogen down to the sofa beside her.

George saw his uncle and let go of his soft toy to kick his legs and lift his arms to be picked up. With a smile that caught at her stupid, susceptible heart, Jasper lifted him and cradled him against his shoulder. She now knew how strong those arms were, how broad and solid those shoulders.

'I should've known Gloria hadn't told you about our tiff.'

Imogen hauled herself back, studiously averting her gaze from man and baby.

'My only excuse is that I've not been sleeping well and...'

Imogen reached for her aunt's hand. 'Jasper tells me you're having trouble with your latest book.'

'It's a hot mess, but I think I'm finally starting to make progress.'

Katherine's smile didn't quite reach her eyes, so Imogen didn't believe her, and while she didn't want to add to her aunt's stress, she didn't want to keep secrets from her any longer either. 'I didn't know about your falling-out with Mum, Auntie Kay, but there is something you probably should know.'

Katherine stared at her—and so did Jasper as he lowered himself into the armchair opposite. She could feel his attention like a laser beam and she really, *really* wished she could just not be aware of it…not be aware of *him*.

Katherine seized Imogen's shoulders, her face losing all colour. 'Immy, please tell me she doesn't have breast cancer.'

It hit her then how much her grandmother's death had affected the two sisters. 'I promise you, she doesn't have breast cancer.'

Katherine sagged. 'You frightened me out of my wits.'

'I'm sorry, I didn't mean to. There is an issue, but it's not as serious as cancer. Back in November Mum found out she has macular degeneration.'

Katherine stared at her. 'She's going blind?'

Imogen's eyes filled and she nodded. 'She has time yet. They can delay it by giving her injections into her eyes, but eventually…'

'Why didn't she tell me?'

'She was going to tell you in person at Christmas.'

'But I didn't come home.' Katherine tapped a finger against her mouth. 'So that's why she's been so passive-aggressive recently and telling me that my being so far away isn't fair to your grandfather.'

'You know what she's like. She's focussing all of her worry on who's going to look after Granddad if she's blind.'

Katherine stiffened, and then without warning burst

into tears. Imogen wrapped an arm about her shoulders, her throat thickening. 'She's going to be fine, Auntie Kay, I promise you. Like I said, there's time. It could be years before her eyesight becomes truly bad. There's time for everyone to adjust, to put strategies into place. And there's no need for you to come home—not for good. Dad and I can look after Granddad—'

'Darling girl, that's not your job.' Katherine lifted her head and wiped her eyes. 'The thing is…'

Katherine's expression had ice fist-bumping down Imogen's spine. Jasper leaned towards them. 'What is the thing?' she croaked.

'Just before Christmas, I found a lump in my breast.'

Imogen's hand flew to her mouth. Her heart pounded so hard it was nearly impossible to breathe. 'You spent the holidays getting tests?'

Oh, please, don't let Auntie Kay have cancer, please—

Katherine's gaze dropped. 'No.'

No? But… Grandma had *died* of breast cancer. Katherine had seen the effects, had—

'I went to a little village on the mainland and worked on my book. And waited for the lump to go away.'

Her mouth went dry. 'Auntie Kay…'

Jasper shot to his feet, his face set, though his eyes blazed. He still held the baby against his shoulder as if it were the most precious thing in the world—cradling him there as if he wanted to protect him from all hurt.

Katherine glanced from one to the other. 'I meant to.' Her bottom lip trembled. 'But I was afraid. I didn't realise that's the way I'd react. I couldn't face the thought of…' She covered her face briefly. 'But if I do have breast cancer and if I die and if Gloria goes blind then…who will look after your grandfather? Your uncles won't know what to do. And I—'

'Kate.' The quiet authority in Jasper's voice had them

both turning to him. 'That's an awful lot of ifs on very little evidence.'

Had he meant to repeat the words she'd said to him earlier?

His brows drew down over his eyes. 'Why didn't you tell me?'

'We don't talk about personal matters, Jasper.'

'But this is your health!'

'I was hoping it'd go away. I know that probably sounds stupid to you both, but—'

'No,' Imogen said. 'I get it. But, Auntie Kay, we have to get you examined.'

Katherine hesitated and then nodded. 'I'll make an appointment tomorrow.'

Jasper widened his stance. He looked suddenly immovable. 'We can do better than that. I'll organise a seaplane for first thing in the morning, and I'll have you seen by a team of Brazil's best medical professionals ASAP.'

Katherine thrust out her jaw. 'Don't come over all high-handed with me, Jasper. You can't force me into anything I don't want and—'

'Kate, I would never force you into anything against your will. *Never.*'

Jasper wasn't his father. She could see now how he'd modelled himself to become the exact opposite—the protector rather than the abuser. She wanted to leap up and hug him—for his kindness to Katherine, but also for all the constant restrictions he placed on himself, for the sacrifices he made without asking for anything in return. A man like Jasper deserved to be surrounded by family and love.

The fight drained out of her aunt. 'I know. I'm sorry. It's just that things are going to start moving so quickly now and it feels as if everything will start spinning out of my control.'

Imogen seized her hand. 'As soon as we have answers,

it'll stop the spinning.' She tightened her grip. 'You know that in the majority of cases lumps are benign.'

'But what if it's not? With my history…'

Fear clutched at Imogen's heart.

'We take it one step at a time,' Jasper interspersed calmly. 'If it isn't benign, then we'll make a plan. You'll take a deep breath and consider all your options. We'll find a way forward, Kate. You're healthy and still young. I promise, you won't be on your own.'

Katherine pulled in a deep breath and nodded. Imogen could see her mentally steel herself to face whatever the future had in store. Jasper fumbled with his phone and Imogen leapt to take the baby.

'He was fussing earlier,' Katherine murmured, 'so I brought him downstairs. But he seems to have settled again now.'

'I'll go put him down.'

It took her next to no time to put the sleepy baby to bed. She started back towards the living room but halted in the shadows at the top of the stairs when her aunt said, 'Jasper, I can't afford the kind of treatment you're talking about.'

Jasper's head lifted from where he furiously texted on his phone. 'Healthcare benefits were part of your employment package.'

Katherine snorted, and Imogen didn't blame her. The man was a *terrible* liar.

He dragged a hand down his face. 'Okay, I have a lot of money. It's just sitting there doing nothing. Please let me do this for you. Let me do something good with it.'

The room blurred, and Imogen's throat thickened.

'You've been a rock—one of the few stable elements in my life. You mean a lot to me. You're like…family.' He gave a half laugh. 'The family I wished I had. Not the messed-up excuse that I got. Please let me do this one thing for you.'

'You can't refuse that, Auntie Kay.' The words burst from Imogen as she flew down the stairs. *Accept his offer*, she wanted to yell. It had been made with a good and pure intent.

'Immy's right. I can't refuse you when you put it like that. Thank you, Jasper. I'm grateful…and touched.'

Katherine rose and gave him a hug. Her eyes were wet when she released him several moments later and his were suspiciously bright at well.

'So you'll be ready to leave at six in the morning?'

Katherine nodded.

Imogen eased forward. 'Can I help with anything?' She'd sit up all night and hold her aunt's hand if it'd help.

'Thank you, Immy, but no. I'm going to pack a few things and then do some breathing exercises. A bit of quiet now is what I need.'

She watched her aunt leave the room before swinging to Jasper. 'Thank you. A million times, thank you.'

'It's nothing.'

'It's everything! To know we'll have an answer one way or another soon…' Didn't he know what a big thing that was? 'Knowing will help. I know she's been hiding from it, and I know she's afraid.' Imogen was terrified so it must be a thousand times worse for her aunt. 'But getting an answer—knowing—is good. And you're making sure that happens as soon as possible.'

'It's the least I can do.'

It was more than most would've done. She didn't say as much, though. It was taking all her strength and concentration not to get caught up in the clear grey of his eyes and the beguiling breadth of his shoulders.

'You'll be okay here on your own for a couple of days with George while Katherine and I go to the mainland?'

She wished she could go too but she swallowed and nodded. 'Of course. Eduardo's here if I need help with anything.' She lifted her chin. She wasn't adding to the expense or the hassle of the trip. She could talk to her aunt every day on the phone.

Those eyes didn't leave her face. 'You want to be with your aunt.'

It was a statement, not a question. 'I wouldn't be human if I didn't want that. But it's neither here nor there. You're…'

She trailed off when he punched a number into his phone and lifted it to his ear. 'Antonio, is there room for another two passengers—one adult and one baby?'

Imogen's heart thumped.

'Excellent. Thank you.'

'It's really not necessary,' she whispered.

'Your aunt will be happier if you're with her. And it's your aunt we need to think about.'

'I swear to God you just became my new favourite person, Jasper.'

Just for a moment his eyes crinkled. And she wanted to hug him so badly things inside her hurt. As if he read that thought on her face, he took a step back. 'Pack light. One small bag. Plan for a two-night stay. If we need anything else, we can buy it on the mainland. I'd better finish making the arrangements and pack for me and George.'

She watched him leave. 'Goodnight, Jasper,' she murmured once he'd disappeared from view.

Her new favourite person? She swallowed. She hadn't been joking.

She was in trouble. Big trouble.

Jasper had made arrangements for the seaplane to take them to the port of Santos—an hour away—and from there a limousine took them to São Paulo. He'd ordered Evan to find him the best darn medical facility in the city. His assistant had gone above and beyond. Not only had he shortlisted five hospitals with excellent reputations, but he'd also managed to book Katherine into one of them for a biopsy that very morning. He didn't know what strings Evan had pulled or how much money it was going to cost, but he didn't care. Kate deserved the absolute best.

He sank into a chair in the hallway outside her door, dropping his head to his hands. Why hadn't he taken better care of Kate? Why hadn't he insisted on taking her and Eduardo to the mainland once a year for medicals?

He'd become unforgivably self-absorbed since arriving on Tesoura. He'd lost a part of himself when Bronwyn, Emily and his mother had turned their backs on him. He'd shut himself off emotionally, fooled himself into thinking that large donations to women's refuges could replace emotion and caring. But he'd been wrong.

The door to Kate's room opened and he straightened. He didn't want either woman to see how worried he was. He needed to be strong for them. Imogen's ashen face as she walked out squeezed his chest tight. He drew her down to the seat beside him. George continued to sleep in blissful ignorance in the nearby stroller. 'Your aunt is in excellent hands.'

'I know. And I'm so grateful to you, Jasper.' She sent him a brave little smile that twisted his insides. 'They're about to take her down for the biopsy, but she wants a word with you before she goes.'

With a nod, he shot to his feet and strode into Kate's room. 'How are you feeling? Is there anything I can get for you?'

'Now that I'm here, I'm feeling remarkably calm.'

He sat on the edge of her bed. 'Is there anything you'd like me to do?'

'Actually, there is.'

He leaned towards her, all attention. 'Name it.'

'I'm going to be busy with tests all day, Jasper. I don't want Imogen fretting any more than she already is. Besides, a hospital waiting room is no place for a baby. I want you to take her out to see the sights—get her mind off things for a while. I don't want to see either one of you until visiting hours this evening.'

'But—'

She raised an eyebrow and he swallowed back his protests. 'I've a novel I wouldn't mind finishing. I have a pen and notepad because a new story idea has come calling, which is far from convenient considering I haven't finished my current one yet but playing around with that will keep me busy. And I have a playlist full of my favourite songs. I've everything I need to keep me calm and occupied.'

He read the subtext. Him and Imogen fussing and hovering would add to her stress—their anxiety would feed hers. He flashed to Imogen's pale face and nodded. Sitting here worrying wouldn't do her any good either. He fished out his phone and brought up a list of current 'things to do' in São Paulo and scanned the offerings. His lips lifted, and he met Kate's gaze. 'Done. Now is there anything I can get or do for you before I whisk Imogen away for the day?'

'I have everything I need, thank you. You've gone above and beyond.'

He rose, hesitated and then leaned across to press a kiss to her cheek. 'We're just a phone call away. If you need us…'

She nodded, blinking hard, and then she rolled her eyes as two orderlies came into the room pushing a wheelchair. 'Honestly, is that necessary? You are aware that I haven't lost the use of my legs?'

Jasper hid a smile. She pointed a finger at him. 'Now, I'm looking forward to being regaled with your adventures later this evening, so don't let me down.'

He saluted and left the room. Imogen glanced up and he forced a cheerfulness he was far from feeling. 'Come on.' He took the stroller and started to wheel it down the hall. 'We've been banished.'

She rose automatically but she didn't move. 'By who?'

He linked an arm though hers and urged her forward. 'Who do you think?'

'Oh, but—'

'Imogen, Kate is going to be busy with tests all day. It's not like we're going to get a chance to see her between those tests or to sit with her.'

'I know. I just… I want to be close in case she needs us.'

'She has both our numbers on speed dial.' He forced himself to release her. Touching her made him…actually it unmade him. 'Do you know what she's looking forward to?'

'What?'

'Us regaling her with our adventures for the day.'

'But—'

'Wondering what we're getting up to is one of the things that will help her get through today.'

She worried at her lip.

'And you know how she hates fuss of any kind.'

She worried harder and he wanted to wrap her in his arms and tell her everything would be all right. Only he didn't know if it would be. Panic tried to let loose inside him, but he reined it in. 'And this isn't a place for a baby.'

She glanced at George and her shoulders slumped. 'Okay, but if you think some cathedral or museum is going to take my mind off what's happening here you have rocks in your head.'

'That sounds like a challenge.' He pushed the stroller into motion again, and her eyes widened at what he expected was the smug expression on his face. 'I'll bet you lunch at an authentic Brazilian eatery that it does.'

Her jaw dropped. 'You're on,' she said with a glare.

Twenty minutes later a taxi set them down at their destination—the museum of contemporary art. Imogen watched the taxi depart. 'Your Portuguese is very good. When did you learn?'

'When I first arrived on Tesoura. It seemed the polite thing to do.'

He'd banished himself to an island and had learned a language he hardly ever used because he never went anywhere, and he never saw anyone. What kind of sense did that make?

He shook the thought away as she glanced at the building in front of him. 'So this is a…museum.'

'Not just any museum. Here, you take the top and I'll take the bottom.' He gestured to the stroller and together they manoeuvred it up the stairs.

'What's so special about—?'

She broke off when she saw the sign advertising the current exhibition, and he grinned at her expression. 'You mean besides the fact that there's currently a costume exhibition showing here?'

The woman was a dressmaker, a seamstress—she'd worked in Paris and was opening her own sewing school in a couple of months. He figured the one thing in this entire amazing city that had the potential to charm her, to fire her enthusiasm and imagination, was a historic collection of amazing clothes.

She slammed her hands on her hips, and he could see her try to work up some righteous outrage. 'You exploited my weakness for a free lunch?'

'Hey, whatever works.'

She glanced at the sign again. 'Well, it looks as if lunch is definitely on me.' She threaded her arm through his and he had to grit his teeth against the rush of warmth that sped through him. 'C'mon, I can't wait to see this. When Aunt Katherine hears about it, you're going to get the biggest gold star.'

The next two hours flew by. The clothes on display were utterly amazing—everything from indigenous ceremonial robes, intricate Renaissance ball gowns, to costumes used in popular soap operas. There were hats and shoes, under-clothes and tools of the trade that meant very little to him. It wasn't the items on display that held his attention, but Imogen's rapt delight. Her explanations of the techniques used and her appreciation for the fine craftsmanship had him transfixed.

'Your sewing school is going to be amazing.'

She stilled but didn't look at him. 'What makes you say that?'

'You have a real passion for all of this. And passion is the thing that makes the difference. People are drawn to it. It gives you the energy and drive to succeed. It means that when you hit a road bump, you'll find a way around it.' He could almost sense the doubts piling up inside her. 'And you shouldn't let that stupid ex-boyfriend of yours convince you otherwise.'

She swung to him, her mouth dropping, but then she turned back to the displays and he let the matter drop. Her passion challenged him in ways he hadn't expected. He'd been passionate once—passionate about building his company into a globally recognised brand; passionate about doing all he could to help his mother and sister; passionate about neutralising his father and the harm he did.

He'd let his passion die. And in the process, he'd become a robot. His chest cramped. His passion for life and justice might've died, but it didn't mean he had to become a miserable excuse for a human being.

He shook the thought off and picked up George's tossed bunny for the fifth time. George squealed in joy when Jasper handed it to him…again.

He was convinced Imogen would've happily spent the entire day perusing the collection, but George's eventual protests warned them he'd had enough of being cooped up in his stroller.

She turned with a smile. 'Lunch?'

'I know the perfect place.'

Her lips twitched. 'I just bet you do.'

He took her to Ibirapuera Park. At 158 hectares, it was one of the largest urban parks in Latin America. They bought *pastel de queijos*—delicious deep-fried snacks stuffed with savoury fillings—and meat patties formed around wooden skewers called *kibe*, and sat on the grass to eat them. They spread out a small blanket for George, and he belly-crawled between the two of them, munching on a rusk and cooing his delight at being freed from his pram.

Buskers started up nearby and Imogen leaned towards them as she listened. 'My father would love this so hard.'

Her sound-recording father? He straightened from where he'd been leaning back on his elbows. He'd been trying to think of a way to keep her occupied for the afternoon, and he might've just found it. 'Would you keep an eye on George for ten minutes while I slip off?'

'Sure.'

It took him fifteen minutes, but it was worth it when he lowered his bag of purchases to her lap. She pulled out the mini cassette recorder and the stack of tiny tapes he'd bought, and she turned to him with a question in her eyes. 'I thought you might like to record these guys for your dad…and maybe send your parents a kind of São Paulo diary. I mean, I know you can do that stuff on your phone, but reception is pretty dodgy at Tesoura, and if you wanted to continue the diary there… Anyway, I thought your father might enjoy the older technology.'

'Oh, Jasper, that's a brilliant idea!' She leaned across to George, who sat between them, and tickled his tummy. 'Your uncle has the best ideas, George.' She glanced up, her eyes shining. 'Thank you, it was the perfect thing to do.'

He didn't know how she did it, but she made him feel like a superhero.

She slipped a tape into the recorder and immediately

gave the date and location, introducing both George and Jasper and making them say hello into the machine. George's hello was inaudible as he tried to eat the recorder. She rescued it with a laugh and then rested back on one hand and gave her impressions of the city. She recorded the nearby buskers—but not until she'd bought their CD and asked their permission. When they found out she was from Australia they played a Brazilian version of 'Waltzing Matilda' that absolutely delighted her.

Her fun and excitement infected both him and George. Though eventually George snuggled down on his blanket with his bottle, his eyes growing heavy as the afternoon began to lengthen. Imogen collapsed to her knees beside Jasper, gesturing to the buskers. 'They're amazing. My father will love them. This day has been amazing, Jasper. It shouldn't have been but...*you're* amazing.'

And then she leaned forward and pressed her lips to his in a brief, exuberant kiss that had every pulse in his body thumping.

She eased away, still smiling, but it faded as she stared into his eyes. Her lips parted and a yearning he couldn't refuse stretched across her face. In that moment he was lost. Curving a hand around her nape, he drew her head back down to his again and he kissed her with a hunger he didn't bother trying to conceal. Somehow, she ended up in his lap, curled there as if she belonged, her fingers threading through his short hair, her tongue tangling with his and driving him mad with need.

He only came to when a group of passing youths catcalled. *Damn.* What on earth was he thinking? They were supposed to be looking after a baby, not necking like a couple of teenagers!

He set her away from him with more speed than grace. 'I'm sorry. I promised that wouldn't happen again.'

She paled at whatever she saw in his face. He pulled in a deep breath, tried to moderate his voice. 'Are you okay?'

'I'm fine.' She lifted her chin. '*I'm* not the one who's sorry that happened.' The green in her eyes flashed. 'I *like* kissing you, Jasper. I… I like you.'

He saw then how invested she was becoming—in him… in them. But there was no them. And if he let her continue thinking that, he'd hurt her. Badly. With a force of will, he hardened his heart. 'I like kissing you too, but it won't happen again. Emotions are running high today.'

Her gaze narrowed. 'It's more than that and you know it.'

'And I don't need the complication in my life,' he continued as if she hadn't interrupted. He hated the swift shaft of pain that darkened her eyes. 'Your aunt would never forgive me if I scratched that particular itch with you, especially if I let you think it meant more than it did.'

He waited for her to call him a jackass, but she didn't. She merely turned her back on him and her attention back to the park.

Damn! His life was on a Brazilian island. Hers was in Australia. Their lives were going in totally opposite directions. Perhaps that in and of itself wasn't such an insurmountable obstacle if it weren't for other things. But there *were* other things—his father, his own reluctance to trust again, his lack of faith and hope. Just…*no*! He wasn't prepared to go through any of that again.

He couldn't give her the kind of long-term relationship she wanted and deserved, so he had no business kissing her. What she deserved was a wholesome, undamaged man who wasn't carrying a ton of baggage and didn't have a family like his waiting to close its jaws about her. She deserved a man who could commit to forever. A man who could protect her rather than one who would bring trouble to her door.

And that man wasn't him.

CHAPTER NINE

IMOGEN STARED AT the doctor the following morning. 'The lump is benign?' she repeated.

'We're ninety per cent certain it's benign,' the doctor clarified. 'We only have the preliminary results—it'll be another five days before the full report is available—but the signs are good.' The doctor smiled. 'But, *sim*, I am confident all is well.'

Jasper leaned towards the statuesque white-coated woman. 'So you don't think Katherine has cancer?'

'That is correct.'

With a whoop, Imogen hugged her aunt, though she was careful not to hug her too tight in case Katherine was still sore from her biopsy. 'Best news ever!'

She turned back to find that Jasper had seized George from his stroller and was holding him aloft like some kind of victory trophy. George loved every moment of it, squealing and kicking his legs.

Katherine seized the doctor's hand and pumped it up and down. 'Thank you so much, Doctor. I can't thank you enough.'

'It will be thanks enough, *minha amiga*, if you keep up to date with your mammograms and promise to make an appointment with your doctor if anything ever again gives you cause for concern.'

'I've learned my lesson. So... I can go now?'

The doctor consulted Katherine's chart. 'I'm afraid not. Mr Coleman has booked you in for a complete medical check. But you should be done by four o'clock this afternoon.'

Katherine turned to Jasper as soon as the doctor left and raised an eyebrow. Imogen did her best not to think about how she and Jasper would survive another day in each other's company.

Not after he'd kissed her. And then acted like a jerk. When prior to that he'd been...

She swallowed. When he'd been every dream she hadn't known she'd wanted. He'd been kind and fun, warm and witty, he'd made her laugh when she hadn't thought that possible. He'd given both her mind and her hands something to do, and while that hadn't rid her of worry for Katherine, it had made it bearable.

Until he'd kissed her, that was. She'd forgotten everything then—Katherine, George, herself. The kiss had been perfect.

Until it wasn't.

'Imogen, help me out here.'

She snapped back to find an exasperated Katherine staring at her. She'd missed the beginning of the conversation, but she could guess it. 'What's the harm in getting the tests done, Auntie Kay? Mum's wishing she'd gone for an eye test earlier.' She glanced at her watch. 'It's only another six or so hours. I'm happy to hang here and keep you company.'

She didn't want to spend another moment with Jasper, thank you very much. Their stilted conversation and taut silences were wearing on her nerves. After yesterday's kiss he'd retreated with so much unholy speed it'd left her feeling tainted and ugly. And stupid.

It shouldn't matter so much. It shouldn't *hurt* so much. But it did.

Katherine blew out an exasperated breath. 'Fine, I'll

have the tests, but I don't want either one of you hanging around the hospital. Go out and see the sights. Have fun.'

Ha! Fun and Jasper no longer went together in the same sentence.

Jasper cleared his throat. 'I actually have some work I need to do.'

He didn't look at her as he spoke.

'Work when you get home,' Katherine protested. 'You and Imogen should go enjoy yourselves.'

'That's okay, Jasper doesn't need to act as my tour guide,' Imogen inserted in her most cheerful voice—so bright it bounced off the walls like a shiny new ten-cent piece. 'What I'd really like to do today is hit the shops. I want to buy souvenirs for everyone back home. I was reading about a market that's under one of the art galleries and it sounds fab—I'm hoping to pick up some pretty, locally made jewellery, maybe find a fabric store or two. I doubt it'd be Jasper's thing.'

'I'd be happy to accompany you.'

But he said it with such a lack of enthusiasm it made even Katherine roll her eyes. Imogen did her best to stop her insides from shrivelling. 'Not necessary. And I'm happy to take George so you can concentrate on your work.' George would be a welcome distraction.

'I can manage.' He set George back in his stroller.

She folded her arms. 'You know he hates being cooped up inside all day.'

His eyes flashed. 'So I'll take him to the park.'

Ha! So he wasn't as cool and reserved as he'd like her to think.

Katherine glanced from one to the other, and Imogen immediately curbed her impulse to get another rise out of him. It was childish. And it'd only make her feel better in the short-term. It'd be best to do what he was doing—put him out of her mind completely. 'Are you sure you wouldn't prefer a bit of company, Auntie Kay?'

'Absolutely not.'

'Then is there anything you'd like me to get for you while I'm out?'

Her aunt made a list, and Imogen didn't know why Jasper hung around if they were going their separate ways for the day. 'You didn't have to wait,' she said as they walked to the elevator.

'I wanted a word with you before you took off.'

But when several people joined them in the elevator he didn't speak again until they stood alone in the wide hospital foyer. The waiting made things inside her clench up. 'It's great news about Katherine's results,' she finally prompted when he'd remained silent for too long.

He turned to her as if he'd forgotten she was there. Which was great for a girl's ego. She pressed her lips together hard and didn't say a word.

'Look, Imogen, about what happened in the park yesterday—'

'Are you just going to apologise again?' she cut in. 'And remind me you're not interested in a relationship again, blahdy-blah?'

His eyebrows rose. 'Blahdy-blah?'

She lifted an eyebrow of her own, and eventually he nodded. 'Pretty much.'

She gave an exaggerated roll of her eyes designed to annoy him. 'Then *puhlease* spare me and take it as read, okay?' She had the satisfaction of seeing his jaw clench, but it didn't help, not in the slightest. Just as she'd known it wouldn't. 'Was there anything else?'

'Yes,' he snapped, drawing himself up to his full height and becoming a stranger—an autocrat—and it reminded her fiercely that he was her billionaire boss and she was nothing but his lowly maid. 'Can you cook?'

That made her blink. 'I'm no chef, but I can cook a meal without burning it.'

'I want to give Katherine a week's holiday. I'd like to reassign your duties to meal preparation. You've taught me enough now about how to look after a baby that I'm confident I can take care of George without assistance. Needless to say, I'm grateful for all the help you've given me where he's concerned.'

But her help was no longer required. She heard that message loud and clear. This was Jasper Coleman reasserting his authority. She wanted to tell him he was being a pompous jackass. But he wasn't. He was drawing strict and rigid boundaries between them, leaving her in no doubt that he'd meant all he'd said about relationships and complications.

And the sooner her heart got that message, the better. She folded her face into polite lines. 'That won't be a problem. I'd be delighted to assist, sir.'

He blanched at her *sir*. She refused to let herself feel anything. She simply waited for him to either give her further instructions or to dismiss her. Actually, this subservience thing wasn't too hard once she put her mind to it.

'Have a pleasant day, Imogen.'

'Thank you, sir.' She bent down to tickle George's tummy and then turned and walked away before she cried.

After her third day of being Tesoura's head chef, Imogen told herself that she'd finally found her equilibrium. She and Jasper hadn't been able to maintain such an intense formality with each other, not with Katherine playing spectator. But as they hardly spent any time in each other's company, maintaining a polite facade proved no great hardship.

As long as she didn't look at him. As long as she didn't remember the way he'd kissed her in the park. As long as she recited, *You're just the maid* over and over in her mind.

What was proving harder to ignore at the moment was a baby's insistent crying. She turned her clock to face her—2:38 a.m. It appeared Mr I'm-Confident-I-Can-Look-After-George-on-My-Own-Without-Assistance wasn't doing so well in the parenting stakes at the moment.

She was tempted to roll over and pull a pillow over her head, and if it was only Jasper who'd suffer she would. But George...

With a sigh, she hauled herself out of bed, mentally checked what she was wearing—a baggy T-shirt and a pair of tracksuit bottoms, which were far from glamorous but at least covered her decently enough—before heading in the direction of George's wails.

She found Jasper pacing the living room with a distressed George, who was refusing to take his bottle.

Jasper's eyes flooded with relief when he saw her, but he said, 'I'm sorry I disturbed you. I needed to heat up a bottle and he cries even harder when I put him down.'

She ignored Jasper—it seemed wise—to focus all her attention on the baby. 'Hey, little man. What's the problem?'

He lifted his head to stare at her and held out his arms, his cries easing. She took him and cuddled him close. 'Aw, poor baby. You're hot.'

He opened his mouth and made angry noises and she cooed back soothing sounds as she ran her hand over his damp hair. 'I know, you're trying to tell me what's wrong, aren't you?'

His crying subsided into hiccups and she took the opportunity to run a finger along his gums. Poor little guy had a tooth coming through. Without glancing at Jasper—it was better not to look at him or to think about him, especially not at this time of night—she started for the nursery.

'What are you looking for?' Jasper said when she tried to search one of the bags one-handed.

'His thermometer.'

He took the bag, found the thermometer and handed it to her. She took George's temperature, crooning to him the entire time.

'Do I need to call a doctor?'

She shook her head, finally risking a glance his way. He looked deliciously dishevelled and heartbreakingly worried. 'His temperature is only up a tiny bit. How long has he been like this?'

'Nearly two and a half hours.'

No wonder he looked so frazzled. 'Why didn't you come and get me?'

'Because I didn't want to come across all feeble and pathetic. But you were my next port of call. How did you get him to stop crying?'

She grimaced. 'I'm going to try and break this as gently as I can—this is a temporary respite. George is teething.'

The nursery was too small, too intimate, too much. She moved towards the door, nodding at the bag Jasper had discarded. 'Let's go back downstairs, but bring that with you.'

She put teething gel on George's gums. But it evidently brought him little relief, as he soon started crying again.

She watched Jasper pace the floor in growing agitation, biting the inside of her lip. 'Would it help if I told you this was entirely normal?'

'A little.' But his eyes said otherwise.

Whatever else had happened between them, she couldn't deny that he loved his nephew. She flashed to the day of Katherine's scheduled biopsy—the way he'd taken her to the exhibition and had then urged her to record a message and playlist for her parents, the way he'd helped draw her mind from her worry. She needed to find a way to distract him like that.

'Can you access Jupiter's social media account from your phone?'

'Yes.'

'I think we should post something to her timeline now.'

He pulled out his phone. 'What do you want it to say?'

'Pacing the floor with a teething nine-month-old. Have tried a bottle, teething ring and teething gel so far, and lots of walking and rocking. So far nothing has helped. Any tips?'

He glanced up and she couldn't read the expression in his eyes. 'If you say one thing about bed hair,' she warned.

'There's absolutely nothing wrong with your hair, Imogen. You're hoping Emily reads this, aren't you?'

She shrugged.

'You're a genius.'

'*Not* a genius. Just not afraid to ask for help. There's a wealth of experience out there on social media. Why not tap into it?' If, at the same time, they could pique a mother's maternal concern…

His phone pinged.

'Guardian Angel 27 says "Pray".'

'Helpful.'

More pings sounded. 'Janice sends "lots of hugs".'

It was nice of her, but not exactly helpful either.

'"Iced water",' he read out.

Her lips twitched. 'That's a little ambiguous. Are we supposed to give it to him to drink or douse ourselves in it?'

His gaze didn't leave his phone. 'Um… "Hang him upside down whilst you drink a margarita."'

'Just…no.'

He scanned through the replies that were evidently pouring in, and then stilled. 'You won't believe this, but Emily has just responded.'

She leaned towards him. 'What does she say?'

'That last time her bub was teething, putting him in his stroller with his comfort toy and pushing the stroller back and forth helped.'

'I'm putting him in his stroller.' She started for the front foyer, which was where the stroller was currently parked.

'I'll grab his bunny.'

Jasper's heart pounded as the baby's cries started to abate.

Imogen nudged his foot and he realised she'd been talking to him and he hadn't been paying attention—hadn't heard a word.

'Tell her George's crying is easing and that it looks like it's working.'

He started typing on his phone.

'Georgia!' she corrected. 'Say Georgia.'

He backspaced, heart and head both racing. He nearly handed her the phone, his fingers feeling like thumbs, but…

But he was finally talking to Emily. His sister. After two years she'd finally spoken to him again, and he hadn't realised it would mean so much.

A personal message hit his inbox, and he immediately opened it. Need help.

He wanted to ring, but if Aaron was nearby… 'What can I do?' he typed back.

His phone rang. 'Emily?'

'Jasper.'

He didn't bother with preliminaries or pleasantries. 'What do you need?'

'I need to get away from Aaron. If he gets hold of me now, he'll kill me.'

He doubted she was exaggerating. 'I can get you on a plane first thing in the morning, for either Rio or São Paulo. Hold on…' He strode into his office, aware of a silent Imogen coming to stand in the doorway with the stroller to watch and listen as he made the travel arrangements on his computer. 'Have you got pen and paper there, Em?'

He gave her the flight details. He organised a bodyguard

to accompany her from Sydney to Rio. He organised a private charter from Rio to Tesoura.

'Are you safe from Aaron tonight?'

'I'm at a safe house. He's away on business but will be back tomorrow. Look, Jasper, he's involved in some kind of money-laundering racket, and I've been helping the police with their enquiries. It's about to come to a head soon…'

'Does he know that?'

'I don't know, but I don't want to be anywhere near him when he does.'

'I won't let that happen. Give me the address of where you're staying. I'm sending that bodyguard tonight.'

'I'm going to have to ditch my phone. He'll be able to track me on it.'

'I'll have a new one couriered to you.' She needed to be able to contact him in case anything happened.

'How's…how's George?'

'He's the sweetest, happiest little guy, Em. I don't know how you've managed it.'

'I've missed him so much, but Aaron has been so…unpredictable lately.'

Jasper closed his eyes.

'I needed to send George somewhere safe—away from everything that's happening here—in case things blew up earlier than expected.'

'Where does Aaron think he is?'

'With Auntie Pat. I told him I wanted to go and stay with her for a few days while he was away on business.'

He'd bet Aaron hadn't liked that. Pat was their mother's sister, and she loathed Keith. Which meant she probably loathed Aaron too.

'Tomorrow you and George will be reunited and safe, I promise.'

'I can't thank you enough, Jasper.'

'No need.'

They rang off. He turned to meet Imogen's gaze. She looked as if she meant to take a step towards him but pulled back at the last moment. 'Emily is coming?'

He nodded.

'That's…that's amazing news.'

She glanced down at the stroller, stopped pushing and lifted crossed fingers. Not a peep came from George. He'd finally fallen asleep.

With a brisk movement, she turned and headed upstairs. Jasper eased past the pram and followed her. 'What are you…?'

He trailed off when she checked the two currently vacant guest rooms. 'We'll give her this one.'

It was the room next to George's and had its own en suite bathroom. She grabbed a fresh set of sheets from the linen cupboard and started to make up the bed. He immediately kicked forward to help. 'There'll be time to do this tomorrow, you know?'

'I know, but I'm awake now.'

She shot him a grin and it made things inside him burn. He'd missed that smile. And her sense of fun. He shook himself. It didn't matter how much his heart protested. The distance he'd deliberately put between them was still for the best.

'I warn you now, though, breakfast is going to be a lacklustre affair.'

'Forget breakfast. I'll get some cereal and toast when I'm ready. Sleep as late as you like. I plan to.'

'Liar. You probably won't sleep a wink until Emily is here.'

She was probably right.

He followed her gaze as it ran about the room. 'What?'

'This is a nice room, but I'm wondering how we can make it more homey. I'll put a vase of flowers on the dresser.' She glanced in at the en suite bathroom. 'I bought some pretty toiletries while I was on the mainland. They'll do nicely in here.'

His chest hitched. 'You don't have to give your things away, Imogen.'

'I don't mind. Besides, I think your sister deserves a little pampering. And I know you'll want her to feel…'

'Safe? Unafraid?'

She nodded. 'But also at home. As if nothing bad could possibly happen to her here. That it's okay for her to let down her guard and rest.'

She put it into words better than he ever could have.

She glanced at him then with unabashed admiration. 'You thought of everything—on the fly—without a moment of panic, when she rang and asked for help. You were confident and in command of the situation—which must've been so reassuring for her. It was amazing to witness. She's lucky to have you, Jasper.'

An itch started up between his shoulder blades. Nothing could happen between him and this woman—he would not let his family destroy her the way it had him and Emily. But he owed her. And he could give her something now—a part of himself he'd never given to anyone. 'Immy, I've played that scenario—Emily ringing me like that—in my mind hundreds, maybe a thousand, times.'

Shortening her name seemed natural and right, so he didn't bother questioning it. 'Ever since I arrived on Tesoura I've wanted Emily to call and ask me to help her break free from Aaron.' He gave a low laugh. 'Which probably means I have some kind of saviour complex.'

'Nonsense.' She moved a step closer, her hands pressed to her chest. 'It means you love your sister and you want her to be safe and happy.'

He tried to not look at her chest, at the way her hands—pressed against thin cotton—highlighted curves that made him ache. He forced his gaze back to hers. 'On the outside

I might've appeared calm during that phone call, but on the inside, I was anything but.'

Her eyes softened and her lips parted. Wind roared in his ears and fire licked along his veins. He eased back a step, feeling anything but calm now. She glanced at him and then at the freshly made bed and colour mounted high on her cheeks. Everything inside him clenched. *No!* He would not take advantage of this lovely woman. 'I've been meaning to ask, when are you returning to Australia?'

She stared as if she hadn't heard him, and then her head rocked back. 'I… I hadn't set a firm date.' She swallowed. 'You evidently think I should.'

He forced himself to nod. 'You have the launch of your sewing business to prepare for, and…' His mind went blank as he fought the urge to take his words back and beg her to stay.

Her chin lifted but the sparkle in her eyes had dulled. 'I'll talk it over with my aunt and let you know.' She edged towards the door. 'I'm going back to bed. George?'

'I'll take care of him.'

She left, but it was a long time before he could move, before he could rid himself of the foul taste that coated his tongue.

The reunion between Emily and George was a revelation. The way George's face lit up…the love in Emily's face… It made Jasper's throat thicken and he had to clear it a couple of times. Imogen, who hovered nearby ready to leap in and help with anything if it was needed, swiped at her eyes.

She went to disappear back into the kitchen, but he caught hold of her hand. 'Emily, this is Imogen. And heaven help us all if she hadn't been here to help with George—teaching me all I needed to know about babies.' And about being an uncle, he realised now. She'd helped to thaw some of the frozen parts inside him. So had George.

'He's been a perfect doll,' Imogen assured Emily now. 'Haven't you, little man?' she said, tickling his tummy and making him gurgle out a delighted laugh.

Jasper froze. The tableau that the two women and the baby made…the fact his sister was *in his house*…

He recalled a time when he'd once gone skiing. He'd become so cold that when he'd walked back inside the warm lodge, his face and extremities had burned and ached for a full ten minutes before they'd started to feel normal again. That was how he felt on the inside now.

'I know how long that flight is from Sydney,' Imogen said. 'I'm thinking you'd probably love a chance to freshen up. Why don't I show you to your room?'

He trailed along behind them. So many emotions pounded through him in such quick succession it left him feeling disembodied. Happiness, grief, anger, protectiveness, relief—they all wrestled inside him.

'It's a beautiful room.' Emily's gaze zeroed in on the photo of George sitting on the bedside table. Imogen had taken it on her phone and had sent it to Jasper to print out before she'd placed it there in a pretty frame. 'Oh, Jasper, thank you so much!'

She threw an arm about his neck—her other held George clasped to her hip. George cuddled Jasper's arm and something that had been broken inside him started to knit back together.

When Emily released him, Imogen moved across to the bedside table and opened the top drawer. 'I took the liberty of grabbing you a few personal items.'

Emily moved across to glance inside. She stilled before meeting Imogen's gaze. 'Thank you.'

Curiosity shifted through him and he started to move across, and then stopped. They were probably referring to feminine hygiene products. Not that he was the least squeamish or embarrassed about such things, but a woman was entitled to her privacy.

'Is there anything else you need? Anything else I can do?' Imogen asked.

Emily shook her head. 'You've been so kind, thank you.' She glanced at them both, hesitating. 'I'd just love an hour to rest and…and to spend some time alone with George.'

She looked scared—as if she was afraid he would refuse her that…as if she'd started to equate all men's attitudes and behaviours with Aaron's and their father's. It pierced him to the core. 'Take as long as you want. Let me—' it occurred to him then that she might be more comfortable around another woman '—or Imogen know if there's anything you need or anything we can do.'

She nodded, and he left the room, stumbled down the hall to his own bedroom. Slumping down to the bed, he dropped his head to his hands and tried to stem the tears that scalded his eyes.

There was a soft sound in the doorway, and then a pair of arms went around him and pressed his head gently to the softness of her stomach. Imogen. He didn't need to open his eyes to know her. He knew her by her scent, by the sound of her movements, and by the way his every atom came to life at her nearness. He wrapped his arms about her middle and held her tight until the burning stopped. Only then did he ease away.

'Sorry.' His voice came out gruff. He felt vulnerable, exposed…embarrassed. 'What a big baby. I—'

She cupped his face and lifted it to meet her gaze. 'This is a normal human response to an overload of emotion. You've been on this island on your own for far too long, have kept too much bottled up.' She bit her lip, her eyes troubled. 'And despite her make-up, I know you saw her bruises too.'

He had. They were old bruises and were fading, but it

hadn't stopped him from wanting to punch something—preferably Aaron. 'She's so thin.'

She swiped the pads of her thumbs beneath his eyes. 'That, at least, is something we can fix, right?'

He nodded. She dropped her hands and eased away. 'It's time for me to get back down to the kitchen.'

With a smile, she was gone.

Over the course of the following week, Emily did put on weight—her cheeks filled out and her eyes started to lose their shadows. Katherine received her full test results, which verified the findings of the preliminary report—she didn't have breast cancer. It gave her the impetus to finish her book and send it off to her editor, and to resume her housekeeping duties. Meanwhile, Jasper desperately tried to think of a way to tempt Imogen back into the water for her daily swims.

She hadn't been for a single dip since they'd returned from São Paulo. He had an uncomfortable feeling he was to blame, but he didn't know how or why, and he desperately wanted to make amends. She'd arranged her return flights to Australia and now only had another week before she left. That was all—*one single week*! He wanted to make it as pleasant for her as he could.

And he definitely didn't want to think about how he'd feel once she was gone.

'What's on your mind?' Emily said from her spot on the floor where she played with George.

'Imogen.'

'Hmm…'

He glanced up at the knowing note in his sister's voice when the front door crashed open with a bang that made them all jump. Aaron appeared in the doorway. His shadow seemed to darken the room. Emily gave a strangled cry, her hand flying to her mouth. Jasper shot to his feet. Little George pulled himself up on unsteady legs and hurled himself at Jasper, clinging to his leg and hiding his face against it.

'I knew this was where you'd be, you traitorous cow!'

Jasper fought the urge to move across and punch the other man. Emily and George had seen enough violence, had been through enough.

At that moment Imogen came walking down the stairs with an armful of dirty linen. 'Do we have another visitor?' she called out cheerfully. 'Should I make up another room?'

'No need,' Aaron said with a snarl as she reached the bottom of the stairs. 'My wife, son and I won't be staying.'

'I see.' She pursed her lips, staring up at him. She looked tiny beside him. 'I take it you're Aaron?'

He gave a thin-lipped smile that made Jasper's heart pound so hard it almost hurt. He handed Jasper to Emily and started across the room, but before he could reach them, Imogen calmly lifted an arm and sprayed Aaron full in the face with something that had the other man immediately screaming and dropping to his knees. 'Agh, help! She's thrown acid in my face!'

She stepped over him and handed the can of spray to Emily. 'I knew that was going to be a good investment. Pepper spray,' she added for Jasper's benefit. 'I know it's not legal in New South Wales, but when I saw a can of it in São Paulo I figured it wouldn't hurt to have some.'

He didn't know what to say. He couldn't believe how… how *efficiently* she'd handled a potentially deadly situation.

Katherine came through from the kitchen. 'I've called the police. They're on their way.' She tossed Jasper a roll of duct tape. 'Tie him up for his own safety. Before Imogen is tempted to hurt him some more. And, Jasper,' she added, 'I wouldn't be too gentle about it if I were you.'

As much as he wanted to, he couldn't hit a defenceless man, and at the moment Aaron was nothing but a helpless, snivelling mess.

The police arrived an hour later and took him away. Emily and George retired to her room for a rest. Katherine returned to the kitchen. Jasper stared at Imogen. 'You really are something.'

She shrugged, but it didn't hide the way her hands had started to shake. 'I was pretty amazing, huh?'

He pulled her into his arms, pressing his lips to her hair. 'You scared me half out of my wits.'

CHAPTER TEN

KEITH COLEMAN ARRIVED two days later.

'Jasper,' Katherine called out from the living room. 'Your father is on the supply boat. It'll have docked by now, so he'll be here any minute.'

Jasper came out from his office where he'd been digitising Imogen's tapes for her. He couldn't decide if he was surprised by this turn of events or not. He glanced across at Emily, who'd paled, but she kept a resolute angle to her chin. Beside her, George crab-walked the length of the sofa, holding on to it for balance. The kid was going to be a runner when he grew up—a top-class athlete.

When he glanced back up, Imogen had appeared at her aunt's shoulder. Everything inside him clamoured at the mere sight of her. Ever since he'd watched her approach Aaron, fear had filled his soul. He'd wake in the middle of the night in a cold sweat from dreams where she was in trouble and he couldn't get to her in time.

Not that she'd needed him to come to her rescue two days ago. She'd rescued all of them instead.

The fact was she didn't need *him*.

The front door rattled and then shouting and pounding followed when it didn't open.

George fell to his nappy-clad bottom. Emily picked him up and cuddled him. Katherine's brows rose. 'The door's locked?'

'Oh, didn't I mention it? I've taken to locking it.' Imogen shrugged with an utter lack of concern.

Jasper wanted to smile at her complete disregard for his father's impatience—growing louder by the second. And then he wanted to hit something. Was she afraid to stay here since Aaron's unexpected arrival? Was—?

'Should I get it?' She pointed to the door.

He blew out a breath and nodded. 'Chin up, Em. I won't let him hurt you.'

'I know. It's like this is the final hurdle, and then I'll be free.'

He kept his gaze trained on Imogen as she moved towards the door. She opened it with a scolding, 'Heavens, what a racket. Really, sir, the doorbell is in perfect working order. Now, how can I help you?'

'I'm Mr Keith Coleman, and I demand to see my daughter and son. I *will* see them and no damn servant is going to stop me.'

Jasper moved into view before Keith could push Imogen out of the way. If his father touched her, he knew he wouldn't be able to think straight. And it'd be better for all concerned that he kept this as civilised as possible. From behind Imogen, he met Keith's glare. 'If you so much as lay one finger on any person here on my island, I will beat you to a bloody pulp and then take you a mile out that way—' he pointed seawards '—and drop your sorry butt overboard.' He kept his voice pleasant for George's and Emily's sakes.

Keith's mouth worked, but no sound came out.

Imogen glanced at Jasper and he nodded. She opened the door wider. 'Why don't you step inside, Mr Coleman?'

Keith straightened his suit jacket before stalking into the living room.

Emily stood and Jasper went to stand beside her. Imogen moved back beside her aunt. Keith sneered at them all. 'You think you have the upper hand, but you're wrong.'

Once upon a time a veiled threat like that would've had Jasper turning cold with dread. Now he saw through the bluster to the ugly bully beneath.

Keith stabbed a finger at Emily. 'I demand you return to your husband immediately.'

'You want her to return to a dangerous criminal?' Jasper kinked an eyebrow. 'How very egalitarian of you.' He couldn't believe his father hadn't washed his hands of his son-in-law and put as much distance between himself and Aaron as he could, given Aaron's allegedly illegal activities.

The older man dismissed that with a wave of his hand. 'It's all a misunderstanding. And one that will be more quickly cleared up with Emily at home by her husband's side.'

'That's not going to happen.' Emily lifted her chin. 'I won't be returning to Aaron. Ever. I'm filing for divorce, and I hope he rots in prison.'

Keith's eyes narrowed to slits. 'If you don't do as I say I'll have you declared an unfit mother. I'll sue for custody of George.'

'You can try, but you won't succeed. I've been planning my escape for months. I know my rights. I've photographic evidence of the bruises Aaron's given me. And I think it's safe to assume that Jasper will provide me with the very best family lawyers available.'

'Goes without saying,' Jasper murmured, proud of the way she held her ground.

'And if you do take this to court, Father, I'll tell the police that you and Aaron wanted me to perjure myself in court and say that Jasper's attack on Aaron two years ago was unprovoked.'

'Why, you little—' He broke off, his eyes narrowing. 'Your mother will pay for your disobedience.' He clenched a hand, that fist leaving none of them in doubt as to how he meant to make her pay. From the corner of his eye, Jasper saw Imogen flinch and had to bottle down his instant desire to plant a fist in his father's face.

He wasn't his father.

'Mother doesn't deserve the way you treat her, but I can't take responsibility for that any more.'

Emily's words made Jasper blink. Had she stayed with Aaron all this time to protect and support their mother?

Giving a derisory snort, the older man turned his attention to Katherine. 'I know what you've been up to. I've been keeping tabs.'

Katherine's eyes went mock wide. 'How thrilling for you, Keith.'

'I could make you a laughing stock—expose the ludicrous stuff you write to everyone you know.'

Jasper's gut clenched, but Imogen gave a barely stifled giggle. 'He has no idea about the world of genre fiction, does he, Auntie Kay?'

'None.'

Imogen winked at Jasper, who must've also looked at a loss because she added, 'Katherine's more likely to be swamped by adoring fans than mocked. I mean, there's bound to be the odd literary snob, but—'

'But not anyone we need concern ourselves with,' Katherine said.

'I know who your agent is. I know the name of your editor. Your publisher is a member of my club.'

Ice tripped down Jasper's spine. Keith would ruin Kate's career? The sense of déjà vu, of helplessness, rose up through him.

Katherine folded her arms. 'The thing is, publishing houses can be sold. I'm quite certain that Jasper could be prevailed upon to buy a publishing house, and to maybe even make me one of his lead authors.'

His panic dissipated, his heartbeat steadied. 'I've always fancied becoming a patron of the arts.'

The smile Imogen sent him was worth the price of two publishing houses.

'I know all about *you* too, Imogen Hartley. And you needn't think you're out of my reach.'

Jasper's every sense went on high alert.

'If you and your aunt don't want any trouble, you'll both leave this island now…*today*.'

'Or?' she inquired with a polite lift of her brows.

'Or you'll find the lease for your business premises has disappeared and the space mysteriously let to someone else. Or maybe the zoning laws will have changed…and then your planning-permission paperwork might go astray.'

She glanced at Jasper. 'He really is an unpleasant piece of work. You and Emily have my sympathies.'

Acid burned his chest. She was leaving in five days anyway. Her leaving today would make no difference. This wasn't her fight. She had a life to get back to. He steeled himself for her nod of acceptance and tried to control the nausea swirling through him.

She folded her arms. 'You're a slimy eel of a man, Mr Coleman.'

Jasper stiffened. What was she doing? Couldn't she see the danger of kicking the hornets' nest?

'You don't see it, do you?' she continued. 'The tables are turning…the power is shifting. Jasper would buy me the perfect premises and hire a business lawyer on my behalf—just to make sure all my paperwork was in order—if I asked it of him. And I'd rather take my chances with him than with you, thank you very much.'

He stilled. It hit him then—Imogen would always choose to do what was right rather than what was easy. She wasn't like Bronwyn. She was a woman who would stay and fight for him. For a moment he could barely breathe.

And then his heart swelled.

'But he won't be able to prevent the bad publicity of a smear campaign. I'll make sure word gets around that your workmanship is substandard and your ethics questionable.'

The threat rocked her, Jasper could see that, but her chin didn't drop. 'Like I said, I'll take my chances.'

'You're fools, the lot of you. You—' he swung back to Jasper '—will return to Australia at my side tomorrow and help me fix this sorry mess or I'll destroy them all.'

Jasper's mind raced. Imogen's words going round and round in his mind—*the power is shifting.* Why hadn't Keith disassociated himself from Aaron? Why hadn't he claimed ignorance of the man's activities and thrown him to the wolves? Keith had done that more than once in his political career to so-called trusted colleagues. Unless…

Jasper widened his stance. Unless he was involved in Aaron's illegal activities too.

All the pieces of the puzzle fell into place. The reason Keith had championed Emily and Aaron's relationship. The reason he'd renounced Jasper before his son could work out what was going on. His desperation now.

Jasper no longer feared his father. He might not be able to nullify all the harm Keith could do, but the women in this room had just shown him how he could mitigate it.

He didn't want to mitigate it, though. He wanted to *demolish* it. He recalled his father's threats to Imogen, and his resolve hardened to tempered steel. He wasn't letting the man get away with that. He was *not* going to let him hurt Imogen. Not now. Not ever.

His every thought sharpened—honed by years of imagining all the ways he could bring Keith to justice. An image fixed itself in his mind. He'd been digitising Imogen's tapes. That recording equipment was sitting in the top drawer of his desk.

Keith obviously interpreted Jasper's silence for apprehension because he gave a triumphant laugh that made Jasper's skin crawl. 'You always were a soft touch. It was your downfall. You'll do what's right by these women.'

'Why don't we take this discussion into my office? Katherine, could you organise refreshments, please?'

Katherine didn't so much as blink, but Emily grabbed his arm and stared up into his face with earnest eyes. 'Don't do this, Jasper. *Please.*'

It hurt that she had so little faith in him, but he couldn't blame her—not given her experiences with their father and Aaron.

He ignored Emily's plea to glance across at Imogen. 'Make up a guest room for my father.'

Her brow pleated. 'What are you doing? Why don't you just boot him off the island and—?'

'I'm doing what's necessary.'

'But—'

He moved across to her. 'Don't make things harder than they have to be.' He made sure the words carried across to his father. He made sure his next ones didn't. 'Slap me across the face and flounce off to the kitchen.'

She took a step away from him her eyes going wide, and then her face darkened, and she did as he'd requested—she slapped him.

The imprint of her hand burned against his cheek and he wanted to kiss her. He squashed the impulse as the kitchen door slammed behind her. Emily raced off after her with George in her arms, while he gestured for his father to precede him into his office.

'She's a fiery little piece,' Keith said.

'And fired after that little display,' Jasper returned.

'Pity, you could've had some fun taming her.'

His father's words made his stomach turn, but he didn't betray it by so much as a flicker of an eyelash. He waved to a drinks cabinet on the other side of the room. 'There's a very good aged single malt there. Help yourself.'

While his father's back was turned, he moved behind his desk, opened his top drawer and placed a blank cassette into the mini-recorder before slipping it into the pocket of his jacket. This morning when he'd pulled on a suit jacket, he'd told himself it was an attempt to return to a sense of normalcy—that he was once again ready to take a conference call if the occasion required it. Imogen had taken one look at him and had shaken her head. He was glad now he'd taken the trouble, though. The jacket felt like armour.

His father returned with two glasses of whisky. Jasper took one and sat, gestured for his father to take a seat too. 'You ought to know I'm not the inexperienced boy I once was. The business world has taught me a lot. It's not possible to achieve the amount of success I have while keeping all of one's ideals and scruples…intact.'

He pretended to sip his Scotch as he let his father draw conclusions—undoubtedly unfavourable—about his son's business practices.

Imogen's face rose in his mind, solidifying his intent. 'I'm not easily browbeaten. And I'm not going to pretend I am now.'

'If you don't do as I tell you, those women will suffer. I'll make it a personal crusade. While I'd be a fool to say such things in front of witnesses, accidents can be arranged.'

'Yes, they can.'

He let those words sink in before continuing. 'However, while your threats have little impact on me, I *am* a businessman. I like to make money. And I find myself growing tired of island life.'

Keith's eyes narrowed. 'What are you proposing?'

'I won't make Emily return to Aaron.'

His father started to rise. 'But—'

'The man's a fool for getting caught. I'm sure there's a way to…deal with him.'

Keith subsided, his eyes starting to gleam. 'Deal with him how?'

'I'm sure you can think of something. I'll only agree to return to Australia if you cut me in on whatever scheme you and Aaron have going.'

Keith started to laugh. These were the kinds of deals his father was used to making. 'You think I'd trust you with anything of that kind?'

'Money can buy a lot of things. Including information.'

Keith leaned back as if he held all the cards. 'Are you offering me money?'

'No, I don't owe you a thing. You owe me. And if I return to Australia…' He let the sentence hang for a moment. '*If* I return to Australia it'll be on an equal footing, *not* as your dogsbody.'

Keith's face twisted, and he slammed his glass down. 'You want to cut me out—take control of everything!' Because that was the way his father's mind worked.

Jasper gave a negligent shrug. 'Just like you, I find I have a taste for power. I want to be top dog.' He wanted to make sure Keith could never threaten Imogen again.

Keith thumped his chest. 'I'm top dog. I'm the one who has the contacts and knows how everything fits together. If I cut you in, it'll be on my terms.'

'But that said,' he continued, as if his father hadn't spoken, 'I'm sure my money could be put to use in advantageous and creative ways that would be in everyone's best interests.'

He broke off when a knock sounded. Katherine entered with a tray bearing coffee and warm scones. She set it on the desk. 'Will there be anything else?'

Jasper glanced at his father and let his lips lift as if in expectation that a deal would be struck soon. 'I think we'll have the fillet steak for dinner tonight, Katherine.'

It was his father's favourite, and predictably the older man preened as if he'd somehow won. Stupid man. Keith was going to find out exactly what happened when he threatened the people his son loved.

Katherine closed the door on her way out. Jasper set a mug of coffee in front of Keith. 'I'll need some kind of guarantee before I commit any money to the project.'

Keith seemed to think that over, knocked back the rest of his Scotch before setting it down with a nod. 'I can tell you enough to realise any financial investment you make would be well rewarded.'

Jasper lifted his coffee to his lips. 'I'm listening.'

'Let me get this straight,' Emily repeated. 'Jasper *asked* you to slap him?'

Imogen nodded. 'He's up to something. He has a plan, so don't lose heart. Your father doesn't frighten him.'

Emily let George scramble down from her lap to retrieve his bunny. 'I hope you're right.'

She was right. Jasper had a plan. She just prayed he could pull it off.

'I must say, Immy, you certainly responded to his request with…enthusiasm,' Katherine said.

'I wanted to be convincing.'

Had she channelled all her anger into that slap? Anger that he'd kissed her and then rejected her. Anger that it continued to mean so much. She swallowed. 'Do you think I hurt him?'

Katherine's eyes danced. 'Let's just say that I think it'll keep him focussed.'

She'd hated hitting him. The moment after she'd struck him, she'd wanted to take that beautiful face in her hands and kiss it better—it was why she'd flounced away in such a rush. Instinct told her that Jasper was playing some deep game, and the stakes were high. She'd help him in whatever way she could—because she trusted him and wanted to support him—and he'd be grateful. But she had to be careful not to read anything more into it than that.

She wasn't giving him any further reason to tell her that while he was attracted to her, he didn't want anything more. He'd been honest with her from the start. Why couldn't she have got that straight in her head? Why did she have to go and fall for him?

'Right, Imogen, you'd better go and get that room ready.'

Emily twisted her hands together. 'I don't want to sleep in the same part of the house as my father.'

Imogen didn't blame her. 'My room has twin beds if you want to bunk in with me. I mean, it's nothing fancy, but…'

The relief that raced across Emily's face was all the answer she needed. 'C'mon, I'll make up a room for Sir Keith the Jackass and then we can move your things downstairs for the night.' Including that can of pepper spray.

The rest of the afternoon dragged by, the suspense that hung in the air making it hard to concentrate on anything. Emily had her dinner in the kitchen with Imogen and Katherine. Jasper and his father ate in the dining room where Imogen couldn't help noticing how at home Keith made himself.

Ha! What did she mean, *couldn't help noticing*? She was spying. Of course she could help noticing. She was *deliberately* noticing.

And what she deliberately noticed was that Keith did most of the talking—all of it bragging and big-noting himself, name-dropping and blowing his own trumpet in relation to his access to Australia's highest political powers. The slimy toad. Jasper, on the other hand, kept calmly plying the man with a very good burgundy—four bottles of the stuff, to be precise—and very little of it made its way down its owner's throat. She crossed her fingers and hoped that whatever Jasper's goal happened to be, he achieved it.

'Your father can drink a lot,' she said, closing the

kitchen door quietly and returning to the table where Katherine had brought out a deck of cards and told them they were playing gin rummy. George had long since been put to bed in his cot in Imogen's room.

'Like a fish,' Emily agreed. 'Jasper's going to need a lot of wine if he's hoping to get him drunk.'

Katherine dealt out the cards. 'Then it's just as well your brother keeps his cellar well stocked.'

They played cards for nearly two hours. The next time she peeked, Imogen watched Jasper half carry his very drunk father upstairs, presumably to bed. When he came back downstairs, he went straight into his study without so much as a glance in the direction of the kitchen.

She shifted her weight from one foot to the other, biting the inside of her cheek. She really wanted to go to him, but on what pretext? If he wanted her, he knew where to find her.

Acid burned her stomach. He didn't want her, though. As much as she might want to, she couldn't lose sight of that fact.

Katherine gave her a nudge. 'Go and find out if there's anything else he needs, and tell him we're locking ourselves in.'

She turned in surprise.

Katherine held up a key. 'The staff quarters lock.'

'Is that necessary?'

'It'll make Emily feel safer.'

She was halfway to Jasper's office when she realised her aunt hadn't actually answered her question. Which was probably an answer in itself. Stomach churning, she tapped on the open office door. Jasper glanced up from where he furiously typed on his computer. 'There's nothing else I need for the evening, Imogen,' he said, pre-empting her. 'You're free to retire.'

Lucky her.

'Emily is bunking in with me tonight. And George.'

He nodded and returned to his computer. 'Was there anything else?' he finally said, not looking at her.

Her chest tightened. He wasn't going to tell her what he was up to? What his plan was? She frowned at a spot on the carpet. 'Katherine told me to tell you we're locking ourselves in.'

He swivelled to face her. 'That's not necessary. But if it makes you feel better…'

What would make her feel better was if he swept her up in his arms and kissed her, told her he'd die without her. Her lips twisted. But that evidently wasn't going to happen.

His eyes swept across her face, and his jaw clenched. He turned back to his computer. 'Goodnight, Imogen.'

She turned and left without uttering another word.

'What did he say?' Emily said the moment she marched back into the kitchen. 'How did he seem?'

High-handed. Remote. Autocratic. She bit the words back. They weren't fair. 'Preoccupied…and uncommunicative.'

'Never mind.' Katherine marshalled them towards the staff quarters. 'Tomorrow may reveal all.'

Imogen tried to rein in her confusion, her hurt. Jasper didn't owe her anything beyond a fair wage and decent working conditions. Her pique faded, but she refused to let hopelessness take its place. Her future held lots of good things—oodles of them. It just didn't include Jasper.

She lifted her chin. Being here on the island had taught her an important lesson. Sometimes you had to take a risk—and if you worked hard and planned well it paid dividends. Some risks *were* worth taking. Look at Aunt Katherine—she'd dared to dream, and it had led to a publishing deal. Emily had risked her own safety to forge a new life for her and George.

Katherine and Emily had faced their fears and both their lives were the better for it. She could face her fears too.

She *wasn't* stupid. She *wasn't* naïve and unprepared. She and her business *would* thrive. As for Jasper…

Instinct told her he was taking a big risk now. With all her heart, she hoped it paid off, hoped he vanquished his demons where his father was concerned. And that he had the chance to lead a good and happy life. Her eyes burned. It was what he deserved.

CHAPTER ELEVEN

EDUARDO APPEARED THE following morning as Imogen served breakfast in the dining room. He hovered by the kitchen door, evidently waiting for her.

The scent of freshly cooked bacon—normally a smell she relished—made her stomach turn. Or maybe that was simply her employer's guest. She finished refilling Jasper's and Keith's coffee mugs before moving across to him. She listened as he gave his message in halting English.

'Is there a problem?' Jasper demanded in some kind of boss voice that set her teeth on edge.

She moved back to the table, hands folded at her waist. 'Eduardo tells me there's a boat here. The skipper claims he's been hired to take someone to the mainland.'

Keith smirked. 'Now you'll get your comeuppance, missy. You might think twice before losing your temper again.'

The passage to the mainland was for her? But...she had another four days before she had to leave. She wasn't ready to go yet. She—

'Call the others in, Imogen.'

As Eduardo hadn't left the doorway, and Katherine and Emily had come to stand behind him, Imogen didn't need to call anyone over. They all moved to stand beside her.

'I have something here I think you'll all be interested in hearing.'

Jasper pulled her mini-recorder from his pocket and hit

play. She listened, at first in confusion, but then in growing comprehension as Keith's voice droned on, bragging about offshore bank accounts, complex financial transactions designed to camouflage where money came from, Ponzi schemes and the killing to be made in digital currencies. On the tape, Jasper asked leading questions about how Keith saw his son fitting into this mini-empire of white-collar crime, and Keith gave detailed explanations. She couldn't believe the man had fallen for it! His enormous ego and inflated sense of his own power—his stubborn belief that he could still cow and manipulate Jasper—was his undoing.

'You recorded me?' Keith leapt to his feet, ejected the tape and ground it beneath his heel on the tiles, before shredding the roll of plastic film that had recorded his damning words. He bared his teeth, his breath noisy in the silence. 'You're going to pay for this.'

Jasper didn't appear the least bit perturbed by Keith's actions so she chose not to be either.

'You were so confident you could get me onside. And so ridiculously sure that you were safe telling me everything because there was no one else to bear witness—your word against mine. And as you'd already discredited my character back in Australia, who'd believe an embittered son over a respected politician, right?'

Keith gave an ugly laugh and held up the shredded tape. 'And without this, it's still your word against mine.'

'The tape you're holding is a copy. After I put you to bed last night, I spent the rest of the evening digitising the contents of the tape and sending the electronic file through to the Australian Federal Police. The original is in my safe.'

Keith's face turned purple and then grey.

'As we speak, your house in Sydney is being searched. I've spoken to Mother and told her what's happening, and she's decided to throw her lot in with me rather than take any more abuse from you.'

'She wouldn't dare! I'll—'

'You'll do nothing, because more likely than not you'll be banged up in a jail cell next door to Aaron. You're in no position to do anything.'

'The ungrateful—'

'When you hit someone enough they'll eventually bite back.'

Imogen watched the scene play out in front of her and wanted to cheer…and throw up…and hug Jasper, Emily and George…and the Australian Federal Police.

'You're now a person of interest and a warrant has been issued for your arrest. Police officers will be here in—' he glanced at his watch '—an hour or two, I suspect. So you can wait for them, or you can take your chances evading them on the mainland and leave on the boat that's just arrived. Up to you.'

The older man slammed to his feet. 'I'll make you pay for this. All of you.'

He raced upstairs—presumably to pack. 'Don't let him out of your sight,' Jasper said to Eduardo.

Less than thirty minutes later, the boat pulled away from the dock with Keith Coleman on board.

'Why did you let him go?' Emily almost wailed as she stared after the departing vessel.

'I didn't let him go, Em. Two of the local *policia* are on board, as he'll find out soon enough. They'll hold him until someone more senior arrives to deal with him. I just wanted to prevent any further unpleasantness happening on my island.'

They returned to the house, and Jasper explained how his plan had formed and how he'd executed it. While Keith hadn't been so unguarded as to give up the names of his associates, he'd given enough information that the police were sure they'd be able to make further arrests in the near future.

Emily laughed and cried.

Imogen let herself out of the house and made her way along the beach, keeping to the shadows of the palm trees. She should be feeling exultant—and a part of her was. But it also felt as if a line had just been drawn in the sand. It brought home to her the fact that she'd be leaving in four days and would never see Jasper again.

She scrambled up the steep track of the headland at the end of Jasper's beach. Ever since arriving she'd been meaning to climb it. *No time like the present.*

She was breathing hard when she reached the top, but the view rewarded her efforts. A sapphire sea glistened in the sun, ruffled here and there by a playful breeze. That breeze might stiffen later this afternoon, creating white-caps, but for now it merely caressed and stroked. A few giant rocks rested between the island and the horizon, giving depth and definition to all the amazing blue.

Turning to survey the vista behind, she was greeted with lush greenery. The wooded hill that was Tesoura's interior hid the far coastline from view. Birdcalls rang throughout the forest, hinting at the abundant life hidden there. Below to her left, Eduardo's pride and joy— the garden—reigned in emerald splendour with Jasper's mansion gleaming white and magnificent in the midst of it. Beyond that stretched the lagoon with its tiny dock and barely a ripple disturbed its surface.

If only she could channel some of that tranquillity into her own soul. Finding a flat rock, she sat and stared out to sea. Wasn't there some poet who'd claimed beauty could heal the hurts of the world? She rested her chin on her hands and glared at the glory spread before her, waiting for it to weave its enchantment and magically glue her heart back together.

Stupid heart.

Stupid her for giving it away so easily where it wasn't wanted.

Stupid.

Her eyes burned but she forced her chin up. Falling in love with Jasper wasn't stupid. It seemed almost…inevitable. He was wonderful. Falling in love with him simply went to show what excellent taste she had. It was just a shame he didn't love her back.

She didn't know how long she sat like that before she heard Jasper beating up a path towards her. Cool reason told her it had to be Jasper. Katherine would simply wait until Imogen came down if she wanted to speak to her. Emily would be busy with George, and Eduardo with his garden.

There was nothing cool about how she felt at the thought of seeing him now, though. She tried to school her features. She told herself to be cheerful. She might be in love with a man who didn't love her back, but she still had her pride.

'Hey!' she said, leaping to her feet when he broke through the undergrowth and crested the summit. With a superhuman effort she kept a grin on her face. 'Here's to the man of the moment!' She gave him a round of applause. 'You were amazing back there—all cool, calm and focussed—like some white knight on his charger.'

'I—'

'I mean—' she knew she was babbling but couldn't stop '—how good did it feel to slay that particular dragon?'

'I…'

She skipped forward to high-five him, but rather than slapping his palm to hers, he caught her hand, lacing his fingers with hers, and not letting go. 'You left.'

The hurt in his eyes nearly undid her. She couldn't tell him the truth—that she'd needed time alone. She couldn't tell him that in vanquishing his father he'd forced her to face the fact that he didn't love her. She could no longer pretend that he was trapped by his family and circumstances.

But that was her problem, not his.

His fingers curled around hers as if they'd never let her go.

Wishful thinking.

Everything inside her throbbed. Her smile had fled, but she refused to let her chin drop. 'I wanted to give you and Emily some time alone together. To process all you've managed to achieve, to celebrate the fact you've broken from your past.'

'You left,' he repeated, his brows lowering over his eyes. 'You don't see it, do you?'

'See what?'

'Without you, Imogen, there wouldn't have been anything to celebrate.'

What was he talking about?

'Without you, I don't want to celebrate.'

Her heart all but stopped.

Jasper swallowed. He'd screwed up, hadn't he?

This lovely woman had offered him a glimpse of another life—a life he desperately wanted—and he'd flung it back at her. She'd offered him her heart. Not in so many words, but they both knew that had been the subtext of their conversation on the beach that night after their kiss.

She'd been prepared to see where things between them might go, but he'd dismissed the idea. Ruthlessly. He winced, imagining how hard-hearted she must've thought him. She'd accepted his rejection with equanimity—hadn't tried to change his mind, had respected his wishes.

And then he'd kissed her again in São Paulo and had rejected her all over again. That had been unforgivable. He didn't blame her for locking her heart up tight against him now.

She pulled her hand from his, her brow wrinkling as if she was trying to make sense of what he'd said. 'I can't take credit for what happened this morning.'

She might've closed her heart to him, but he could open his to her. 'This morning had everything to do with you.' He clenched his hand, trying to keep a hold of the feel of her, wanting it imprinted on his mind. 'If it weren't for you, I might never have believed that Emily was in trouble in the first place.'

'I know you believe that, but I don't. It was you who worked out how to contact her. And when she did make contact, it was you who got her to safety.'

'It was also you,' he pressed on, 'who made me fall in love with George.'

She rolled her eyes. 'I think you'll find George was responsible for that himself.'

'You taught me how to be an uncle.'

It appeared he'd finally shocked her into silence. Her mouth opened, but no words came out.

He widened his stance. 'Yesterday afternoon when my father threatened Emily, I was angry. When he threatened Katherine, I was outraged. But when he threatened you, I wanted to kill him.'

Even now the memory had everything inside him clenching up tight. 'I knew I could counter the harm he threatened. You all showed me how to do that—and I'd have been happy to do it. But the thought of you having to put up with his spite, being persecuted for no other reason than the fact that you're a good person...' Both his hands clenched. '*That* was the moment I decided to take him down.'

The green highlights in her eyes seemed to alternately flash and dull, like the sun on a moving sea. She moistened her lips and an ache started up inside him. 'Why?'

His mouth dried, but he was through with lies and deceit. 'Because I love you.'

She froze. She blinked. She didn't utter a single damn word.

Give her more, you idiot.

Reaching out, he touched her cheek. 'I know I've given you no reason to believe me—that I've run hot and cold. And I don't blame you if you don't return my feelings, but I can't let you leave this island believing you don't mean anything to me.'

Her lips parted. He wanted to kiss her so badly he started to shake with it. But then she backed up a step and the hope he'd stupidly let loose drained away and the day darkened as if a cloud had just passed across the sun.

He glanced up at the sky. Not a single cloud marred the endless blue—not even on the farthest horizon. Turning back to Imogen, he pressed his lips together to stop from begging her to give him another chance. He didn't regret telling her how he felt; he didn't regret telling her he loved her, but he wouldn't harass her. He'd had enough of men hassling women to last him a lifetime.

She thumped down to a rock as if her legs had given way. She swallowed and gestured to another rock nearby. He took it, hating how much distance it put between them. From here he couldn't reach out and touch her.

That's the point.

'If you'd prefer to be alone, I can leave.'

'I don't want you to leave, I'm just… I know my silence must sound deafening to you, but…' Her eyes narrowed. 'I'm trying to decide if I believe you or not.'

He froze. Did that mean…? Was she saying…? He didn't bother trying to rein in his hope. 'Why do you doubt me?' If he knew that, he might be able to allay it.

She covered her face with her hands, and he understood they weren't playing games here—they were in deadly earnest. 'Because it's what you do, Jasper—it's your modus operandi.' She pulled her hands away. 'You want to protect women… And children.'

She thought that was a bad thing?

'After meeting your father—' she shuddered '—I can see why you don't want to be anything like him.'

He remained quiet, focussed.

'You know that I'm not immune to you. I know you know that.'

His heart pounded.

'And I'm worried that if you think you're hurting me, you'll give me what you think I want regardless of the cost to yourself.'

He leaned towards her. 'You think I'd tell you I loved you to make you happy rather than because it's true?'

Her tongue snaked out to moisten her lips. 'That's the thought that's crossing my mind.'

Damn. He tried not to notice the shine on her lips, tried not to let it distract him. 'You're right insofar as the thought of hurting you makes me feel physically ill.'

Although the sun beat down on them with benevolent warmth, she'd gone pale. His heart gave a sick kick.

'But you're wrong too,' he forced himself to continue. 'I would never lie about loving you. It would hurt you tenfold in the long run because you'd eventually work it out. How could I do that to you—a woman with so much love in her heart and so much joy for life and so much to look forward to?' He shook his head, praying she'd believe him. 'If I thought you loved me, but I didn't return that love— I'd have to tell you. It'd be a clean break. Painful at first, no doubt, but I know you'd move on.'

She blinked.

'That kind of lie—the kind you're accusing me of—is a trap. It'd be a trap for the both of us and I've seen what traps do to people. I don't want that. Not for me. And I sure as hell don't want it for you.'

She rested her elbows on her knees, her chin in her hands as she stared—almost glared—at him. It shifted her towards him fractionally and he wasn't sure if she was aware of that or not. There had to be some other way he could convince her, something he could—

'You told me that Tesoura is your home. That you have no plans for ever leaving.'

'I was wrong.' He spoke without hesitation. 'Running away like I did was the coward's way out.'

She straightened. 'That's not fair! You had every reason for needing a bolt-hole. You are *not* a coward.'

Her defence warmed him. He wanted to take it as a good sign.

She thrust out her chin. 'And you're not an emotional coward either. You just told me you loved me without knowing if I'd say it back. That was pretty brave.'

He still didn't know if she was going to say it back. But he didn't point that out.

'Regardless of what happens between me and you, Imogen, I'm returning to the real world. I want to be close to my family. I have my heart set on living in Wollongong, but if that's not possible then I'll get a place somewhere in Sydney.'

Her eyes widened at his words.

'I know you don't see it, but you've made me a new man.'

Please let her see that.

'You helped me deal with the bitterness and resentment I'd let fester inside me. But that's not all. You've given me hope.' He wanted her to feel the truth of his words in her bones. 'I'm not talking about the hope that something might happen between the two of us. I'm talking about the hope that I can live a good life again—that I can be an uncle to George, a brother to Emily, a son to my mother, and maybe even a husband and father myself one day. I'm planning to reconnect with the friends I've shunned these last two years, and I'm going to get hands-on again with my business.'

She straightened; her hands pressed to the spot above her heart. Tears sparkled on her lashes.

'You want to know the exact moment I realised I was in love with you?'

She nodded.

'The moment you appeared in the living room in the middle of the night to help me with George when he was teething. I'd never been so darn happy to see anyone. And before you say otherwise, it had nothing to do with George. Seeing you simply made the hard stuff easier to bear. Seeing you made me feel that some piece inside me that had been missing had just been found. I felt…whole.'

Her lips parted.

'When did I *actually* fall in love with you?' He shook his head. 'Probably the moment I saw you dancing with that stupid vacuum cleaner.'

'But…you yelled at me.'

'I didn't yell!' He grimaced. 'Though I was admittedly less than cheerful at the time.'

She kinked an eyebrow at his understatement.

'That was the moment everything started to change, and I didn't want it to. I was pushing back against it, trying to maintain the status quo. I'm sorry I was so bad-tempered. You didn't deserve it.'

The expression in her eyes made his heart beat hard. 'You want to know when I first realised I was in love with you?' she asked.

Every cell inside him fired to life at her words. He tried to keep his feet on the ground, not to get carried away. Her confession didn't mean she still loved him. But her smile…

'It was the moment you made arrangements for me to travel with you and Aunt Katherine to São Paulo. I told you that you were my new favourite person.'

He remembered the exact moment.

'As soon as the words left my mouth, I knew they were true. I think it all started, though, that day on the beach.'

'When we kissed?'

'No. Though *that* was a revelation.'

She could say that again.

'I'm talking about the day you fell for George. When he grabbed on to you and you just couldn't hold out against him any longer. I think that was the moment when my heart waved a white flag and surrendered.'

But he'd rejected her twice since then. Had he trampled so hard over her heart that she didn't have any love left for him now? He wanted to drop to his knees in front of her but forced himself to remain where he was. 'Imogen, I've just spoken about the future I want. What I want more than anything is for that future to be with you. I don't expect you to trust me immediately.' Desperation clawed at him. 'But please let me see you a little when I'm back in Sydney. Let me prove to you—'

Her smile transformed her face and he couldn't speak as his throat closed over.

'No, Jasper, that's not a deal I want to make.'

But she smiled in a way that lifted rather than felled him.

'The deal is that you see me a lot. *A whole lot.* Didn't you hear what I just said?' She surged to her feet, and so did he. 'I love you too.' She moved across to stand in front of him, reaching up to touch his face, her eyes soft and her lips even softer. 'I love you.'

And then she was in his arms, her arms wound tight around his neck and her hair tickling his face. He wrapped his arms around her waist and closed his eyes, giving thanks to whatever deity had sent her into his life.

She eased back, her mouth millimetres from his. 'Deal?' she whispered.

'Deal,' he murmured, catching her lips in a kiss that promised a lifetime. He'd finally found the one place he belonged—with Imogen—and he meant to treasure it, to treasure her, forever.

EPILOGUE

Three years later

JASPER GLANCED AROUND the monstrosity of an open-plan kitchen/diner that Katherine had told him was an utter necessity and had to pinch himself. It was crammed to its vaulted ceilings—ceilings Imogen had swooned over—with Christmas cheer, with excited chatter and laughter, and with all the things he'd known Christmas could hold for other people but had never expected to experience for himself.

Several people toasted him as he came into the room and he grinned. It was official—he and Imogen had been added to the Christmas hosting rota. He had to pinch himself again.

His wife hadn't been kidding when she'd said the holiday was a big deal for her family. Tonight, they were hosting the Christmas Eve party; tomorrow Imogen's parents—two of the nicest people he'd ever met—were hosting the traditional all-day Christmas lunch, while the day after that her uncle Robert and aunt Sarah were hosting the Boxing Day wind-down.

And he loved it. All of it. With a passion that almost seemed unholy.

And the house he and Imogen had designed for the ten-acre block of land he'd bought in Wollongong—with its extraordinary ocean views—provided the perfect back-drop for all this warmth and belonging. Everything was… *perfect.*

Almost perfect. His father had another five years to serve on an eight-year jail term, but as far as Jasper could tell not a single person missed him. Aaron had already served his eighteen-month sentence and had relocated to Darwin. Jasper's lips tightened. But only after striking a devil's bargain. In exchange for start-up funds for a bar and restaurant, Aaron had signed away all his custody rights to George. Jasper still couldn't believe the man had suggested such a thing—George was a joy, a delight, a treasure. But if that was the way Aaron felt, then it was better for George to have nothing to do with him.

He pushed the sombre thought away. Tonight was for fun and laughter and giving thanks. Moving behind Imogen, who was putting the finishing touches to a cheese and fruit platter, he slipped his arms about her waist. 'Anything I can do to help?'

She gave a delicious shiver when his lips touched her nape. 'I don't think so—the food's all ready.' They'd prepared a buffet-style feast and had set up picnic tables and blankets on the lawn outside. The evening was balmy and the sky full of oranges, pinks and mauves as the sun started to set. 'But please tell me someone is supervising the children in the pool.'

'Your aunt Fiona and aunt Stacey are keeping a close eye on proceedings while your uncle Jordan and uncle Dennis discuss the merits of different car motors.'

Imogen laughed. 'If they keep that up my aunts might just push them in the deep end.'

'And your cousins are teaching George how to dive.' George, who was nearly four and utterly fearless!

'Good for them.' She set a final bunch of grapes to her platter with a flourish and then turned and looped her arms about his neck. 'So how are you enjoying our very first party in our gorgeous new house?'

'I love it. When can we have another one?'

He didn't try to temper his excitement, his enthusiasm… his joy. He knew it must be shining from his face, but he didn't have to be wary or guarded here—not among these people who'd embraced him and claimed him as one of their own.

Her face softened. 'You deserve all of this, Jasper. All of the fun and holiday spirit and love.'

'I don't know about that.'

'I do,' she said, her voice a soft whisper against his skin.

They'd married eighteen months ago, and he hadn't known it was possible for one man to feel so lucky—loving her was the smartest thing he'd ever done. That love filled his chest now, making him feel weightless, as if he could float up to the highest point of the ceiling.

She glanced beyond him, her luscious lips curving into a smile. 'It's nice to see your mother and Emily enjoying themselves.'

He followed her gaze to the terrace outside, where his mother and sister were firmly ensconced in a circle of Imogen's family—all of them laughing and seemingly talking at once. It'd taken time for the shadows to retreat from their eyes. They'd bear scars forever, he knew that, but it didn't mean they couldn't be happy in the here and now.

He'd had three cottages built on this ten-acre block, each with its own private garden. Emily and George were in one, Katherine in another, and the married couple he and Imogen had hired as housekeeper and gardener were living in the third. He'd wanted to build one for his mother but she hadn't let him. She'd sold the house in Sydney to buy a modest unit in Wollongong's town centre, within easy access to them all. He hoped that, given enough time, both Emily and his mother would find a love like his and

Imogen's—a love that healed and renewed; a love that made the world a place full of hope and possibility.

Imogen reached up on tiptoe to press her lips to his and a familiar surge of heat licked along his veins. Whatever she saw in his face made her chuckle. 'Hold that thought until the party's over.'

He had every intention of doing exactly that. For now, he contented himself with reaching for his phone and selecting a song from his playlist. He spun her in his arms as sixties Southern Californian surf music poured from the speakers. 'Pretend I'm a vacuum cleaner and dance with me.'

She threw her head back and laughed, her dark curls bouncing with effervescent good humour. 'Best offer I've had all night!'

He made a mental note to better that offer when they were alone.

His heart nearly burst when the entire kitchen and dining room erupted into a storm of dancing. Katherine and Imogen's mother, Gloria, started a complicated dance that had them both breathless by the end and everyone else clapping madly. Katherine's writing career was going from strength to strength and Gloria, in her spare time, had taken it upon herself to become Katherine's marketing manager. He suppressed a grin. So far the arrangement was working beautifully even given the occasional inevitable bump along the way.

'Food's up,' Imogen hollered when the song ended.

They ate. They socialised. They sang Christmas carols for the children. At nine o'clock the fireworks he'd arranged—with all the associated council permits and fire safety precautions in place—created a magical display that delighted child and adult alike.

After that, sleepy children were put to sleep in spare bedrooms or on the sofas in the lounge room while the adults continued to revel for another couple of hours. Eventually, though, the guests started to excuse themselves. Jasper saw the last of them off and then wandered back through the house to find his glorious wife.

She stood outside on the terrace, staring at a moonlit sea. She turned to greet him with a smile as big as her heart, and full of love. For him. The knowledge awed him. 'That was one of the best Christmas Eve parties ever, Jasper. If we're not careful we might just find ourselves hosting it every year.'

'I wouldn't mind.'

She poked him in the ribs before sliding an arm about his waist. 'You'd *love* it.'

He grinned, tucking her in more firmly against his side. 'That was the best Christmas Eve ever.'

'Which is what you said last year…and the year before that,' she teased.

'And I'll probably say it again next year.' He sobered, glancing down at her. 'They keep getting better. I don't know how, but they do.'

She sobered too. Moving out from beneath his arm, she took his hand in both her own. 'I think this one is extra special.'

'It's the first time we've hosted one of the Christmas events.' *That* was a big deal. 'And we did it in our dream home.' To be honest, though, wherever Imogen happened to be was his definition of dream home.

'Not just that—this whole year has been amazing.'

Her and Lauren's sewing business had become a soaring success. They now ran a very exclusive fashion house— The House of Tesoura. Emily had started her own PR company, and the fashion house had been her first client. Both businesses were thriving. 'You've achieved amazing things this year, Imogen. The House of Tesoura is the toast of the town.'

'I'm ecstatic about that, of course—' her eyes danced '—and over the moon that I can blow raspberries at all of the naysayers, but that's not what I'm talking about. I'm talking about the plans we discussed a few months ago. I feel as if we're on the cusp of an exciting new adventure.'

He swallowed and his heart started to thud. 'You mean…about starting a family soon?' He was almost too afraid to hope. He already had so much.

'That's exactly what I'm talking about.' She bit her lip and then took his hand and laid it flat against her abdomen, her eyes shining and her lips trembling.

A jolt shot through him like electricity—he went rigid, and then a wild, glorious excitement coursed through him. 'You're…?'

She nodded. 'I found out yesterday. I wasn't going to tell you until tomorrow. I thought it'd be the best Christmas present ever. But I've been bursting with the news… and now seemed like the perfect time.'

He couldn't push a single word past the lump in his throat.

Imogen was pregnant.

His hand curved against her in wonder.

They were going to have a baby.

'Happy?' she whispered.

With a superhuman effort, he swallowed down the lump. 'I thought I was happy two minutes ago. This—' he shook his head '—it's almost too much.'

'No, it's not, darling Jasper.' She reached up to touch his face. 'It's just right. It's exactly as it should be.'

'I'm the luckiest man alive.' Cupping her face, he lowered his mouth to hers and told her in a language that needed no words exactly how happy he was.

* * * * *

HER RIGHT-HAND
COWBOY

MARIE FERRARELLA

To
Charlie,
My one and only
Love,
After fifty-one years together,
You still make the world fade away
Every time you kiss me.

Chapter One

It felt familiar, yet strange.

The closer she came to the sprawling two-story ranch house, the simple five-word sentence kept repeating itself over and over again in Ena O'Rourke's brain like a tuneless song. Part of her just couldn't believe that she had returned here after all this time.

She could remember when she couldn't wait to get away from here. Or rather not "here" but away from her father because, to her then eighteen-year-old mind, Bruce O'Rourke was the source of all the anger and pain that existed in her world. Back then, she and her father were constantly at odds and without Edith, her mother, to act as a buffer, Ena and her father were forever butting heads.

The way she saw it, her father was opinionated, and he never gave her any credit for being right, not even once. After enduring a state of what felt like constant warfare for two years, ever since her mother lost her battle with cancer, Ena made up her mind and left the ranch, and Forever, one day after high school graduation.

At the time, she had been certain that she would never come back, had even sworn to herself that she wouldn't. And although she wavered a little in the first couple of years or so, as she struggled to put herself through college, she had stuck by her promise and kept far away from the source of all her unhappiness.

Until now.

She swung her long legs out of her light blue sports car and got out. She had sincerely doubted that a man who had always seemed to be bigger than life itself was ever going to die.

Until he did.

Bruce O'Rourke had died as tight-lipped as he had lived, without ever having uttered a single word to her. He had never even tried to get in contact with her. It was as if, for him, she had never existed.

It figured, Ena thought now, slowly approaching the house where she had grown up. Her father hadn't bothered to get in contact with her to tell her that he was dying. Instead, he had his lawyer summon her the moment he was gone. That way, he hadn't given her a chance to clear the air or vent her feelings.

He hadn't wanted to be held accountable.

Because he knew he had driven her away, she thought now, angry tears gathering in her eyes.

"Same old Dad," she bit off angrily.

She remained where she was for a moment, just staring at the exterior of the old ranch house. She had expected to see it on the verge of falling apart. But apparently her father had been careful not to allow that to happen. He had taken care of the homestead. The house looked as if it was sporting a brand-new coat of paint that couldn't have been more than a few months old.

She frowned to herself. Bruce O'Rourke took a great deal more care of the house and the ranch than he ever had when dealing with her. Her mother, Ena recalled with a stab of pain, was the only one who could effectively deal with the man. What Edith had advised her on more than one occasion was to just give the man a pass because he was under so much pressure and had so much responsibility on his shoulders. It wasn't easy, the genteel woman had told her in that soft low-key voice of hers, trying to keep the ranch going.

"So you kept it going while pushing me away—and what did it get you in the end, Old Man? You're gone, and the ranch is still here. At least for now," she said ironically. "But not for long. Just until I can get someone to take it off my hands. And then I'll finally be done with it, and you, once and for all," Ena concluded under her breath.

She was stalling. She supposed she was putting off dealing with that oppressive wave of memories that threatened to wash over her the moment she walked through the front door and into the house.

But she knew that she couldn't put it off indefinitely.

Taking a deep breath, she squared her shoulders and took another tentative step toward the house. And then another until she reached the steps leading up to the wraparound veranda. The place, she recalled, where her mother and father used to like to sit and rock at the end of the day.

As she came to the second step, Ena heard that old familiar creak beneath her foot.

Her father never had gotten around to fixing that. She

could remember her mother asking him to see to it and her father promising to *"get to it when I have the time."*

"Obviously you never found the time to fix that that, either, did you, Old Man?" she said, addressing the man who was no longer there.

"Is that a Dallas thing? Talking to yourself?" a deep male voice behind her asked.

In the half second that it took Ena to swing around to see who had crept up so silently behind her, she managed to compose herself and not look as if the tall, handsome, dark-haired cowboy behind her had launched her heart into double time.

"Is sneaking up behind people something you picked up while working here?" Ena countered, annoyed.

Her father had had that habit, materializing behind her when she least expected it, usually to interrogate her about where she had been or where she intended on going. And no matter what she answered, her father always sounded as if he disapproved and was criticizing her.

The cowboy, however, sounded contrite. "Sorry, I didn't realize I wasn't making enough noise for you." He then coughed and cleared his throat. "Is that loud enough?" he asked her with an easy grin.

Ena pressed her lips together and glared at him without answering.

The cowboy nodded. "I take it from that look on your face that you don't remember me," he said.

Ena narrowed her clear blue eyes as she focused on the cowboy, who must have towered over her by at least a good twelve inches. There was something vaguely familiar about his rugged face with its high, almost gaunt cheekbones, but after the restless night she had spent and then the long trip back, she was *not* in the mood to play guessing games with someone who was apparently one of her father's ranch hands.

"Should I?" she asked coldly.

Mitch Parnell winced. "Ouch, I guess that puts me in my place," he acknowledged. He pushed back his worn Stetson and took off his right glove, extending his hand out to her. "Welcome home, Ena."

The deep smile and familiar tone nudged forward more memories from her past. Her eyes slowly swept over the dusty, rangy cowboy. It couldn't be—

Could it?

"Mitch?" she asked uncertainly. But even as she said his name, part of her thought she was making a mistake.

Until he smiled.

Really smiled.

Even as a teenager, Mitch Parnell had always had the kind of smile that the moment it appeared, it could completely light up the area. She and Mitch had gone to high school together, and for a week or two, she had even fancied herself in love with him—or as in love as a seventeen-year-old unhappy, lost girl desperately searching for acceptance could be.

Her mother had died the year before and communication between her father and her had gone from bad to worse. It felt as if the only times Bruce O'Rourke spoke to her, he was either lashing out at her or yelling at her. Hurting, she had been desperate to find a small haven, some sort of a retreat from the cold world where she could pretend she was loved and cared for.

But at seventeen, she had been awkward and not exactly skilled in womanly wiles. Consequently, she just assumed that Mitch had missed all her signals. It even felt as if he had dodged all her outright romantic gestures. In any event, she wound up withdrawing even further into herself, biding her time until she finally graduated high school and could flee the site of her unhappiness.

At the time, Mitch had just been someone she'd gone to school with. If anything, he had been a further reminder of her failure to make a connection with someone. She didn't associate him with her father's ranch. Had he come to work here after he had graduated high school? The few conversations they'd had back then, he had never mentioned anything about wanting to work on a ranch. Seeing him here was a surprise.

It occurred to her that she knew next to nothing about the good-looking guy she had briefly thought of as her salvation.

"Mitch?" she repeated, still looking at him, confused.

Pleasure brought an even wider smile to his lips. "So you do remember me." There was satisfaction evident in his voice.

Ena fervently hoped that he merely thought of her as someone he'd gone to school with and not as the girl who had made an unsuccessful play for him. This was already awkward enough as it was.

"What are you doing here?" she asked.

"I work here," Mitch answered. His tone was neither boastful nor solicitous. He was merely stating a fact. "As a matter of fact, your dad made me foreman of the Double E almost three years ago."

Ena stared at him, trying to comprehend what Mitch was telling her. When she'd left, her father only hired men to work on the ranch who he'd either known for years or who came highly recommended by men he had known for years. Apparently, some things had changed in the last ten years.

"Where's Rusty?" she asked, referring to the big barrel-chested man who had been her father's foreman for as long as she could remember.

The smile on Mitch's lips faded, giving way to a somber expression. "Rusty died."

She stared at Mitch in disbelief. "When?" she finally asked.

This was almost more than she could process. Rusty Hayes had been the man who had taught her how to ride a horse. When she was really young, she remembered wishing that Rusty was her real father and not the man who periodically growled at her and even growled at her mother on occasion. Rusty had been even-tempered. Her father couldn't have been accused of that.

"Three years ago," Mitch told her. There was sympathy in his eyes. "You didn't know," he guessed.

"There's a lot I didn't know," Ena bit off. "My father and I didn't exactly stay in touch," she added angrily, trying to process this latest blow.

Mitch continued to look at her sympathetically. "So I gather." She was still standing on the top step of the veranda. He decided that maybe she needed a gentle nudge. "Would you like to go in?" he asked.

The question seemed to snap her out of the deep funk she had slipped into. Ena pulled her shoulders back as if she were gearing up for battle. "I lived here for eighteen years. I don't need your invitation to go in if that's what I want to do," she informed him.

Mitch raised his hands up in mute surrender. "Didn't mean to imply that you did," he told her, apologizing without saying the actual words. The next moment, he saw her turning on her heel. She walked down the three steps, away from the porch. "Are you leaving?" he asked her in surprise.

"Are you trying to keep tabs on me?" she demanded.

To Ena's surprise, rather than answer her, Mitch began to laugh. Heartily.

Scowling, she snapped, "I wasn't aware that I had said something funny."

It took him a second to catch his breath. "Not exactly funny," he told her.

Her eyes had narrowed to small slits that were all but shooting daggers at him. "Then what?" she asked.

This whole situation had made her decidedly uncomfortable, as well as angry. This person she had gone to school with—and had briefly entertained feelings for—was acting more at ease and at home on this property than she was. For some reason, that irritated her to no end.

Mitch took in another deep breath so he could speak. "I was just thinking how much you sounded like your father."

If he had intentionally tried to set her off, he couldn't have found a better way. Anger creased Ena's forehead.

Struggling not to lose her temper, she informed him, "I am *nothing* like my father."

Mitch's response was to stare at her as if he were trying to discern whether or not she was kidding him. Before he could stop himself, he asked in amazement, "You honestly believe that?"

"Yes," Ena ground out between clenched teeth, "I honestly do."

The smile on Mitch's face was almost radiant. He pressed his lips together to keep from laughing again, sensing that she really wouldn't appreciate it if he did. But he couldn't refrain from saying, "Wow, you really *are* like your father."

No wonder her father had made this man his foreman. Mitch Parnell was as crazy in his own way as her father had been. "Stop saying that," she insisted.

"Okay," he agreed good-naturedly, relenting. "But it doesn't make it any less true."

Ena curled her fingers into her palms. She wasn't going to give Mitch a piece of her mind, even though she would have liked nothing better than to tell him what an infuriating idiot he was. Which only left her with one option.

Ena turned on her heel and headed back to her vehicle—quickly.

Mitch followed at a pace that others might refer to as walking briskly, but he cut the distance between them so effortlessly it didn't even look as if he was walking fast.

"Hey, was it something I said?" he asked. "If it helps, I can apologize," he said, although he had no idea what he could have said to set her off.

But because he had just lost a boss who over the years had become more like a surrogate father to him, Mitch was willing to apologize to Bruce's daughter. He knew that having her here would have meant a lot to his boss. Besides, he had looked into Ena's eyes, and while she probably thought she had covered up things well, he had glimpsed pain there. Having her run off like this wasn't going to eliminate that pain.

"I came to see the ranch house," Ena informed him crisply. "And I saw it. Now I'm going to see my father's lawyer and find out what he has to tell me so I know exactly where I stand."

"You're talking about your dad's will." It wasn't a guess on Mitch's part.

Ena's antenna went up. The accounting firm in Dallas where she had worked her way up to a junior partnership had seen all manner of fraud. Fraud that had been the result of greed and a sense of entitlement. Initially, when she had first encountered it, she had been surprised by the way people treated one another when a little bit of money was involved. But eventually, she came to expect it, just as she now expected to have to fight Mitch on some level because he had probably come to regard the ranch as his own and had hung around, waiting for her father to die. He undoubtedly expected to have her father leave the ranch to him.

Maybe, for all she knew, Mitch had even helped the situation along.

Well, too bad, she thought. If her father *had* left the ranch to his "trusty foreman," Mitch Parnell was going to have one hell of a fight on his hands.

Calm down, Ena. You're jumping the gun and getting way ahead of yourself, she silently counseled.

But she wasn't here to try to prove that Mitch had somehow brought about her father's demise because he had designs on the Double E. She was here to try to make the best of the situation, sell the ranch and move on. With any luck, by the end of the week she could put her whole childhood behind her once and for all.

Starting up her car, she half expected Mitch to run up to her window and try to stop her—or to at least say something inane such as "Don't do anything hasty." But as she pulled away, the foreman remained standing just where he was.

She could see him in the rearview mirror, watching her and shaking his head.

The smug bastard. Was he judging her?

Deep breaths, Ena, she instructed herself. *Deep breaths. You can't let someone out of your past get to you. You're here to listen to the reading of the will and to sell the ranch. The sooner you do that, the sooner*

*things will get back to being normal and you can go
on with your life.*

A life she had fought hard to forge, she reminded
herself. On her own. Without asking for so much as a
single dime from her father.

She was proud of that.

At the same time, the fact that she had had to do it
on her own, without any help, or even an offer of help,
from her father managed to sting bitterly. It reinforced
her feelings of being by herself. She hadn't always been
alone. There'd been another child, her twin brother,
but the baby had died at birth. While her mother had
treated her as if she were a perpetual special gift from
Heaven, she had always felt that her father resented that
she had been the one to live and her brother had been
the one to die.

"Sorry, Old Man," she caught herself saying as
she drove into town, on the lookout for the attorney's
office—there had been no lawyers in Forever when she
had left. "Those were the cards you were dealt. You
should have made the most of it. I would have made you
forget all about the son you never had. But you never
gave me the chance." She shrugged, her shoulders rising and then falling again carelessly. "Your loss," she
concluded.

The next moment, not wanting to put up with the silence within her car a second longer, Ena turned on the
radio and let Johnny Cash mute her pain.

Chapter Two

Mitch watched as Ena's rather impressive but highly impractical car—at least for this part of the country—become smaller and smaller until it was barely a moving dot on the winding road.

She had come back, he marveled. He'd had his doubts there for a minute or two after Bruce O'Rourke had died and Cash, her father's lawyer, had sent a letter to notify Ena, but she had come back.

Ena was even more beautiful than he'd remembered, Mitch thought. Hell, every memory involving her was sealed away in his mind, including the very first time he ever laid eyes on her.

He smiled to himself now, recalling the event as if it were yesterday. It was a Tuesday. Second period English class. He'd been a new transfer to the high school and had just been handed his class schedule. He'd walked into Mrs. Brickman's class fifteen minutes after it had officially started.

Everyone's eyes in the class had been focused on "the new kid" as he walked in the door, doing his damnedest to look as if he didn't care what anyone thought of him, even though he did.

And then, as his eyes quickly swept over the small class, he saw *her*. Ena O'Rourke. Blue eyes and long blond hair. Sitting up front, second seat, fourth row. He caught himself thinking that she was the most beautiful girl who had ever walked the face of the earth.

He'd almost swallowed his tongue.

It took everything he had to continue with his blasé act, appearing as if he didn't care one way or another about any of these people.

But he did. He cared what they all thought.

Especially the blonde little number in front.

And because she had suddenly become so very important to him, he deliberately acted as if he didn't give a damn what any of these people thought of him. Especially her.

With a Navajo mother and an Irish father, Mitch felt as if he had one foot in each world and yet belonged nowhere.

He remembered Ena smiling at him. Remembered Mrs. Brickman telling him to take the empty seat next to *Miss O'Rourke*.

Remembered his stomach squeezing so hard he could hardly breathe.

Wanting desperately to come across as his own person and not some pitiful newcomer, he had maintained an aloof aura and deliberately kept everyone at arm's length, even the girl who reduced his knees to the consistency of melted butter.

Why had he ever been that young and stupid? he now

wondered. But life, back then, for an outsider hadn't been easy.

It hadn't become easier, he recalled, until Bruce O'Rourke had gruffly given him a chance and hired him to work the ranch shortly after his parents died, leaving him an orphan.

Funny the turns that life took, he mused.

Mitch observed Wade McCallister making his way over to him. The heavyset older man looked more than a little curious. He jerked a thumb at the departing vehicle. "Hey, boss, was that—"

Mitch didn't wait for the other man to finish his question. He already knew what the ranch hand was going to ask and nodded his head.

"Yup, it was."

Wade had worked off and on at the Double E Ranch for a long time. Long enough to have known Bruce O'Rourke's daughter before she was even a teenager.

Turning now to watch Ena's car become less than a speck on the horizon, Wade asked, "Where's she heading off to?"

"She's on her way to talk to the old man's lawyer," Mitch answered. Even the dot he'd been watching was gone now. He turned away from the road and focused his attention on Wade.

Wade's high forehead was deeply furrowed. The ranch hand had never been blessed with a poker face. "She's gonna sell the ranch, isn't she?" the older man asked apprehensively.

"She might want to," Mitch answered. "But she can't." His smile grew deeper. "At least not yet."

"What do you mean she can't?" Wade asked him, confused.

Wade had known Bruce O'Rourke longer than Mitch

had. But Wade didn't have a competitive bone in his body and he wasn't insulted that his normally close-mouthed boss had taken Mitch into his confidence. As a result, Mitch had been devoted to the old man and everyone knew it. While the rest of them had lives of their own apart from the ranch, Mitch had made himself available to Bruce 24/7, ready to run errands for him no matter what time of day or night. No job was too great or too small as far as Mitch was concerned.

"The old man put that in his will." He had been one of Bruce O'Rourke's two witnesses when his boss had had the will drawn up and then had him sign it. Afterward, Bruce had expanded on what he had done. "He said the ranch was hers on the sole condition that she stay here and run things for six months."

It sounded good, but it was clear that Wade had his doubts the headstrong girl he'd watched grow up would adhere to the will.

"What if she decides not to listen to that—what do you call it? A clause?" Wade asked, searching for the right term.

Mitch nodded. "A clause," he confirmed. "If she doesn't, then the ranch gets turned over to some charitable foundation Mr. O'Rourke was partial to."

The furrows on Wade's forehead were back with a vengeance. "Does that mean we're all out of a job? 'Cause I'm too old to go looking for work with my hat in my hand."

Mitch shook his head and laughed at the picture the other man was attempting to paint. "Too old? Hell, Wade, you're not even fifty."

Wade wasn't convinced. "I'd have to pull up stakes and try to find some kind of work somewhere else, and

I'm comfortable where I am." The ranch hand's frown deepened. "Like I said, too old."

"Well, don't go packing up your saddlebags just yet," Mitch told the man he regarded as his right-hand man. "Even if the ranch does get sold down the line, whatever organization takes over is doubtlessly going to want the ranch to keep on turning a profit. But don't worry," Mitch assured the other man. "The old man was banking on the idea that once his daughter gets back to her roots, she's not going to want to let this place go."

Wade, however, wasn't convinced—with good reason, he felt. "You weren't here when she left. To be honest, I'm surprised the old man's daughter came back at all."

"Oh, I don't know," Mitch said, thinking back to his own childhood and adolescence. It had taken him time to make peace with who he was and where he had come from. Now he was proud of it, but it hadn't always been that way. "Our past has a greater hold on us than we'd like to believe."

But Wade was still far from swayed. And other problems occurred to him. "Even if she does wind up keeping it, she's bound to make changes in the way the ranch is run."

Mitch was used to Wade's pessimism. It hadn't been all that long ago that he had been just like Wade, seeing the world in shades of black. But then Bruce had taken him under his wing and everything had changed from that day forward.

"Let's not get ahead of ourselves," Mitch advised. "Let's just see how her visit with the old man's lawyer goes."

Wade took in a deep breath, centering himself. "Okay, you're the boss, Mitch."

Mitch grinned. "That's right. I am. At least for now," he allowed, deliberately playing on the other man's natural penchant for gloom and doom.

For Wade's sake, as well as for the sake of all the other men who worked under him at the Double E Ranch, Mitch maintained a positive attitude. The old man had taught him that there was nothing to be gained by wallowing in negative thoughts, saying that he himself had learned that the hard way. If things went well, then being negative was just a waste. And if things didn't go well, there was no point in hurrying things along. They'd catch up to him soon enough.

Besides, who knew? Mitch thought. Maybe coming back here would help heal whatever was broken within Ena's soul.

"C'mon," Mitch urged, turning toward Wade. "We've still got work to do."

Forever had built up since she'd been here last, Ena thought as she drove down the town's long Main Street. The last time she'd been here, the town's medical clinic had been boarded up, the way it had been for close to thirty years. From what she could see by the vehicles jammed in the small parking lot, the clinic was open and doing a healthy business.

She smiled to herself at her unintentional pun.

And that was new, Ena noted as she continued to travel along Forever's Main Street. Slowing her vehicle, she took a closer look at what appeared to be—*a hotel?*

Surprised, she slowed down even more as she passed a small welcoming three-story building. Yes, it was a hotel all right.

Was there actually an influx of tourists to Forever

these days? Enough to warrant building and running a hotel? Was it even profitable?

Ena looked over her shoulder again as she passed the new building. She had never thought that progress would actually ever come to Forever. Obviously she had thought wrong.

The law firm where she was supposed to go to see her father's lawyer was new, as well—as was the concept of her father actually *having* a will formally drafted and written up. If her father had actually *wanted* to put down any final instructions to be followed after his demise, she would have expected him to write them down himself by hand on the inside of some old brown paper grocery bag, its insides most likely stained and making the writing illegible.

To see a lawyer would have taken thought on his part, a process that she had a hard time crediting her father with. Anyway, to draw up a will would have been an admission of mortality, and from the bottom of her heart, she was certain that her father had honestly believed he was going to live forever.

He'd certainly conducted himself that way while she lived here.

Ena realized that she was driving past the diner. She caught herself wondering if that, too, had changed. Was Miss Joan still running the place? She couldn't bring herself to imagine that not being the case. Miss Joan had been a fixture in Forever for as long as she could remember.

When she'd been a young girl, Ena could remember that she'd been afraid of the sharp-tongued woman. It was only as she got older that she began to appreciate the fact that everyone turned to Miss Joan for advice or support, even though, at least on the surface, Miss Joan was a no-nonsense, opinionated, blustery woman who could cut to the heart of any matter faster than anyone she'd ever met.

Ena made a mental note to stop by the diner when she finished with her father's lawyer. She wanted to see for herself if Miss Joan was still running the place.

And, while she was at it, she wanted to ask Miss Joan why *she* at least hadn't gotten in contact with her to tell her that her father was dying of cancer. Never mind that she hadn't given the woman her address or phone number and had maintained her own silence for ten years. Miss Joan had her ways of getting in contact with people. She always had.

After pulling up in front of the neat, hospitable, small freshly painted building with its sign proclaiming Law Offices, Ena carefully parked her sports car.

As she emerged out of the vehicle, she saw a couple of vaguely familiar-looking people passing by. They were looking in her direction as they walked. By the expressions on their faces, they appeared to be trying to place her, as well.

Getting this uncomfortable bit of business over and done with was the only thing on her mind at the moment. She looked away from the duo and went up to the law office's front door.

Ena had barely rung the bell when the door swung open. She found herself making eye contact with a tall, good-looking, blond-haired man she didn't recognize. The man had a friendly, authoritative air about him despite his age, which she judged to be somewhere around his late thirties.

Ena dived right in. "Hello, I have an appointment with Cash Taylor," she told the man.

Warm, friendly eyes crinkled at her as he smiled.

"Yes, I know. I'm Cash—and you're right on time," he told her. "That isn't as usual as you might think." Cash opened the door all the way. "Won't you come in?"

"Thank you," Ena murmured, making her way into the small homey lobby. And then she turned toward Cash, waiting.

"My office is on the right," he told her, sensing his late client's daughter was waiting for him to tell her which direction to go in.

There were two main offices in the building. Cash had one, while the sheriff's wife, who had initially started the firm when she married Sheriff Santiago, had the other. Both were of equal size.

"This is new," Ena heard herself saying as she followed Cash into his tastefully decorated office.

"It is," Cash agreed. "Although I can't take credit for it. My partner started the firm when she decided to stay in Forever after she married Sheriff Santiago."

"Sheriff Rick's married?" Ena asked, surprised by the information.

Cash nodded. "Married and a father. So am I." Not that she probably remembered him, Cash thought. However, there was someone she probably did remember from her early days in Forever. "You might know my wife. She was Alma Rodriguez before she decided to take a chance on me," he told her with an engaging smile.

The surprises just kept on coming, Ena marveled. "You're married to Alma?"

Cash was obviously proud of that fact. He nodded. "You've been gone ten years, is it?" As he sat down at his desk, he checked the notes in the open file before him. "I guess you have a lot of catching up to do."

"I don't plan to stay here long enough to catch up,"

Ena politely informed him. "I'm just here long enough to get the property ready to put up for sale and then I'm going back to Dallas."

Cash frowned slightly. "I'm afraid you're going to have to postpone your return back to Dallas," he informed her politely.

Ena's eyes widened as she stared at the lawyer. "Wait, what? Why?"

Cash realized that he had forgotten one very important step. Extending his hand to her, he said, "First of all, please allow me to express my condolences on the death of your father—" He got no further.

Ena waved her hand, symbolically wiping away whatever else he had to say along those lines. She didn't want his sympathy or anyone else's.

"You can save your breath, Mr. Taylor," Ena said. "My father's been dead to me a long time, just as, I assume, I have been dead to him."

Cash shook his head, wanting to correct her mistaken belief. "I'm afraid I—"

"If he didn't tell you, Mr. Taylor, let me," Ena volunteered. "From the minute I was born, my father and I never got along. After my mother died, that hostility just increased by a factor of ten. I took off the day after I graduated from high school. And I've never looked back." That wasn't strictly true, but she saw no point in elaborating.

Cash nodded. "Yes, your father told me."

Ena shifted in her seat, uncomfortable at the very idea of being here. "To be honest, I'm not really sure why he left the ranch to me. I just assumed he was going to run the ranch forever."

"Unfortunately," Cash began, "*forever* had a timetable."

He lowered his voice a little as he added, "And we are all very sorry to have lost him."

Right. He had to say that, Ena thought.

"Uh-huh," she finally responded, only because she felt she had to say something.

"As for leaving the ranch to you," Cash continued genially, "you are the only living member of his family."

She wanted to be on her way back to Dallas. "All right, so tell me what I need to sign or do to get this sale moving along," she requested. As far as she was concerned, this was already taking too long.

"What you *need to do*," he informed her, "is to stay here for the next six months."

Ena stared at the man opposite her in disbelief. "You're serious?" she asked, stunned.

Cash nodded. "Absolutely. Those are the terms of your father's will." To prove it, he read the brief section to her.

Ena made an unintelligible noise. "Even from beyond the grave, that man found a way to put the screws to me," she cried.

"In your father's defense, I think that he thought of it as a way to bring you back to your roots," Cash told her.

"My roots," she informed him stubbornly, "are in Dallas."

"That might be," Cash conceded. "But your father saw it differently."

Ena rolled her eyes. "My father saw *everything* differently. He made it his mission in life to contradict every single thing I said or did," she informed him.

Cash did his best to attempt to smooth over this obviously rough patch. "I realize that there was some bad blood between you years ago—"

"There was *always* bad blood between us," she informed the lawyer tersely. "The only reason it wasn't spilled was because my mother—who was a saint, by the way, for putting up with the man—acted as a buffer between us. Once she was gone, there was no one to step in and try to make my father be reasonable—so he wasn't. Everything that ever went wrong was, in his opinion, my fault."

Ena stopped abruptly, catching herself before she could get carried away.

"I'm sorry," she apologized. "My father always had a way of bringing out the worst in me. How long do I have to decide whether or not I'm going to abide by the terms of this will of his?" she asked.

"I'm afraid you have to if you want to keep the ranch," Cash told her.

"So I guess that's the decision before me," she said. "Whether or not I want to keep the ranch. Tough one," she said flippantly. "How long did you say I have before I have to give you my decision?"

Cash stared at her. For the moment, she had managed to stump him.

Chapter Three

Knowing some of the circumstances behind Ena's relationship with her father, Cash cleared his throat and tried to be as diplomatic as possible. "I realize that the situation between you and your father wasn't exactly the best."

Ena suppressed the involuntary harsh laugh that rose to her lips. "I take it that you have a penchant for making understatements, Mr. Taylor."

"Call me Cash." He didn't comment on Ena's observation. "Things aren't always the way that they seem at first glance."

Ena folded her hands before her on the desk. Her knuckles were almost white. "If you're referring to my father," she told the lawyer evenly, "Bruce O'Rourke was *exactly* the way he seemed. Cantankerous, ornery and dead set against everything I ever said or did." She drew back her shoulders, sitting ramrod straight in the chair. "My fate was sealed the day I was born, Mr. Taylor—Cash," she corrected herself before the lawyer could tell her his first name again.

"That's being a little harsh, wouldn't you say?"

"No," she replied stiffly, "I wouldn't. If anything, I'm being sensitive. My father was the harsh one." A dozen memories came at her from all directions, each with its own sharp edges digging into her. Ena winced as she struggled to block them all out. "He never forgave me for being the one who lived," she told Cash quietly.

Cash looked at her, completely in the dark as to her meaning. "I'm sorry?"

She had probably said too much already. But word had a way of getting around in this little town and if he didn't know about her father's tempestuous relationship with her, he would soon. He might as well hear it from her. This way, he'd at least get a semblance of the truth. It was his prerogative to believe her or not.

"I had a twin brother. It turned out that my mother was only strong enough to provide the necessary nourishment and bring one of us to term." She took a deep breath as she regarded her folded hands. "My brother didn't survive the birth process. I did. My father had his heart set on a boy. I was just going to be the consolation prize." She raised her eyes to meet Cash's. "He never got over the fact that I survived while my brother was stillborn. My father spent the rest of his life making me regret that turn of events."

Deeply ingrained diplomacy kept Cash from arguing with Ena's take on the matter. Instead, he said, "Still, he did leave the ranch to you."

"No," she contradicted, "he dangled the ranch in front of me and left me with a condition, which was something he always did." She thought back over the course of her adolescence. "He enjoyed making me jump through hoops—until one day I just stopped jumping."

Over the course of his career, Cash had learned how to read people. Right now, he could anticipate what his late client's daughter was thinking. "I wouldn't advise doing anything hasty, Ms. O'Rourke. Give the terms of your father's will a lot of thought," Cash advised.

"I've already thought it over," Ena informed the lawyer, "and I've decided not to play his game."

Cash's eyes met hers. "Then you're going to let him win?"

Ena looked at the attorney sitting on the other side of the desk. Her brow furrowed. "Excuse me?"

"Well," he began to explain, "from what you've said, your father always made you feel that you were a loser. And if you walk away from the ranch, you'll be forfeiting it, which in effect will be making you a loser. And that, in turn, will be telling your father that he was right about you all along."

Ena scowled at the lawyer. "You're twisting things."

The expression on his smooth face said that he didn't see things that way. "Maybe, in this case," he responded, "I'm able to see things more clearly because I don't have all this past baggage and animosity coloring my perception of things." He slid to the edge of his seat, moving in closer to create an air of confidentiality between them. And then he punctuated his statement with a careless shrug. "I'm just saying…" he told her, his voice trailing off.

He was doing it, Ena thought, irritated. Her father was boxing her into a corner, even though he was no longer walking among the living. Somehow, he was still managing to have the last say.

Ena frowned. As much as she wanted to tell this lawyer what he could do with her father's terms, as well as his will, she knew that Cash was right. If she tore up the will and walked out now, that would be tantamount to giving up—and her father would have managed to ultimately win.

She hated giving him that, even in death.

Blowing out a breath, she faced her father's lawyer with a less-than-happy look.

"I have to stay here for six months?" She asked the question as if each word was excruciatingly painful for her to utter.

"You have to run the ranch for six months," Cash corrected, thinking she might be looking for a loophole. There weren't any.

"Can I delegate the work?" Ena asked, watching the man's face carefully.

"You mean from a distance?" Cash asked. She wanted to oversee the operation from Dallas, he guessed.

"Yes," she said with feeling. "That's exactly what I mean."

"No." The lone word shimmered between them, cloaked in finality. "Your father was very clear about that. He wanted you to be on the ranch while you oversaw the work that needed to be done."

Ena swallowed a guttural sound. It was all she could do to keep from throwing her hands up in frustration. "I don't know anything about running a ranch. My father told me that over and over again," she emphasized. "He deliberately kept me away from the day-to-day process—other than mucking out the stalls. *That* he was more than happy to let me do."

"Obviously he'd had a change of heart about the

matter when he had me write up the will. And anyway," Cash went on, "you have some very capable men working at the Double E. I'm sure that they all would be more than willing to help you."

He was right and that was exactly her point. "So why can't I just tell them to use their judgment and keep the ranch running just the way that they always have?" she asked.

The look on Cash's face was sympathetic. He could see how frustrating all this had to be. "Because your father's will was very specific," he told her.

Ena's laugh was totally without any humor. "Yes, I'll bet. It probably said, 'Keep sticking pins in her side until she bleeds.'"

For the first time since they had sat down together, she saw the lawyer grin. "Not even close," Cash assured her.

She wasn't so sure. The sentiment was there all right, just probably hidden between the lines. "You obviously didn't know my father as well as you thought you did."

"Or maybe you're the one who doesn't know the man, at least not the way he was in his last years. It's been ten years," Cash reminded her. "People change in that amount of time, Ms. O'Rourke."

"Normal people do," Ena agreed. "But not my father. He was as set in his ways as any mountain range. To expect that mountain range to suddenly shift would be incredibly foolish."

"So you're turning your back on the will?" Cash concluded.

"No." She saw that her answer surprised him, so, since he'd been the one who had attempted to talk her out of forfeiting her claim, she explained. "Because you were right about one thing. If I just metaphorically toss this back in my father's very pale face, then he will have won the final battle and I'm not ready to let that happen. So," she continued, taking in a deep breath, "even though it's going to turn my whole life upside down, I'm going to stay on the Double E and work it so that I can meet those terms of his. And when I do, I'm going to sell that burdensome old homestead so fast that it'll make your head spin, Mr. Taylor."

Cash smiled at her. "I believe that at this point I'm beyond the head-spinning stage. Don't forget," he reminded her, "Miss Joan is my step-grandmother. Thanks to her, very little surprises me these days. By the way, she asked me to remind you that if you haven't yet. She's waiting for you to drop by to go see her."

Ena shrugged away the reminder. "I don't want to bother her. She's working."

The expression on the lawyer's face told her that he saw right through her excuse. "You *have* met Miss Joan, right?"

Ena stiffened. She had no idea why he would ask her something like that. He had to know the answer was yes. "Yes, of course I have."

"Then you know that she's *always* working," he reminded her. "I don't think that the woman knows how *not* to work."

If Ena had had any lingering doubts that Cash Taylor was actually related to Miss Joan, that put them all to rest. The man was obviously familiar with the diner owner's stubborn streak, as well as her way of overriding any and all who opposed her no matter what that opposition was rooted in.

Ena inclined her head, conceding the point. "You're right. I guess I'll stop by and see her before I leave town today," she told him, hoping that was enough to table this part of the discussion.

Nodding, Cash smiled and then extended his hand to her. "Well, welcome home, Ms. O'Rourke. I just wish this could be under better circumstances."

"So do I, Counselor. So do I," Ena responded with feeling. "Anything else?"

Cash shook his head. "No, I believe we've covered everything."

Gripping the armrests, Ena pushed herself to her feet, ready to take her leave as quickly as possible. "Then I'll be going now. Thank you for telling me about my father's will—and for your guidance," she added.

Although she silently thought that she could have done *without* his guidance since it made her agree to put up with her father's terms. She was, in essence, playing the game in her father's court. Which would make her victory when it came—and it would—that much sweeter.

She just needed to remember that.

On his feet as well, Cash said with genuine feeling, "My pleasure, Ms. O'Rourke. Here, I'll walk you to the door."

"That's really not necessary," Ena said, attempting to deflect the offer.

"I don't know about that. Miss Joan would give me a tongue-lashing if she found out that I'd forgotten my manners. Besides, one of us needs to stretch their legs," he added with a wink.

The "trip" to the law office's front door was an exceedingly short one. She was standing before it in a matter of seconds. Cash managed to open it one moment earlier, holding it for her.

"And don't forget to swing by Miss Joan's—when

you get the chance," he added politely. "She really would love to see you."

Ena nodded, although she sincerely doubted that Miss Joan would actually *love* to see anyone, especially someone who had walked away from Forever ten years ago. She knew for a fact that Miss Joan had little patience with people who felt that they needed to run away from Forever in order to either make something of themselves or, at the very least, find something more meaningful to do with their lives.

Feeling less than triumphant, Ena got into her sports car and drove the short distance to the diner.

She almost wound up driving *past* the diner. After listening to her father's will being read, she really was *not* in the mood to politely listen to someone tell her what was best for her. Miss Joan was not exactly a shy, retiring flower. But she also knew that offending the woman was not exactly the best course of action. So, at the last minute, Ena backed up her vehicle and pulled into the small parking lot.

Because of the hour, the lot wasn't packed.

Or maybe, Ena mused, business had slacked off. She knew that things like that did happen. She had seen it occur more than a few times during her years living in Dallas. One minute a business seemed to be thriving, even turning people away. The next, that same business was trying to figure out just what had gone wrong and why their patrons had forsaken them and were now frequenting another establishment.

But then those businesses, especially the restaurants, had a great many competitors. It was a toss-up as to which of them could come out on top and lure customers away from the others.

As far back as Ena could remember, Miss Joan had

had no competition. There was only one other establishment in Forever. That was Murphy's, owned and run by three brothers who proudly proclaimed the establishment to be a saloon. The Murphy brothers had a running agreement with Miss Joan. They didn't serve any food—other than pretzels—in their saloon and Miss Joan didn't serve any alcoholic beverages in her diner. That made Miss Joan's diner the only "restaurant" in town.

So if the good citizens of Forever wanted to grab a meal during their workday, they would all need to head out to Miss Joan's. Ena caught herself wishing that the diner were crowded now. That way, she could just pop in, officially tell Miss Joan that she was back in town, then slip quietly out. If there was any extra time, she might possibly tell the woman that she was debating temporarily sticking around in Forever, at least until such time as she met the conditions of her father's will and could sell the ranch.

Although she doubted that was necessary. Miss Joan had a way of knowing things before anyone told her. She just *intuited* them. Some hinted it had something to do with a Cajun ancestor in her family tree, but Ena doubted it. There was just something about the woman that couldn't really be pinpointed. She was just uniquely Miss Joan.

Getting out of her vehicle, Ena slowly approached the diner. She climbed up the three steps leading to the diner's door even more slowly.

Staring at the door, Ena decided that this wasn't one of her better ideas, at least not now. With that, she turned away from the door.

She had made it down all three steps when she heard the diner door behind her opening.

"You waiting for trumpets to herald your entrance

to my diner? Or maybe I should be dropping handfuls of rose petals in your path?"

Ena would have known that voice anywhere. Stiffening her shoulders, she turned around and looked up at the small compact woman with deep hazel eyes and hair the color of not quite muted flame. Miss Joan had caught her in the act of escaping. She should have seen this coming.

"I thought you might be too busy for a visit right now," Ena told her.

Miss Joan continued to stand there, one hand fisted on either side of her small, trim waist as she looked down at the girl she viewed as the newly returned prodigal daughter.

She shook her head. "Ten years and you still haven't learned how to come up with a decent excuse. Not that that's a bad thing," Miss Joan said. "At least they didn't teach you how to lie in Dallas. Well?" she asked expectantly when Ena continued to stand where she was. "Are you posing for a statue? Because if you're not, stop blocking the stairs to my diner. Use them and come in, girl."

Miss Joan didn't raise her voice, but the command was clearly there.

Moving like a queen, Miss Joan turned around and walked back into the diner. Everything about the way she moved clearly said that she expected Ena to follow her inside.

Ena's internal debate was very short-lived. She decided that coming into the diner was far easier than walking away from what was clearly a mandate from Miss Joan.

Ena quickly hurried up the three steps. With each step she took, she told herself that she wasn't going to regret this. After all, she had spoken to Miss Joan hundreds of times before. This would just be another one of those times. Lightning was *not* going to streak across the sky and strike her the moment she entered. She was just paying her respects to an old friend.

A rather scary old friend, she thought as she pushed the diner door open with fingertips that were positively icy.

Chapter Four

"Take a seat at the counter, girl," Miss Joan instructed without sparing Ena so much as a glance over her shoulder.

Miss Joan waved a very thin hand toward an empty stool that just happened to be right in the middle of the counter. It was also directly in front of where the woman usually stood when she was observing the various activities that were going on within her diner.

When Ena complied, Miss Joan got behind the counter and asked, "You still take your coffee black?"

"I do," Ena answered.

Nodding, Miss Joan filled up a cup straight from the urn. The coffee in the cup was hot enough to generate its own cloud directly above the shimmering black liquid. Years of practice had the woman placing the cup and its saucer in front of Ena without spilling so much as a single drop.

"Are you hungry?" Miss Joan asked.

Ena shook her head. "No, ma'am, I'm fine," she answered.

Miss Joan's eyes narrowed as they pinned hers with a penetrating look. "When did you eat last?" she asked.

She should have known that she couldn't get away with such a vague answer. She would have no peace until she gave Miss Joan something a little more specific. "I had something at a drive-through early this morning," she told the woman.

"You're hungry," Miss Joan declared in her no-nonsense voice. "Angel," she called out to the chef she had come to rely on so heavily. "I need an order of two eggs, sunny-side up, two strips of bacon, crisp, and one slice of white toast, buttered." Her eyes met Ena's. "Did I forget anything?"

Ena moved her head from side to side. "No. You never do." It was as much of an observation as it was a compliment.

Other than the fact that Miss Joan's hair looked a little redder than it had when she'd left Forever, the woman hadn't changed a bit, nor had she missed so much as a beat, Ena thought. There was something to be said for that.

Waiting on the order, Miss Joan crossed back to Ena. "You back for good?" the woman asked bluntly, not wasting any time beating around the bush.

She wanted to yell out "No," but instead, she proceeded with caution. "I'm taking it one day at a time."

Miss Joan surprised her by letting the response stand. "That's as good a plan as any," the woman allowed. One of her old-timers seated at the end of the counter called out her name and Miss Joan glared in the man's direction. "Can't you see I'm busy talking to Bruce O'Rourke's prodigal daughter?" Shaking her head, she looked back at Ena. "Some people act as if they were raised by she-wolves and have no idea what it means to have manners."

Just then, Angel placed the order on the counter between the kitchen and the main room. "Your order's ready, Miss Joan," Angel told her.

"I see it, I see it. Keep your shirt on," Miss Joan replied testily. Picking the plate up, she brought it over to Ena and put the meal in front of her beside the half-empty coffee cup. Moving seamlessly, she automatically filled the cup up. "Let me know if there's anything else that you need."

Ena had been debating whether or not to say something from the moment she had finally walked into the diner. She decided that she had nothing to lose. "There is something."

Miss Joan retraced her steps and returned to the center of the counter. She looked at the young woman expectantly. "Okay, go on." But before Ena said a word, Miss Joan held her hand up to temporarily stop her. The man at the end of the counter had apparently leaned in to listen to what was about to be said. "This doesn't concern you, Ed," Miss Joan said sharply. "Drink your coffee." It was an order.

"Yes, ma'am," the old-timer murmured, picking up his cup.

Miss Joan's eyes shifted back to Ena. "All right, go ahead."

Ena pulled her courage to her. "Why didn't you try to find a way to get word to me?" she asked, the question emerging without any preamble.

Miss Joan raised one of her carefully penciled-in eyebrows. "About?"

The woman knew damn well what this was about, Ena thought, exasperated. But because this was Miss Joan, she played along and answered, "My father. And before you say that you didn't know how to reach me, your step-grandson knew where to find me in order to send that letter notifying me about my father's death and the fact that there was a will. We both know that nobody knows *anything* in this town without you knowing it first."

"You're giving me way too much credit, girl," Miss Joan said, deflecting the comment.

"That's not true, Miss Joan, and you and I know it," Ena informed her. Her voice grew even more serious. "Why didn't you let me know my father was dying?"

Miss Joan moved in closer over the counter, lowering her voice. "Because your father didn't want me to let you know."

Anger mingled with frustration flashed through Ena's soul. "The noble warrior, dying alone, was that it?" she asked sarcastically.

Miss Joan didn't react well to sarcasm, but for once, she let it slide. She answered the question honestly. "You left ten years ago and stayed away all that time. Your father didn't want some spark of belated guilt being the reason you came back. Besides," she continued, "your father wanted you to remember him the way he was, not the shell of a man he became just before he died."

Ena stared at Miss Joan. She wasn't sure what to believe. "So it was *vanity* that kept him from getting in touch with me?"

Miss Joan shrugged at Ena's conclusion. "If that's how you want to see it. But I always thought you were smarter than that."

"How else am I supposed to see it?" Ena asked, raising her voice.

Miss Joan looked at her sharply. "Eat your breakfast before it gets cold," she ordered just before finally turning her attention to the man seated at the end of the counter.

Any appetite she might have had was gone now, but Ena knew better than to just walk away without at least eating some of the breakfast in front of her. Miss Joan would take that as an insult, not just to her but also to the woman she had working in her kitchen. Miss Joan had never been big on compliments, but in her own way she was fiercely protective of the people she took under her wing.

So Ena forced herself to eat as much as she could keep safely down, then, when she was certain Miss Joan was otherwise occupied, she quietly slipped away from the counter. Ena left a twenty-dollar bill beside her plate, thinking that would cover breakfast and then some.

She had reached the entrance and had almost made good her getaway when she felt a hand on her arm. Startled, she looked and saw that the hand belonged to a waitress she didn't recognize.

The waitress, a girl who might have barely been out of high school, pressed the twenty she'd left on the counter into her hand. Ena looked at the waitress quizzically.

"Miss Joan told me to tell you that she never said anything about charging for the meal," the waitress told her.

Ena looked down at the twenty. *Damn that woman, always getting in the last word*, she thought. Just like her father.

Out loud, she observed, "I guess she never said a lot of things."

"Do you want me to tell her that?" the waitress asked.

Ena shook her head. "No, never mind. Here," she said, trying to give the money to the waitress. "Consider this a tip."

But the other woman kept her hand tightly closed. "Can't," the waitress protested. "I didn't earn it and Miss Joan wouldn't like me taking money like this for no reason."

With that, the waitress turned on her heel and retreated back into the diner.

Ena sighed. *Looks like we're not in Kansas anymore, Toto*, she thought. Ten years in Dallas had caused her to forget just how frustratingly set in her ways Miss Joan could be.

The next six months were going to be hell.

But that didn't change the fact that Miss Joan's step-grandson was right. If she walked away from the ranch, her father would have won their final battle. There was no way she was about to allow that to happen. She couldn't bear it.

"Into the valley of death rode the six hundred," Ena murmured under her breath, quoting Tennyson's epic poem "The Charge of the Light Brigade." She felt as if she were going through the motions of reliving the actual events depicted in the poem.

Except that she was determined to come out of this alive and victorious.

"Hey, boss," Roy Bailey, one of the hands working on the Double E, called out into the stable. Mitch was inside working with an orphaned foal that was having a great deal of trouble taking his nourishment from the bottle that was being offered to it. "I think she's back."

"You're going to have to be more specific," Mitch responded, raising his voice while keeping his attention on the foal. "Which *she* are you talking about?"

"He means Mr. Bruce's daughter," Wade answered, speaking up for the other ranch hand. "And from what I can see, she doesn't look all that happy."

"I'm guessing she's had the terms of the will spelled out for her," Mitch said. "Hey, Bailey, take over trying to feed this little guy," he instructed the ranch hand, holding out the bottle to him.

Bailey looked rather reluctant, although the hired hand took the bottle from Mitch. "I'm not good with a bottle," he protested.

"That's not the way I hear it," Mitch said with a laugh. "Just hold the bottle. With any luck, the foal will do the rest," he told Bailey.

Rising to his feet, Mitch dusted off his hands. He stepped out of the stables just as Ena was making her way to the ranch house.

He cut her off before she had a chance to mount the steps leading to the porch. Bailey was right about Ena's appearance, he thought.

Out loud, Mitch observed, "Well, you certainly don't look very happy."

Startled, she looked in his direction. Her expression hardened. "I'm not," she told him.

"I take it that your dad's lawyer told you the terms of the will?"

Mitch put it in the form of a question, but he already knew the answer. She wouldn't have been frowning that way if she had been on the receiving end of news that she welcomed.

"Yes, he did," Ena said grimly.

He looked at her for a long moment. "Is that scowl on your face because you've decided not to stay—or because you have?"

Diplomacy was obviously a lost art out here, Ena thought.

"That's pretty blunt," she observed. "You certainly don't believe in beating around the bush, do you, Mitch?"

"Only when it's fun," he said. Then he sobered and added, "But no, not usually. And not, apparently, in this case." His eyes searched her face, looking for a clue. "So, you haven't told me. Are you staying?" he asked, phrasing his question in another form.

Her eyes narrowed. Was he being cute or was he just toying with her? "Do I have a choice in the matter?"

He spread his arms wide. "You could leave," he reminded her.

"Right," she said sarcastically. "And forfeit my birthright?" she asked, stunned that he would even suggest that.

"Is that important to you?" Mitch asked. He was curious to hear what her response to that would be.

"Honestly?" she asked. When Mitch nodded, she told him, "What's important to me is not letting that old man win."

There was that stubborn spirit of hers again, Mitch thought. "Despite whatever I might have alluded to earlier, I don't really think it matters all that much to him one way or the other," he told her, covertly observing her expression. "The old man is past the point of caring."

"Well, I'm not and it does to me," Ena informed him. "And I'll be damned if he gets to ace me out of something that's been in the family for three generations just because I had the *audacity* to be born a female and not his male heir."

He, for one, thought that her having been born a female was a great boon to the world, and especially to him, but he wasn't about to voice that sentiment to her, at least not right now. It would get him into a lot of hot water for a hell of a whole lot of reasons.

"Just so I'm clear on this, you're going to stay on and run the ranch?" he asked, waiting for a confirmation from her.

Ena closed her eyes. The frustrated sigh came up from the bottom of her very toes. "It certainly looks that way," she replied, opening her eyes again.

If he let himself, he could get lost in those eyes, Mitch thought. He always could.

"You're going to need help," he concluded.

"Ordinarily, I would take that as an insult," she told him. She liked to think of herself as self-sufficient and independent, but she also knew her limitations. "But right now, I have to admit that you're right. I'm going to need help. A *lot* of help. To be perfectly honest, I don't really know the first thing about running a ranch—" She saw him opening his mouth to say something and she got ahead of what she knew he was going to say. "And yes, I know I grew up here, but just because you grow up next to a bakery doesn't mean you have the slightest idea how bread is made. Especially if the baker won't let you into the kitchen."

He looked impressed by the fact that she could admit that. "Best way I know how to get started is to just jump right into the thick of things and start working," he told her. She was looking at him quizzically, so he explained, "There's a foal in the stables whose mama died giving birth to him and he needs to be fed if he has any chance of surviving."

The very abbreviated story unintentionally brought back painful memories for Ena. Her mother hadn't died in childbirth, but her twin had. She could definitely relate to that foal on some level.

"Take me to him," she told Mitch.

Mitch suppressed a smile. He'd been hoping for that sort of reaction from her.

"Right this way, Ms. O'Rourke," he said politely, leading the way into the stable.

The foal was skittish when she came up to him. Ena was slightly uncomfortable as she glanced toward Mitch for guidance.

"Just start talking to him," he told her.

"What am I supposed to say?" Ena asked, at a loss for how to proceed.

Mitch shrugged. He'd never had to think about it before. "Anything that comes to mind. Pretend you're talking to a little kid," he suggested.

But she shook her head. "Still not helping. Not many little kids need an accountant," she pointed out.

He thought for a moment, searching for something she could work with. "Tell him how good-looking he is. Every living creature likes to hear that," he told her.

Ena wasn't sure about that. "Really?" she asked him uncertainly.

"Really." Rather than demonstrate, he thought it best to leave it up to her. "Come on," he coaxed. "You can do it. You know how to talk. I know you do," he insisted. "I've heard you."

Ena looked at him sharply. Was he telling her that he remembered going to school with her? That he'd eavesdropped on her talking to someone? Just how much did he remember? Because she instantly recalled the less-than-flattering memories of all but throwing herself at the mysterious new stud who had walked into her school and her life. She also painfully recollected having him politely ignore each and every one of her passes. If he did remember all those passes that fell by the wayside, then working with him to run the ranch was not an option. She didn't handle humiliation well and she'd worry that he was laughing at her.

"What do you mean by that?" she asked suspiciously, bracing herself.

"Just what I said," he answered innocently. "I've heard you. You talked to me when you came here this morning."

"Oh," she responded, simmering down. "That's what you meant."

"Yes. Why?" Mitch asked. "What did you think I meant?"

"Never mind," Ena told him, waving away the foreman's question.

Taking the bottle from one of the men she gathered was working with Mitch, she turned her attention to the foal. The wobbly colt all but attacked the bottle, sucking on it as if his very life depended on it.

He was probably right, Ena thought. "What a good boy," she murmured to the foal, pleased by the success she was having.

Chapter Five

Mitch stood off to the side of the stall, observing Ena as she fed the foal.

"See, it's coming back to you," Mitch told her. The bottle was empty but the foal was still trying to suck more milk out of it. Drawing closer to Ena and the foal, Mitch took the bottle out of her hand and away from the nursing foal. "You're a natural."

Ena shrugged. "It doesn't take much to hold a bottle. The foal's doing the work. It's not like I'm forcing the liquid down his throat."

Mitch shook his head. He didn't remember her being like this when they were in school together.

"I would have thought that being away from here would have made you less defensive, not more," he said. "There's nothing wrong in accepting a compliment."

"I don't need you to tell me what's right and what's not right," she informed him.

Mitch was not about to get embroiled in an argument, not over something so minor.

"Sorry," he apologized. "I meant no disrespect," he assured her easily. "Nobody is looking to trip you up here."

"I know that," she snapped.

The smile on his face was just this side of tight. She was inches away from an explosion, but for now he kept his peace. "Good. Just so we're clear."

Looking to change the subject, Ena glanced back at the foal. She ran her hand lightly along his back. To her surprise, the foal didn't back away. "What's his name?" she asked Mitch.

The foreman watched her face for a reaction. "I was thinking of calling him Bruce, after your dad," he told her. "Seeing as how he was born seven days after your dad passed on."

Ena's first thought was to say that her father wouldn't have appreciated the sentiment or being linked to the foal. But then she decided that her father *might* have liked that. He had certainly been attuned to anything that had to do with the ranch.

Far more so than anything that ever had to do with her, she thought ruefully.

"Well, maybe he would have liked that after all," she finally told Mitch. "But if this foal grows up to have a stubborn streak a mile wide, you can blame it on his name."

Mitch laughed softly, stroking the foal's back. "Your dad was a very stubborn man," he agreed. "But seeing how hard he had to work to keep this place going, he sort of had to be."

Unlike his laugh, Ena's was depreciating, bordering on almost dismissive.

"You don't have to tell me how hard my father worked. That man made sure he drove his point home about how hard he worked every time he'd lecture me—which was all the time," she underscored.

She was trying to draw him in again, Mitch thought, trying to get him into an argument with her. But he stood firm.

"Everybody's got a different parenting style," Mitch replied.

"That's being rather generous," Ena commented coolly. When he looked at her confused, she elaborated, "To call what he did *style*."

Mitch knew that Bruce O'Rourke could be difficult, but he had also mentored him and in effect became like the father he no longer had. He felt as if he had to speak up in the man's defense.

"Aren't you being just a little hard on him?" Mitch asked her.

Ena's answer was immediate. "Not nearly as hard as he was on me." She said the words almost pugnaciously, as if she were ready to fight Mitch on this.

Mitch debated his next words, then decided that he wasn't speaking out of turn. She needed to know this. If he let it go, he'd be doing both her and Bruce a disservice.

"You know," he told her, stepping away from the foal so that he could have her undivided attention. "Your father was heartbroken when you took off the way you did the day after graduation."

She would have given anything if that were true. But she knew that it wasn't. For some reason that was beyond her comprehension, Mitch was being defensive of her father.

"For him to have been heartbroken," she informed

Mitch stiffly, "he would have had to have a heart. And how do you know what he felt? You weren't even here then."

"Actually, I was," Mitch corrected her. "I came to work for your father the day after we graduated." He remembered seeing her at the ceremony. He doubted that she had taken notice of him. The moment it was all over, he'd rushed off to see her father because he had interviewed for a job with the man a couple of days earlier. "I think we missed each other by a few hours. Your dad seemed pretty distraught when I saw him," he recalled.

Ena frowned. "Now you're just making things up," she accused. "You don't have to speak well of him on my account. As a matter of fact, I'd rather you didn't, because then I'd know you're lying." He was making her father out to be some sensitive, kind man and she knew that the man was far from that. "You forget, I lived with the man for eighteen years and I know *exactly* what he was like."

"Men like your father have a hard time letting their feelings show."

Ena didn't see it that way. "He had no trouble letting his anger show. I never had to guess when he was angry—because he was angry *all* the time."

She couldn't remember *ever* hearing so much as one kind word from her father, or any words of encouragement for that matter. All her father could do was point out her faults—at length.

This was going nowhere, Mitch thought. For now he gave up. Inclining his head, he said, "All right, have it your way."

"It's not *my* way. It was his," she insisted. "Now, if you don't mind, I'd like to table this discussion for the time being. I'm going to go into the house and settle in." Walking out of the stable, she headed back to where she had parked her vehicle.

To her surprise, Mitch walked out of the stable as well and followed her to her car. Turning on her heel, she looked at him, thinking he had some more words of "wisdom" to impart.

"What?" she demanded.

"I thought I'd carry in your suitcases for you," he offered.

His amicable offer caught her off guard and effectively took her edge off. She couldn't very well yell at him after that.

"Suit*case*," she emphasized, opening the trunk. "Not *cases*."

He watched her reach in and take out a compact white carry-on. "I guess you believe in traveling light," he noted.

There was a reason for that. "I only intended to stay a couple of days," she replied. "Apparently that's changed," she added with a sigh of resignation.

Executing a smooth movement, Mitch took the suitcase from her and walked toward the house with it.

"Do you want me to gather all the hands together?" he asked, looking at her over his shoulder.

She didn't understand why he would make that kind of offer. "Why would I want that?"

He thought it was self-explanatory. There were a few new hands here since she'd left, men who had been hired on after he had started working here. "I thought so you could meet them officially."

She supposed that was a good idea, but she wasn't up to that right now. There was one killer of a migraine forming right behind her eyes. Once one of those got going, it didn't stop until it all but consumed her. She had felt it starting in the lawyer's office, right after he had explained the will to her.

The migraine had her father's name on it.

Just like in the old days, Ena thought.

"This is a small town and word spreads fast so I'm guessing that the new *hands* all already know who I am. As for the individual hands, I'll meet them on the job. Best way to get to know someone is by seeing the level of their work." She almost winced when she realized that she had just quoted one of her father's edicts. Damn the man for getting into her head. "But right now, I'm going to go and lie down."

"Not feeling well?" Mitch asked sympathetically.

It almost sounded as if he cared, Ena thought. But why should he? He was probably hoping that she'd take a turn for the worse so that he could get the ranch from her—cheap. She was willing to bet that her father's "foreman" had fancied himself running the place—until he'd heard about the will.

"Sorry to disappoint you, but it's nothing fatal," she told him. She struggled to block the shiver and only partially succeeded. "It just feels that way." Ena saw the tall cowboy looking at her as if he couldn't comprehend what she was saying to him. "I get migraine headaches," she explained. "I realize that a person can't die from that—they just want to. Or at least I do when it goes into high gear like this."

"You take anything for it?" Mitch asked, closing the front door behind them.

"Why? What are you planning on giving me?" She winced again. "Sorry, bad joke. But I can't do any better right now."

Mitch nodded. "I'll bring this into your room," he said, lowering his voice. And then he stopped to consider what he'd just said. "Will you be taking over your father's bedroom?"

She looked at him as if he were crazy. Why would she want to do that? "Oh, lord, no. If I do that, I won't sleep until I get back to Dallas. My father would haunt me if I'm in his room," Ena told the foreman.

Rather than just go along with what she'd just said or gloss over it, Mitch asked, "Then you believe in spirits?"

"Not *spirits*," she corrected. "*Spirit*. Just one. Singular," Ena stressed. "A ghost. If there's a way for my father to come back and haunt me, he'll find it and I'd rather not be camped out in his room when he does. No, I'll just take my old bedroom," she told Mitch. Then she added, "It's the first room on the right at the top of the stairs."

He was already heading up the stairs. "Yes, I know," he told her.

"How?" she asked him, puzzled.

She had never had him over when they were in school together. Because he had in essence rebuffed her advances, there had never been any reason to invite him to her house.

"Your father pointed it out to me," Mitch explained. "Said that way, when he came up at night, you could stand there and look down at him."

Flashes of light were interfering with her ability to see right now, but she tried to stare at Mitch. "He didn't say that," she protested.

"I was there, but have it your way," he told her with a shrug. "I don't intend to mark the first day of our working relationship with an argument."

Our working relationship. That sounded way too structured to her. She didn't want to think of her being here in those terms. As far as she was concerned, this was just a day-to-day thing and if there was any chance she could find a way to change it, sell the ranch and take off, she planned to do it. But only *after* she got rid of this awful brain-numbing migraine.

"We'll talk later," she told him, waving him on his way. "After I get the little drummer boy out of my head," she murmured.

Gripping the wooden handrail, she focused on putting one foot in front of the other until she had finally managed to get herself to her room.

Mitch had reached it before she did and he put her suitcase just inside the door. "Let me know if there's anything that you need."

She waved her hand at him, indicating that he should just go. "What I need," she said with effort, "is not to be here."

The corners of his mouth curved. "Other than that," Mitch qualified.

But she had already closed the door on him, shutting out his words and his presence.

Ena found her way over to the double bed. Gingerly, she lay down on the gray-and-blue comforter. The fact that her room had remained just the way she'd left it registered belatedly somewhere amid the growing throbbing pain.

Shutting her eyes, Ena willed herself to fall asleep.

Unfortunately, her brain wasn't being receptive. She tried pulling the covers over her head, but that didn't help, either.

Neither did the almost imperceptible knock on her door that came almost half an hour later.

Ena stifled a moan. She wanted to pretend she hadn't heard it and not respond, but something told her that the person on the other side of the door would just persist in knocking, so she surrendered.

"Yes?" she asked weakly. Even the sound of her own voice was making the migraine worse.

"Do you mind if I come in?"

It was Mitch, she realized. *Now what?* She sighed, remaining where she was, a prisoner of this throbbing hotbed of pain.

"Might as well," she said in a whisper. "This migraine isn't going anywhere and neither am I."

She heard the door opening. She didn't hear it close. Was that for her protection? Or his?

It wasn't until she finally pried open her eyes that she saw that Mitch was carrying something. Up until this point, she had been doing her best trying to block out everything, including the ranch, all without much success.

He brought the cup over to her bedside, but she wasn't looking at that. She wanted to know why he was here. "What is it?"

Mitch nodded at the mug he was holding. "I thought this might help."

What was he talking about? "*What* might help?" Ena asked. Very slowly, she pulled herself up into a sitting position. The very act threatened to split her head right in half. The pain was also making her nauseous.

"This." He indicated the large mug he was holding. She caught a whiff of something aromatic and warm— tea? She wasn't in the mood for guessing games. Or for tea.

"What is that?" Ena asked, opening her eyes and trying to focus. She thought she saw steam curling from the mug in his hand.

"Something that is going to help make that headache of yours go away," he told her.

She truly doubted that. "Arsenic?"

"Nothing quite that drastic," Mitch assured her with a chuckle.

"Then it won't work," she told him. "Take it away."

Mitch didn't move a muscle. "Give it a try. What do you have to lose?"

"Miss Joan's breakfast."

"I promise this won't make you sick," he coaxed.

"All right, I'll drink it if it'll get rid of you," she muttered, resigned.

Ena took the mug into both her hands. For a moment, she let herself absorb the warmth. It was comforting, but she strongly doubted that whatever was in the mug would do anything to help alleviate the savagery that was going on in her head.

"What is this, really? Chamomile tea?" she asked, looking down at the dark liquid that was shimmering before her.

"No. Just something my mother used to whip up using herbs and a little of this and that for her friends when they had migraines. It's all natural," he assured her.

"So's a coyote, but I wouldn't bring it into my room and pet it," she retorted.

"Just drink it," Mitch urged.

She supposed she had to give it a try since he had gone out of his way to throw this together. But she really had her misgivings that this aromatic brew was going to help. She just hoped that she wasn't going to regret being so trusting.

"This and that?" she echoed.

Sensing that she wasn't going to drink the tea he'd

made without having him elaborate, he gave her the names of the ingredients that his mother had taught him to use.

Ena stared at him. "Are those real names, or are you making things up?" she asked.

"You can look the names up when you feel better. The remedy is something that my mother's mother passed on to her. And, if I'm not mistaken, her mother's mother before that, although I wouldn't swear to that part. All I know is that everyone who ever tried this *tea* had positive results."

"Okay." Ena took a tentative sip and immediately made a face. "Really? Positive results? This tastes awful."

"I didn't say that anyone said it tasted good, only that it worked well." He had a feeling that she needed to think this was her idea, not something he had talked her in to. "Try it or don't try it, it's up to you," Mitch told her. "I'll see you later—or tomorrow."

Ena sat there with the mug in her hand until he had let himself out, closing the door behind him. Then, taking a deep breath, she brought the cup back up to her lips. Still holding her breath, she drank the entire mug in what amounted to one long endless sip.

Finished, she shivered as she struggled to assimilate the bitter brew.

Setting the mug down, she lay back in bed and closed her eyes, sincerely hoping she wasn't going to throw up. Or die.

Chapter Six

It was gone.

Ena was on the verge of drifting off to sleep when she suddenly realized that the killer migraine that had been threatening to take off the top of her head for the last hour had totally disappeared. It was if it had never existed at all.

Ena gingerly raised herself up to a sitting position, afraid that any sudden movement on her part would cause the migraine to return with a vengeance. She held her breath.

But the migraine didn't return at all.

Still worried that this was all just wishful thinking on her part, Ena tested the extent of her "miracle recovery" by slowly moving her head from side to side once, and then again.

Nothing.

She swung her legs off the bed, putting her feet on the floor. Ena slowly stood up. Still nothing.

Although she didn't suffer from migraines frequently, whenever they did come, the migraines hit with the force of a neutron bomb exploding in her head. Every shattered fragment lingered, sometimes for an entire day.

Ena looked at her watch. It had been less than twenty minutes since she'd ingested that mouth-puckering tea concoction that Mitch had brought to her and as odd as it was for her to believe, the tea had eradicated every last bit of her temple-crushing headache.

She felt almost giddy with relief. There was no way, given the short amount of time that had passed, that this was just a coincidence and her migraine hadn't just vanished. Ena had lived through far too many of these episodes to believe that.

Ena went down the stairs, still taking things slowly. Reaching the landing, she looked around for Mitch. She was certain he would be waiting to observe the effects of his mother's magical tea.

A thorough look around the ground floor told her that Mitch wasn't anywhere in the house.

From the house Ena went directly to the stables. Her thinking was that was the last place he had been before bringing her suitcase into the ranch house for her. She wasn't about to say she was looking for him. Ena intended to use the foal as an excuse for her being there, saying that she wanted to see how the colt was doing.

If she wasn't mistaken, the foal needed to be fed every few hours. Mitch had said that it had been born only a few days ago.

Mitch didn't seem to be around. Wade and another ranch hand she didn't recognize were the only ones in the stables.

Disappointed, Ena asked Wade, "Have you seen Mitch around anywhere?"

Rather than give her a verbal answer, Wade pointed directly behind her. Startled, Ena spun around on her heel and found herself looking up into Mitch's face.

His gleaming white teeth almost blinded her. He looked extremely satisfied to find her there. "I see that my mother's remedy worked."

Ordinarily, she would have made some sort of an attempt to deny the assumption or even say something disparaging about the bitter drink. But truthfully, she felt far too good about recovering from what she had been sure was going to be an utterly disabling headache. When they hit, her migraines usually laid her low for at least half a day, if not longer.

Her enthusiasm bubbled over, causing her to declare, "It's fantastic." And then she had a question for him, just to make sure that this wasn't some sort of fluke occurrence.

"Does that *remedy* work like this every time?" she asked. There was still a little skepticism in her voice.

"That's what I hear from everyone who's ever tried it," he told her.

She wanted to explore this further. "And you just used herbs and roots and—whatever those other ingredients you said were?" she asked, unable to remember the exact names he had used.

"I did," Mitch confirmed. Then, keeping a straight face, he added, "Plus a little bit of fairy dust mixed in for good measure just at the end."

Ena stopped short, staring at him. Was there another additive in that mixture he hadn't mentioned before? One that wasn't legal? Her concern spiked.

"You're kidding," she cried, her eyes trained on his face.

He let her go on believing the scenario she had conjured up for half a second before saying, "Yes, I'm kidding. My mother used things that she grew in her garden. Herbs that, for the most part, are plentiful and can be easily found around here." Mitch took out a packet from his hip pocket and handed it to her. "The next migraine you get, you'll be ready for it," he promised. "Just dissolve it in hot water."

Ena studied the packet he'd handed her. It looked rather harmless, but who knew? Still, she wanted to believe that he wouldn't put her on.

"And what's in here can be readily found in the area?" she asked.

"Absolutely. All the ingredients grow like weeds around here. Trust me." Mitch saw the momentary doubt that came into her eyes. "And not the kind of weed that's illegal. Nobody would arrest you for *holding* if they found this on you. It just looks like you're about to brew some tea—which you would be if you find yourself having another one of those crippling headaches."

Ena held the packet up, examining it carefully. Another thought hit her. "Did your mother ever try to sell this?"

"You mean to her friends?" Mitch questioned. When Ena nodded, he answered, "No, why would she do that? She would have gladly shared her knowledge. Anyone could have gathered the ingredients, ground them up and made their own serviceable tea."

He was giving people too much credit, she thought. "These might grow everywhere, but not everyone can figure out how much to use and which specimens to pick to make that tea."

Ena no longer seemed leery. Mitch saw the thoughtful look crossing her face. She was going somewhere with this.

"What are you getting at?" he asked her.

She held up the packet. "Have you ever thought of marketing this?"

Mitch laughed, amused. Maybe she *didn't* know what went into running a ranch like this one. "When?" he asked. "In my spare time?"

To his surprise, Ena nodded. "It might be something to think about."

"I'm a cowboy. This is what I know," Mitch told her, gesturing around the stable. "Thanks to your dad," he added. It was only right to give credit where it was due. If Bruce O'Rourke hadn't taken him under his wing when he had, who knew where he would be now?

Mitch saw the frown on Ena's face. "That might not be what you want to hear, but it's true. Just like it's true that I wouldn't have the first *idea* how to begin mass producing what's in that packet—or how to let people know about it."

Those were all things that she knew about. "That could all be worked out," Ena told him, not willing to give the idea up just yet.

Although he liked hearing her be optimistic, this wasn't something he had time for.

"Right now I—*we*," he corrected, ever mindful of the part she played in all this, "have a ranch to run. A lot of people depend on this place to earn a living. Your dad knew that and I'm not about to let him down."

Ena nodded grimly. She could respect that. She just wished that it didn't involve her father, even in spirit. But right now, she wasn't about to ruin the fact that she felt like a woman who had been reborn, thanks to his mother's miracle remedy, so she let his comment go.

"All right," Ena said gamely, "what do you want me to do?"

The question surprised him. He would have expected her to start issuing orders, even if she didn't have the slightest clue what needed to be done. She had been away from this for ten years, and according to what she'd said, her father had never allowed her to be involved in running the ranch to begin with. That she seemed apparently willing to take a back seat—at least for now—gave him hope that they would be able to work well together.

It was a far cry from the woman who had burst onto the scene this morning.

He didn't have to think to answer her question. "Off the top of my head, the stalls need cleaning, the feed needs to be distributed and that foal you were feeding earlier is hungry again."

"You mean Bruce?" she asked, knowing full well that he did.

"Yes," Mitch answered, obliging her, "I'm talking about Bruce."

She smiled slowly, thinking of the foal she had made a connection with. "I guess I can manage that." She looked around. "Where's his bottle?"

Mitch sent one of the hands, Billy, to fill and retrieve the bottle for her. That done, he began to leave the foal's stall.

Ena had thought he was going to stay here with her. "Where are you going?"

"Remember those other chores I just mentioned that needed doing? They're not going to do themselves, plus there's other things to see to. And you've got this," he said with just the right touch of confidence. He didn't want to oversell it in case it blew up on him.

"Yes, I've got this," she echoed just as Billy returned with a full bottle for the foal.

Mitch flashed a smile at her a second before he walked out.

She took the bottle Billy held out to her, nodding her thanks.

"Okay, Bruce," Ena said, still feeling rather strange to be using her father's name in reference to the foal. "Let's get to it. I've always wanted to know what it felt like to have you eating out of my hand, Bruce."

"Ma'am?" the cowboy asked just as he was about to leave the stall and join Mitch.

Ena waved away his puzzled look. "Just a private joke. It's Billy, right?" she asked, looking at the cowboy she judged to be a few years younger than she was.

"Yes, ma'am." As an afterthought, the cowboy removed his hat and held it in his hand. "Billy Pierce."

"Nice to meet you, Billy Pierce," she said warmly. "Have you been working here long?"

"Just a little over two years, ma'am." He looked at her with genuine sympathy. "I am sorry about your dad passing."

He had to say that, Ena thought. But she wasn't about to pull the young cowboy into the resentment she was experiencing, so she merely acknowledged his comment by saying "Thanks." When the hired hand continued to stand there, she felt compelled to ask, "Is there something else, Billy?"

Billy nodded his shaggy blond head. "Your dad was a good boss to work for."

That she hadn't been expecting. She had never thought of her father as being either good or fair. She truthfully had never thought of her father interacting with anyone else outside of her, and her mother while Edith O'Rourke had been alive. She had just assumed that he had been hard as nails with everyone.

"So I'm told," Ena replied quietly. "You'd better get going and do whatever Mitch has you doing," she gently prodded the young man.

The startled look on Billy's face told her that he had momentarily forgotten about that. "Oh, right," Billy responded. With that, he quickly left the stall.

"Looks like it's just you and me, Bruce," she said to the foal. The colt was busy going at the bottle she held in her hand, madly sucking at its contents. "I really wish that Mitch had given you a different name. You're way too cute to be called *Bruce*."

The foal made a noise, as if he agreed with her assessment.

The timing was so perfect that she had to laugh despite herself. Ena ran her hand along the foal's neck, petting the animal.

"Don't worry about the name, it doesn't matter. I have a feeling that we're going to be fast friends after the dust settles," she told the foal. "So, what do you think?"

It was probably her imagination, but she could have sworn that the foal made eye contact with her for a moment, then whinnied as if he were in agreement with her judgment.

Ena nodded. "We'll see, boy. We'll see," she promised.

"So, how's it going?" Mitch asked, popping in for a moment just in time to see that the foal had finished feeding.

"He ate everything," she announced, then held up the empty bottle to prove her point to him. "Okay, what's next on the agenda?"

He smiled at the foal. He knew he shouldn't but he thought of the foal as more of a pet than just another horse. "Now I take the foal with me and see if I can get Paulina to adopt him."

"Paulina?" she echoed, confused. What was he talking about?

The stable door was open. He stepped over to the side so that she had a better view of the mare he was talking about.

"That dapple-gray mare over there." Mitch pointed to the horse on the far side of the corral. "She lost her foal in the spring. Breech birth, almost lost them both," he told her. "The vet had to make a quick choice."

"Bet my father didn't like losing a foal," Ena commented. It wasn't actually a guess. She knew how her father thought.

"He didn't," Mitch replied, "but he told the doc that he understood about her making a choice and he appreciated her saving Paulina."

She stared at him, amazed. "My father said that?" she asked incredulously. That didn't sound a thing like the man she'd known. "You sure it was him? You don't have him confused with someone else?"

"I'm sure," Mitch told her. "I told you, your father changed. Maybe having you take off that way when you did made him reevaluate the way he'd been doing things up to that point."

Ena snorted. "Now I know you have him confused with someone else. My father *never* thought he was in the wrong. Besides, if my father had this big epiphany the way you claim he did, why didn't he try to find me? I didn't disappear off the face of the earth," she stated. "I even sent him a couple of Christmas cards those first two years so he wouldn't think that I was dead."

Mitch bit the inside of his lip. He really wanted to say something, but he knew that it was too soon for that. Saying it might make her turn on her heel and retreat. And right now, he needed her to stay, as per the will, because that was the only way she would be able to eventually sell the ranch—or hold on to it if she changed her mind about its disposal. He was hoping for the latter.

Either way, she was the one who needed to do this.

"You want to come with me while I make the introductions between Paulina and Bruce?" he asked. "I might need a little help in keeping Bruce calm and he really seems to have taken to you."

Ena nodded. She liked being part of the process, she thought. "Sure. What do you want me to do?"

"Just keep the colt steady while I get this rope on him," he requested. Making a loop to slip over the foal's head, Mitch talked to the animal in a calm, gentle voice the entire time. "This isn't going to hurt a bit, Bruce. We just want to make sure you don't run off before you get to meet your new mama. That all right with you, boy?"

Ena listened to Mitch talking to the foal as if Bruce were capable of taking in each word. "You think he understands you?" she asked the foreman skeptically.

"Maybe not the words," Mitch allowed. "But definitely the tone. And by and by, he'll pick up on the words, as well," he told her confidently. "You just have to remember to keep talking to him as if he understands every word—and eventually, he will," he concluded. Mitch glanced at her, making a decision. He'd been vacillating about this over the course of the day, ever since she'd shown up. But she needed to hear this. She needed to appreciate the man that her father was. "Your dad taught me that," he told Ena.

"Uh-huh," she murmured, humoring Mitch.

She was making agreeable noises, but he wasn't fooled. Still, if he said it often enough, Mitch thought, he'd get her to believe it eventually, just like with the foal.

Chapter Seven

The mare, Paulina, seemed to have her doubts about nursing the foal that had been presented to her. At first, she wouldn't have anything to do with Bruce, but the foal was nothing if not persistent. Each time the mare nudged him aside, the foal just kept coming at her.

For her part, Ena did her best to bring the two animals together, coaxing the mare into accepting the barely two-week-old colt.

Eventually, just before she was about to throw up her hands and give up, Ena's persistence paid off. Expecting another repeat performance by the mare in which Paulina pushed the foal away, she was extremely pleased when Paulina *didn't* kick the foal aside the way she had done several other times.

"I *knew* you'd come around eventually," Ena told the mare. "Couldn't resist that sad little face forever, could you?" she asked. The mare seemed to look at her, then looked away, giving her attention to Bruce. "That's okay, you don't have to say anything. I understand where you're coming from." Ena laughed softly. "The little guy got to me, too."

"Is she answering you?" Mitch asked, grinning as he walked up behind her.

It took everything Ena had not to jump when she heard the sound of his voice. She had been totally sure that she was alone with the mare and the foal.

"Have you ever thought of investing in a pair of spurs?" she asked.

She actually sounded serious when she asked the question, which in turn confused him. "Why?" he asked.

"Because that way you couldn't sneak up on a person," she told him.

Now it made sense. "I wasn't aware that I was doing that," Mitch told her.

"You were," she assured him. Looking at the mare and foal, she noted that neither had reacted to Mitch's presence. They obviously had stronger nerves than she did. Either that or they were just comfortable around him. "I never hear you coming," she accused.

"Sorry. I'll try to walk louder," Mitch promised, amused.

She didn't appreciate Mitch's comment, or his amusement. "Just clear your throat or make some kind of other noise when you're coming up behind me. That's all I ask."

Mitch winked at her, instantly causing a knot to form in her stomach.

"I'll cough," he told her. Then he turned his attention to the real reason he had swung by her. "So, how's the bonding session going? Any luck?"

Ena nodded. "I think that Bruce may have had a little breakthrough with his new mother. The last time he came up to nurse, Paulina didn't kick him away," she told Mitch proudly.

"Hey, that *is* progress. Great work," he declared, congratulating her. "I didn't think we'd get anywhere with Paulina for at least a couple of days." Mitch grinned. "Good thing for Bruce that you came home when you did." When he saw the look on Ena's face when he said that, Mitch had a feeling he knew where he had gone wrong. "You don't think of this as being your home, do you?"

Rather than saying yes or no, she raised her chin defensively. "Home is my apartment in Dallas," she told him. "This, the ranch, is just my birthplace."

"Well, whatever you choose to call it, you coming back here at this time saved me a lot of work," he told her. "Paulina tends not to be all that pliable," Mitch confided. Then he said warmly, "Thanks."

Granted she was secretly proud of herself, but admitting that made her seem somehow vulnerable in her own eyes. So she dismissed his compliment. "I didn't really do anything. It's just nature's way of filling a vacuum."

Mitch could only shake his head. "You are a really hard woman to give a compliment to, you know that?"

Ena handed over the rope that he had put around the foal's neck. "Watching this little guy eat made me realize how hungry I was. I'm going in to see if I can scour up something to eat," she told Mitch, walking away from the mare and what appeared to be the mare's newly adopted foal.

Mitch watched her go. He was about to tell her that

she didn't need to *scour* anything, because when he had gone in to check, The housekeeper, Felicity, was preparing a fried-chicken dinner. She'd probably finished by now and most likely was waiting on "the new boss lady" to come in.

But that was an experience she needed to have firsthand, he thought. So he let Ena go to the ranch house while he got the new "mother" and her foster colt bedded down for the night.

The second Ena walked in through the door, she could smell it. Someone had cooked something.

Chicken?

Had Mitch prepared dinner for them while she'd been busy with the foal and his new "mother"? If that were the case, why hadn't he said anything to her?

She was on her way to the kitchen by way of the dining room when she stopped in her tracks.

The table was formally set.

Had Mitch done that, too? He didn't strike her as someone who would do something like that, not formally at least. He struck her more of the anything-goes type, which meant that she'd have to get her own silverware and dinner plate.

By now she caught another scent. Flowers? No, she detected lilacs, which had to be a cologne. Not the kind that doubled as an aftershave lotion.

Had he brought in a woman to do the cooking?

Ena wasn't sure what to expect as she walked toward the kitchen. While her mother had been alive, all the meals had always been prepared by her. After her mother had passed away, her father had a series of housekeepers who did the cooking and cleaning.

None of them lasted longer than three months. Most

handed in their notices sooner, unable to put up with the demands that her father always issued. When she'd walked in the front door, Ena had been ready to take over the kitchen despite the long day she had put in.

But it didn't look as if she had to.

Just as she was about to troop into the kitchen to find exactly who was behind this scent that had come wafting in to greet her, Ena all but collided with a small compact-looking woman, standing no taller than five foot one.

The woman wore her salt-and-pepper hair up in some sort of hairstyle she'd fashioned that looked like it was half a twist, half a bun. Judging from the dusting of flour that was on the top of her blouse and apron, the woman Ena had narrowly avoided tripping over was the source of not just the cologne but the delicious aroma tempting her, as well.

The woman was carrying out a platter filled with fried chicken pieces.

"Ah, you are here at last," the woman declared with latent satisfaction. "The food was not going to remain warm much longer. Sit," she ordered, gesturing at the place setting at the head of the table.

Ena didn't recognize this miniature tyrant of a woman at all. If she was one of the housekeepers her father had gone through, she had no recollection of her.

Looking at her, Ena said, "And you are…?"

"Busy," the woman responded crisply. "And you will be underfoot if you come into my kitchen." She nodded toward the front door. "Mr. Mitch should be here any minute. With the others," the housekeeper added.

"The others?" Ena repeated, confused. "What others?" she asked.

"The men who work on the ranch, of course," the woman told her.

Of course? There was no *of course* about it. The scenario the woman was describing was a far cry from the almost solitary meals that she had taken in this room with her father the last two years before she'd left.

"Don't they eat in the bunkhouse?" Ena asked, still confused.

"Mr. Bruce said it would be easier for me if everyone ate in here. That was why he had this big table made."

Now that the woman mentioned it, Ena noted that the dining room table was close to one and a half times larger than the one that had been there the last time she had eaten in this room.

"I see you've met Felicity," Mitch said, walking in. "Dinner smells great, Felicity," he told the housekeeper.

Felicity looked unfazed by the compliment. "It tastes even better if you eat it warm."

Ena stared as Mitch took his seat to the right of her chair. She wasn't accustomed to having a foreman eat with her, much less having all the hired hands piling in, as well. "When did all this happen?" she asked, trying to wrap her head around the fact that, according to the housekeeper, this had been her father's idea.

"A few years back." He saw the skeptical expression on Ena's face. He had a feeling he knew what she was thinking. That her father hadn't been behind the suggestion. "I told you your father had changed," Mitch reminded her.

"Was this your idea?" Ena asked, watching as the ranch hands filed in and took their seats around the table.

He wasn't going to tell her that he'd had nothing to do with it, Mitch thought. "Let's just say it was a joint idea, one that your dad agreed only made sense." He could see that she had more questions for him. He second-guessed her. "Your dad saw the advantages of a good meal being the easiest way to keep his men working like well-oiled machines. And Felicity's meals were fantastic," he added. "So if Felicity had to cook for everyone, everyone might as well be in the same room to eat those meals. That made it easier on Felicity." Mitch looked around the table. "Dig in, men. We've got a big day ahead of us tomorrow," he told them.

"Every day's a big day," Wade said as Mitch's lead ranch hand helped himself to several big pieces of Felicity's fried chicken.

Ena's brow furrowed. "What's tomorrow?" she asked, looking from Wade to Mitch.

"Wednesday," Mitch answered simply.

"What he means to say is that every day really *is* a big day." Billy spoke up, trying to make the foreman's comment less mysterious.

"That's just his way of keeping the rest of us from slacking off," Wade told her in between sinking his teeth into the chicken thigh he had speared.

"Why don't you try the mashed potatoes?" Mitch urged, holding out a big serving bowl toward Ena. "In case you didn't know, Felicity makes the best mashed potatoes around," he told her.

How could she know? Ena wanted to ask. She hadn't even known about Felicity until just now.

"It's true," Billy confirmed eagerly, jumping into what he thought was a conversation. "Even better than my mama's."

"You didn't have a mama," one of the other ranch hands teased. "Everyone knows you were hatched out of an egg."

"That's enough," Mitch announced forcefully. "I'm sure that Miss O'Rourke doesn't want to hear you all behaving like a bunch of schoolboys. Do you?" he asked, looking toward Ena for backup.

If she were being honest with herself, Ena wasn't sure if she felt the hired hands' behavior was irritating or entertaining. It was certainly a far cry from what she remembered meals being like when it was just her father and her.

Back then, the air was either filled with recriminations all surrounding her behavior or it was filled with silence because she couldn't find a topic that was safe to broach to her father without hearing any criticism. Ena liked neither, especially not the criticism.

Deciding it was safer to be easygoing, Ena said, "I don't mind."

Her answer immediately won over every man at the table. They all grinned at her almost in unison—and then they all started talking at once, asking her questions, offering comments and information.

Some also told her which of the horses might be ready to be auctioned off and which of the stallions should be kept as breeding stock.

Ena did her best to try to keep everything that was being said at the table straight, but it was all too easy to just lose the thread of what someone was saying, or who was saying it.

By the time dinner was over and the hired hands finally all took their leave, going to the bunkhouse, Ena felt as if her brain were exploding. Not the way it had when she was having a migraine, but it was still being overtaxed.

The expression on Mitch's face when he looked at

her was nothing if not sympathetic. And then he smiled at her. "Worn-out yet?"

"Oh, I'm way past worn-out," Ena told him. She really hated admitting a weakness, or appearing vulnerable. But she felt that on some level, she and Mitch had a bond. So she asked, "Is it like this all the time?"

"This was a slow day," he replied.

Her eyes widened like cornflowers searching for sunlight. "You're kidding."

"Maybe just a little," he admitted, trying to put her at ease, at least to some degree. "But not nearly as much as you'd like me to be. Ranching isn't for sissies," he told her. Then he waited a beat before adding, "That's something else your dad liked to say."

"Yes, I'm familiar with that saying of his," she replied, her face clouding over. "Do you make a habit of quoting my father?"

Maybe he'd overstepped here, but since he had taken that step, he couldn't retreat. That would be counter-productive.

"Only if the occasion calls for it," he told her. "I guess I just wanted you to appreciate the man your father was. He changed from the image you've been carrying around in your head," he explained. "He was a man who decided to take a chance on an eighteen-year-old orphan when he didn't have to—and all common sense told him not to."

He saw her mouth harden just a bit around her jawline and her eyes flash.

"Too bad he didn't want to do that with the daughter he *did* have," Ena murmured.

Abruptly, she pushed her chair back from the table and stood up. Instead of heading for the stairs, the way he thought she would, Mitch saw her heading toward the kitchen. Thinking he might have to avert a situation in the making, he quickly hurried after her.

"That was a very good meal, Felicity," he heard her say to the housekeeper. "I enjoyed it a lot."

The woman turned her head in Ena's direction, her expression ambiguous. And then she smiled at her. "It was my pleasure, Miss Ena," she told the young woman with feeling.

"How long did you work for my father?" Ena asked.

Felicity didn't have to pause to answer. "Eight years."

"You stayed with him for eight whole years?" Ena asked, stunned.

"Yes, I did," the housekeeper replied without any hesitation.

"That's amazing," Ena marveled.

Felicity didn't see what the big mystery was. "Mr. Bruce paid well and he was a good man to work for. He was hard, but he was also fair."

Ena had to admit that she was nothing short of amazed.

The housekeeper wasn't the first one to call her father a good man or say that he was a fair man to work for. Had her father actually undergone some sort of earthshaking rebirth in his later years? Because no one would have ever referred to Bruce O'Rourke as being *good* back when she had lived with him.

She felt almost angry that he had changed this much in his later years—because her mother hadn't been the beneficiary of this miraculous personality change. He had been this really difficult man to deal with back in those days. While Ena was happy that other people found him a good, decent man to work for, she was highly resentful that her father hadn't come around this way while her mother was still alive.

Ena felt tears forming.

Bruce O'Rourke had cheated her mother, Ena thought bitterly. This was just one more thing that she couldn't forgive her father for.

Chapter Eight

Ena hated having to be in a position where she was forced to make excuses. Doing so brought back painfully uncomfortable memories. Suddenly, she was an adolescent, standing before her father and explaining why she had done, or had not done, something. Which was why she avoided the entire scenario if she possibly could.

But she couldn't this time. Couldn't avoid the call she was going to have to make to Jay Whittaker at her firm in Dallas.

Whittaker wasn't exactly her boss so much as he was the senior partner in the accounting firm where she had worked ever since she had graduated from college. But even though he wasn't her boss, she always had the feeling that the vastly competitive man was persistently watching her, waiting for her to slip up and make some sort of mistake. It wasn't anything he had ever actually said to her as much as it was the attitude he seemed to exude. He enjoyed bullying people. It made him feel important.

But Ena knew that the longer she put off calling Whittaker, the longer the call and its outcome loomed over her.

So the following morning, right after spending a restless night followed by breakfast she couldn't really get down, she put in a call to the Dallas office. It was 8:20 a.m., the time when Whittaker always showed up in the morning. She knew it was because he liked getting the jump on the people he worked with.

Sitting in the small crowded room her father used to call his den, Ena listened to the phone she'd dialed on her father's landline ring.

The phone on the other end was picked up after two rings. Ena willed the knot in her stomach to go away.

"Mr. Whittaker, it's Ena—" she began, only to have the scratchy-sounding voice belonging to Jay Whittaker cut her off.

"When can I expect you back?" Whittaker asked bluntly without any polite exchange between them. "Friday?"

Typical, she thought before trying again. "No, I'm afraid not—"

"What do you mean *afraid*?" Whittaker asked, interrupting her again.

Whittaker was accustomed to firing out questions rapidly and getting back answers the same way. Ena was certain that the man had never had a leisurely conversation in his life.

Putting the call on speakerphone, she wearily attempted to explain, "My father had an unexpected clause in his will—"

"What kind of clause?" Whittaker asked her impatiently.

"The kind that is going to wind up making me stay here for the next six months," she answered through clenched teeth.

As much as she didn't like being controlled by her father or being forced to stay here in order to comply with the will, Ena liked having to explain herself to Whittaker even less.

"Six months?" The base of the landline all but vibrated from the impact of his high-pitched voice. Ena was just grateful she wasn't holding the receiver against her ear.

Ignoring the man's very obvious display of anger, Ena plowed straight to her point. "I'm going to have to request a leave of absence."

"Well, I'm sorry," Whittaker said in a tone that told her that he was anything *but* sorry, "but you can't ask for one out of the blue. The firm can't—"

She didn't wait for him to finish. "You can call it a family emergency," she informed him. "I have enough vacation time accrued over the last six years to actually cover the time I'm going to need," she pointed out, her voice growing in strength.

The one thing she hated more than having to explain herself was having to ask for a favor. But strictly speaking, this couldn't be called that.

Only Whittaker would think of it in those terms.

"And you expect your job to just be here *waiting* for you once this so-called *emergency* of yours is over with, is that it?" Whittaker asked, a nasty edge to his voice.

Ena tried another approach. She really didn't want to make waves. In general, the firm had been good to her. Whittaker was the only one who had ever been difficult to deal with.

"I can go over some of the work that needs to be done from here. I can work on it in the evening and email it to the office. My assistant at the firm can handle the rest," she assured Whittaker. "Don't worry, the work will be covered."

Whittaker sounded far from placated. Or maybe he just wanted to use this as an excuse to get her out of the way, Ena thought as she heard him say, "I'll have to bring this to Mr. Blackwell's attention."

"I realize that. But you don't have to." Before he could say anything to contradict her, Ena told him, "I'm going to be making a formal request for this leave and sending it to Mr. Blackwell as soon as I get off this phone."

That temporarily took the wind out of the other man's sails. Whittaker made a disgruntled noise. "You realize that the reason you were hired ahead of the other applicants was because you didn't have any baggage. We thought that would prevent this sort of thing from happening and hampering the company."

"The firm isn't being hampered. It's just being mildly inconvenienced," she told him firmly. "Believe me, I'm not happy about this."

"That makes two of us," Whittaker bit off. He made another aggravated sound, then told her, "I want regular updates from you. I'll have one of the assistants send out one of your accounts to you the second I clear this with Mr. Blackwell."

With that, Ena heard the connection terminate. Swallowing a few choice words, she leaned back in her chair.

"Nice guy," Mitch said, coming into the den. "He your boss?"

Startled, she turned her chair in Mitch's direction. She hadn't realized anyone was there. She still wasn't getting used to him materializing out of nowhere.

"He thinks he is," she said, frowning. "Whittaker's in charge of one group. I have another. Nobody's really the *boss* except for Aaron Blackwell, the man who started the firm," she told Mitch. She pushed her chair back and rose to her feet. "I didn't realize that you were eavesdropping."

"I wasn't. You had that guy on speakerphone and I think the horses in the stable heard him," Mitch quipped. "Sounds like a charmer," he commented. "He always that pleasant?"

"Even before his wife left him," Ena replied.

"Well, I can definitely see why his wife left him," Mitch commented. "Listen, I know your dad's will said you had to work on the ranch for six months, but it didn't specifically say *constantly*."

She looked at him as they walked out of the house. "What are you getting at?"

"Maybe you could go to Dallas a couple of days a week, hold that guy's hand, so to speak, if you need to. I wouldn't want to see you get fired," he told her.

What he meant was that he didn't want to see her self-esteem take a beating, even though the whole idea behind Bruce O'Rourke's will was to get his daughter to change her mind about running the ranch rather than selling it.

"Whittaker can't fire me," she told Mitch.

He wondered if she was just saying that because the truth embarrassed her.

"He certainly sounded as if he thought he could," Mitch said.

"Well, he can't. Especially since I do have all that

vacation time accrued." She slanted a glance toward Mitch. He meant well and she appreciated that. "But thanks for the thought," she murmured.

"Don't mention it," he told her. "Why don't you come to the stable and see how Bruce and his new *mother* are doing?" he urged.

Because of the way her mind had been trained to work, anticipating the worst, Ena immediately thought something had gone wrong. "Is there a problem?"

The smile on his face alleviated her initial anxiety. "On the contrary, I think you helped fill a need in both their lives."

"You were the one who suggested it," she reminded him. She didn't want him to think she could be manipulated with empty flattery.

"I did," he agreed, "but you were the one who kept encouraging the little guy to keep trying even after he'd been rejected over and over again."

She looked at him in surprise. "How would you know that?"

"I have my spies," he teased. And then he said, "Billy told me."

She jumped to what was, to her, the natural conclusion. "You had him watching me?"

"No," Mitch replied patiently, "*he* made that choice on his own. If you ask me, I think that Billy has a crush on you."

She thought Mitch was kidding, then realized he wasn't. Ena sighed. That was all she needed: to have a wet-behind-the-ears cowboy following her around like a puppy dog.

"Well, I didn't ask," she informed Mitch, dismissing the entire incident.

"Point taken," the foreman replied with a good-natured grin.

Ena picked up her pace as she walked toward the stables. Despite everything, she was eager to see for herself how well the foal was getting along with his newfound "mother." She silently admitted that she needed that sort of boost to her frame of mind, which was at the moment, despite what she had said, at a low point thanks to Whittaker. Not to mention the feeling that she was in over her head when it came to the ranch.

The second she walked into the stall, she was saw that the mare was indeed allowing the foal to nurse. And when Paulina decided that her new foal had had enough, she made her wishes known by forcefully nudging the colt aside.

Mitch watched in silence right beside Ena.

"No matter what you say, that's all thanks to you," he finally told her. He could tell that compliments made her uncomfortable, so he dropped it at that. "Seen enough?"

Obviously, that was her cue to leave, Ena thought, so she began to walk out again. "Yes. What do you have in mind now?"

For the briefest of seconds, her question gave birth to an entirely different response than he was free to make. Because what he had in mind was nothing he was able to actually say.

So instead, he said, "Nothing out of the ordinary. Just the same old routine as yesterday." And then he thought of an alternative. "Unless you feel like helping fix a part of the fence that's just about ready to fall apart."

"Sure," she told him almost eagerly. "Where is this fence that's on the verge of crumbling?"

His suggestion had been an offhanded comment,

thrown in on a whim, nothing more. He hadn't expected her to respond in such a positive way.

"It's just at the end of the northern pasture." Mitch looked at her somewhat uncertainly. "You sure you want to do this?"

"I wouldn't have asked if I didn't. I like working with my hands," she told him.

Mitch picked up one of her hands and carefully examined it. It was just as he'd thought.

"Your skin's smooth and your nails aren't broken. You'll forgive me if I have my doubts about your claim about working with your hands."

She tossed her head, sending her blond hair flying over her shoulders. "Just take me to what you need fixed and prepare to eat your words, Parnell."

For her to be that confident in her abilities could only mean one thing. "So your dad did have you working on the ranch," Mitch concluded.

"No," she contradicted. "I took a woodworking class after hours at the high school. My father made it clear that he didn't think I could do anything. I took that class just to show my father that I actually *could* be handy."

"And did you show him?" he asked as they headed toward his pickup truck. The back was loaded with posts, planks of wood and the tools that were necessary to do the required work.

Ena shrugged in response to his question. "I never got the chance. I figured I'd do it the day after graduation. But then there was this one last knock-down, drag-out argument between us just before the graduation ceremony." Her face clouded over as she relived every single detail in her head. "I took off the next day."

"Maybe you should have waited," Mitch said.

"Things might have turned out differently between the two of you if you had."

"I really doubt it," she said, climbing into the passenger side of the cab. She knew he was thinking about the way her father had supposedly changed over these last ten years. "I think he changed because you came into his life."

Mitch started up the truck, then looked at her, stunned. "Me? No, I think you got that wrong." As a matter of fact, he was quite certain of it.

But Ena shook her head. "I don't think so. You turned out to be the son he had always wanted. Once you came into his life, from what you've said, it looks to me that he started to be less angry at the world and started turning into a human being."

But Mitch didn't quite see it that way. Bruce had been fair with him, but he didn't feel that the older man had thought of him as a son in any way—even though for his part, he had regarded his boss as a second father.

"I think you just might have put the carriage before the horse," he told her.

She wasn't going to spend any more time arguing with Mitch about this.

"Whatever. Let's go see about that fence that needs fixing," she told him.

He was more than happy to oblige.

"I take it back," Mitch told her almost two hours later.

He and Ena had been working on the fence this entire time, taking down the sagging poles and replacing them, then nailing in new lengths of wood between the poles. It was going faster than he had anticipated. They were more than half-finished. He hadn't expected that, certainly not from her.

"Take what back?" Ena asked, taking a short break. She did a quick survey of her own work and was basically satisfied, although she noted that there were areas where she could have done a better job.

"You still have pretty hands, but you certainly know your way around fixing a fence," Mitch told her with a grin. "That shop teacher would certainly have been proud of you. Was it Mr. Pollard?" he asked, remembering the class he'd had with the man, except back then, Pollard had doubled as a football coach.

It had been years since she had thought about the potbellied shop teacher with the sagging trousers that he was forever hiking up. Envisioning him now, she recalled that he'd also had unruly yellow-white hair that looked like a haystack that was being blown around by a fierce wind.

Ena nodded in response to his question. "Yes, it was Mr. Pollard." More memories came back to her. "That man insisted on keeping us trapped in that room for the first half hour of each session while he regaled us with all these stories about the projects he'd made and how he always kept his students in line, no matter how unruly they tried to be."

Mitch was more than familiar with the man's shortcomings. "Well, he might have liked to hear himself talk, but he seemed to have done a good job teaching you how to work with wood."

She slanted a look in his direction. "Is that a compliment?"

"If you have to ask, I guess I wasn't being clear enough, but yes, that was a compliment. You did a really good job—and so did Mr. Pollard," Mitch added.

"Too bad your dad couldn't see this." He gestured toward the fence they were just working on. "He would have been really impressed."

But Ena wasn't buying any of it. "I really doubt that."

Mitch remained firm. "I don't."

Ena was silent for a long moment. And then she suddenly turned toward him. "Mitch?"

There was a different look in her eyes that caught his attention immediately. "Yes?"

"Where's he buried? My dad," she added in case he thought she was asking about Mr. Pollard or someone else for some reason.

Ena didn't know if her father had been buried, or if he'd been cremated and his ashes scattered somewhere. It hadn't even occurred to her—until just now.

"In the farthest corner of the cemetery," Mitch told her. "Just behind the church."

"The church?" she repeated in surprise. "My father never stepped one foot into a church in his entire life. Not even when my mother died." She recalled that awful day. It had rained appropriately enough. Nothing else had been appropriate about that pain-filled day. "He had her buried on the ranch."

"Your father changed his mind about that," he said, watching the surprised look on her face. "He had her casket exhumed and transferred to the cemetery. Miss Joan actually talked him into doing that," he explained. "She told him that your mother would be more at peace there. Shortly after that, your father made it known that he wanted to be buried next to his wife when his time finally came."

"So that's where he's buried? In the church cemetery?" Ena asked in surprise. That didn't sound like her father, she thought.

"Yup. Right alongside your mother. The whole town turned out for the funeral," he added.

"Did you pay them?" she asked, surprised by Mitch's statement. She couldn't recall her father *ever* having any friends. Why would anyone attend the funeral of a man they hardly knew?

Mitch almost laughed at her question but managed to catch himself just in time.

"No, but I think Miss Joan threatened a few people into going. Nobody says no to that lady. Not if they ever want to be able to eat at her diner again."

Ena nodded her head. That made more sense, she thought.

Chapter Nine

"Would you like me to take you?" Mitch offered when Ena had made no further comment about her father's burial plot.

Did he think she was a helpless female incapable of finding her way around? She wasn't sure if she should be insulted or if this was Mitch's attempt at being chivalrous.

"I grew up here, Parnell. For the most part I know every inch of this postage stamp–sized town. I can certainly take myself over to the cemetery—*if* I wanted to go."

"I didn't mean to imply that you couldn't. I just thought you might like some company."

Ena looked at him. That wasn't what he meant, she thought. "You mean moral support, don't you?" she corrected him.

But Mitch stuck to his guns. "No, I mean *company*

but if that's the way you want to see it," he went on amicably, "then I'm not going to argue with you."

"No?" she questioned, annoyed. "I thought you liked arguing."

"Not even remotely," Mitch replied. When she still didn't answer his initial offer to accompany her to the cemetery, he decided to prod her a little more. "So?"

Right now, Ena found that she couldn't deal with the thought of looking down at the ground that was covering the loud, angry man who had once been her father. So instead of giving Mitch an answer one way or another, she waved at the partially completed section of the fence and said, "Let's just finish this, okay?"

Mitch inclined his head, acquiescing. "You're the boss."

For a moment, that gave Ena pause as she rolled the foreman's words over in her head.

"Yes," she finally agreed, brightening at his response. "I am."

Although, if she were being truthful with herself, it was hard for her to think of herself in those terms. Her father had been the boss on the Double E. With his death, all that there was left behind was a vacuum, not a place for her to take over and fill.

Logically, Ena knew she should aspire to that title, but it honestly held no allure for her. She felt the same way about becoming the boss at the accounting firm where she worked. She had drive and ambition, but having others bow and scrape before her didn't interest her in the slightest. She had always been far more interested in doing the work than in pontificating to those who were working for her.

However, for argument's sake, she agreed with Mitch's pronouncement that she was the boss. In her estimation it was the fastest way to get things moving along—and that, in her estimation, was all that really counted.

"Are you tired?" Mitch asked out of the blue after they had been at repairing the fence for close to another full hour.

"No," Ena answered a bit too quickly and, she realized, a bit too defensively. "Why?"

"No real reason." It was a lie actually, Mitch thought. He decided to be honest with her. "You just seemed to have slowed down, that's all."

It wasn't that she was tired. She'd slowed down because she felt that as soon as they finished repairing the fence, Mitch would ask her again if she wanted to visit her father's grave. She really didn't want to have that discussion. Didn't want Mitch thinking that she was afraid to go see the grave for some reason.

It wasn't fear that was keeping her from going. It was dealing with the idea of seeing both her parents in the ground while she was still alive and well, doing her best to come to grips with the whole scenario in which she was now all alone in the world.

"You're imagining things," she told Mitch dismissively.

Again he gave her no argument. "Maybe I am. Maybe I'm tired, too."

He was humoring her, saying that he was tired for her benefit, she thought. Under normal circumstances, she might have very well called him out on the lie. But in her present state of mind, she didn't want to get into it. It was better this way.

She was about to say that she felt like working longer, but he seemed to have anticipated that, as well.

"Hey, what do you say we call it quits for now and hang up our tools for the day?" Mitch's tone sounded pretty final.

Ena decided to take him up on his suggestion. The truth was she had pushed herself a bit too much just to prove that she could handle the work and now she was regretting it. Or at least her arms and shoulders were. She was really going to be sore tomorrow.

"Fine with me," she answered, trying to sound non-chalant. "Do you want to go back to the stable?"

"Eventually," he told her, putting the tools into the truck's flatbed.

Eventually. Okay, here it came. The last thing she needed was to have him lecture her about paying her "respects" to her father and that she would feel better once she made herself deal with that. Mentally, she dug in, waiting for Mitch to fire the first shot. She deliberately ignored the fact that being near him like this raised her body temperature and caused her heart to beat faster than it was supposed to. She tried to tell herself that she was utterly oblivious to him and the effect he had on her—but deep down inside her soul, she knew she was lying.

"And what is it that you intend on doing now?" she asked, spoiling for a fight and hoping that would get her mind off the rest of it.

Finished with the tools, he opened the driver's-side door. "I thought I'd swing by town, pick up some more supplies. We're running short on a few things."

"And that's it?" she questioned, stunned and disappointed, as well. "You're going shopping?"

"Yes, unless you have something else you want to do instead," he answered her innocently, knowing he was goading her. He loved seeing the fire enter her eyes.

Someday soon, he promised himself, that fire would be meant for him—and in a good way.

"Let me get this straight. You want to go into town to pick up some supplies," she repeated incredulously.

"That's what I said, yes," he told her, keeping a straight face.

"That sounds like an errand," she protested. "Don't you have someone you could tell to do that for you?"

"I could," Mitch agreed. "But I like looking around the general store for myself, in case there's something I forgot to put on the list. Besides," he said honestly, "I like mingling with people. It allows me to stay in touch with what's going on in town."

"So this isn't your way of getting me to swing by the church cemetery?"

"You made it sound like you didn't want to, so why should I do that?" he asked her.

Her eyes narrowed. "You're playing mind games with me."

"I think you're overthinking this and giving me way too much credit. I don't have time for mind games. I've got a ranch to run—for you," he added pointedly. "Now, if you like, I can bring you back to the stable or the ranch house," he added, "before I go into town for those supplies."

He was good at playing the innocent man, she'd give him that, Ena thought. She debated which way to play this for a moment, then made up her mind. This could work out after all.

"No, that's all right. I'll come into town with you. It might not be such a bad idea to look around for a bit," she told him.

He wasn't about to get sucked into a discussion over

this. "Whatever you say. Like I said before, you're the boss."

If that was true, she thought, slanting a glance in his direction, why did she have this feeling that she'd somehow been played?

Maybe Mitch was right. Maybe she was guilty of overthinking everything. Even so, she couldn't shake the feeling that the man was somehow very subtly manipulating her.

Lost in thought, she really hadn't done very much by way of helping him to secure the tools into the back of the truck. They went to stock up on supplies. Since Mitch was driving the pickup, it gave Ena a real opportunity to look around as they approached town.

Nothing had really changed in Forever, she thought. Oh, there were some new additions and perhaps there was a slightly busier air about the small town than there had been ten years ago. But for the most part, it still felt like the tiny town that half the more mournful country songs were written about. The kind of town it was good to be *from* but definitely not one to be living in at the present time.

She was just asking herself what she was doing back here when Mitch pulled up to an open spot right in front of the general store. The engine made a stuttering sound as he turned it off.

She could feel his eyes on her. When she turned toward him, he said, "You don't have to come in if you don't want to."

Was he trying to tell her something? Her years in the business world had made her suspicious of everything, unable to take *anything* at face value.

"Why wouldn't I want to?" she asked him.

"I was only thinking that you might not want to have

to put up with a whole bunch of questions fired at you. You remember what people are like in Forever," Mitch reminded her. "Always full of questions because nothing much goes on in their lives without gossip. They'd want to know if you were going to stay on now that you're back—and they'd probably ask you why you took off the way you did. They might even—"

Ena shut her eyes as she put up her hands to block the onslaught of words. "Stop. You've made your point. You might have thought of this earlier," she told the man in the front seat next to her.

His expression was easygoing and totally devoid of guilt. "You're right. Sorry," he apologized.

"Well, we're here now," she said with a sigh. "You talked me into it. I'll just stay in the truck," she decided.

Maybe he should have been more forceful about taking her back to the ranch house, Mitch thought. "I'll hurry," he promised.

Ena shifted in her seat. The truck's seat was definitely not made with comfort in mind. "You do that," she told him.

So much for reverse psychology, he thought as he walked quickly to the general store. He'd thought if he'd told her what she would be facing coming into the general store with him, Ena would have come with him just to prove that she could put up with a shower of questions and emerge unscathed.

Maybe he should have just let her get out of the truck and come with him without saying anything to encourage her to hang back. He had been certain that her desire to be the one in control would have had her coming into the store with him.

Well, he'd gambled and lost. No big deal, he told himself. Now all he could do was just hurry down the shopping list he'd brought with him and hope that Ena wasn't going to be in an irritated mood when he got back with the supplies.

"You in a hurry, Mitch?" Wallace Page asked.

The owner of the only store of this kind in Forever, Wallace, watched the foreman from the Double E Ranch move through the store, grabbing items and piling them all up on the counter. He didn't recall ever seeing Mitch move around so fast.

"You might say that," Mitch answered, depositing another large item on the counter, then heading back to the shelves for a sack of something else. "I've got someone waiting in the truck."

"Oh, so it's that way, is it?" Wallace said with a knowing laugh.

"No," Mitch denied patiently as he went to fetch another item on his list. "It's not any way, Wallace." Done, he quickly surveyed everything he'd picked up. "Just total all this up for me, please."

"Sure thing." The man's fingers flew over his almost ancient cash register keys, an item he had inherited from his father. "Need help getting these things to your truck?"

"All I need is to use the wagon to get it all out there," he told the owner.

"You want me to put it on the Double E's account?" the storeowner asked once he had finished totaling it all up.

"Like you always do, Wallace," Mitch responded.

"Hey, is that the O'Rourkes' girl with you?" Wallace suddenly asked. He craned his neck, trying to get a glimpse of the interior of Mitch's truck from his vantage point through the store's front window. The man's thin, pinched face fell. "Guess not," the man said, disappointed.

Mitch turned to look toward his truck. He was surprised to see that the passenger seat was empty. They were too far from the ranch for Ena to suddenly decide that she was going to walk home.

So where had she taken off to? When he'd left her, he hadn't gotten the impression that she wanted to go see anyone.

"I thought you said you had someone waiting for you in the truck," Wallace said, confused.

Still not willing to identify who he had brought with him, Mitch shrugged. "Guess they got tired of sitting around and waiting and decided to take in the local color."

Wallace cackled. "That's a good one, son. We all know that Forever doesn't have any local color," the general store owner declared with a shake of his head. "But maybe someday…"

"Yeah, maybe someday," Mitch agreed absently, hardly hearing what Wallace had said. "I'll see you next week, Wallace," he said.

Trying not to appear as if he were in a hurry—or worried—Mitch quickly unloaded the various boxes and sacks in the giant-sized wagon, then pushed the cart over toward where the other carts were lined up.

He debated driving around to look for Ena, but he didn't want to move his truck in case she had just gone for a walk and was returning to the vehicle. The idea of a walk, however, was highly doubtful.

"Where are you?" Mitch murmured under his breath, scanning the immediate area.

He thought of going to the diner, but if Ena *hadn't* gone there, Miss Joan would somehow intuit that there was something wrong and launch into her own version of the third degree. He didn't want to have to go through that unless it was absolutely necessary and he had no other recourse.

Standing there, looking up and down the streets of Forever, Mitch studied the various buildings in the area, thinking.

And then it occurred to him where Ena must have gone.

Still leaving the truck parked in front of the general store, he quickly hurried past the medical clinic and Murphy's, as well as a few other familiar places, until he reached the church.

Instead of going inside the recently renovated building, he went around it until he came to the back end of it.

The cemetery was located a small distance way.

Mitch walked quickly toward it. At first, it appeared that there was no one inside the gated area. And then, as he came closer, still scanning the area, he saw her.

Ena.

Mitch quickly lengthened his stride until he was inside the gated area.

For a moment, he debated whether or not he should withdraw and leave her alone before she saw him. He knew that she had to have gone through some rather deep soul-searching before she had talked herself into coming over here.

But he did want to be there for her in case Ena suddenly felt she needed him.

Looking around, he found a large tombstone that, if he stood just right, would block him from her sight. So he stood off to the side, observing her. Watching for some sort of sign that she suddenly desired him to be there for her, or to talk to. Whatever it took, Mitch wanted to be ready. He knew what it felt like to suddenly find himself all alone, the way she did now with her father's passing.

Being very careful to be as quiet as he could, Mitch realized that she was talking to the small headstone he had put up.

"Still calling the shots, aren't you, Dad?" Ena was saying to the headstone that had her father's name on it. "I see you moved Mom. At least you picked a better place for her this time than you did the last time. She never did like that old oak tree, you know, not that you cared about something like that.

"I guess this means that Mom's going to have to listen to you talk for all eternity." Ena shook her head. "That's not fair, you know. The poor woman earned her rest after having to put up with you for all those years. But then, you were never all that interested in what was fair, were you?"

Ena fell silent for a moment, searching for words. "I want you to know that you lucked out. That guy you took under your wing, the one you probably wished was your kid instead of me, well, he turned out to be a good man. He's running the place and doing a really good job. You would have been very proud." She pressed her lips together. "Maybe you should have left the ranch to him. He certainly earned it. But then, you probably never made him feel the way you made me feel."

"He regretted that, you know."

Startled because she was so engrossed in talking to the spirit of her father, she hadn't realized that someone was there, listening to her.

Ena turned around to find herself looking up at Mitch.

Chapter Ten

Ena's defenses instantly went up. How long had the man been standing there, listening to her "talk" to her dead father?

Annoyed and embarrassed, she could feel her cheeks growing hot.

Her eyes blazed as she looked at him. "Are you spying on me?" she demanded.

"No, I went out looking for you," he explained calmly. "When I came out to the truck with the supplies, you weren't sitting in the cab. You'd told me that you were going to wait in the truck until I got back, so when I didn't see you, I got concerned."

She supposed that if she weren't so embarrassed because Mitch had overheard her "talking" to her father, she might have found his concern to be almost touching. But she *was* embarrassed, and right now, she just wanted to move past this whole incident and forget that it had ever taken place.

"There was no reason for you to be worried," she told him gruffly. "It's not like I could have been kidnapped by some drug lord or something. This is Forever, for heaven's sake. *Nothing* ever happens in Forever," she maintained flatly.

"I wouldn't be so sure if I were you," he told her. "Things happen here." He saw the skeptical look on her face and pressed on, "*Life* happens here. The sheriff met his wife here because Olivia came searching for her sister when Tina ran off with the father of her baby. Everyone wound up here," he told her.

"Well, they weren't from around here originally," Ena stressed, as if that made her point.

"Yes, but they live here now. At least Olivia and Tina do, along with Tina's baby. And it might interest you to know that Tina is now married to one of the town's doctors—Dr. Davenport, who also came from the Northeast. New York City to be specific. And theirs isn't the only story like that.

"My point," Mitch continued, "is that we don't live in some kind of bubble here. People from all over the country come through here, and when they do, they bring life with them. And they *choose* to stay here."

Ena closed her eyes and sighed, giving up. "Okay, you made your point. But nothing dramatic happened to me," she informed him. Then, to explain why she'd left the truck, she said, "You talked about my father and my mother being buried in the church cemetery and I thought that I'd just come take a look at their headstones for myself. Mystery solved."

Her expression was almost stony, he thought, trying to guess what was going on in her head.

"And now that you did?" Mitch asked. When she

didn't say anything in response, he tried to prod her a little. "Any thoughts?"

Ena glanced back at the two tombstones that marked her parents' graves.

"Yes," she said grudgingly. "You picked out nice headstones."

"Actually," he told her, "your father picked those out. Since he knew he was dying, he wanted to tie up all the loose ends that he could while he was still able to get around. He went to that mortuary in the next town and made all the arrangements. Your dad was a very determined man. He kept on working until he was too weak to get out of bed."

Try as she might to block out the wave of intense guilt that had suddenly risen up, it managed to break through, drenching her. She hated feeling this way and attempted to deflect her guilt by blaming the man next to her.

"You should have found a way to locate me and let me know that my father was dying." There was unmistakable hostility in Ena's voice.

His answer was the same as Miss Joan's had been. But it was prefaced with a twist she hadn't expected. "He already knew where you were but he didn't want to disrupt your life."

Ena stared at Mitch, stunned. "Wait, he *knew* where I was?" That wasn't possible, she thought. She had moved twice since the last Christmas card she'd sent to her father years ago.

Mitch hesitated. He was telling tales out of school, but he supposed at this point, what did it matter? She needed to know that her father *did* care about her despite whatever she thought she knew.

"Your father had a private investigator track you down," he told her.

That just confused things further for her. "I don't understand. If he went to such great lengths to have me found, why didn't he come to see me?"

That was simple enough to answer. "He went to such great lengths because he wanted to make sure you were still all right. The private investigator he'd hired told him that you had put yourself through college and that after graduation, you'd found an accounting position with a good, reputable firm.

"The private investigator assured your father that you were doing well. But you know your dad, he wasn't just going to accept the man's word for that so the investigator produced pictures as well as written evidence to back up what he was saying. It was all included in the report he wrote up for your father. I can show it to you if you'd like," Mitch offered.

It still didn't make any sense to her. "But if he had all that information, if he knew where I was, why didn't he even *try* to come see me?"

"My guess is that your father was a proud man. His feeling was that you left him. He didn't leave you. He undoubtedly thought that the ball was in your court—meaning that it was up to you to come back."

She could see that under normal circumstances, but not in the end. "But when he knew he was dying, he could have gotten word to me—"

"Again, he was a proud man," Mitch repeated. "He didn't want pity to be the motivating reason you came back."

Ena shook her head, frustrated. She glared at the headstone. "The man's dead and he's still making me crazy."

"I guess that was his gift," Mitch told her with a quiet smile.

She wouldn't have called it a gift. "How did you put up with him?" Ena asked.

"Oh, he had his good points." Mitch looked at the headstone and thought of the man buried there. "He treated me fairly, gave me a roof over my head, became like a second father to me. A stern father," he granted, "but to a kid without anyone, that was a lot."

For a moment, she felt a little jealous of the relationship between her father and the foreman. A relationship she would have given anything to have. "I guess he was lucky to have you."

"That went both ways," Mitch told her. And then he added contritely, "Look, I'm sorry I intruded on your time here. Why don't I go back to the truck and wait for you there? Take all the time you want, then come find me when you're done. The truck's still parked in front of the general store."

Now that Mitch had walked in on her, Ena felt awkward about spending any more time there. Anyway, she had basically said everything she had wanted to say to her father.

"I'm done," she announced.

Mitch looked at her uncertainly. "Are you sure?"

Ena shrugged. "There's just so much a person can say to a headstone," she answered glibly.

"Your mother was there, too," Mitch gently pointed out.

"I don't need to look at a piece of stone to talk to my mother. I talk to her in my heart," she informed him. Turning, she began to walk toward the cemetery exit. "Didn't you say you loaded up the truck with supplies?" she asked.

"I did."

"Well," she said impatiently, "isn't there something in those supplies that's melting or rotting or coming apart by now?"

"No, but I get the message," he told Ena, the corners of his mouth curving ever so slightly. "You want to go back to the ranch."

That was putting it rather bluntly, but there was no denying that he was right. "Very good. What gave me away?" she asked him sardonically.

"I guess it was just my steel-trap mind," he responded. "I also have the ability to read minds on occasion, so if I were you, I'd stick to thinking pure thoughts."

She laughed at that, her mood mercifully lightened. "I suppose that means I can't fantasize about strangling you?"

"Not at the moment," he answered, then grinned. "But maybe later."

Bemused, she shook her head. "You are one very weird man."

He flashed another grin at her, and although she tried not to let it get to her, she couldn't deny that it did.

"I'll take that as a compliment."

Ena frowned at him, but her heart really wasn't in it. "I'm not sure that I meant it as one."

"That's okay," he told her, enjoying himself. "I can still take it as one."

The ride back to the ranch was less awkward than the one she had experienced coming into the town. It was as if, because of the things that Mitch had shared with her, an unspoken truce had been struck up between them.

In addition, Ena no longer felt that Mitch had some

sort of hidden agenda when it came to her or to running the ranch. She'd decided that Mitch was on the level and that he just wanted to live up to the promise he had made to her father.

Ena glanced at Mitch's chiseled profile. For a moment, she had to admit to herself that she was glad that he had been there in her father's last days.

I guess you really did find the son you always wanted, Dad. Sorry it couldn't have been me, she thought as they approached the ranch house.

Even in her present mind-set, it still took Ena several days before she worked up the courage to finally walk into her father's room.

In part it was because she didn't want to deal with any unanticipated painful old memories. Being in her father's house was difficult enough for her. Entering the man's room, his "inner sanctum" so to speak, was another matter entirely. In addition, she didn't want to accidentally stumble across anything that might make those old memories even worse.

Mitch hadn't said anything about it, but maybe her father had taken up with someone in the last years of his life. Someone who had replaced her mother in his eyes.

Ena wasn't certain how she would deal with that.

Yes, her father had had every right to see someone. After all, he had been a widower and he had also been a grown man who needed companionship.

But after the surly way he had been toward her mother, there was a part of Ena that felt her father had no right to look for and find that sort of happiness with someone else.

So she wavered about walking into his room. Eventually, she lost her temper with herself. This was stupid.

She was a grown woman. She could handle whatever she might find—not to mention that there might be nothing to find.

With effort, Ena managed to steel herself, blocking out any extraneous thoughts that could get in her way and torpedo what she was attempting to do. She was strictly on a fact-finding mission, she told herself. She wanted to get a sense of how her father had spent the last ten years of his life, and while asking Mitch questions would certainly help fill in the gaps, Mitch might have his own agenda when it came to dealing with this. He might be trying to keep things from her because, for whatever reason of his own making, he wanted her to think well of her father.

Too late for that, she thought, although she had to admit that some of her thoughts had been tempered and softened a bit because of the things that Mitch had told her.

Still, she didn't want the foreman to influence the way she ultimately viewed her father's last days. All she had to do was summon eighteen years of bad memories and any good things that Mitch might have had to say were in serious jeopardy.

The second she finally walked into her father's bedroom, a sense of his presence instantly seeped under her skin. He'd been dead for a month and she could swear she could still smell the soap he always used.

She slowly looked around the exceptionally masculine room.

"Well, I'm here, Old Man. You got your way. At least for now," she qualified. "You got any hidden surprises to spring on me? Something to make me feel that I wasn't a total fool for coming here?" Ena walked around the room, touching things. Thinking. "Because if you think that the ranch is my consolation prize for enduring everything that went down between us, you're wrong. I don't want the ranch. I *never* wanted the ranch. That was always your thing," she said, addressing the air with a touch of bitterness in her voice.

"I'm planning on selling the ranch the first chance I get once the deed is officially in my name. So I'm going to put up with those conditions you stuck into the will. I'm going to live up to my end of it, and you, you're going to live up to yours. Pardon my pun," she told her father's spirit whimsically.

Roaming around the darkly furnished room, she thought of how he had removed all traces of her mother from what had once been their bedroom. Even the curtains that she had put up were gone. Her father had hung drapes in their place.

Opening his closet showed her that he had taken all her mother's clothing and put them away, as well. Most likely *gave* them away.

But there was no evidence that her father had taken up with another woman. There was no trace of anyone else in the room. No clothing, no small bottles of perfume left behind and forgotten. Not so much as an empty makeup container.

Still, she was her father's daughter, which made her inherently want to be completely thorough. So she moved around the room, opening doors and drawers, rummaging through any and all places, trying to find something that didn't belong.

Ena was very nearly finished with her search when she found it.

A rectangular box shoved all the way into the recesses of her father's closet.

The lid on the box was secured by several large

rubber bands the size of small bungee cords. The fact that it had so many cords aroused her curiosity.

Moving very carefully, she took off one cord after another until she could finally lift the lid off unimpeded.

This had to be it, Ena thought. Whatever was inside here probably had to do with her father's mystery lady. The person he had at least hoped to replace her mother with.

Ena sat down on the edge of the bed with the box next to her. Taking a deep breath, she braced herself, then slowly lifted the lid.

There were several envelopes in the box, all addressed to her father.

Recognition was immediate.

The handwriting was hers.

The envelopes had been from her, sent to her father those first two Christmases so that he wouldn't worry that something had happened to her. She'd been so sure that he had thrown them away. He certainly hadn't acknowledged them.

She could remember waiting each year, long past Christmas, for some word from him, but there hadn't been any.

Her hands trembled a little as she took out the first card. The note she had written to her father fell out. When she picked it up, she could see that the paper was worn, like it had been taken out and read over and over again, then carefully returned to its envelope.

She took out the last one. This note looked like the first note had: worn from frequent handling. The notes hadn't been crumpled in anger or torn the way she would have expected. Just worn because they'd been read and reread countless times.

By a man who would have loudly protested that he didn't care—but obviously had.

She sighed, holding the letters in her hand. Her eyes stung and she blinked, determined not to shed a single tear.

But she ultimately lost that battle the way she knew she would.

Chapter Eleven

It was turning into one big perpetual juggling act.

Because Ena didn't want to run the risk of possibly losing her position in the hierarchy at the firm where she had worked so hard to get ahead, three days a week Ena got up before the crack of dawn to work on the accounts that had been forwarded to her via email. She took them on because she had always believed in shouldering her responsibilities, not shirking them, and these were her accounts.

But as the days went by, she began to feel that her heart wasn't in this as much as it had been. While there was a certain satisfaction working with numbers, it wasn't the same sort of satisfied feeling she derived from working with the horses.

Besides, she discovered around the latter half of the second week she was there, if she were really looking to balance a ledger, she had her father's accounts to work with.

Or, more to the point, to set right.

"You really didn't have a head for figures, did you, Old Man?" she marveled, addressing the hodgepodge that Bruce O'Rourke had undoubtedly referred to as his accounting method.

As Ena paged through the worn ledger that looked as if it had been used as a doorstop more than once, she was stunned to see that her father had left some columns completely blank and others without any totals whatsoever. Toward the latter half of the book, there was hardly a balanced statement to be found.

Piecing things together, Ena concluded that her father had stopped keeping records, or at least accurate records, somewhere around the time that her mother had taken ill. And it had all gone downhill from there.

Prior to that, the columns had all been neatly written. She looked closer and saw that every number was written in her mother's very precise handwriting.

"She was your accountant, wasn't she, Old Man?" Ena murmured.

She frowned, flipping through the pages. It looked as if not only wasn't her father's heart in the work but he had barely paid attention to it, and when he did, it all looked as if it was haphazard and slipshod.

Getting this in order was going to take a monumental effort, she thought.

"There you are," Mitch declared as he came into the den. "I was looking for you. Felicity said you had breakfast early. Are you ready to get to work?" he asked.

She spared him a quick glance. "I *am* working," she informed him. "Did you know that my father's records were a complete mess?"

Mitch shook his head, although her question didn't

surprise him. "He never let me look at any of that. Always said that he had it all under control."

She frowned as she turned another page, all but shuddering at what she found. This was going to take her weeks and weeks to straighten out, if not longer, she thought in mounting despair.

"Well, he lied," she told the foreman.

"Maybe he didn't realize how bad this was," Mitch guessed.

That, she thought, was being far too kind. "Oh, I think he knew exactly how bad this was. He probably didn't care. To him, ledgers and accounts weren't what ranching was about. That kind of thing was just a nuisance that he felt just got in his way." She thought back to her childhood. "As long as he made enough money selling horses to pay his men and to keep the ranch afloat, he figured he was doing all right."

"But he wasn't?" Mitch asked, waiting for her to fill in the details.

Ena flipped to another page. It was just as awful as its predecessors. Closer examination showed her that there were entries on those pages without any sort of rhyme or reason.

She sighed. "So far from all right that I don't see how it didn't catch up to him long ago."

"Does this mean you're going to lose the ranch?" Mitch asked. It was obvious that he was concerned.

Ena shook her head. "Not if I can help it. It's going to take some clever calculating and manipulation of figures, but I think that the situation might be salvageable."

"Well, if anyone can do it, you can," Mitch said with confidence.

Ena blinked. Now he was just trying to butter her

up. "How can you say that? You don't know anything about my work."

"No," Mitch agreed. "But I do know you," he pointed out. He paused for a second, debating whether or not to say the next words. He decided he had nothing to lose. "Knew the kind of person you were all the way back in high school. You're not someone who just gives up. You dig in and fight for what you want."

She looked at him, surprised by what he had said. "All those years back in high school, I thought you didn't even know I existed. Other than just to nod at." And that had only been when she nodded first.

His smile widened as he looked at her. "Oh, I knew. And I paid attention."

She thought back to the way she had tried to get his attention. No matter what she had done, he had just ignored her. Or at least that was the way it had seemed.

"Then why—"

"Didn't I ever ask you out?" Mitch guessed at the rest of her question. "Because I felt that you were out of my league and I didn't want you to shoot me down when you figured that out. I had a very fragile ego back then. Put that together with being the *new kid* as well as being in the foster system, and I just didn't have enough courage to ask you out and risk ultimately getting turned down. Besides, I knew who your father was and, to be honest, I was pinning all my hopes on getting a job on his ranch when I graduated."

She hadn't realized that. She just thought it was a coincidence that he had wound up working here. "So, in a way, this was because of my father?" she asked incredulously.

He couldn't very well say no after he'd told her the first part. "In a very roundabout way," Mitch allowed.

"For the most part, it was because you were such a big deal and I didn't have the nerve to fall flat on my face—so I never asked you out."

"Huh," she said, turning the swivel chair around to face him squarely. The chair squeaked as it turned, making her wince. "I wouldn't have pegged you for a coward," she told Mitch.

"I'm not—anymore," he told her. "And I've got your father to thank for that. He helped me build up my confidence, made me feel that I was capable of doing things."

Listening to him, Ena shook her head. "It still doesn't seem like we're talking about the same man. The Bruce O'Rourke I knew never built up anyone's self-esteem. As a matter of fact, the old man seemed to thrive on destroying self-esteem."

"Maybe your leaving was what changed him," Mitch told her. "Because according to some of the old-timers who were there when I started to work on the ranch, your dad had the kind of disposition that made rattle-snakes duck and hide."

Ena laughed despite herself. "Now *that* sounds like my dad," she told him.

He liked hearing her laugh. She looked good in a smile, he thought. It just brightened her whole face. "Like I said, he changed after you left. Because of that—and thanks to you—he became a fair boss. Stern, like I said, but really fair. And I found that I could always talk to him."

She was really having trouble making her peace with what Mitch was telling her.

"Well, that made one of us, because I certainly never could, not even when my mother was alive. After she died, life with my father became just like doing time in hell."

There was sympathy in his eyes as he looked at her. "Was he that bad?"

"He was actually worse, but I don't use that kind of language, so my description of hell is going to have to do," Ena told him.

Mitch came around the desk, and to Ena's surprise, he took her hand, coaxing her up out of the chair. "Why don't you leave all that for now?"

"But it's been in this state for *years* now," she complained.

"That's my whole point," Mitch told her. "If it's been that way for all this time, it can certainly last for another day. No need to kill yourself to try to get it fixed as fast as you can. As a matter of fact," he said, considering the ordeal she was determined to take on, "tackling this behemoth in stages might be a better way to go if you think about it. This way, you won't wind up completely wiped out."

"Stages, eh?" she asked and Mitch nodded in response. "You, Parnell, have a very unique approach to working," Ena told him.

"It's called prioritizing, and it seems to have worked out for me so far so I feel like I can honestly recommend it to you." His voice grew serious. "There's nothing to be gained by working yourself into the ground like that. If you're *not* wiped out, you can come back and work on this another day. So, how about it?" he asked. "You know the foal's been asking for you."

"Right," she said with a laugh. "And did he *ask* for me by name?"

Mitch winked at her as he said, "Well, as a matter of fact…"

The man was incredible, Ena thought, amused. "Well,

if we're dealing with a talking foal, let's not keep him waiting," she responded. "Let's go pay the little guy a visit."

"Now that's the ticket," Mitch encouraged. Then, without thinking, he put his arm around her shoulders and guided her out of the den and toward the front door as if they were old friends.

Ena felt something warm sparking within her chest and moving through her limbs. For now she decided to just enjoy it without analyzing it any further.

She was spreading herself thin and she knew it, Ena thought. But unlike what Mitch had suggested, she couldn't seem to get herself to prioritize the various duties that faced her.

There was doing the daily work on the ranch—something she knew Mitch and the hands who were working here could have taken on themselves, but that wasn't the point, according to the terms of her father's will. She was here to do the work, not shirk it.

There was also the huge mess that was otherwise known as her father's accounts. They were *so* jumbled up she knew it was going to take her *days*, if not longer, to untangle and straighten out. And then, of course, there were the accounts that were being emailed to her from Dallas. Accounts that she had insisted she could work on while away from the office.

Maybe she had taken on more than she was equipped to handle, Ena thought, staring at her father's ledger. After all, she wasn't exactly some sort of superheroine. She knew that.

But her pride wouldn't allow her to let anything she had taken on slide. So she found a way to spend time on all of it. The days were for the ranch, the early mornings and late evenings were for the accounts she had told her firm she would look into. And the four and a half minutes that were leftover were for her father's all but hopeless accounts.

That was what she was working on now, sitting in the den at her father's old scarred desk, struggling to keep her eyes from closing and desperately trying to figure out an old entry she had come across.

It made less than no sense to her.

Ena sighed, massaging the bridge of her nose, trying to keep at bay a possible headache that was forming right between her eyes.

"Whatever made you think you could tackle math, Old Man?" she murmured, looking at the page she had open. "This would have made more sense if you'd let your horse handle the accounts."

"You do realize that you need to get some sleep, right?"

Startled, she looked up. Mitch had come into the room. She hadn't even heard him walk in. But then, she was getting used to that.

"What I need is to understand why my father thought he could handle the books and why in heaven's name he didn't just get someone to do it for him," she said with a sigh. She fought a strong urge to toss the ledger across the room—or out the window.

"Could be that he was as stubborn as you are," Mitch speculated.

She didn't like being compared to her father. Ena raised her chin defensively. "At least I know my limits," she told him.

Mitch perched on the edge of the old desk, looking down at her. "Do you?" he asked, amused.

Her eyes narrowed as she pinned him with a look. "Just what is it that you are insinuating, Parnell?" she asked.

"Not insinuating," he responded. "I'm stating it blatantly. You're trying to do too much and you're looking to get yourself sick."

Ena could feel her temper rising. "Not my intention," she retorted.

"Maybe not," Mitch allowed. "But that's the end result. You're trying to juggle too many things at once, and eventually, one of those things is going to fall and hit you right in the head."

"Colorful," she commented cryptically.

"Also true," Mitch insisted. "Call it a day and go to bed," he advised.

She felt really punchy at this point and it was making her cranky. "You're not in charge of me, Parnell."

"No, you're right, I'm not. But that doesn't mean that I want to stand by and watch you get sick—and if you keep on going like this, trying to do two and a half jobs, you just might. Your dad wanted you to work the ranch. He didn't mean that you should go on doing your other job and also cleaning up his account books at the same time. I'm fairly sure of that," Mitch added with just the slightest touch of sarcasm.

That only served to make Ena angrier. "That's because he didn't think I could do anything," Ena said, remembering the way her father used to regard her.

"So now, by knocking yourself out this way, you're going to *show* him, is that it?" Mitch asked.

"Of course not," she snapped. When he continued to look at her with that "knowing" expression on his face, she had to struggle to hold on to her temper. "I can't *show* him because he's dead."

"That's right, he is," Mitch agreed quietly, his eyes still on hers. "So killing yourself like this really serves no purpose."

"Other than fulfilling the terms of the will, allowing me to continue to hold on to my job in Dallas, not to mention not losing the ranch to a bunch of bill collectors my father somehow either forgot to pay or just hoped would go away," she said, her voice building with each word she said.

Mitch slid off the desk and came around to look over her shoulder at the ledger that was opened on the desk.

"Is it really that bad?" he asked her.

She felt hemmed in right now and scrubbed her hand over her face. "Well, it's definitely not good."

"Can you do anything about it?" Mitch couldn't help thinking of all the people he worked with—people who were counting on the ranch continuing to operate so they could earn a living.

Ena pressed her lips together as she looked at the ledger entries—the ones she could make sense out of. "Depends on whether I can talk some people into granting the ranch extensions until we can get everything under control." She shook her head, her eyes all but glazing over. "He really should have asked for help with all this."

"Not in his nature," Mitch told her. "You know that."

"Yes, if I know anything, I know that," she agreed. She leaned back against the chair, stretching her shoulders. Her eyes kept insisting on closing. "You're right. I should go to bed."

Finally! "Glad to hear that," Mitch said.

"Just as soon as I get up enough strength," she mumbled.

The next thing he knew, Ena had fallen asleep right in front of him, still sitting back in the chair.

Chapter Twelve

Mitch touched Ena's arm. She didn't react. She was sound asleep.

"Well, I guess strength isn't going to be coming anytime soon. Looks like you just completely ran out of energy," he observed, looking at Ena. And then he assessed the situation. "Well, you certainly can't sleep in this chair. If you do, everything's going to ache when you wake up in the morning. You won't be any good to anyone then, least of all yourself."

There was only one thing to do. He needed to get her into her bed.

As gently as possible, he slipped his arm under her legs. Getting a secure hold, he picked Ena up from the chair. She stirred and made a noise, but her eyes remained closed.

Mitch released the breath he was holding, and he started to walk slowly. Leaving the den, he headed for the stairs.

Ena stirred again. Mitch walked even slower, certain that she was going to wake up at any second. But instead, she curled up into him as if he were a living, breathing pillow.

You're really making this hard, Ena, Mitch thought, doing his best not to allow the warmth he felt emanating from her body to infiltrate his. But it wasn't easy, especially not when working so closely with her had brought back all his old feelings for her, all those carefully blocked-out desires.

It was harder now. He was no longer that awkward teen pining after someone he felt was out of his league. He had gained self-confidence since then and holding her in his arms like this just brought all those old sensations back to him.

Vividly.

"You really know how to get to a man," he murmured to her under his breath.

Careful to take the stairs slowly because the last thing he wanted was to wake Ena, he moved up the steps cautiously, watching her face as he did so.

Midway up the stairs she sighed and seemed to curl into him even more, nestling her face against his chest. All sorts of stirrings were dancing about in the pit of his stomach.

Funny, he thought, after all this time, she was still the only one who could make him feel this way. Not that he was all that experienced. He wasn't a womanizer by any means, but then he wasn't exactly a shrinking violet, either. There had been women in his life, women from both his late mother's world as well as his late father's. There had been a mixture of both cultures.

But there had never been *the* woman.

He had just assumed that he wasn't meant to feel that

wild, heady, intoxicating excitement that a man experienced when the right woman crossed his path.

And then, suddenly here she was, the woman who somehow could raise his body temperature just by *being*, and here he was, carrying her up to her room.

To put her to bed and then just slip away, he silently reminded himself.

Clay Washburn, his best friend back when he and Clay had barely been teens, would have just shaken his head in despair.

He hadn't thought about Clay in years. Not since the car accident had happened, the one that had robbed him of his teen confidante.

He thought of him now. Clay had been a ladies' man, able to completely charm any woman who crossed his path within moments of the occurrence.

But although he thought of Clay fondly, he had never aspired to be anything like that himself. Being a ladies' man just wasn't his style. It required too much work, too much planning and he had never even had a desire to win a woman over.

Not until now.

Don't go there, Mitch warned himself. *She is not here to be seduced by you. She's here so she can fulfill the terms of her father's will. She's not here to get to know you better.*

Why couldn't it be both? Mitch wondered suddenly. After all, there was no rule that said it couldn't be both.

He was tired. That was why his mind was straying like this. He'd definitely be able to think more clearly in the morning, he promised himself, carefully shouldering open Ena's bedroom door.

Still moving very slowly, Mitch stepped inside the room.

There was only a crescent moon out and it illuminated almost nothing. The bedroom was more or less totally in pitch-darkness.

Even though he'd left the door open when he walked in, Mitch made his way to the bed very carefully. He made sure to take incredibly small steps so he wouldn't trip over anything or bump into something that would ultimately jar Ena awake.

So he stood inside the doorway for a second, waiting for his eyes to adjust to the dark. He wanted to be able to make out shapes that were in the room.

Once his vision had adjusted, Mitch made the rest of his way toward the bed. Reaching it, he very carefully laid Ena on top of the comforter.

A small bereft sort of sound seemed to escape from her lips and he froze.

Mitch debated covering her, then decided that he had pressed his luck too much as it was. If he tried to put the comforter over her, Ena could very well wind up waking.

"See you in the morning," he told Ena softly as he began to retrace his steps and retreat from Ena's bedroom.

"If you're lucky."

Mitch stopped dead and then slowly turned around. Was he hearing things, or had she suddenly woken up and spoken to him?

He had his answer when he finally looked at her face. Ena's eyes were open and she was smiling directly at him.

"You're awake," he said needlessly.

Ena grinned, even though she really did look tired. "Looks that way, doesn't it?"

Crossing back to her, he had one question. "When did you wake up?"

She looked a wee bit guilty as she said, "Just when you started going up the stairs."

That didn't make any sense to him. She was so independent—why would she have allowed him to carry her into her room if she was awake? "Why didn't you say anything?"

"Because I was really, really tired and it felt really nice to be whisked off to my room like that. Besides, I was curious if you were going to try anything," she told him, growing very sleepy again. Ena sighed as she curled up on the bed. "Nice to know that you're a gentleman."

"Yeah," Mitch muttered. "Nice for one of us at least," he said under his breath.

She heard him, but she was really too tired to call him out on it.

Besides, there was time enough to do that in the morning. After she got her rest...

Ena was asleep before she could even finish her thought.

The following morning the full significance of what had transpired the night before hit her. Mitch Parnell was the rarest of birds, an actual gentleman. He'd brought her up to her room, and even though he had thought she was asleep, he hadn't attempted anything.

However, Ena couldn't help thinking it meant he wasn't remotely attracted to her. But even though it could be deemed as being self-centered on her part, she was fairly confident that he *was* attracted to her.

The thought made her smile.

Widely.

"Well, someone certainly looks happy this morning," Felicity commented when Ena walked into the kitchen.

"I just got a really good night's sleep," Ena told the housekeeper. The latter was standing by the stove, looking like she was about to spring into action at any moment.

Hearing what Ena had just said, the housekeeper nodded her salt-and-pepper head.

"It is about time." When Ena looked at her quizzically, the woman said, "I am not deaf. I hear you working and moving things around in your father's den. I know you are working two jobs."

"Three," Ena corrected her. "But who's counting?"

The housekeeper's lips curved just the slightest bit. "You seem to be," Felicity noted. "Otherwise you would not have corrected me."

"Fair enough," Ena allowed. She looked around again. "Where's Mitch?"

"Mr. Mitch has already had his breakfast," Felicity told her.

Ena hadn't expected that. "Why didn't he wake me up?" she asked.

"Because he didn't want to," Felicity said simply. "Mr. Mitch left strict orders not to wake you," the housekeeper said, anticipating Ena's next question. "But he also said to make sure you had breakfast when you did come down."

"Where is he this morning?" Ena asked the woman.

Felicity gave her a stern look, as if she knew that her late boss's daughter would dash out the moment she had that information. "Mr. Mitch said I could tell you only *after* you have had breakfast."

Ena's good mood was quickly evaporating. "Felicity, I'm not in the mood to play games."

"Good, because I am not playing games," the woman informed her. "I am listening to Mr. Mitch's instructions," Felicity declared with more than a touch of pride.

Ena's eyes narrowed. She made one final attempt to get the woman to give up the information.

"You do know that I'm the one who pays your salary," she reminded Felicity.

"What I know is that Mr. Mitch is concerned about you and what he said to me makes good sense." Felicity looked at her sternly. "Now, the sooner you eat your breakfast, the sooner I can tell you where to find Mr. Mitch and the other men. Now, then," she said, giving her a penetrating look, "what is it that you would like to have for breakfast?"

Ena sighed. She had a feeling that Felicity could go on like this all day until she surrendered—so she did. "Scrambled eggs."

The housekeeper nodded, looking pleased. "Very good. Toast?"

Ena shrugged. "Sure, why not?" she said. Then she specified, "One slice."

The housekeeper opened up the loaf of bread and deposited two slices into the toaster.

"Two is better," the woman said with a finality that told Ena the matter wasn't up for discussion. She was getting two slices and that was that. And then she asked, "Coffee? Orange juice?"

Ena wasn't in the mood for either, but that wasn't the way this game was played and she knew it, so she replied, "Whatever it takes for you to tell me where Parnell is."

The housekeeper smiled with satisfaction. "Coffee and orange juice it is," she declared, pleased that Ena had come around.

Moving quickly, it only took the woman less than five minutes to whip up the aforementioned breakfast and put it on a plate.

"You will chew this slowly," the housekeeper told Ena as she set the plate of scrambled eggs and toast down in front of her. She eyed Ena and told her, "Foxing food down is bad for you."

Caught off guard, Ena stared at the housekeeper for a long moment—and then a light suddenly went off in her head.

"You mean *wolfing*," Ena corrected the older woman.

Felicity shrugged indifferently. "Fox, wolf, they are both small sneaky animals that like to eat on the move," she said, eyeing Ena to get her point across. "You will eat what I have made sitting down and you will eat it slowly."

There was no mistaking that the housekeeper had just issued an order.

Resigned, Ena did as the woman specified.

She fought a very strong urge to ask the housekeeper if she wanted her to chew each bite a certain amount of times. With her luck, the woman would answer in the affirmative and then pull a high number out of the air, making sure she followed through.

So Ena sat at the table and dutifully ate her breakfast.

Felicity's voice droned on in the background, telling her something to the effect that she, Ena, was very lucky to have someone as thoughtful as *Mr. Mitch* looking after her.

And then Felicity dropped a bombshell.

"He looked after Mr. Bruce, too, when Mr. Bruce got sick," she told Ena proudly.

"He did?" she asked. This was the first she had heard about this. Mitch had never mentioned doing this.

Felicity nodded. "He did," she confirmed. "Looked after Mr. Bruce like a son. *Better* than a son," she corrected. "I was here, of course, doing what I could to help out, but Mr. Bruce was too proud to accept my help. It was Mr. Mitch who took care of him, who helped him get dressed in the morning and into bed at night. Mr. Mitch made Mr. Bruce feel that he—Mr. Bruce—was doing him a favor by allowing him to help. He is a very good man, Mr. Mitch," Felicity said with feeling.

"So I'm beginning to learn," Ena said quietly. Finished with breakfast, she placed her utensils in the middle of the plate and pushed the plate away into the center of the table. "All right, I've satisfied his conditions, *now* will you tell me where I can find Mitch and the other men?" she asked, looking at Felicity expectantly and waiting for the woman to live up to her end of the bargain.

The housekeeper volunteered the information as if it was only logical and Ena should have figured it out for herself.

"Mr. Mitch said that he and the other men would be breaking in the new horses."

"Does that mean that he's at the corral right now?" Ena asked.

"Not the one closer to the house," Felicity specified. "He uses the corral behind the second barn to break in the horses."

Ena didn't bother asking why the change in venue had been made. She just wanted to get out and find Mitch. Felicity's revelation just now had caused a host of questions to pop up in her head.

"Thank you," Ena said as she rose to her feet. After draining the last of her coffee, she put the cup down, then told the housekeeper, "The breakfast you served this morning was very good."

Felicity nodded, accepting the words as her due. "I know."

Ena smiled to herself as she left the kitchen. Felicity was in a class by herself. She couldn't help wondering if the older woman and her father had clashed. Most likely on a daily basis. But the woman spoke fondly of her father, so either she had a high tolerance for frustration, or, at bottom, Felicity and her father understood each other.

Better woman than me, Felicity, Ena thought.

Leaving the house, she stood outside for a moment, looking around and absorbing her surroundings.

It was a beautiful, crisp morning. A good morning to be alive, Ena thought. She had skipped working on the accounts that her firm had forwarded, as well as playing hooky from working on her father's hodgepodge of a ledger this morning. And if she were being totally honest with herself, she had to admit that ignoring both things felt good.

She also realized that she was actually looking forward to working with the horses today. She liked ranch work. She could get back to the grind of working on her father's ledger and the accounts later this evening, but right now, she was eager to find Mitch. For a number of reasons.

Chapter Thirteen

If Ena hadn't already known where she was going, the sound of raised, cheering male voices would have guided her to the right destination. Mitch had told her yesterday that the focus today was going to be breaking in some of the newer horses. He'd even mentioned that the process on some of the horses had already been started.

What she hadn't expected—but looking back, Ena realized that she should have—was that the man who was doing the breaking was Mitch.

Her breath caught in her throat as she came closer to the corral and saw what Mitch was doing. All the wranglers were there, surrounding the corral, most likely for moral support, she thought. Taking a place between Wade and Billy, Ena watched Mitch hanging on to a dapple-gray stallion. There was a great deal of daylight between Mitch and the saddle as the stallion bucked like crazy, trying to get Mitch off his back.

"Why is Mitch on top of that horse?" she cried, directing her question toward Wade. Ena couldn't look away, afraid that at any second, Mitch was going to go flying into the air. She could feel her heart climbing up higher into her throat, lodging itself there.

"Best way anyone knows to break in a horse," Wade replied calmly.

"Shouldn't someone else be doing this instead of Mitch?" Ena asked. If anything happened to him, the Double E would be out a foreman—among other things. This was just crazy, she thought.

"Nobody's better when it comes to breaking horses than Mitch," Billy piped up. It was evident that the younger hand had a serious case of hero worship when it came to the foreman.

"Don't worry," Wade assured her, sensing her agitation. "Mitch knows what he's doing."

She was clutching the top rail of the fence and her knuckles were turning white. She wasn't even aware of breathing.

Ena never took her eyes off the bucking horse and his rider.

"What he's doing is rattling around what few brains he's got in that head of his," Ena declared angrily, her voice rising as the stallion became more and more frenzied.

"This isn't Mitch's first rodeo—or his first bucking bronco," Wade told her, adding confidently, "He's gonna be fine." Then, as some of the others gasped, Wade cried, "Wow!" when Mitch looked as if he was about to rise up even higher from his mount and was in danger of literally going flying. "That was a close one!"

With each attempt, the horse, aptly named Wildfire, seemed more determined than ever to throw off the man on his back. Bucking and tossing his head, Wildfire's frenzy grew in scope.

And then, with one more incredible upward leap, Wildfire threw Mitch off.

Ena screamed as Mitch hit the ground, watching in horror as the back of his head bounced as it made contact with the hard dirt.

For a dreadful second, the foreman appeared to be too stunned to get up.

Nobody moved.

Not waiting for any of the ranch hands gathered around the perimeter to do anything, Ena maneuvered herself through the space in the corral's railings. But before she could run to Mitch, Wade had caught her by the arm.

Frustrated, she tried to yank her arm away and looked at the older man accusingly.

"Give him a minute," Wade counseled.

"To do what? Get stomped on?" Ena cried angrily. "He's lying there like some kind of rag doll. He's a *target*," she pointed out, exasperated.

Turning back, she saw Mitch shake his head as if to clear it. Then, moving quickly, he caught hold of the stallion's dragging reins and pulled Wildfire back. That threw the animal off balance for a split second. Mitch used that sliver of time to climb back into the stallion's saddle.

Ena watched, horrified. "Is he crazy?" she demanded, looking from Wade to Billy.

"If he doesn't get back up on the horse, that stallion is going to be twice as hard to break," Wade told her matter-of-factly, never taking his eyes off the resilient foreman.

"So one horse doesn't get broken. At least Mitch

won't break his neck—or worse," Ena said, not under-standing what the big deal was.

"Mr. Mitch isn't going to accept that," Billy told her solemnly. "Mr. Mitch never met a horse he couldn't break," the young wrangler added proudly.

"Make sure you write that on his tombstone," Ena said, disgusted.

But angry as she was at what she viewed to be a stu-pid move on Mitch's part, she couldn't get herself to tear her eyes away from the horse and his would-be master. She caught herself praying that Mitch wouldn't come flying off the horse again. This time he was liable to split his head wide open.

The minutes ticked by. Wildfire bucked less and less until, eventually, the horse grew tired of trying to throw Mitch off his back altogether and surrendered. The last couple of minutes, the once-wild horse became totally docile. Triumphant, Mitch allowed Wildfire one final peaceful go-round as the horse moved along the perim-eter of the corral.

Billy ran up to Mitch and eagerly took the reins from the foreman's hand as the latter slid off the newly tamed stallion's back.

"I *knew* you could do it, sir," Billy told him, beaming.

Ena was right on the hired hand's heels, less than a half beat behind him. She did a quick survey of the man standing in front of her. Something was off—she could feel it.

"Are you all right?" she demanded, still looking at Mitch.

"Never better," he responded, flashing a satisfied grin. "Why?"

"Because I watched you smash your head," she told him impatiently.

"Oh, that's nothing," he said, waving away her concern. "It's a hard head," he laughed.

One of the men called to him and Mitch turned to look in his direction. He turned a little too quickly and seemed to waver a little unsteadily on his feet.

Ena saw his face turn slightly pale. He stood very still for a second, as if he was trying to regain his balance.

"Are you all right?" Ena repeated, growing really concerned.

"I said I'm fine," Mitch insisted.

"And I just saw you turn pale right in front of me," Ena countered.

He could see the men looking at him, probably not knowing what to think. He had to put this to rest. "Must be your imagination," he replied, shrugging off her concern.

But Ena wasn't about to be put off. Drawing closer to him, her eyes narrowed as she looked into his. "I don't think so. You came down really hard when you hit your head."

"It's not the first time," he told her glibly. "All part of the work."

"You could be walking around with a concussion," she said pointedly, getting in front of him so he couldn't walk away from her.

His smile was tolerant. "Why don't you let me worry about that?" he said. Then, looking over her head toward Wade, he said, "Wade, where's the other horse you wanted me to break?"

Wade began to answer, then saw the warning look in Ena's eyes. He quickly improvised. "The horse was taken back to his stall."

"This is the first I've heard of it. Why?" Mitch asked.

"Um, he didn't look all that well to me," Wade told him, saying the first thing that came to his mind. He shrugged helplessly. "Why don't you take a break from taming the horses for today?"

For the first time, Ena saw Mitch getting annoyed. "What, she get to you, too?"

"She's making sense, sir," Billy said, timidly adding his voice to Wade's. "You did hit the ground pretty hard, sir."

"Right. I'm the one who fell so I should know how hard I hit the ground and I said I was fine, damn it!" Mitch insisted.

But the next move Mitch made completely contradicted his assertion. Turning away from Wade, Billy and the woman who he felt had put them up to this, Mitch felt his knees almost buckle right under him.

Grasping the first thing he could reach so that he could remain upright, he wound up clutching Ena's shoulder.

That made her point, Ena thought.

"I think we both know that I'm right." She glanced at Wade and Billy. "Can I get you two to watch him while I go get the truck?" she asked.

Second-guessing her intent, Billy said, "We can get him back to the house for you, ma'am."

"Thank you but I'm not going back to the house," Ena told the younger wrangler. "I'm taking Mitch into town so he can see one of the doctors at the clinic."

Mitch stiffened. "I don't need to see a doctor," he protested.

"Maybe not," Ena replied and for a second Mitch looked relieved. But not for long. "But the doctor needs to see you. It's called taking precautions."

"It's called a waste of time," he countered, frustrated.

"Po-ta-toe, po-tah-toe," Ena responded. Then she added, "Humor me."

"Look, thanks for your concern, really, but I don't have time for this," Mitch told her.

He shut his eyes for a second because things were spinning. Mercifully, when he opened his eyes, the world had settled down again.

But Ena looked as determined as ever to get him to the doctor.

Completely unaffected by Mitch's protests, Ena calmly said, "We're making time for this." She looked at the two men she was entrusting to remain with Mitch. "Watch him," she ordered. "Tie him up if you have to. I'll be right back."

"You know that this is totally unnecessary!" Mitch said, calling after her. "I'm really fine!" He craned his neck so that his voice would carry as she hurried away from the corral.

Ena was back faster than he had anticipated. She was driving his truck.

"What did you do, run?" he asked.

"As a matter of fact, I did," she said, sounding a little breathless as she got out of the cab of the truck. "I was afraid you'd bully these guys into letting you just walk away. And before you say anything about the cost, don't worry. I'm going to take care of it."

"It's totally unnecessary," Mitch maintained. "If you have your heart set on throwing your money away, you can do it by paying off some of those accounts for the Double E that you said were in arrears."

"I am working on that," she assured him. "But just as important as paying off the accounts is having a living, breathing foreman. Get him into the truck, boys," she said, addressing Wade and Billy.

"I can get in on my own," Mitch retorted, pulling back from the two wranglers.

Ena shot him a look that said she was coming to the end of her patience. "Then do it!"

"Lady sounds like she means business to me," Wade told Mitch. "Don't worry, I'll hold down the fort while you're gone."

He was talking to Mitch, but it was Ena who responded, "I appreciate that."

"Well, I don't," Mitch said, speaking up as Wade hustled him into the passenger side of the truck.

"You don't count right now," she told him just as she climbed up into the driver's seat. Seated, she looked out the window at Wade and Billy, as well as the others. "I'll be back as soon as I can," she promised.

"Hey, this is my truck, you know," Mitch pointed out indignantly.

"I know," she replied, putting the key into the ignition again.

"Well, if you know that, then why are you driving it?" he asked.

She didn't want to say anything in front of his men because he might feel that she was undermining him. But now that they were alone, she could tell him the reason she was so concerned. "Because one of your pupils is dilated and a lot bigger than the other one."

He had no idea what that meant or why she thought it was a reason to be dragging him off to the medical clinic. "What? What does that even mean?"

"It means that you might have a concussion and I want to get you checked out to make sure that we're not ignoring something serious."

He sighed. "Concussion again," he repeated in disgust.

"Yup. And I'll keep saying that word until the doctor can rule it out," Ena told him.

"I don't remember you being this stubborn when we were in high school together," he told her.

"Well, guess what? I am," she said brightly.

He crossed his arms in front of his chest, the picture of the immovable object—or so he hoped. "We're going to be stuck at that medical clinic all day and maybe I won't get in to see the doctor anyway."

"That's okay. We'll take our chances," she said philosophically. She'd started driving toward Forever, but the truck bucked a little before it got back into gear. "What's wrong with this thing?"

"It doesn't like strangers driving it," he answered without any hesitation.

"Too bad," she told him. Glancing over toward him, Ena saw that Mitch hadn't put his seat belt on. "Buckle up, cowboy."

"Why? Am I in for a bumpy ride?" he asked dryly, quoting an obscure movie reference he remembered having heard once.

The smile she threw him sent a chill down along his spine. "You have no idea," she promised, pressing down on the accelerator.

The medical clinic was crowded, just as he had predicted. Debi, one of the two nurses who were coordinating the various patients seated in the waiting area, looked up from her computer and asked, "May I help you?"

Ena had no qualms about telling the young woman, "Yes, this is an emergency."

"Are you hurt?" Debi asked, quickly scrutinizing her.

"I'm not, but—" Ena lowered her voice because she knew that Mitch wouldn't want anyone overhearing the reason she had dragged him in to see the doctor "—he was breaking in a horse and the horse threw him. He flew off and hit his head. One of his pupils is dilated."

Mitch closed in on Ena. "She's worrying needlessly," he told Debi.

"Why don't we let one of the doctors determine that?" Debi suggested kindly. "I think that Dr. Dan is up next, unless you'd rather see—"

"Dr. Dan will be fine," Mitch said, eager to get out of there. "But really, this isn't necessary. I've got work to do."

"And we're going to get you doing it as soon as possible." Debi looked around at the waiting room and rose slightly in her chair to get a better look. "You folks mind if I squeeze Mitch here in ahead of you?" she asked the patients waiting to be seen.

Ena braced herself to try to appeal to these people, some of whom she recognized but others were complete strangers to her.

She had prepared herself needlessly, however, because the people in the waiting room quickly gave their permission, willingly stepping back so that the cowboy they all knew could go in first.

"Sure, he can have my spot," one man toward the back of the reception room said.

"I certainly don't mind waiting," a young woman told Debi.

"Got nothing waiting for me at home except for Carrie, who is dying to tell me I told you so, so sure, he can go in ahead of me," an older man responded, waving Mitch in.

"I knew your dad." Another man spoke up, looking at Ena. "He would have wanted me to let Mitch here go in if he's hurt."

"I'm not hurt," Mitch insisted, raising his voice to get his point across.

"That's what we're trying to determine," Ena reminded him. "If you don't have a concussion, you can give me all the grief about it you want on the way back. If you do have one, then I get to say I told you so and your soul is mine," she told him.

"Hey, that sure sounds like a fair bargain to me," an older woman said, then cackled at the possible outcome of the confrontation.

"Looks like you get to go in next, Mitch," Debi told him, coming around toward him from behind her desk. "Just follow me."

"I'll wait here," Ena told him.

She would have preferred going into the exam room with him, but she knew she couldn't very well go in and hold his hand. He wouldn't stand for it, and besides, she wasn't related to him.

She watched Debi lead Mitch in through the door that led to the exam rooms in the back of the clinic.

With a sigh, she moved away from the reception desk and found a seat in the waiting room.

Chapter Fourteen

"Waiting is always the hardest part, honey."

The remark came from an older woman sitting in the waiting room. The woman was to Ena's right and she leaned forward in her seat to give their exchange a semblance of privacy. Smiling, the woman patted Ena's hand as if they had some sort of bond between them, even though Ena didn't recognize her.

Ena forced a smile to her lips. "I guess it is," she replied politely.

"Oh, I know it is because you're stuck out here, letting your imagination run wild. If you were in there with him, asking questions and finding things out, it would be a lot easier for you, trust me," the woman told her with confidence. Her face brightened. "But he'll be out by and by."

Ena forced a smile to her lips and just nodded in response.

The smile the woman flashed at Ena was genuine. "You don't remember me, do you?"

Ena had to admit that the woman's voice sounded vaguely familiar, but her face wasn't. Ena shook her head. "I'm sorry—"

The matronly-looking woman laughed. "Oh, don't be sorry, dear. The last time I saw you, I had brown hair instead of all this gray and you were this cute little senior going to high school along with my daughter, Sandra."

The name instantly triggered a memory. "Mrs. Baker?" Ena cried uncertainly, looking more closely at the woman in the waiting room.

Shirley Baker laughed, delighted. "So, you do remember me."

"Of course I do," Ena answered, genuine pleasure filling her voice. "How's Sandra doing?" she asked, grateful to be able to actually carry on a conversation instead of doing what the woman had said, letting her mind come up with awful scenarios about Mitch's possible condition.

Mrs. Baker beamed. "Sandra's doing just great. She's married now. Gave me two beautiful grandbabies," the woman said proudly. "They're two and four. I watch them for her when she works at the hotel. I'm taking the day off today, getting my semiannual with the doctor," she confided in a lower voice. And then she went on to say in a louder voice, "We've done a lot of growing here in Forever since you've been gone."

Ena nodded. "I noticed."

Shirley Baker's expression turned sympathetic. "I was sorry to hear about your dad. He was a good man. A lot of people came to his funeral," she said, obviously thinking Ena would take comfort in that. "Almost everyone in town paid their respects."

"So everyone keeps telling me." Because this woman was someone she had once known, Ena knew the woman was undoubtedly wondering why she hadn't attended her father's funeral. "I didn't know he was ill until he was gone," she started to explain.

Mrs. Baker reached over and squeezed Ena's hand. "Nobody's blaming you, dear. Family ties aren't always the easiest to maintain," she told Ena. "I just wanted you to know that when my Henry died, your dad was the first one at my door, managing things for me until I could get my head together and deal with things myself. I don't know where I would have been without him."

"My father did that?" Ena asked incredulously.

She couldn't remember a single instance over the years when her father actually went out with friends or, for that matter, even mentioned having any. How had that solitary man transformed himself into the perennial good neighbor?

Mrs. Baker nodded. "Your father."

"When I fell off my tractor and wound up breaking my leg, it was your dad who came over every day after he finished his own work to help out with mine. And when he couldn't come over, he sent that foreman of his over. The one you brought in to see the doc," Jeb Russell told her, adding his voice to Shirley Baker's.

That started the ball rolling. Within minutes, other people in the waiting room were speaking up, telling Ena about things that her father had selflessly done for them when they found themselves suddenly in need of a good neighbor.

Ena felt both stunned and overwhelmed. It was hard for her to reconcile this version of her father with the one she had grown up with and had always known. She felt cheated because he had never been this way with her and he had never allowed her to witness what was obviously a new, improved version of Bruce O'Rourke.

After she had left home, the man *had* reinvented himself.

Why this new, improved version never attempted to get in touch with her—especially after he had had her tracked down—was still very much a mystery to her. Yes, Mitch had given her a reason, but it was a relatively poor one and it didn't really begin to provide her with any answers to her questions.

When the door leading to the examination rooms in the rear of the medical clinic opened and Mitch came out, Ena was busy talking to another one of the patients. She didn't see him at first. When she did, she immediately shot up to her feet and quickly crossed over to the reception desk.

She saw a tall kind-looking man in a white lab coat talking to Mitch. He had to be the doctor, she decided. Why was he still talking to Mitch?

Was something else wrong?

Apprehension immediately returned to her in spades as she came closer.

"How is he?" she asked the man in the lab coat without any preamble.

Dr. Daniel Davenport turned his head in her direction. "You must be Ena O'Rourke," he said, putting out his hand to her.

Ena shook his hand without really taking note of what she was doing. She was completely focused on Mitch. "I am. How is he?" she repeated.

"You're right," Dan said to Mitch, who was standing right next to him. "She is really is as direct as her father was."

Ena immediately wanted to deny the similarity, but doing so would take her down another path and she didn't want to distract the doctor. She wanted her question answered.

Now.

Rephrasing her question, she asked, "Does he have a concussion?"

"I did a CAT scan. He does have a concussion, but it is only a very mild one," Dan told her.

Mitch appeared vindicated. "See, I told you I didn't have to come in," he said to her.

Dan continued talking as if Mitch hadn't said a word. "But you were right to bring him in," he said to Ena. "It's better to check these things out than to experience regrets later on." He glanced toward Mitch, then told Ena, "I'd definitely recommend a couple of days of rest for him."

"Rest. Got it," Ena said as if she was making the doctor a promise. "Anything else?" She wasn't about to rely on Mitch to tell her the doctor's instructions once they left here.

"He should be all right after that," Dan responded. "But if he experiences any complications—dizziness, nausea, trouble sleeping, that sort of thing," he elaborated, "I want you to call the clinic immediately and bring him back here."

"We won't have to make that call," Mitch told the doctor.

"Unless we do," Ena said, overruling Mitch.

Dan laughed quietly as he watched the couple leave his waiting room.

"I'd say that he's met his match. What do you think?" he asked the nurse.

"I think that you're right, Doctor," Debi told him, then handed Dan the medical file for the next patient waiting to see him.

"See, I told you that there was nothing to worry about," Mitch said as they walked back to his truck in the parking lot.

"That is *not* what I heard the doctor say," Ena responded.

"Maybe you should have had your ears checked while we were there," Mitch suggested.

Reaching his truck, he was about to open the driver's-side door. Ena managed to block his hand with her own, keeping him from opening the door.

"What are you doing?" Mitch asked, looking at her in confusion.

"I'll drive," she informed him.

Mitch was far from pleased. "The doc said I was okay."

"No, he said you had a mild concussion and to watch you for a couple of days," Ena corrected. "The man said nothing about watching you drive," she stressed. "Now, get into the truck on the passenger side—unless you want to stand here for the better part of the day and argue about it."

Mitch sighed and shook his head, then stopped abruptly, the color suddenly completely draining from his face.

Ena was instantly alert. "Did you just get dizzy?"

He expected her to gloat or utter those awful words: *I told you so.* When she didn't and exhibited concern instead, Mitch decided that maybe he should stop giving her a hard time. He acted grateful instead.

"Maybe I will sit in the passenger seat for now," he told her.

"Good choice," she agreed. She waited for Mitch to climb into the truck on the other side, fighting the urge to offer her help. She already felt she knew how he would react to that. "Ready?" she asked once he'd closed his door and buckled up.

"For your driving?" he quipped, covering up the fact that, just for a second, he'd felt dizzy again. "Not really."

Ena got in on the driver's side. "I'll have you know that I'm a very good driver."

"You forget, I've already had a sample of your driving. I was with you when you drove to the clinic," he reminded her. "Dallas must have different driving standards than we do."

"Dallas," she informed him coolly, "has decent roads."

"Does that mean that you don't speed there?" he asked, feigning surprise.

"I *didn't* speed to the clinic," she told him. "I was just trying to get you to the doctor before you could come up with a reason to bail on me," she informed him stiffly.

"Does that mean that you're going to be taking your time driving back to the ranch?" he questioned.

"Now that we know all you really need is some bed rest," she said, easing back on the accelerator, "yes, I'm going to be taking my time getting back to the Double E."

Mitch frowned when she mentioned bed rest.

"If you're expecting me to just lie around for the next two days—" he began.

Ena cut him off. "Yes, that's *exactly* what I'm expecting."

"Then I suggest you prepare yourself to be disappointed. I've got far too much to do to lie around like a lump for two days."

Her eyes narrowed. "I can have you tied to your bed."

For a second, he allowed himself to build on that image, but then, shaking it off, he said, "As tempting as that sounds, no, I'll have to pass on that."

"Did I give you the impression that this was up for a vote?" she asked. "If I did, then I'm sorry because it's not. You have no say in this. It's just me and the doctor." And then she relented. "We can compromise, and you can be on my dad's old recliner instead of a bed."

She had noticed the old chair the other day. It was shoved over in a corner of the living room. She could clean it up so that Mitch could use it.

"It's only a compromise if you put that recliner out in the middle of the corral so I can do the work I signed on for," he informed her.

"If you're going to give me a hard time," she fired back in a steely tone, "I wasn't kidding about having you tied up."

He laughed shortly at her threat. "Sorry, I don't mean to insult you but you're not strong enough to do that."

She was not the weakling he took her to be, Ena thought. "You'd be surprised," she told him. Then she went on to say, "But who says I was going to be the one to tie you up?" When she saw the perplexed expression on his face, she told him, "I'll get Wade, Billy and Felicity to hold you down and tie you up—and if they're not enough, I can always call in Miss Joan. If anyone can *make* you rest, it's Miss Joan."

He sighed. "Okay, Uncle," he cried, surrendering. "You win."

Ena laughed. "I figured threatening you with Miss Joan would tip the scales in my favor. This is for your own good," she told Mitch.

He was cornered and he knew it. There was no use in fighting the matter. Even so, Mitch blew out a frustrated breath.

"You really are a lot like your father," he told Ena. He saw her stiffen. "That's not a bad thing, you know."

"So I've been hearing," she said with a touch of exasperation in her voice. She still hadn't made her peace with the fact that her father had made this transformation *after* she had left town. "Those people in the waiting room, they all told me about what a good man my father was, how helpful he was, volunteering to help his neighbors when they needed him."

"He was and he did," Mitch affirmed.

"Where was this version of him when I was growing up?" she asked.

"I really can't answer that for you," Mitch admitted. "He was being busy, I guess. Maybe being overwhelmed by all the things he was trying to do. What matters, in the end, was the man that he became." He hoped she could take some comfort in that.

But it was obvious that she didn't. "I wouldn't know about that."

"I can tell you about him," Mitch volunteered. "So can some of the others on the ranch."

"When we get to the ranch, you're going to be resting, remember?" Ena reminded him.

"The doctor didn't say anything about resting my jaw muscle," he said.

"I'll place a call to the doctor when we get home,"

she said with such a straight face, he didn't know if she was being serious. "Maybe he just forgot to mention that little thing."

There was silence for a few minutes as Ena continued to drive, and then Mitch spoke. "I'm probably going to regret this…" he began, then stopped for a beat.

"Regret what?" she asked when he didn't continue.

"Saying this," he told her.

"Saying what?" she asked impatiently. The man could draw out a single syllable.

He took a deep breath, as if he needed the extra air to push the word out of his mouth. And then he finally told her, "Thanks."

"You're thanking me? For dragging your stubborn hide into town and to the doctor?" she guessed.

"No," he admitted, "for caring enough to see that something was off."

"Then you *are* dizzy," she said triumphantly because he'd finally admitted it.

"Was," Mitch corrected. "And I'll admit that it might not have been the worst idea to have me checked out. The doc told me that he'd seen a few of these cases go sideways."

Ena smiled. "So, let me get this straight. You agree that I did a good thing, overruling you and bringing you in to get checked out, is that it?" she asked him. He could hear the smile in her voice.

"Don't let it go to your head," he warned.

Her smile widened, her eyes crinkling as she spared him a look. "Too late."

Mitch sighed, feigning aggravation. "I knew I was going to regret this."

"Not as much as if we hadn't gone in and you suddenly started experiencing all the complications that go along with a head injury," she said seriously.

"This seems to be a personal crusade of yours," he commented.

"In a way, I guess it is." She paused for a moment, debating whether or not to share something with Mitch. To be honest, she was surprised he didn't already know, seeing how close he'd gotten to her father. "My uncle— my dad's younger brother—got thrown from a horse when I was a kid. He wasn't even trying to tame it. The horse was spooked by a rattler, reared, and my uncle just fell off. Hit his head, thought nothing of it and shook it off. A week later, he was dead," she said flatly, holding thoughts of the incident at bay. After all these years, the memory still hurt just as sharply as it had that day. "The doc at the hospital said the injury had caused a blood vessel to break and he bled out." She paused for a long moment before she could continue. Glancing at Mitch, she told him, "I just wanted to be sure that didn't happen to you."

"Oh. Well, thanks for that," he mumbled.

"Yeah, just remember that when I tell you to rest," she said.

This time he kept the words that rose to his lips in response to himself. He figured he owed it to her.

Chapter Fifteen

"This isn't necessary, you know," Mitch insisted as he watched Ena making up the sofa in the spare bedroom.

She didn't even bother stopping what she was doing to look in his direction. Instead, she focused on turning the sagging sofa into something that she would be able to sleep on.

His late boss's daughter had to be the most stubborn woman he had ever encountered, Mitch thought. He tried dissuading her one more time, although he had a feeling it was futile.

"I'm perfectly capable of spending the night in my bunk at the bunkhouse," he told her. "Or, if you don't trust me, I can sack out on the recliner."

When they had returned from the medical clinic, Ena had covered the faded leather chair with a sheet, as well as a comforter. Mitch had grudgingly spent the rest of the day there.

However, he had to admit that he had enjoyed having Ena make him dinner. She'd insisted that he eat that in the recliner, as well. Because Felicity had the afternoon off, Ena had made the meal—boiled chicken along with a bowl of homemade chicken soup. Mitch felt as if he were five years old again, but it was nice to be fussed over, although he would have never admitted it out loud.

But now, in his opinion, she was really going too far.

"You're sleeping here," she told him with finality as she finished making up the sofa. "And so am I."

Mitch blinked, wondering if he was hallucinating or if his hearing was suddenly going. He swallowed because his mouth had gone dry. "How's that again?"

"You heard me," she told him, turning around to look at him. "I'm sleeping in here."

That caught him completely off guard. He thought of the times he'd fantasized about just this sort of thing when they were back in high school. "Not that I mind," he told her in a hoarse voice. "But why?"

"I want to be here in case you have a seizure during the night," she said matter-of-factly.

"A what?" He stared at her. Was she kidding? But one look at her face and he saw she was serious. "Look, I appreciate you being concerned, but you've been watching way too many doctor programs on TV," he insisted. "I told you, I'm fine."

"Yes, I know what you keep saying," she replied. "But the doctor said you have a mild concussion." She waved at the sofa. "This is just precautionary. But if, during the night, you suddenly have a seizure or start throwing up, someone has to be here to look after you. Although it pains me to say it, none of those guys in the bunkhouse would know the first thing to do if that does happen."

He looked at her rather skeptically. "Oh, and you do?"

"Yes, I do," she informed him, adding, "I've had some first aid training."

Mitch wasn't sure if he believed her, but he supposed it was possible. He let her words sink in.

"Wow, you're just full of surprises, aren't you?" he marveled, giving her the benefit of the doubt.

She knew what he was trying to do—and she wasn't about to be diverted. "Don't turn this around, Parnell. We're talking about you, not me."

She was like a bulldog, he thought. Once she latched onto something, he couldn't shake her loose.

He decided to try another approach. "So I'm getting the bed and you're getting that lumpy thing over there that's supposed to pass as a sofa, is that it?" He frowned, looking at it. "That doesn't look very comfortable."

"Don't worry about me," she said, dismissing his observation.

Mitch looked thoughtfully at the double bed that was up against one wall. "You know, this bed's big enough to accommodate two people."

"Whatever you're thinking, Parnell, it's not happening," she informed him. "The whole idea of all this is for you to get some rest, not get yourself all worked up."

And that was as close to the subject of lovemaking as she intended to get—at least until he was completely out of the woods.

"We could each stay on our side of the bed," Mitch proposed, not ready to abandon the subject just yet.

She refused to allow herself to be tempted—even though she was. "This isn't a negotiation."

"So you're just going to be a dictator now?" Mitch asked.

It would have been more effective without the mischievous smile, she thought. Doing her best to sound tough, she said, "Watch me."

That was just the problem. He had been watching her. A lot. And the more he watched her, the more he found himself wanting her. Having her hovering over him like this, ministering to him, only made his longing grow that much stronger.

"You know," he said, lowering his voice seductively, "I usually sleep in the nude."

Now he was just saying anything to get a rise out of her, Ena thought. She would have known about a pajamaless sleeping habit if Mitch actually had one. There were no such things as secrets on the ranch. But for the moment, she pretended to believe him. "Not tonight you're not."

Resigned, Mitch gave up and lay back in the bed.

"All right," he told her. "You win."

"The outcome was never in doubt," she informed him. "See you in the morning, Mitch," she said, lying down on the sofa and shutting off the lamp on the side table. The room was suddenly bathed in darkness.

"You're sleeping in your clothes?" Mitch questioned. He was still dressed himself, but that was only because he'd been hoping to retreat back to the bunkhouse before she had become a human watchdog.

"I am tonight," she answered.

Ena tried to fluff up her pillow. It wasn't cooperating. Neither was the sagging sofa. It wasn't easy finding a comfortable position on it.

Mitch could hear her moving around and guessed

that the sofa was even more uncomfortable than she had bargained on.

"Offer still stands," he told her. "There's plenty of room in the bed."

"Go to sleep, Parnell," Ena ordered.

"Yes, ma'am."

"And stop grinning," she said. "I can hear the grin in your voice."

Which only made him smile more. But he dutifully said, "Yes, ma'am."

Ena remained awake for a while, anticipating any one of a number of things. But eventually, the sound of Mitch's even breathing lulled her to sleep.

The night went by without any further incident.

Ena had had every intention to get up before Mitch was awake. But when she finally opened her eyes, the first thing she was aware of was that Mitch had his head propped up on his fisted hand and he was looking at her.

Intently.

She frowned as she instantly sat up, still not totally conscious. She dragged her fingers through her hair, doing what she could to make herself appear presentable. It was hopeless, she decided.

She fixed Mitch with a glare. "Why aren't you still sleeping?"

"Because I'm an early riser," he replied. He'd been awake for a while and had spent the time just watching her sleep. "Do you know that you wrinkle your nose when you're sleeping?"

"I'll be sure to make a note of that," she replied crisply.

But Mitch wasn't finished with his observation yet. "It's kind of cute."

She supposed he was just trying to be nice. "Glad you approve of my wrinkled nose. More important, how are you feeling?"

He looked at her. "Like a slug who wants to get back to work."

Ena nodded, taking his answer in stride. "In other words, normal."

"Yes," he said, seizing on the word. "Normal!" All he wanted was for her to treat him as if everything was back to normal.

"Good." She smiled sweetly at him as she kicked off the covers and got off the sofa. "Then you have one more day to go."

Mitch gave her an exasperated look. "Ena O'Rourke, you are a cruel woman."

She wasn't doing this to win points with him. "Cruel or not, the doctor said to have you rest for a couple of days and we're sticking to that."

"I warn you, I'm going to go stir-crazy," he complained as he watched her head toward the room's doorway.

"Nobody ever went stir-crazy in two days," she assured him.

His mood grew just the slightest bit more desperate. "Then I'll be the first."

"You know, you could try being patient," she told Mitch.

He'd already thrown off his own covers and was sitting on the edge of the bed, itching to get moving. "Not in my nature."

"Learn," she told him as she left the room. "I'm going to see about breakfast."

Refusing to remain confined, Mitch brushed his

teeth, threw some water on his face and went down into the kitchen.

She'd expected him to protest, then give in the way he had yesterday. But that didn't seem to be happening, she thought when she saw him coming into the kitchen.

"What are you doing here?" Ena asked.

"Stretching my legs," he lied. "I was getting cramps in them because of all that *resting* I was doing."

Felicity, busy making breakfast, looked thoughtfully from Ena to the foreman who had just walked into her domain. She didn't ask any questions, but it was obvious from the look on her face that she was filling in the blanks for herself.

"Hungry?" she asked Mitch.

Mitch grinned. That was a question that he could answer without hesitation. "Starving."

The housekeeper nodded. "That is a good sign," she said with approval.

Ena had told the housekeeper about Mitch's visit to the medical center the moment she saw the woman. She was attempting to enlist Felicity's help.

"The doctor said he should rest," she insisted.

Felicity glanced over at the foreman. "And by the looks of him, he did. But too much rest makes a person feel useless and lazy. That is no way to run a ranch," the housekeeper concluded with authority.

Ena threw up her hands, knowing she couldn't fight both Felicity and Mitch.

"All right, if you promise not to exert yourself and to let the other hands do all the heavy stuff, you don't have to go back to bed after you eat. Good enough?" she asked Mitch.

The smile he flashed her caused her stomach to

tighten as a little thrill worked its way down her spine. It almost made her surrender worth it.

If she worried that the others would rag on Mitch for allowing himself to be restricted by her, she could have saved herself the grief. When the ranch hands saw him that morning, they greeted Mitch as if he were a conquering hero coming home from war.

Things quickly went back to normal after that. Mitch couldn't have been happier.

Because she had allowed her other responsibilities—both the accounts from her firm as well as the accounts in her father's poor excuse for a ledger—slide, she began putting in more time working on them. So much so that she was back to losing sleep because she stayed up late and was up early, doing her best to attempt to catch up.

At times it began to feel like a losing battle, but she wasn't about to give up, even though she felt herself fading.

Every shred of time she had was utilized.

"Hey, ever hear that old chestnut 'Physician, heal thyself'?" Mitch asked her one evening several weeks later.

He was standing in the doorway of the study, watching her working after she had already put in a full day's work on the ranch. Something stirred within him. Damn, but he had never gotten over her, he thought.

He walked into the room.

"I'm aware of it," she told Mitch without looking up. Having put in time on her firm's accounts, she was back to trying to figure out what to do about rectifying her father's rather creative record keeping.

"Then maybe you should think about giving it a try," he said.

"Later," she responded. "If you hadn't noticed, I'm busy right now."

"I noticed," he answered. "Seems to me that you're busy all the time."

She was getting cross-eyed, trying to follow the numbers on the page. "Uh-huh."

"You're not listening to me, are you?" he asked.

"Uh-huh."

That was what he thought. This time, he put his hand down on the ledger, blocking her view.

"Hey!" she cried in protest, looking at him.

He could be just as stubborn as she was, Mitch thought. And this was for her own good. "You need a break."

"What I *need* is to get this done," she countered, physically removing his hand from the ledger.

He could have kept his hand there if he wanted to. Instead, he let her move it. But he needed to get her to see things his way—for her own good.

"You're going to make yourself sick, you know that. You're not just burning the candle at both ends—you're burning the candle in the middle, too," Mitch insisted.

She closed her eyes, searching for strength. "Thank you for your concern, but—"

Mitch didn't let her finish. "Does this conversation sound familiar to you?" he asked. Because she didn't say anything, he went on, "Let me refresh your memory for you—you and I had this exact same conversation a few weeks ago, except I was the one being lectured and I was the one insisting I was fine. You, in your infinite wisdom, pointed out that I wasn't." He looked directly into her eyes. "Allow me to return the favor now," he requested.

Ena sighed, knowing Mitch was right. That didn't

make it any easier for her to back off. "You can be a royal pain, you know."

He grinned at her and said, "Right back at you."

Dead tired, she still made an attempt to reason with him. "Look, I can let the accounts from my old firm go for the time being. I can say that I've decided to take a prolonged vacation and focus on the ranch for now—but that hodgepodge that my father called a ledger? I can't just ignore that. Too many things are coming due soon and if I don't find a way to get creative and to manage to secure an extension on the bank's note, the ranch is going to be under new ownership and it's not going to be mine, Parnell."

He looked at her thoughtfully. "Maybe you can find a way to make the bank give you that extension you mentioned. The bank really doesn't want your ranch. It's more profitable for them if you keep the ranch and repay the loan."

Ena scrubbed her hands over her face and then looked at Mitch. "You know, for a cowboy, you think like an accountant."

"I'll pretend you didn't say that," Mitch told her, keeping a straight face. "Look, there's a party this weekend. I know for a fact that the bank manager is going to be there. Maybe if we approach him in a friendly, neutral setting, he might be open to seeing things your way. Maybe you'll even come up with a viable suggestion about a repayment schedule by then."

She hadn't gotten past the first sentence. "A party?"

He nodded. "Miss Joan's holding the party for Dr. Dan and his wife. It's celebrating the clinic being open for ten years. Everyone's invited," he added before she could protest that she hadn't gotten an invitation so she couldn't go. "You wouldn't want to insult Miss Joan by not attending."

She rolled her eyes. "Heaven forbid."

"Not to mention the fact that you could use the break," he told her. "By my count, you've been doing nothing but work ever since you got here and you above all people know that you need to balance that out," he told her.

"I balance it out," she protested. When he looked at her, she told him, "I sleep."

"Not much fun in that," Mitch told her. "C'mon, you'll be killing two birds with one stone. You'll be approaching the bank manager on neutral ground and you'll be getting some much-needed recreation. You know what they say, all work and no play, et cetera."

Ena raised her eyes to his. "Are you saying that I'm dull?" she asked, playing out the rest of the saying in her head.

Mitch smiled at her, his eyes saying things to her that he couldn't say out loud.

Her breath caught in her throat as she tried to ignore the way her pulse had picked up, responding to the way he was looking at her—and making her want things that would only cause problems in the long run.

"No, I'd never say you were dull," he told her. "Anything but dull," he added with enthusiasm, his words all but caressing her face.

"Is that a compliment, Parnell, or am I just being extremely punchy?" she asked.

"That was a compliment," he assured her. "You are the most well-rounded, fascinating woman I have ever met and I certainly wouldn't think of insulting you," Mitch said. He cleared his throat before he said anything else. "So, about that party…" He allowed his voice to trail off as he waited for her to agree.

She sighed. "When did you say it was?"

Mitch knew that meant yes. "This Saturday."

Ena shrugged. "All right, I'll go. For the good of the ranch—and not to insult Miss Joan."

His grin widened. "Good idea."

Chapter Sixteen

Mitch glanced up at the sky. He was able to tell time by the position of the sun as easily as if he were looking at his watch. Right now, it was getting late.

"We'd better start getting ready if we're going to make that party that Miss Joan's throwing," he said to Ena as he stripped off his gloves. He shoved them into his back pocket and started to head out of the corral.

"Yeah, about that," Ena replied slowly, deliberately avoiding Mitch's eyes. She always felt as if his piercing blue eyes could see right through her and she really didn't want to deal with that right now.

Looking at the ground, she told him, "I'm not going." When Mitch said nothing in response, she could feel herself beginning to fidget inside. She was anticipating an argument. "A party's no place to talk business, and besides, there's just too much to do here." She waved her hand at the straw they had been spreading around in the stalls that was a long way from finished. "I can't just take off and play hooky for the better part of the day. What if something goes wrong?"

More silence.

She pressed her lips together, already knowing what he had to say about that. "Okay, so the hands might be able to handle it, but I'd still rather be here myself—just in case," she insisted.

Running out of words, Ena finally looked up at Mitch. The man could be so infuriating.

"Well? Aren't you going to say *anything*?" she asked.

The foreman looked at her with a calm, knowing expression on his face. "Scared?" he asked.

Ena was instantly incensed. "No, I'm not scared," she snapped indignantly.

"Good," he concluded, "then you can go." He glanced at his watch. The minutes were ticking away, and he hated arriving late. "I'll be over to the house to pick you up in an hour. Is that enough time, or do you need more to get ready?"

She didn't know what sort of women he was used to, but she certainly didn't need an hour to get dressed. "I don't need more time—"

He cut her off. "Great, then I'll be there sooner," Mitch told her. He started to leave the corral, then stopped and looked over his shoulder. "You're not walking," he observed. Instead of asking her why, he offered, "I can take you back to the ranch house on my horse."

Ena sighed and finally walked out of the corral. Then with a determined gait, she walked right past him.

"Guess we don't need the horse," he said, addressing Ena's back.

Ena didn't turn around to answer him. All things considered, she felt it was better that way.

* * *

"Wow, I forgot how well you clean up," Mitch said when, true to his word, he arrived at the ranch house less than an hour later to pick her up. Felicity had opened the door to admit him in.

"If that's your idea of a compliment, I think you need to work on your technique," Ena told him, trying very hard not to let him see that his reaction had secretly pleased her.

He nodded solemnly.

"Duly noted," Mitch responded. "But just so you know, that did come from the heart." His eyes swept over the deep blue dress, appreciating the way it clung to her curves—just the way he would have liked to if things were different. "Maybe I should bring my gun with me," he debated.

Ena picked up the shawl she was bringing with her. She had found it earlier in the recesses of her closet. She had forgotten to pack the shawl and take it with her when she'd left ten years ago. The shawl had belonged to her mother. A bittersweet feeling had filled her when she had thrown the shawl over her shoulders and looked herself over in the mirror earlier. She'd come very close to crying.

"Why?" she asked Mitch, now puzzled by his desire to bring a weapon with him. Forever was nothing if not peaceful.

His grin told her the answer was self-explanatory, but he indulged her anyway. "To make sure that nobody gets any ideas about getting you to spend your time exclusively with them." His eyes swept over her again. "You are really something in that dress," he told her.

Ena looked at him for a long moment. And then she

nodded at his compliment. "I guess that's an improvement—as long as you don't wind up shooting anyone."

"Only if I have to," Mitch deadpanned. And then he smiled at her and, his voice softening, said, "You do look really nice."

"Thank you. So do you," she told him, returning the compliment.

Mitch's smile deepened, causing two dimples to appear in his cheeks and turning his rugged face into a boyish one.

"Thanks," he told her. Then he added, "Let's just say you bring out the best in me."

With that, he presented his elbow to her.

Ena was tempted to ask if he thought she was going to trip over something, but she refrained. This wasn't the time to be flippant or act independent. Instead, she quietly slipped her arm through his.

"Well, don't you two look pretty," Wade declared with a wide grin when he saw them leaving the house and walking toward Mitch's freshly washed truck.

Mitch didn't rise to the bait. "You're just jealous," he told the wrangler he considered his right-hand man.

"Yeah, I am," Wade admitted. He never took his eyes off Ena. "You look nice, boss." This time his words were directed toward Ena.

She smiled at him. "Thank you," she murmured.

"Get back to work," Mitch told the other man, pretending to be stern. And then he winked at the ranch hand. Wade nodded, then went back to the corral.

Helping her into the passenger side of his truck, Mitch took Ena's hand in his. He looked at her, slightly surprised.

"Your hand's icy." The weather didn't warrant that.

"Are you cold?" he asked. Maybe she needed something more than just that shawl. "I can go back in and—"

She shook her head. "I'm just nervous," she confessed.

So much for getting her something warmer, Mitch thought. Rounding the hood of his truck, he got in on the driver's side.

"Why?" he asked. This wasn't like her, he thought.

She shrugged as he started up the truck. "I haven't seen a lot of these people in ten years. They're probably all going to be judging me when they see me, wondering where I've been and why I wasn't there at my father's funeral."

"No, they won't." He sounded so sure of his answer that, for a second, Ena clung to it. "They'll all be envious that you got to leave Forever and make something of yourself. Truth is," he told her, "a lot of them wanted to do just that, but for one reason or another, they never did. But you're the one who did. You got to live an adventure."

"An adventure, huh?" His description amused her. "Funny, I just thought I didn't have a choice. It was either leave Forever, or slowly die by inches in front of a man who hated me since the day I was born. At least," she said with a deep sigh, "that's what I thought at the time."

He glanced in her direction. "And now?"

She thought of all the things Mitch had told her about her father, about the way the man had claimed to feel toward the end of his life.

"And now I'm not so sure." She took a breath, collecting herself as she looked at him. "Can't you drive this thing any faster?"

"I could," Mitch allowed.

He was driving slowly because he wanted to have more time with Ena. There were always other people—the wranglers, not to mention Felicity—around and they couldn't have these more personal conversations with all those ears listening in. But they were alone now, so she couldn't feel that anyone was eavesdropping on their conversation even if it *did* get personal.

"Then do it," Ena instructed.

Which was her way of saying that she didn't like the way this conversation was going, Mitch thought. Well, at least he had broken some ground. That was good enough for now.

Pressing down on the accelerator, he said, "Yes, ma'am," and they took off, going twice as fast as they had been.

Because Murphy's had more available space than Miss Joan's diner did, Miss Joan had decided to hold the anniversary party for Dan and the medical clinic there. Which was just as well because the party turned out to be a joint venture out of necessity. Miss Joan provided the food and the Murphy brothers provided the liquid libations as well as the entertainment, courtesy of Liam Murphy and his band. A professional musician who had gone on tour more than a few times, Liam, the youngest of the three brothers, still enjoyed performing in his own hometown. And no matter where his tour took him, Liam never felt more appreciated than he did back in Forever, where it had all begun.

"This is nice," Ena had to admit as she and Mitch walked inside Murphy's.

Looking around, she found that she recognized several faces. And then several more.

Everywhere she looked within the packed saloon, she

discovered even more faces that were at least vaguely familiar to her. The nervousness she had managed to disguise began to dissipate in earnest.

And then, suddenly, the crowd parted, shifting to either the right or to the left, creating a space for a rather elegant-looking Miss Joan to make her way over to them.

Ena hardly recognized the woman.

"You got her to come," Miss Joan said to Mitch, sounding genuinely pleased. Her eyes crinkled just a bit as she said, "Nice work."

Mitch nodded, pretending to accept his due. "I only had to handcuff her to the back of the truck for part of the way."

"No, he didn't," Ena protested. Mitch looked so serious she was afraid Miss Joan might believe the fantastic claim.

Miss Joan raised a brow in Ena's direction. "Then he had to do it the whole way?" Miss Joan sounded completely serious. Ena began to vehemently deny the statement—and then she heard Miss Joan's high-pitched laugh. "Just having a little fun with you, dear. Just like you should be having," the woman added. She nodded in approval as Liam and his band started up another number. "Good music," she noted. She turned her hazel eyes back toward Ena standing beside Mitch. "Dance."

It wasn't a suggestion.

Mitch slipped one hand around Ena's waist and wrapped his other one around her hand.

Ena looked at him in surprise. "What are you doing?"

"Just following Miss Joan's orders," he told her. "If we don't," he whispered against her ear, "Miss Joan's liable to take out a gun and start shooting at the floor around our feet the way they used to when they wanted to get someone to dance in those old cowboy movies."

He had to be kidding, Ena thought. "Miss Joan wouldn't do that," she protested.

"Maybe not, but I'm not brave enough to find out," Mitch said as he began to sway with her to the slow song that Liam was playing.

Ena wanted to protest that she didn't want to dance, especially not to a slow song, but she didn't want to cause a scene, either. So dancing with Mitch turned out to be the less problematic of the two alternatives—even if it was so close.

Leaning into him, Ena tried as hard as she could not to let herself enjoy what was happening. But she had to admit that it was really difficult for her to remain aloof. Especially since she really *was* enjoying dancing with Mitch. Enjoying being held by him. With so very little effort, she knew that she could allow herself to get carried away.

She had to remain vigilant, Ena silently told herself. Otherwise, she could easily wind up melting— and people would talk.

"People are watching us," she told Mitch, feeling more than a little self-conscious. But even so, the warm feeling she was experiencing only seemed to increase in scope.

"That's because they're all jealous of me," he told her in an easygoing voice.

"No, they're not," she protested.

"Sure they are," he contradicted. He drew his head back for a moment, his eyes looking into hers. "And why not? I'm dancing with the most beautiful woman here."

She struggled to keep her distance, at least emotionally. "I had no idea you were this smooth," she told him.

"If you're referring to my dancing, I've been practicing," Mitch admitted. And then he added, "With Felicity."

"I wasn't talking about your dancing technique, I was referring to your tongue," she clarified.

"Oh. Well, what can I say? You inspire me," he replied.

Despite trying to maintain an emotional distance between them, she couldn't help laughing.

"What's so funny?" he asked.

"Back in high school, you just kept to yourself. I tried to get your attention a few times," she admitted. "But you always acted like I didn't exist."

"I told you," he reminded her. "I knew that you existed. I also knew that your father existed, and if I made one move on you, just one, I knew that man would skin me alive."

She shook her head. He couldn't have believed that. "You could have made all the moves you wanted. My father wouldn't have cared."

"Just because he never said it out loud didn't mean that he didn't care," Mitch told her. "All you had to do was look into that man's eyes and you knew that he cared. A lot."

He was just trying to make her feel better, she thought. But he couldn't because she knew the truth about the situation.

"Yeah, right." The two words fairly dripped with sarcasm.

"Trust me," he assured her. "It's a guy thing. One guy knows what another one feels. And that man cared," Mitch told her. "He just didn't know how to let you know that."

They would just go round and round about this and not get anywhere. She wanted to drop the subject—

permanently. "I don't feel like talking about my father," she told him, laying her head on Mitch's shoulder as the band started to play another song.

Mitch felt all the powerful emotions he was trying so hard to keep under lock and key struggling against their restraints. For now, he would just focus on holding her and nothing more.

"I never said a word," he told her.

Taking a breath, he found himself breathing in the scent of her hair.

Careful, he warned himself. It was all too easy to get carried away. All it took was one misstep on his part and he could wind up regretting it forever if he scared her off.

It was an evening Mitch didn't want to see end, but perforce, it had to.

But not before he had managed, with Miss Joan's help, to get Ena together with A.J. Prescott, the bank's manager.

More than anything, when Miss Joan brought the man over, Ena just wanted to turn around and run. Dozens of reasons why she shouldn't have this impromptu "meeting" popped up in her head.

However, sensing that it was a now-or-never situation, Ena knew she had to plead her case with Prescott since it was his bank that held the mortgage note on the Double E Ranch.

Keeping in mind what Mitch had told her, that the bank preferred not to foreclose on properties but have them be productive moneymakers, Ena sucked up her courage and laid out her plan on how to make the horse ranch more profitable.

Somewhere along the line, as she talked almost nonstop to the manager, she also brought up the "miracle cure" for migraines by Mitch's mother. When Prescott looked intrigued, she proposed a side business in which she and Mitch could sell the homemade product, comprised of natural ingredients that had already individually been approved by the FDA. She was certain that people would react to the product the way she had. The added proposed sales would be enough to put them over the top as far as being able to keep the ranch running and in the black.

All she needed was for the bank to approve an extension.

Prescott remained quiet for a very long moment. Then, looking over toward Miss Joan, who was standing several feet away from Ena, he finally nodded.

"Considering your father's long-term history with our bank, I'm sure that we will be able to arrange what we call a good faith extension. I'll have McGreevy, our loan officer, draw up the terms and you can look them over. If you find them satisfactory, you can sign the document and keep the ranch. You're better suited to ranching than the bank is," Prescott told her with a smile.

"That's enough business talk for now," Miss Joan declared, coming in between Ena and the manager. "Have some more apple pie, A.J.," Miss Joan suggested. "And you, I believe you owe that studly foreman of yours another dance. Go, dance with him before I do," she urged, putting her hand to Ena's back and pushing her in Mitch's direction.

Ena smiled, feeling both empowered and giddy at the same time because of what had just transpired in the saloon.

"Yes, ma'am," she told Miss Joan as she went to do as the woman advised.

Chapter Seventeen

"You know, for someone who dug in her heels about attending that little shindig today, you wound up practically closing the place down," Mitch laughed as he drove them back to the Double E Ranch. The last time he had looked at his watch, it was almost eleven thirty.

She pretended to frown at him. "Don't lecture me, Parnell. This is the first time I've felt this kind of relief in a long time. I guess I just lost track of time," she confessed.

"Hey, this isn't a lecture," he protested. "I know better than anyone how hard you've been working since you got here. Don't forget, I was the one who suggested that you come to this thing in the first place and blow off some steam," Mitch reminded her.

She hadn't meant to sound as if she was blaming him. "I wound up doing more than that, thanks to you and Miss Joan," she told him. The truth of it was things had gone so well she felt as if she were flying. "It looks like we're going to be getting that extension on the ranch's loan."

He had been standing to the side at the time, acutely aware of everything that was happening because he was so in tune to her body language. He smiled at her now. "You're the one responsible for that, Ena. We had nothing to do with it."

He was the one who had given her the courage to step up and make her pitch to Prescott, not to mention that if it weren't for him, she wouldn't have thought up her strategy with his mother's migraine cure.

"You're the one who got the ball rolling," she pointed out.

"And you're the one who knocked that ball out of the park," he stressed, picking up on her metaphor as he brought his truck to a stop in front of the house. He got out, rounded the truck's hood and came up to the passenger side. "End of the line, boss lady," he said, opening the door for her.

Ena took his hand and got out. "I don't want this day to be over yet," she told him. "Would you like to come inside for a drink?"

She'd already had a couple after her business with Prescott had concluded and Mitch wasn't certain how well she held her liquor. He didn't want alcohol to be the reason things got out of hand.

"Are you sure that's such a good idea?" he asked, bringing her to her door.

Her lips quirked in a bemused smile. "Are you accusing me of trying to get you drunk so I can have my way with you?"

He wasn't sure if she was serious, but he took no

chances. "No, I didn't mean that. I just thought that you might—"

Ena laughed, unlocking the front door. "Relax, Parnell, I'm just kidding. And you don't have to worry about me, either. The one thing I *did* inherit from my father is his ability to hold his liquor. It would take a lot more than two drinks to have any sort of effect on me."

"What would three drinks do?"

"Might make me smile wider," she answered with a wink.

Maybe it was okay to come in for that drink, Mitch decided. "I'd like to see that," he told her. "Okay, you talked me into it," he said, following her inside. "Just remember, this was your idea."

"Funny, I seem to remember that this was yours," she said innocently, closing the front door behind him.

"I don't mean going to the celebration in the first place," Mitch told her. "I'm talking about having a nightcap."

Turning on the light beside the door, Ena crossed to where she knew her father used to keep the liquor. There were still a couple of bottles in the cabinet.

"Less talking, more doing," she said, taking out a half-filled bottle of Wild Turkey whiskey. There were a few mismatched glasses on the counter; she selected two.

"You know, someone else might point out that that's a really loaded statement," Mitch said as he watched her fill two glasses halfway with the amber liquid.

"Someone else?" she echoed, handing him his glass. "But not you?"

He accepted the glass from her and took a sip just to strengthen his resolve. Maybe it was just his imagination, but she looked even more desirable than usual in the low light.

The liquid coursed through his veins, doing little to subdue what was going on inside of him.

His eyes met hers and he could feel his pulse quicken. "You're making it really hard for me to remember my place, boss lady."

Ena shifted. She was only inches away from him. There was just enough space for a breath of air to come between them.

And then even that space was gone.

She had yet to take a sip of her drink. Instead, she raised her eyes to his. "And just what is your place, Mitch?"

Her low voice instantly undulated all along his skin.

"Back in the bunkhouse." He nodded vaguely in the general direction.

"But you're not back in the bunkhouse right now," she pointed out quietly. "You're here, with me."

Heaven help him, good intentions or not, he was really losing ground here, not to mention he was also losing his resolve. The only way he had a chance of doing the right thing was to say something clumsy and crass to her to make her back off.

"Are you trying to seduce me, boss lady?" he asked her.

Rather than take offense, or back off the way he thought she would, Ena merely asked him, "What makes you think that?"

"Every fiber of my being," he answered. Mitch was really struggling now not to just grab hold of Ena and pull her into his arms, giving in to the waves of desire that were insisting on persistently washing over him and drenching him.

Damn, he should have stayed firm and not come in, he thought. Instead, all he could focus on now were her lips as she spoke to him, drawing him in further and further.

"So what's stopping you?" Ena asked.

He was brutally honest in his response. "My sense of self-preservation."

Ena rose on her toes, her tantalizing mouth within an inch of his. "I'm not planning on destroying you," she whispered.

He could feel her breath on his skin, could feel himself weakening as desire blossomed full bore within him, growing so quickly in proportion that it stunned him even as it took him prisoner.

"You might not be planning on it," he told her, his throat growing dry, "but that doesn't mean it's not going to happen."

She turned the tables on him and said the one word that he had said to her when he was trying to get her to attend the party earlier.

"Scared?"

His answer wasn't the one she was expecting. "Terrified," he confessed.

She wasn't sure she understood. "Of me?" she asked in disbelief.

"No, of me," he told her. He curled his fingers into his hands. "If I let go right now, I'm not sure if I can stop myself. Or even manage to hold myself in check."

Ena put her hand on his chest. Warmth instantly generated from the points of contact. "What if I told you that I'm not afraid?"

"I'd tell you that you should be." He said the words so quietly they sounded more like an invitation than a reason for her to flee.

"Let me be the judge of that," she told him, her lips so close to his now that he could almost taste the words as she uttered them.

And that finally did it. Mitch lost what little control he was trying so desperately to hang on to.

The next second, he was no longer attempting to block his urges. Instead, he pulled Ena to him, his arms wrapping around her as he lowered his mouth to hers.

And then he did what he'd been wanting to do since the very first moment he had laid eyes on her back in high school, more than ten years ago.

He kissed her.

His kiss deepened to the point that he lost all concept of anything beyond the small circle that the two of them created. Lost himself in the taste, the feel, the very scent of her.

This was exactly the way she had imagined it would be, Ena thought as her heart leaped up.

Better.

The delicious taste of his lips against hers reduced her to a mass of swirling, molten desire.

Her arms went around his neck and she completely lost herself in him, experiencing not just the rush of desire but all the vast cravings and appetites that were created in its wake.

She couldn't remember the last time she had even had any time to enjoy the company of a man in her life, much less want to make love with him the way she now ached to do with Mitch. Work had always seemed so much more important to her than just a passing dalliance.

But that was because none of the men she had encountered while building up her professional life had ever been anything like Mitch.

There was something about Mitch that made her want to break all the rules she had set for herself and not give a damn that they were being broken.

Technically she was his boss, but she didn't want Mitch to think of her that way now. She just wanted them to be on the same equal footing for one precious evening.

She wanted to make love with him—and to have him want to make love with her, as well as *to* her.

Suddenly, Ena felt herself tottering on the brink of disappointment when Mitch drew his head back and looked at her.

"Are you sure about this?" he asked.

"Are you having second thoughts?" she heard herself asking. Maybe he didn't find her desirable and here she was, forcing herself on him. The thought stung more than she would have imagined.

She had no idea how to pull out of this tailspin that was about to claim her.

And then Mitch said, "Oh, Lord, no. You're a beautiful, desirable woman and no sane man would want to step away from you, much less have second thoughts about what's happening here. But I don't want you getting the wrong idea," he told her, even though just voicing those words cost him, because more than anything in the world, he didn't want her pulling away from him.

Ena's heart was racing so fast she thought it was going to break her ribs and leap out of her chest. She also knew that she was in danger of totally crumbling if he stopped what was about to happen right now.

"What's the right idea?" she asked in a barely audible whisper.

Oh, to hell with it, he thought. He'd done his best to be noble but he was only human. "The right idea is that

I'm having trouble keeping my hands off you because I've had fantasies about you from the very first time I saw you." Then, to prove that this wasn't just a line, he told her exactly when that was. "February 6, second-period English class."

And just like that, Ena melted. "Damn," she murmured, "you couldn't have said anything sexier if you tried."

His eyes crinkled as he smiled at her. "Guess I'm doomed."

Ena threaded her arms around his neck again and smiled up into his eyes. "Guess you are."

This time when their lips met, she secretly marveled that something akin to a spontaneous combustion didn't occur. There was certainly enough heat being generated between them to cause it.

She felt his lips slip down her throat, then press warm kisses along first one side of her neck, then the other, creating all sorts of havoc within her stomach and limbs.

Lost in the sensations he was creating, she reached for the buttons of his shirt, but Mitch shifted and suddenly, she felt herself being swept up into his arms. He started walking.

Dazed, confused, she looked at him.

"Felicity might come down for a midnight snack," he told her, heading toward the stairs. "We wouldn't want to broaden her *education*," he warned.

Ena suppressed a giggle.

She realized Mitch was taking her up to her room. Her excitement increased twofold as anticipation of what was to come once her door was closed took hold of her.

She managed to keep herself in check until Mitch

reached the landing. The moment he did, she let her ardor loose.

He had to stop walking for a second as her hot kisses landed on his face, his neck, the lobes of his ears, everywhere she could reach.

The sound of his increasingly heavier breathing told her that she was getting to him, which in turn made her even more excited.

"You are driving me totally crazy," he gasped, trying to catch his breath. His arms tightened around her to avoid dropping her, but, he discovered, it wasn't easy maintaining his hold on her.

The second they were in her room and he had closed the door with his elbow, he crossed to her bed and laid her down. The next second, he joined her, hardly breaking their contact for more than a fraction of a second.

He eagerly undid the zipper at her back, then tugged at the material, sliding her dress down the curves of her body until it was just a discarded scrap of material on the floor.

He couldn't take his eyes off her.

"You're overdressed," she breathed, tugging on his belt and the shirt he had tucked in beneath it.

"I am," he agreed, or at least thought he did. His head was spinning, intoxicated by her to the point that down was up, and up was down, and anything beyond the bed didn't exist. He didn't know if he said the words out loud or only thought them.

All he knew was that he wanted her.

His fingers flew over the buttons of his shirt, undoing whatever she hadn't already opened. He pulled off his boots in what seemed like one uninterrupted movement. His jeans quickly followed his boots, leaving him only wearing one last small article of material.

And then it was her turn again.

Mitch swiftly removed her bra and underwear in what seemed like one fluid motion.

His eyes devoured her. "You're so beautiful it hurts."

"Now that," she murmured as she linked her arms around his neck again and brought him down to her, "is a compliment."

She could almost feel his smile as it spread along his lips. "Glad you approve."

"I do. I do," she declared before she sealed her mouth to his again.

They melded, a tangle of arms and legs and sealed hot body parts, rolling around on the bed and reveling in the sizzling press of two bodies searching for at least a temporary moment of salvation.

He surprised her by *not* immediately taking her. Instead, Mitch further impressed her by showing her how patient he could be. He made love to her by degrees, kissing her over and over again, priming her body for the final ultimate moment.

Mitch artfully heightened her anticipation until she was certain she was going to explode waiting for him to make them one single unit.

Just as she was about to take the lead because she couldn't wait any longer, Mitch was suddenly right over her. He was balancing his weight on his elbows. Then, his eyes on hers, he parted her legs with his knee.

Her breath caught in her throat as he entered her, her heart all but slamming against her rib cage. The next moment, he began to move, slowly, deliberately, each pass increasing in rhythm and speed.

He was going faster and faster. Ena found herself racing with him, determined to reach that final pinnacle when he did. And when they reached it, the explosion shuddered through their bodies. A feeling of joy all but drenched her. The sensation was so much more intense than anything she might have anticipated.

Her arms tightened around Mitch as he held tightly on to her.

She felt his smile against her neck as he slowly descended back to earth, reaching it at the exact same moment that she did.

She didn't want to move. Instead, she just wanted to savor the moment and pretend that it was never going to end.

Even though she knew it would, all too soon.

Chapter Eighteen

Mitch shifted his body, moving to the side so that his weight was no longer on Ena. Propping himself up on his elbow, he smiled at her.

"You were magnificent," he said, his voice caressing her.

"Funny, I was going to say the same thing to you," Ena teased.

Mitch gently brushed his fingers through her hair lightly framing her face. "I was inspired."

Ena raised her eyebrow, amused. "Oh?"

He heard the mischief in her voice and grinned as he drew her closer. "Give me a couple of minutes and I'm sure I'll be inspired again," he promised.

"A couple of minutes?" Ena questioned. "That seems like a long time," she commented, punctuating each and every word with a kiss.

"You've got to remember," he told her with breathless effort, "that you took a lot out of me."

"I know," she said, her eyes crinkling as she continued kissing him between each word she uttered. Pausing for a second to look into his eyes, she resumed pressing kisses to his face and throat. "And I loved every minute of it."

His resistance evaporating, Mitch took hold of her, pulling Ena on top of him. The next second, without any warning, he suddenly reversed their positions so that she was beneath him.

"No more than I did, Ena," he assured her.

And then there was no more talking. Instead, he lost himself in her, taking her back across the wild, passionate terrain they had already crossed only a few memorable moments ago.

Ena slipped into the warm, welcoming embrace that lovemaking created, reveling in the way being with Mitch like this made her feel.

Ena blinked, trying to focus her mind and her eyes as she slowly woke up. Moving her shoulders against the mattress, she stretched, doing her best to come to.

When she did, she realized that the space beside her was empty.

Mitch was gone.

Well, what did you expect? That he was going to serenade you with banjo music the second you opened your eyes? You had a great night, but now it's back to normal, she told herself.

Now the best thing that she could do was to *act* normal. No muss, no fuss and definitely not anything that would make anyone else suspect that they had spent the night together.

Throwing the covers aside, she got up and quickly got ready, telling herself over and over that this was just

another day on the ranch and that there was work that
needed to be done.

Work, Ena reminded herself, that now *could* be done
because she had managed to get the bank to grant them
that much-needed extension.

She caught herself humming as she went downstairs.

"Well, you certainly look happy," Felicity said, greet-
ing her when Ena walked into the kitchen. The woman's
dark eyes swept over her. "Did you have a good night?"
the housekeeper asked.

Ena had no idea if Felicity was making idle conversation or if the housekeeper had somehow sensed what
had happened between Mitch and her last night and the
woman was making a general comment on it.

Hoping it was the former, Ena decided to throw a few
specifics into her answer. "The party at Murphy's was
very lively, so yes, I had a very good time."

The knowing look in Felicity's dark eyes told her the
housekeeper wasn't really referring to that, but at least
for now, to keep things simple, Ena decided that was
her story and she was sticking to it.

"By the way," Ena said innocently, "did Mitch come
by already?"

Felicity shook her head. "No, I did not see Mr. Mitch.
He and the caballeros are working as usual." Making
something on the stove, she briefly glanced in Ena's
direction. "Horses need to be fed and groomed. They
do not care if it is the weekend or not."

"Very true," Ena agreed. She picked up a piece of bread
to put into the toaster. "I'll just grab a piece of toast," she
told the woman.

Felicity turned from the stove and gave her a very
frosty eye.

"No, you will sit down and have breakfast like a

civilized person. Engines do not run on air. They need fuel," the housekeeper declared, leaving absolutely no room for argument.

Ena didn't even have to think about it. "Okay, I'll have breakfast," she said, surrendering.

She felt too good to get into an argument with the woman—all she wanted to do was be able to get out and find Mitch as quickly as possible—not to say anything in particular, just to prove to herself that last night had really happened.

Felicity set the plate down in front of Ena and then stepped back as the latter began to eat. The woman's thin lips puckered into a disapproving frown.

"You are not a vacuum cleaner," Felicity said sharply. "You are supposed to chew your food, not gulp it down in a chunk."

"I am chewing," Ena told the housekeeper, consuming the food the woman had placed in front of her as quickly as possible.

Felicity crossed her arms before her, a monument of disapproval. "Do not blame me if you wind up getting sick," she said.

"I wouldn't dare," Ena murmured under her breath.

Finished, she pushed the plate away from her and got to her feet.

"Thank you," she called out to the housekeeper as she hurried to the door.

Felicity shook her head again, following Ena to the front door.

"A woman is always supposed to keep a man waiting," the housekeeper informed her. But Felicity knew that she was wasting her breath, addressing the air. Ena was already gone.

Even though she had hurried out, Ena heard what

Felicity had said. To be honest, part of her agreed with the housekeeper. That was how the game was usually played, at least in the beginning.

But she didn't want to play any games. She never had. What she wanted was to be able to enjoy Mitch and his company for as long as possible, especially since in her heart of hearts she knew she was supposed to be on a schedule.

She was fairly certain that was how Mitch saw it. He probably assumed that in six months—less now because she'd already put in some time—she would go back to her world. Depending on the situation, she would have either sold the ranch to someone local or, more likely, kept the ranch herself. In that case she would have Mitch run the place for her while she went back to Dallas to do what she did best: work with numbers.

The moment she laid out her plan for her herself, she suddenly realized that she really wasn't as sure about it as she had initially been. Ten years ago she had thought that she wanted to get as far away from ranching as she could. Her goal all along had been to prove to her late father, looking up—or down—from whatever vantage point his life had placed him in, that she was up to the challenge he had laid down for her.

Once that was done, she would go back to life the way it had been.

Except the idea of resuming the life she had had just a little while ago was not as pleasing to her as she had once thought. But that didn't change the fact that she assumed Mitch still thought that she was leaving the moment the six months were up.

Maybe that was why he'd felt free to fool around with her the way he had. Because, from that perspective, there were no strings attached to what they had done, no promises made in the heat of passion that needed to be kept. Last night had been about two consenting adults enjoying one another.

Except that she suspected one of the adults had enjoyed what happened last night a little more than the other had.

And if Mitch became even the slightest bit aware of that, she felt in her heart that it could very well scare him away.

Which meant that she had to keep a lid on things no matter how tempted she might be to say something, Ena firmly told herself.

But it definitely wasn't going to be easy. Ena could feel her heart leaping up the second that she saw him.

For his part, Mitch saw her coming from half a field away. He was grateful he had that much time to steel himself off.

He was certain that Ena wouldn't want anyone else to know about their night together, as magnificent as it had been. After all, she was the owner here and he was, at bottom, just a hired hand. The last thing he wanted was for her to get the impression that he had made love with her thinking that would give him some sort of advantage or even leverage over her.

But damn, just watching her walking toward him had him feeling things, stirring up his insides. It had him wishing that he had spent more time perfecting a poker face.

When she reached the area where he and the others were, Mitch touched the brim of his Stetson as if to tip it to her. "Morning, Miss O'Rourke. Wasn't sure if you'd be joining us this morning," he told her.

"Morning," Ena echoed. "Why wouldn't I?" she challenged. "Horses don't care if it's Sunday." She looked at the horseshoes that were piled up on the ground. "What are you doing?" she asked, directing her eyes as well as her question toward the other wranglers more than Mitch.

"We're shoeing some of the new foals," Wade told her, nodding toward a heavyset wrangler who had on a black leather apron. Ena assumed he was the blacksmith. "The ones that are fully grown," Wade added. "We thought if you sold them at auction that would bring in enough money to keep the ranch going awhile longer."

That surprised her. "You didn't tell them?" she asked, looking at Mitch.

Mitch merely smiled in response. "I figured it was your news to tell."

She would have thought that those would be the first words out of his mouth the second he gathered the other wranglers around him this morning before they started working.

"Tell us what?" Billy asked, looking from Ena to Mitch.

"Go ahead," Mitch urged, nodding at her.

"We saw the bank manager at Murphy's last night—" she began.

"*Miss O'Rourke* saw the bank manager," Mitch corrected.

She just continued as if he hadn't said anything, "And the man agreed to extend the note on the ranch as long as we start showing a profit."

She decided to keep the details about the herbal cure

by Mitch's mother to herself for the time being. It was enough that Mitch knew what she was planning to do with it—and why.

"Can we?" Wade asked, directing the question to Mitch.

Mitch in turn looked at Ena, redirecting the question to her. "I think we can," she said with confidence.

"All right, men, you heard the boss lady. Now, get back to work," Mitch ordered.

As if on cue, activity restarted all around him.

Ena stood off to the extreme right as a number of the wranglers took charge of several of the horses, leading them to a fenced-off area to await being shod. A few of the horses were skittish and had to be calmed.

Mitch has called her *boss lady*, she thought. Was that for the men's benefit, or did he actually think of her that way himself? If he did, then they couldn't really be on equal footing, Ena thought. She didn't want that. She didn't want him feeling that she was above him. That would adversely affect their relationship.

But maybe Mitch didn't think of them as having a relationship, she thought, her stomach twisting as the possibility occurred to her. Maybe it really was just about a good time for him and nothing more.

It should be that way for you, she silently insisted. *It's about time you loosened up.*

She'd never had the sort of wild, carefree adolescence the way she knew that a lot of others had had. She'd been too busy toeing a line once her mother was gone. And after that, once she left home, she had been too busy trying to create a life for herself. Somehow, there had never really been any time to just be young, to explore her own feminine wiles.

Was this how it went between men and women? A

good time was had without any promises of something more? She honestly didn't know. She had never had anyone for guidance when it came to this, no one to look to as a role model.

Her mother, whom she adored, had never taught her anything except how to defer to her father. There had to be more to a relationship than that.

But maybe she was expecting too much from Mitch. Maybe he was just in it for the fun of it and not anything else.

Okay, she decided, she could do that. She could just ride this wave and see where it would take her, enjoying this exhilarating ride for as long as it continued, Ena told herself.

Their eyes met for a second and then Mitch crossed over to her. He didn't want Ena to feel that he was presuming too much, or that he felt that last night had given him a special status with her because he knew that it hadn't.

Still, he didn't just want to leave it at that without saying a word, or worse, pretending that last night hadn't happened. Because it had. It had been glorious, lighting up his life the way it had never been lit before.

He had deliberately left her bedroom while she was sleeping this morning because if he had stayed, he knew he would have been tempted to make love with her all over again. And while they had made love twice the night before, there was something about daylight that forced things into perspective. The last thing he wanted was for her to feel pressured. Nor did he want her to reject him. He really didn't know how he would be able to deal with that.

But there was certainly nothing wrong with his coming up to her at the start of a new day and asking, "How are you feeling?"

That had come out of the blue, Ena thought. Rather than give him a glib answer, she asked in a quiet voice, "About?"

Mitch shrugged vaguely. "Everything," he said, feeling that it was best not to cite anything in particular.

She flashed a noncommittal smile. "I'm feeling just fine."

Maybe he shouldn't have said anything, he thought. "Good. Me, too."

Talk about vague, Ena thought. They could be discussing their feelings about the price of grain or the state of the weather. Was he being vague like this to protect her or himself?

She didn't have a clue. She knew what she wanted him to be saying and doing, but only if *he* wanted to, not because she did.

Ena took a breath. She needed to sort all this out for herself, calmly and rationally. And then, and only then, would she be able to come to Mitch and have that conversation that she felt they both needed to have.

Because being vague like this actually made her feel trapped in limbo.

"You sure you're okay?" he asked her, keeping his own voice low.

"Yes," she answered crisply, her eyes meeting his. "I'm sure."

"Then I'm going to get back to work," Mitch told her. He turned on his heel and went walking back to his men.

She watched as Mitch took measured steps away from her. She couldn't help wondering if the man was aware that his hips moved ever so temptingly with each step that he took.

She found herself suddenly reliving last night. Ena promised herself that she wasn't going to allow what had sprung to life between them to be over, no matter what it took.

Like a flower in the desert, it needed to be watered and nurtured and she intended to do both.

Chapter Nineteen

Well, it was official, Ena thought. It was more than three weeks since she and Mitch had made love. More than three weeks since he had so much as even touched her in a chaste, impartial way.

At this point she was struggling not to let anger get the better of her because she could now add the term *one-night stand* to her dating resume.

There was no other way to describe what had happened between her and Mitch, because ever since that one glorious, delicious night, the ranch foreman hadn't even tried to hold her hand—or any other part of her for that matter.

Ena felt let down and hurt, and had no idea what to make of it because she had never been in this position before.

It certainly didn't help that Mitch acted as if nothing out of the ordinary had happened between them. The way he behaved—since that night—anyone watching him would have said that they were nothing more than two people working on a horse ranch together.

In the beginning, she thought she had done something wrong. After a while, though, she decided that *he* was the one to blame. So when Mitch spoke to her, she did her best to give him a frosty shoulder.

But that gave her no satisfaction. With each passing day, more and more she felt as if she were drowning in a barrel filled with ice water. Drowning and without a single clue how to save herself.

If something didn't happen soon, she knew she was going to go down for the third and final time.

Each day she got up and went through the motions of working on the ranch, while deep within, she felt as if her heart were breaking apart. It was an effort to try to keep her mind on what she was doing.

And then, just when she felt as if she had reached a crossroads, she saw Cash pulling up in front of the ranch house in his car.

Standing close by, Mitch saw the lawyer's car, too. "Wonder what this is all about," he said.

Seeing the car, Ena's first thought was that Cash had found an addendum to her father's will. The way her luck was going, there were probably more hoops for her to jump through before she could finally become the sole owner of the Double E.

When she didn't say anything in response to his question, Mitch asked her point-blank, "Trouble?"

Ena didn't even look his way. She had to harden her heart when it came to this man and it had to start now.

"Nothing that would concern you," she retorted, walking toward Cash's vehicle.

"Ouch," Wade said, overhearing. "That one drew blood." He looked at Mitch. "You two doing okay?"

The answer to that was obvious. "Don't you have work to do?" Mitch asked.

Wade had always known when to step back. "Absolutely," he said to the foreman and began to move toward the corral.

Mitch stood where he was for a minute, then decided that if the lawyer was here because of something that had to do with the ranch, as foreman he would hear about it sooner or later, so it might as well be sooner rather than later. With that thought in mind, he crossed quickly toward Ena and the lawyer. The latter had just gotten out of his vehicle.

Mitch got there in time to hear Ena ask, "What brings you here, Cash?"

"Good news. Possibly," Cash qualified. "That's why I wanted to deliver it to you in person."

Because of the way things had been going, her patience was at a low point. "Well, what is it?" she pressed. "My orchestra has the day off, otherwise I would have already signaled for a drumroll," she told him. Then she immediately said, "I'm sorry. I'm afraid I'm a little testy lately."

"Well, this just might make you less testy," Cash told her with an encouraging smile. "You have an offer to buy the ranch."

"An offer?" she asked, confused. "But I haven't put up the ranch for sale."

"No, but Edward Larabee seemed pretty eager to annex this ranch to make it part of his spread. It seems that he sees himself as being at the head of a horse empire. Someone must have told him that you're not all that thrilled to be back here ranching," Cash speculated.

Ena was acutely aware that Mitch was standing there, taking all this in. That made her even more uncomfortable. "Well, in any case, I can't sell the Double E to him yet. You know that." She pressed her lips together, feeling trapped. "The terms were that I had to stay and work the ranch for six months," she reminded him needlessly.

Cash nodded. "Larabee's aware of that. He's more than willing to wait, as long as when you are ready to sell, you consider his offer before the others."

"Others?" Mitch asked, surprised. "There are others?"

"No, not yet," Cash said. "But once word gets around that the Double E is for sale, there might be others." Cash reconsidered his statement. "As a matter of fact, there most likely will be. I just wanted to come out and let you know about this in case you've started feeling like you're going to be trapped here."

She didn't want that getting around. "I never said I felt trapped," she protested.

Until she had arrived back in Forever, she had been very careful about keeping all her personal feelings to herself.

"You didn't have to," Cash told her kindly. "It was there, in your eyes, for anyone to see." He could tell that wasn't what she wanted to hear. He decided that it was best to wind this up. "Anyway, Larabee wants to be first in line when your required six months are up." He glanced at his watch. "I've got to be getting back."

As he got into his car, he said, "Congratulations. This is good news, I hope." Then, starting up the engine, he drove away.

"Larabee's got a hell of a nerve, making that offer," Mitch said as he watched Cash's car disappear down the road.

"Why would you say that?" Ena challenged.

"Why?" he echoed, wondering why she sounded so irritated. "Because you're not going to sell."

She gave him a withering look. "I'm not?"

"No," Mitch declared. And then he looked at her face more closely and realized that maybe he was taking things for granted. "Are you?"

Ena shrugged. "It's definitely worth thinking about," she answered. "I mean, there's really nothing to keep me here."

"Nothing to keep you here?" he repeated, stunned. She wasn't serious, was she? "You were *born* here."

Ena tossed her head, dismissing his argument. "That's not enough of a reason to keep me here."

He stared at her, completely confused. "I don't understand," he said. "I thought when you convinced Prescott to extend the loan on the ranch—and he agreed," Mitch stressed, "that you'd made your mind up to stay here and run the place."

Shrugging, Ena turned away and began to head to the house. "Not everything is what it seems," she informed him coldly.

That just succeeded in making him even more confused. "What's *that* supposed to mean?"

She didn't bother turning around. "Whatever you want it to."

She was almost at the house when she heard Mitch call after her.

"Bruce'll miss you."

That stopped her for half a second. "He'll get over it," she said, continuing toward the front door.

Mitch stood there, feeling something crumble inside him with each step she took. For one long moment, he debated letting her go, but then something urged him not to, to give this "thing" between them—whatever it was—one last shot despite all his noble attempts at restraint to the contrary.

Ena had reached the house and walked in through the door, afraid that she would break down before she got inside. She had taken two steps into the house when the door behind her flew open again.

"No, he won't," Mitch declared. "And even if he does—I won't," he said, his voice dropping.

No, she told herself fiercely, she wasn't going to fall for that again. Mitch's actions spoke louder than his words and he had practically shunned her these last three weeks. She let herself fall for him, had given him her heart and then practically gotten kicked in the teeth for her stupidity.

Well, not again.

Swinging around, Ena looked at him, her eyes blazing. "Oh, I'm sure you'll get over it in record time. As a matter of fact, I bet that you probably already have."

He stared at her, lost. "What are you talking about?"

"I'm talking about you acting as if I had leprosy." To underscore her words, she hit him in the chest with the flat of her hand. "As if I was someone you had to endure in order to keep your job."

When she went to hit him again, he took a step back, catching her hand before she could make contact. "Still don't understand," he said pointedly.

"Then think about it!" she all but shouted in his face. "We made love, you put another notch in your belt and then you cut me dead. Seems simple enough to understand to me." Her eyes narrowed, shooting daggers at him. "Now, if you have nothing else—"

Mitch caught hold of her shoulders to keep her in place. "I have nothing else if you sell this ranch and leave Forever."

He was worried about his job, she thought angrily. "Don't worry, I'm sure that Larabee will keep you on as foreman. I can even specify that as being one of my terms when I sell it to him—"

"The hell with being foreman." He blew out a breath as he looked up at the ceiling, searching for words. And then he looked at her. "I gave this my best shot, but I can't do this any longer."

It was her turn not to understand. "I'm sure that I don't know—"

Now that he had found the words, he couldn't allow himself to be distracted. "Don't take this the wrong way, Ena, but shut up."

Startled, she stared at him. "What?"

"Shut up," Mitch repeated. "Do you want to know why I stayed away from you? Because I realized that you might think what happened between us was because I wanted to seal my place on the ranch. That you'd think I wanted to help you run the ranch or maybe even something more than that. But I don't care about the ranch," he insisted, then felt that needed clarification. "I mean, I care about the ranch, but definitely not more than I care about you." He saw the disbelief on her face. He wasn't doing this well, he upbraided himself. "Look, this is a whole new place for me." He shrugged helplessly. "I'm shoeing a horse and seeing your face."

Ena tilted her head. "I'm not sure that's a compliment."

"Well, it is," he insisted, "because nothing has ever interfered with work for me before—until there was you." He knew he was saying too much, but now that he had gotten started, he couldn't stop himself. "I want you so much that I literally *hurt* inside. But what I don't want is you thinking that I'm after the ranch. The only thing I'm after is you." He took in a shaky breath. "I felt that way ever since I saw you in Mrs. Brickman's English class and I feel that way now." His eyes looked into hers. "I just don't know how to prove it to you."

Ena smiled. "You just did."

"What?" He didn't know if she was kidding him or not. "How?"

She supposed it was so simple he didn't see it. "Because you remembered when you first saw me. The thing is, you didn't just make that up because I remember it, too," she told him.

That first time was very important to him. Had it actually been that way for her, too? Or was she just pulling his leg for some reason? "You do?"

She smiled at Mitch. "I do."

His mind began racing, making plans. "Look, maybe I can find some work in Dallas," he began.

She stopped him right there. "Why would you want to do that?"

He told her the truth. "Because the idea of my staying here when you leave makes me feel like my insides are all being scraped out."

She smiled at him. "Your insides are safe, Mitch. I'm not going anywhere."

He didn't understand. Was she having fun at his expense? "But you just said—"

Ena stopped him right there. "I say a lot of things when I'm hurt," she told him.

"Hurt?" he questioned. Was she telling him that he'd managed to hurt her? He'd never even considered that was possible.

Ena closed her eyes for a moment, shaking her head. "You are going to require a lot of patience and work."

Maybe this was going to be all right after all, he

thought. "I'm all yours," he told her. "Do whatever you want with me," Mitch said. "As a matter of fact, I insist on it."

Humor entered her eyes. "Careful what you wish for," she warned.

Now that the barriers were finally down, he felt he could be honest about everything. And it was time he told her. "Do you know what I wanted to say to you the first time I saw you?"

"What?"

"I wanted to say 'Will you marry me?'" He saw her looking at him skeptically. "I didn't," he continued, "because I knew who your father was and I was going to ask him for a job the minute I graduated. I was afraid that if he heard that I'd said that to you, he'd accuse me of just saying that in order to make him consider me for that job."

Ena laughed. Boy, had he been wrong. "You obviously didn't know my father."

"I also wanted to say it that night we came home from Murphy's," he told her. "I didn't say it then because you were so confident that you were going to get that extension from the bank and I didn't want you thinking I was trying to take advantage of the situation, you know, marrying you because of the ranch."

"And you started keeping your distance for the same reason," she guessed.

"It made sense at the time," he said, although hearing it out loud now showed him how foolish he had been.

"If you're given to making stupid decisions," she concluded crisply.

He smiled at her. "That being said, I'm through with making stupid decisions."

She had a feeling that there was more. "All right," she said, encouraging him to continue.

He took a breath. "Now, I don't want you to think that I'm rushing you."

"What am I not being rushed about?" she asked.

He took another breath, a deeper one this time. "I have loved you ever since I first saw you in Mrs. Brickman's English class, and when the dust finally settles, I'd like you to consider…" He tried again. "Do you think that you might be able to consider…"

Ena looked up at him. "Are you asking me to marry you?"

He supposed he *was* making a mess of it, he thought. "I'm trying to."

She cocked her head. "But?"

"I guess what's stopping me is I don't think I can handle you saying no."

Her eyes smiled at him first. "Well, lucky for you, I don't plan on saying no—that is, if you ever finally ask."

"Really?" His smile seemed to grow until it encompassed his entire face.

"First you have to ask," she reminded him.

Then, to her surprise, Mitch took her hand and got down on one knee. "Ena Meredith O'Rourke, will you marry me?"

She winced when he said her full name. "Wait, you *know* my middle name?" she questioned in surprise. It wasn't something that she typically told people. She had never liked the name, even though it had belonged to her parental grandmother.

"I know everything there is to know about you," Mitch told her.

She was beginning to believe that, she thought.

"Well, since you know my middle name, I guess I'm

going to have to marry you." She blinded him with her smile and said, "So, yes! Yes, I will marry you."

That was all he needed to hear. Mitch pulled her into his arms and did what he had longed to do for the last three weeks. He kissed her.

And he kept on kissing her for a very long, long time.

* * * * *

MILLS & BOON

Coming next month

HER TWIN BABY SECRET
Therese Beharrie

He laughed. Gave in to the urge to tuck her hair behind her ear as he'd seen her do earlier.

She exhaled. 'What are you doing, Benjamin?'

He dropped his hand, looked at her face. 'I don't know.'

'You do know.'

'No, I don't.' He smiled. Almost as soon as he did, it vanished. 'Except for right now. Right now, I'm contemplating how to get you to kiss me again. I'd say it's an appropriate response to how incredible you look.' He shook his head. 'I was staring earlier because I didn't have anything to say. You're so beautiful. And this dress is…and your hair, your face…' He shook his head again. Offered her a wry, possibly apologetic smile. 'I'm sorry. I think the last couple days have officially caught up with me.'

Her expression was unreadable, but she said, 'It's been a rough couple of days.'

'Yeah.'

'Because of me.' She paused. 'I'm sorry.'

'You don't have to apologise. You already have, at least.'

'Right.' She leaned back against her door, which he realised only now she hadn't moved away from. 'This hasn't been easy for me either.'

'I know.'

'A large part of it is because you get on my nerves. A lot,' she added when he frowned.

'That seems uncalled for considering I just gave you a bunch of compliments.'

'You want acknowledgement for that?'

'A thank you would nice,' he muttered.

'You're right.'

'Sorry—could you say that again?' He patted his pocket, looking for his phone. 'I want to record it for posterity.'

'This, for example, is extremely annoying. But at the same time, I can't stop thinking about the kiss we had the other day.'

He stilled.

'Which gets on my nerves, too. An interesting conundrum. Am I annoyed because I'm attracted to you? Am I annoyed because you annoy me but I'm still attracted to you?' She exhaled. It sounded frustrated. 'I don't have answers, but I keep asking these questions. Then, of course, you do something decent, like pretend to be my boyfriend even though you have no reason or incentive to. You stand up for me in front of my brother, which I found disturbingly hot. In the same breath, you act stupidly, and tell your mother—your *mother*—that I'm your girlfriend. Which, tonight, we have to rectify.'

She shook her head.

'Honestly, Benjamin, these last few days have been the most frustratingly complicated of my life, and I'm an entrepreneur with a crappy family. And I'm *pregnant,* about to become a single mother. Complicated is the air I breathe. But you make things...' She trailed off with a little laugh. 'And still, I want to kiss you, too.'

Continue reading
HER TWIN BABY SECRET
Therese Beharrie

Available next month
www.millsandboon.co.uk

COMING SOON!

We really hope you enjoyed reading this book. If you're looking for more romance, be sure to head to the shops when new books are available on

Thursday 9th January

To see which titles are coming soon, please visit

millsandboon.co.uk/nextmonth

MILLS & BOON

HEROES

At Your Service

Experience all the excitement of a
gripping thriller, with an intense romance
at its heart. Resourceful, true-to-life
women and strong, fearless men face
danger and desire - a killer combination!

MILLS & BOON

HISTORICAL

Awaken the romance of the past

Escape with historical heroes from time gone by. Whether your passion is for wicked Regency Rakes, muscled Viking warriors or rugged Highlanders, indulge your fantasies and awaken the romance of the past.

MILLS & BOON

Desire

Indulge in secrets and scandal, intense drama and plenty of sizzling hot action with powerful and passionate heroes who have it all: wealth, status, good looks… everything but the right woman.